SO-AQI-932

HEART
AND
SOUL

Elizabeth Bennett

JOVE BOOKS, NEW YORK

HEART AND SOUL

A Jove Book / published by arrangement with
the author

PRINTING HISTORY
Jove edition / May 1994

ISBN: 0-515-11372-7

A JOVE BOOK®
Jove Books are published by The Berkley Publishing Group,
200 Madison Avenue, New York, New York 10016.
JOVE and the "J" design are trademarks belonging to
Jove Publications, Inc.

PRINTED IN THE UNITED STATES OF AMERICA

10 9 8 7 6 5 4 3 2 1

For W.E.B.,
heart and soul

One

"*H*ello?" Some sort of bell had been tolling through Cassie's dream, and it had taken five long rings for her to realize hazily that it was the telephone.

"Cassie? Is that you?"

"Miranda . . ." Cassie sat up in bed and fumbled for the light on her night table. "What's going on . . . what's wrong?" There was something in her older half sister's voice—a hesitancy, an undercurrent of panic—that Cassie had never heard before.

"Did I wake you up?" Miranda asked. "What time do you go to bed down there in hicksville, anyway? It's not even midnight in New York." Whatever odd note Cassie had heard in Miranda's tone was gone now, replaced by the seductive contralto familiar to millions of American television viewers. Strong and clear, yet somehow intimate, it was a voice that inspired confidences. People told their darkest secrets to Miranda Darin in front of blinding lights and prying cameras. *Tell me,* the voice would urge. *Trust me,* the beautiful smile promised. And in the next instant, the most terrible truths would tumble out, destroying careers, shattering reputations. And yet, there was something so alluring about Miranda Darin that her top-rated *Breaking News* show never had to search far for the next willing confessor. On that Wednesday evening in

1

March when Miranda called her half sister Cassie, the show had more than thirty stories in various stages of production, enough to keep them going through the rest of the year.

"I know you find this hard to believe," Cassie said with a sigh that expressed her annoyance, "but Raleigh, North Carolina, is still in the same time zone as New York, New York. As well as being in the same century, may I add." Cassie added importantly, "I was out on assignment most of last night, I'm exhausted."

"It's been so nuts here, I'm just glad I had a chance to connect with you," Miranda said. As usual, Miranda ignored Cassie's attempt to establish her own worth and importance. Although even Cassie had to admit that "the assignment" she had referred to was nothing more glamorous than covering a four-alarm blaze at a warehouse on the outskirts of Raleigh, it was still a story. And though it didn't even get a mention outside the *Raleigh News and Observer's* tri-city area, her piece had run on the front page of her own paper that morning. Leave it to Miranda, Cassie thought, to deflate Cassie's first real success since she had started as a staffer on the paper three years before.

"Well, now we're connected," Cassie replied. They hadn't spoken since that past Christmas, and even then their usual ten-minute phone conversation was cut short by a temper tantrum from Miranda's spoiled seven-year-old daughter Heather. A daughter who, like Miranda's self-made millionaire husband, always seemed too busy and important for Cassie to actually meet. She rarely admitted the truth to herself, let alone to the friends and colleagues who envied her relationship to the world-famous Miranda Darin, but she hardly knew her older sibling anymore. Still, Cassie told herself as she shook off the bed sheets and swung her feet to the floor, she knew her well enough to sense that despite what she said, something definitely was wrong . . . it buzzed, like a bad connection, just behind Miranda's words. In a less forced tone, Cassie asked, "How's everyone? Jason? Heather?"

"Just great," Miranda said. "Frantically busy as always, but we're all fine."

"Good," Cassie said, trying to imagine what her sister could possibly want from her. In the last four years, since the plane crash that killed their mother and Cassie's father, the half sisters' relationship had slowly unraveled. The change had actually started years before that terrible morning when they had stood together beside their mother's grave and realized that they had already drifted too far apart to offer each other any real comfort.

"We were hoping you could come visit us this weekend," Miranda said now, "for Easter."

"What?" Cassie replied. "Me?"

"Yes, you and whomever you might want to bring," Miranda breezed on as Cassie listened incredulously. "You're still seeing that handsome young intern or something? What's his name, Cliff? No . . . Carl?"

"Kenneth," Cassie managed to say. "Kenneth Stimpson, and he's already invited me to his parents' place for the weekend. Sorry. You should have phoned sooner." Imagine, Cassie told herself furiously, being called up at the last minute like this and being expected to drop everything and come! They probably had a house guest who had canceled out unexpectedly, and now they needed her to complete their table setting or something.

"But you've got to come," Miranda replied. "Bring this Kenneth, I don't care. You must come."

"Why? What's so important?" Cassie asked, longing to add: *after four years.*

"We're . . . having a big party. Saturday night. Black tie. Some very important people will be there, Cassie. Dan Rather, network big shots. It could do your career a lot of good."

"Since when have you given a damn about my career?" Cassie demanded, unable to restrain herself. The nerve of Miranda! Proudly, Cassie had sent Miranda clippings of her stories from her first reporting slot at a small newspaper in West Virginia. There had been no reply. No note. No nothing. From conversation to conversation, Miranda could barely remember the name of the paper Cassie worked for now. And yet, if truth be known, Cassie had not yet missed one of Miranda's Thursday night *Breaking News* broadcasts in the four years it had been on the air.

"I'm sorry," Miranda said. "You're right to be upset. I've not been . . . I'm not a terrific sister. I know that." There was a long silence on the other end of the phone; Cassie could hear the sound of her own breathing, fast huffs of anger. Miranda cleared her throat and continued, "Did it occur to you, Cassie, that I might be hoping to make up for lost time here? That what I'm trying to say in inviting you up for the weekend is . . . let's try to be friends . . . and sisters again?"

She spoke in a voice that made a person long to confide, that urged one to relax, to float along, to say *yes*. And even though Cassie had a good many reasons to fight against the temptation . . . she had one overwhelming reason to give in. Sadly, it wasn't that she believed for one instant what Miranda claimed: she wasn't hoping to start now a relationship she'd rejected for nearly thirty years. Miranda didn't care about being Cassie's sister . . . or her friend. For some reason that Cassie didn't yet understand, but could clearly divine in Miranda's sudden invitation, her older sister needed her. And that, more than any pretended outpouring of affection, moved Cassie after a moment of hesitation to say: "Well, then, of course, Miranda. How in the world can I refuse?"

After Cassie had put down the receiver, she leaned a little farther across the night table to pick up a silver-framed photograph. She held it lovingly as she looked down at the four faces that smiled back. The picture had been taken five years before. It was the day of Cassie's graduation from Chapel Hill, and the thin black nylon robe had whipped around Cassie's lean frame like a flag against a pole. She squinted into the sun, her pale face and blond hair bleached out by the bright sunlight. Her mother stood beside her, her arm proudly circling Cassie's waist. Cassie's father was on the other side, his eyes shadowed by his strong intelligent brow. A foot to the left of Ted and a little apart, as always, stood Miranda.

If you looked closely you could see a certain resemblance between Cassie and Miranda; the same slightly quizzical tilt to the right eyebrow, a similar gentle groove at the chin, almost identically fine straight hair, though Miranda's, as everyone knew, was shockingly blond—that rare, platinum strain once favored by movie stars—and Cassie's was a far more common strawberry variety. Both half sisters were tall, lean, and fit. Cassie had the kind of straightforward good looks most people called "healthy": glowing cheeks, strong white teeth, a clear-eyed hazel gaze. In Miranda, however, those same features, through some alchemy of fate and genetic structure, had been rearranged into sheer beauty.

It was a fact with which Cassie, ten years Miranda's junior and a lifetime in her shadow, had long since come to terms.

"Beauty isn't anything you earn," Miranda and Cassie's mother had frequently reminded the girls. A dedicated social worker and die-hard liberal, Dorothy Hartley had never seemed particularly proud of her older daughter's stunning good looks. Perhaps they reminded her a bit too vividly of her first husband, Miranda's father, a suavely handsome insurance salesman who went out for a pack of cigarettes two months after Miranda's birth . . . and never came back. It took seven long years before Dorothy found her true love match in Ted Hartley, a civil rights lawyer whom she met on Martin Luther King Jr.'s long Freedom March. With pretty little Miranda in tow, Dorothy and Ted had fallen in love along the dusty roadside leading into Birmingham. Theirs was a passion that only intensified over the years as they committed their lives to helping the poor and underprivileged.

Throughout her childhood in Raleigh, Cassie felt nothing but undiluted love and confidence from her parents. It helped, of course, that they were both so fair-minded and openhearted. It helped that they were so devoted to the ideal that all people are created equal—despite color, race, sex . . . and physical attributes. It helped, but nothing could ever make up for the hurt when people would stop the family on the sidewalk or in the supermarket to exclaim: "What a stunning girl!" Meaning, of course, Miranda.

How often as she was growing up did Cassie silently whisper to herself that beauty wasn't earned? It became her mantra. But as the years went on, and beautiful Miranda also proved herself to be brilliant and hardworking Miranda . . . the weight of her older sister's success became harder to bear. What a relief it was for Cassie when Miranda went off to Columbia University in New York, with a full scholarship, of course. And further relief when Miranda became so caught up in college and the big city that she only managed to get home briefly for long weekends. By then she was already something of a stranger in the busy, always slightly messy Hartley household. With each visit Miranda seemed more glamorous and distant . . . and Cassie felt more tongue-tied and inadequate. But Miranda, her sights set on something far beyond Raleigh and the feelings of her young half sister, barely seemed to notice Cassie's awestruck shyness.

"Well, I'm off to a party with Rick Thompson," Miranda had announced during the Christmas break of her first year of grad school at the Columbia School of Journalism. She stood in the dining-room doorway, a green crushed-velvet dress inching halfway up her long, perfectly shaped thighs . . . the sheath of blond hair falling halfway down her back. No wonder every single one of Miranda's many former high school boyfriends—some of them already married with children—dropped by the house to see her whenever she came home. Like moths mesmerized by a flame, Cassie told herself as she enviously watched her older sister slip into a new suede jacket, these ever-hopeful boys would stand in line to be burned again and again by Miranda's careless affection. A freshman in high school that year, tall, skinny Cassie had managed to receive some tepid interest from a couple of boys in her class, but she already knew she would never inspire the passionate idolatry that seemed Miranda's birthright.

"Rick Thompson?" Dorothy asked, putting down her coffee cup. "Isn't he engaged to Sheila Brandish? And besides, your father and I were hoping you'd come with us to Cassie's sing. She has a solo part this year." It was just a small excerpt from *The Messiah,* but Cassie had been cherishing a secret hope of finally impressing Miranda. Though Cassie had a sweet, if somewhat thin, soprano, Miranda's husky contralto couldn't hold a note of music. Here at last, Cassie felt, was something at which she excelled over her older sister.

"At the high school?" Miranda replied, laughing. "Oh, Mother, please! I thought you liked me to see my old friends when I had a chance . . . and this is supposed to be Raleigh's party of the year. And besides, Cassie understands . . . she knows as well as I do what a drag those awful Christmas sings are, don't you, Cassie?"

"Sure," Cassie mumbled, though after that concert her interest in singing waned. All through high school, Cassie searched for something she could do better than the way Miranda had done it. But no matter what she tried—field hockey, the debating team, cheerleading, the drama club— Miranda had done it first and with greater style. And after a cum laude send-off from graduate school, Miranda's triumphs—now on the far bigger and more important stage of Manhattan—continued unabated: CBS newswriter . . . assistant producer . . . general assignment reporter . . . then the big jump to the Magnum network and a feature reporter slot. Well, everyone knew the story from there. From the evening that *Breaking News* premiered, the beautiful Miranda Darin had captured the undivided attention—and more often than not the hearts—of America.

"You've just got to stop measuring yourself against Miranda's yardstick," Cassie's mother had told her when Cassie headed into her junior year at Chapel Hill and remained uncertain about her major. During the previous semester, she'd switched from art to political science to biology. "You've got to look into yourself—not out at her—and decide what you, Cassie, really want to do with your life."

"What I want," Cassie retorted in a rare moment of honesty about the painful subject, "is to be better than her. No . . . just as good as her. I'm tired, Mother, I'm sick and tired of being best known as Miranda's little sister."

"That's your problem, Cassie," her mother replied. "People see what you show them. You're letting yourself stay in her shadow . . . you're hiding there. Step out of it—find your own patch of light—and believe me, people will start seeing you for who you are."

"Sometimes I wonder who that is," Cassie said.

"Well, I don't for a second," Dorothy replied vehemently. "You're kind. You're thoughtful . . . in a nice dreamy way. You're a good and loyal friend. And in all of these things, honey, you far outshine Miranda. It worries me that for all her success and fame, Miranda has no real good friends back here. You know, she never did. She only bothered with boys—and I'm afraid that was just to see how many she could dangle at one time. She was always too eager to escape to put any roots down. And you need that, Cassie, you must know—deep in your heart—where you come from if you ever want to get ahead in this world. Now I'm going to shut up. I believe I've dispensed enough wisdom for one day."

Shortly after that, Cassie had found the strength of mind to take up the one subject that she'd secretly most enjoyed—and yet most feared would show up her shortcomings in terms of Miranda. She majored in Journalism. And in her own careful, thoughtful way she excelled in it. She was not as glib a writer as Miranda. She was not as demanding or probing a reporter. Obviously she was not as successful. And yet she had found her own patch of sunlight as Dorothy had advised her . . . although sometimes, Cassie had to admit, it did little to comfort or warm.

Cassie put the photograph back on the table and turned off the light. She pulled the sheets around her and stared up into the dark. Even after four years, her parents' death felt recent and wrenching. There was a gaping hole in her life. A whole bombed-out section of her heart that refused to mend. The job helped. Kenneth tried to help. But there were moments, like this one, when Cassie felt the best times of her life were behind her. She had never again shared with anyone the closeness, the understanding—just the pure, unthinking affection—that she had with her parents. She'd certainly never felt it with—or from—Miranda. Perhaps that kind of love was just an illusion of childhood, Cassie thought. Something she could never recapture.

These days it certainly seemed that Cassie's life was riddled with losses . . . and Miranda's, as usual, was just one unbroken line of wins. Cassie ticked them off in her mind as she drifted toward sleep: great looks, brilliant career, handsome and successful husband, pretty daughter . . . easily manipulated younger sister who willingly drops everything anytime she thought to call.

Two

That the Darin residence had once been the home of a Rockefeller relative was a fact that Miranda did nothing to hide. Located on a quiet side street just off Madison Avenue, it was at the very heart of one of the wealthiest square miles of real estate in the world. To the west the town palaces known as "Millionaires' Row" marched up Fifth Avenue. To the east, the high-rise mansions of Park Avenue formed a muted gray wall of privilege and power. Though not particularly distinguished architecturally—it was constructed of molded limestone, roofed with green copper and slate—the Darin residence quietly "fit in" with the other town houses on its street. And that, Miranda Darin had quickly understood, was the first step to being accepted in the rarefied social stratosphere to which she aspired.

For Miranda, like so many beautiful and successful women before her, there was only one mountain left to scale before she could feel she had truly made it in Manhattan: the social one. Britain has its royalty; America has its very, very rich. Those who sit on the museum boards, who head the charity drives, who attend the ballet benefits. Although at first glance it would seem that this wealthy world was open to whoever could meet the price of admission, Miranda had learned painfully fast that this was simply not so.

"Can you imagine?" she'd overheard one social matron whisper to another in the ladies' room after a committee meeting for the Metropolitan Opera fund-raiser Miranda had attended when she had first tried breaking into New York society. "That Darin woman wanting to televise the performance? How tacky can you get? The whole point of a benefit is that you can be assured the slavering masses are kept at bay."

Yes, in the beginning, Miranda had made her share of mistakes. She'd tried too hard. Pushed a little too much. Volunteered too often for too many things. She learned that beauty, intelligence, money, and fame alone weren't enough to help her squeeze into that tight little world. It took time. And patience. Astor, Vanderbilt, Harriman, Rockefeller, Whitney; these were names that had been in the upper echelons of the social register for generations. That Miranda Darin had climbed as far as she had in the past two decades was something of a minor miracle. That she had launched herself so successfully without the help of her financially brilliant yet socially backward husband was a subject of much respectful discussion among those who cared about such matters.

"I've never met him myself," Lucinda Phipps confided to Marisa Newtown on the phone the morning of the Darins' party. "Although I've been told he's quite gorgeous in a badly groomed sort of way. Poor Miranda—she's always so perfect."

"Well, I did run into him once," Marisa said, "when he was picking little Heather up from Dalton. My Laurel's in her class, and when I heard Heather say 'Hi, Daddy!' I just barged right over to his car and introduced myself as one of Miranda's dearest friends."

"And?" Lucinda demanded. "What was he like?"

Marisa inhaled deeply and sighed, letting the suspense mount. "He rolled up his window without saying a single word."

"No!" Lucinda said. "How horrible. Poor, poor Miranda.

No wonder she goes everywhere with Vance Magnus . . . not that that's such a hardship in my opinion."

"Mine either," Marisa agreed. "We should both be so lucky to have Magnus for an escort. Though, I have to admit, Lucinda, that there was something very attractive about that awful man Miranda married. In a dark and dangerous kind of way."

"Oh, do point him out to me tonight," Lucinda said. "If he's there."

At that moment, in an airport waiting room in Baltimore, the question of who was—and wasn't—going to attend Miranda's party was also very much on Cassie's mind. A freak early spring snowstorm had stalled air traffic up and down the East Coast, and Cassie had spent the night in the airport waiting room after her connecting flight from Raleigh to New York had been canceled. Her neck ached, her eyes burned from lack of sleep, the new rayon suit she had bought especially for the plane trip was wrinkled, and her breath tasted sour. For the fourth time in the last hour she tried to phone Miranda's house; each time she got a busy signal. This time, finally, the call went through.

"Who is it?" a girlish, breathy voice answered. Cassie was quick to note the lack of a welcoming "Hello." If she had answered the phone like that when she was a girl, she would have been grounded for a week.

"It's your aunt Cassie, Heather," she replied. "Is your mom there? I need to talk to her."

"I'm waiting for an important call," Heather replied. "I'm sorry, but I've got to keep the line free. Call back in half an hour."

"No—wait—Heather!" Cassie cried, but the phone went dead. Cassie slumped against the phone booth and closed her eyes tight to keep the tears back. Ridiculous of her to feel like crying. But she felt so tired . . . and disappointed. Even if she got to New York in time, she would arrive looking like the rumpled backward country mouse Miranda assumed—and Cassie secretly feared—she really was.

Damn, she should have listened to Kenneth's advice. Sensible as always, he had counseled: "Why not go sometime when it's convenient for you, Cass? It seems to me you're just accommodating Miranda's whim to have you there— on mighty short notice—and throwing our own plans to the wind. You know how much my parents were looking forward to meeting you . . ."

Cassie made her way back to the row of hard plastic molded chairs and sat down. No, she hadn't listened to Kenneth. She had hardly even taken his words into consideration. Because, ever since her sister's call, she had been consumed with the question of why she had been asked to make a command appearance at Miranda's. Cassie knew enough about her sister to know that nothing she ever did was motivated by what Kenneth called "whim." Miranda calculated pros and cons and put into action only that which she considered most effective. Miranda had never, as far as Cassie remembered, done anything on impulse. Or just out of curiosity. That was Cassie's style. And, present case in point, it was a tendency that more often than not got her into trouble. Unlike Miranda, she just wasn't one to think a thing through.

For far too long now, Cassie realized, she had been drifting. Moving from thing to thing, following the course of least resistance. Even her relationship with Kenneth was something easier to continue than to end. He professed his love . . . and she accepted it. Her lack of focus and direction spilled over into her work as well.

"The trouble with you, Cassie," her assistant city editor had told her recently when she had been passed over for a story she'd really wanted, "is that you just kind of waffle around on important assignments. You skirt the crux of the story . . . albeit you always come up with plenty of color. This story about the new zoning laws—we really need someone who's going to go in there and dig." No, she knew that her ACE—as the assistant editors were called—was right. The reporters who got ahead were those who went after stories like bloodhounds on a scent. Cassie tended to collect too many unrelated facts, to research everyone's side of a particular story, to end up with pieces that were long on narrative . . . and short on plot.

Cassie yawned, stretched, and closed her eyes. Exhaustion lulled her. She felt herself floating on a bright, busy river. She heard people chatting vaguely to her right and left, the sound of newspapers crackling, the noise of a loudspeaker reverberating: "Flight 127 to La Guardia now boarding at gate number . . ."

With an effort, she woke, fished around for her dog-eared boarding pass, and shuffled with the others onto the newly de-iced plane. It took less than an hour before they landed in New York . . . and another two hours before Cassie was finally forced to face the fact that her luggage had not made the trip with her.

"I'm sorry, ma'am," a haggard lost-and-found clerk reported "Your bag seems to have gotten rerouted to Denver. Fill this form out, and we'll deliver it to wherever you're staying in New York no later than Sunday night."

"Great," Cassie said, "just in time for my return flight home." She found a ladies' room and did what she could to wash up, using liquid soap and the hot air blower. The once crisp and well-tailored slate-gray suit that she had been so thrilled to find on sale now looked tired and cheaply made. Cassie, who tended to dress in turtlenecks and jeans and other throwbacks to the sixties, had thought when she bought it that the suit gave her a serious, professional aura. In the harsh bathroom light she could she could see what she hadn't noticed at the department store: the fabric made her complexion look sallow, and the lipstick she applied to counter her paleness was far too bright. When she leaned over to adjust her hem, Cassie's wristwatch snagged in her panty hose. A half-inch-wide run spread from midcalf to waist as she straightened up again.

She bought another pair of panty hose at a concession in the airport and, as she waited in the taxi line, tried to figure out how she was going to get them on before reaching Miranda's house. It was already nearly four-thirty in the afternoon, and the party would start at five. She contemplated a return to the ladies' room until she saw the long line that had formed behind her at the taxi stand.

And so Cassie arrived at one of the more glittering cocktail parties of the Manhattan Easter weekend late, poorly dressed, seriously tired, and with a decided limp. As she climbed the curved marble steps to the Darins' ornately decorated wrought-iron front door, she practiced turning her leg with the snagged stocking in and away from view.

Before she could ring the bell, the huge door silently swung open. A man, dressed in white tie but with the slightly sardonic attitude of a head waiter, eyed her critically. On closer inspection, Cassie saw that the man's tuxedo fit poorly, bunching at the waist, too short at the cuffs. Obviously rented.

"Yes?" he demanded, as though he already knew she didn't belong. Cassie could hear the tinkle of glasses, a murmuring sea of conversation in the background. If she'd had any other place to go, she would have turned and fled at that very moment.

"I was invited," Cassie told him weakly. "I'm a guest. For the weekend. All my things went to Denver. Rerouted. Oh, damn," she muttered as she heard the sound of approaching laughter.

"Don't hold the door open, for heaven's sake." Cassie heard Miranda's distinctive voice. "It's freezing. Who is it anyway?"

"I'll take care of it," the man said. "You, come here," he added, grasping Cassie's right arm. "This way." She saw a blur of beautifully dressed people, cream-colored enameled walls, chintz-covered furniture. She stumbled a little as he pulled her up curving back stairs, an aroma of expensive hors d'oeuvres drifting up from below. She followed him down plushly carpeted halls scented with furniture wax and freshly cut flowers. He switched on a light, and the

loveliest bedroom Cassie had ever seen was flooded with
a soft peach-tinted glow. Miranda, or her interior designer,
was clearly mad about chintz: a Clarence House pattern
covered the walls and the magnificent nineteenth-century
mahogany four-poster. A dozen or so antique white lace
pillows had been arranged on the bed with artful grace.
A pair of English decoupage lamps on small yet ornately
carved night tables flanked the bed. Only the white enameled ceiling, wainscoting, and pale cream-colored carpet
offset the lush feminine patterns of the room.

"How beautiful!" Cassie said. Her own bedroom was
comprised of a double mattress covered with a plaid cotton
comforter and a desk made of two filing cabinets bridged
by a battered oak door. Cassie had been very proud of the
handmade desk. Her portable computer fit very snugly into
an inlay of the old oak plank.

"Here." The man opened a door at the far end of the
room. "Take what you need," he said, leaving the door
ajar and walking back toward Cassie. He looked at her
again with the same ironic smile as when he first saw
her and added, "You're about her size. Borrow whatever
you like."

Cassie walked across the room and stared into the small
chamber. It was a dressing room, chintz-covered, of course,
in a light pink geranium pattern. A plush crimson-covered
day bed took up the far corner; the rest of the room was
filled with rack after rack, shelf after shelf of dresses,
skirts, sweaters, pants, shoes, hats, scarves—a full boutique
of designer clothes.

"Are you sure she won't mind?" Cassie called back to
the man who had shown her upstairs, but he was gone.

Miranda must have told him to bring her here, Cassie
assured herself. No doubt Miranda had explained to the
butler or waiter or whatever he was that her sister was
expected to arrive late and that he should show her up
to Miranda's room and tell her to make herself feel at
home. Cassie kicked off her shoes and flopped back on

the chintz-covered bed with a sigh. Did she really dare do what the man had suggested? She looked down at her gray ruin of a suit . . . and recalled the expensive clothes of the guests below.

She smiled as she stepped out of her bedraggled skirt. "I just didn't want to embarrass you," Cassie would tell Miranda later, "in front of all your important friends." Then, feeling surprisingly happy and confident, Cassie walked barefoot into the famous Miranda Darin's dressing room . . . and started to try on her sister's things.

Three

It wasn't as if Cassie hadn't been to some pretty fancy parties before: big weddings, proms, the Christmas bash the paper threw at the country club every year. It's just that no one there rubbed elbows with Morley Safer. Or sipped champagne next to Beverly Sills. Or accidentally jabbed a high heel into one of Senator Anthony Haas's Italian-leather-covered toes.

"Oh, sorry," Cassie said as the Senator turned to see with whom his foot had collided. It was him, in the flesh, Cassie realized, the man who had personified for her parents all the deepest values of the liberal ideology. He was a little shorter than his photos suggested, his face flushed and somewhat puffy. But his blue eyes had the same aggressive expression that Cassie remembered from television debates and magazine interviews. His beautifully tailored Savile Row suit could not disguise his burly working-class physique. He must be in his early sixties now, Cassie thought, as she felt his eyes on her. His sand-colored hair was thinning, exposing a broad powerful brow. His chin and neckline were starting to soften. But Cassie could still feel the famous charisma emanating from the older man. This almost sexual thrall had motivated her parents and hundreds of thousands like them in the sixties to march, to protest, to stand up for what they believed in.

"Miranda—no," the Senator replied somewhat thickly, frowning and looking Cassie over more closely. "But you must be related somehow, yes?" He held out his hand in welcome.

"I'm her sister," Cassie answered, grasping his hand. "Her half sister, really. My parents were tremendous admirers of yours, Senator." How thrilled they would have been to know that Cassie had met this man, to realize that Miranda actually knew him personally! For the first time since being invited, Cassie felt grateful that she'd accepted Miranda's invitation.

"Where is that lovely woman, anyway?" the Senator replied, looking around the crowded living room. "I haven't seen her since I got here . . ."

"I haven't either, actually," Cassie began before she realized that someone else had grabbed the Senator's attention. He was bending down, cupping his hand against his ear, listening to what an older woman in a wheelchair was saying. The woman was dressed in a dark blue sequined evening dress, and ropes of pearls circled her neck. Cassie could tell by the way the Senator treated her that she was someone special. But after the Senator turned away, Cassie once again felt lost. Stepping carefully, she continued to drift through the noisy crowd, searching for Miranda, a small smile fixed firmly in place.

People nodded and smiled back. Obviously she looked familiar to them. The fact that Senator Haas had nearly had mistook her for Miranda secretly thrilled her. Thank God, she told herself, she had had the sense to change into Miranda's things. Dressed in a powder-blue tailored Yves St. Laurent dress with an intricately patterned Hermes scarf draped around her shoulders, Cassie felt slim and pretty. She even fit into Miranda's shoes, choosing an elegant pair of low-slung suede Bottega Veneto pumps. Cassie had drawn the line at trying on Miranda's jewelry, though she had peeked into the antique Japanese chest where her collection was stored. Each cherry-wood drawer contained a small glittering bounty: in one, a nest of gold loop earrings in various sizes and styles; in another, the interweaving strands of a black pearl necklace; still another contained nothing but a small dark blue box. Cassie had opened it to find a flawless octagonal sapphire flanked by tiny diamonds set on a platinum band. The ring alone was undoubtedly worth more than what Cassie earned in a year.

Money . . . Miranda's town house literally smelled of it: the unmistakable scents of Patou and Chanel, the rich mustiness of carefully aged tobacco, the almost sticky sweetness of freshly cut hyacinths arranged in an antique pewter urn at the foot of the stairs. Two of the several downstairs fireplaces were lit—one in the living room, the other in the crimson-walled library—adding a pungent layer of wood smoke to the other mingled aromas.

"Yes, you look much better," said a vaguely familiar voice at Cassie's side. She turned to find the man who had first let her into the house and shown her up to Miranda's room. He held out a glass of champagne.

"Thanks," she said, taking the crystal flute in both hands and smiling at him. He smiled back, and for the first time Cassie registered the fact that he was quite handsome. He was slightly taller than her with coal-black hair, in some need of cutting, combed back from his forehead. His skin had the hardened cast of a construction worker—someone who spent most of his time outdoors, who worked with his hands. But for all that, his eyes were a keen, observant golden-brown, and his smile had a knowing intelligence to it. Cassie decided that he was probably an actor, supplementing a difficult stage career with his catering job.

"Are you having a good time?" he asked. His voice was deep and rough, as though he used it sparingly.

"Well, it's a little difficult since I don't know anybody," Cassie replied. "Though I managed to introduce myself to Senator Haas over there by trampling on his toes."

"I wouldn't worry about that," the waiter said with a laugh. "He's too far gone to feel much of anything."

"You mean . . ." Cassie stared across the room at the famous politician. "He's drunk?"

"Nothing that vulgar," the man explained. "I'd say he's about as meticulously inebriated as he is well dressed. Mind you, he takes great care never to stumble or slur his words. But he's actually blitzed, been drinking vodka since breakfast."

"How would you know?" Cassie asked, unhappy with the news that her parents' idol had feet of clay. She didn't like the waiter's sarcastic tone, yet when she looked again across the room at Senator Haas she could now see the truth in what the man had said: the Senator's gaze was unfocused, his smile slow and a little dazed. And, Cassie remembered sadly, he'd mistaken her for Miranda.

"I know because I keep my eyes open," the waiter told her. "I try to see these people for what they are . . . not what all their expensive haircuts and designer clothes would have you believe."

"Do I detect a note of envy in your voice?" Cassie laughed, though she could see by the waiter's expression that he wasn't amused.

"Why in the world would I envy this crowd?" the man demanded. He had dark expressive brows that came together when he frowned. His eyes, Cassie decided, were the color of amber or rosin, something slightly precious and extremely durable.

"Well, I just assumed, that being a waiter . . ." Cassie replied. "I mean, having to cater to them . . ."

Her explanation was cut short when he said, "You think that . . ." but his question dissolved into laughter. It was a strange sound—part cough, part chuckle, but altogether not a very happy noise, Cassie decided. It ended as abruptly as it began. "You think I'm a waiter?"

Cassie stood erect, not liking his tone of voice at all. What right did he have to be so condescending . . . and yet so secretive? He made her feel as though he knew something—no, a great many things—that she didn't. "Actually

I decided you were a struggling actor and this was what you do to keep bread on the table."

"God, I look that . . . disreputable?" the man said, though more to himself than to her. "I must be doing something right."

"Please enlighten me, then," Cassie replied stiffly. "I don't know anyone here . . . and I obviously misjudged. I'm sorry." She thought of what he said, about seeing people for what they were. No doubt he saw straight through the expensive facade Miranda's silk and suede had temporarily provided her—to the uneasy and uncertain person for whom he'd first opened the door.

But he came to her rescue swiftly, dropping his sardonic attitude. "I apologize. Cassie, isn't it?" he said, holding out his hand. "I'm Jason Darin, Miranda's husband. And, really, I'm sorry I embarrassed you. I thought you knew."

"You're Jason?"

"You're surprised," Jason said, his smile much kinder now. "Tell me—what exactly did you expect?"

"Oh . . ." Cassie circled her hands vaguely. "Something . . . someone far more . . . polished? You know—I mean, are you aware that your tux doesn't quite fit?"

Jason again made the unhappy sound that passed for laughter and said, "Yes, I'm quite aware. I do this to annoy your darling sister. Clothes mean so very much to her."

"I see," Cassie said, her gaze moving from him to the crowded, and now smoke-filled, room. Yes, she was surprised. She had envisioned Miranda's life as one seamless crystal bowl of perfection, filled with the ripest and most expensive cherries. And yet the first person she met—Miranda's own husband—was both something of an outcast and decidedly a critic of Miranda's life-style. "So you don't entirely approve of all this?"

"I bought her this place as a wedding present," Jason replied, though not answering her question. "I'd just closed a fantastic deal—one of the most lucrative real estate projects I'd ever helped broker—and I knew how much she wanted to live around here. With all the other society ladies. She wanted so very much to be a lady."

"It's a beautiful . . . neighborhood," Cassie said lamely. The conversation had veered away from her. Jason seemed to be talking mostly to himself.

"Yes . . . but look who you get for neighbors! You see that old biddy swathed in blue sequins?" Jason nodded to the woman in the wheelchair with whom Senator Haas had been speaking. "She's the Saint Peter of Manhattan Society. She decides who'll get through the pearly gates . . . and who won't. It doesn't matter how much cash you dish out for the New York Public Library Fund or the Metropolitan Opera House. It doesn't matter if you dress up in black tie every night of the week. It doesn't matter if you're a social worker . . . or a child molester. If she doesn't take to you—you're out. She lives half a block down the street. Lovely person to have for a neighbor, don't you think?"

"She doesn't like you?" Cassie guessed.

"Actually, she barely knows me," Jason said. "No. She doesn't or didn't like my wife. Nothing Miranda did—and she tried everything—would break the old coot's resolve to shut Miranda out. Until Miranda found her sponsor. It's really a great deal like joining a fraternity, I suppose. Somehow, though, I doubt the dues you have to pay are worth it."

"What makes you so cynical?" Cassie asked, surprised when she heard herself utter the words she had merely been thinking moments before.

Jason turned and stared at her, his golden eyes darkening. His whole face looked as if a cloud had just passed over it. There was something forbidding about the measuring look he gave her, the set of his jaw.

"That's really none of your business," he said.

"I know," Cassie replied simply. "I don't know why I asked. But I doubt that everyone here is as ferocious as the dragon lady over there." She wanted to see him smile again. She could feel him next to her—a coiled spring of a body—throwing off heat and bitterness. She wanted to see him relax, the way he had for a moment when he had first introduced himself. But, more than anything, she wanted him to open up to her. She realized how much she liked the rusty and strained sound of his voice. "Tell me about some of the others," she urged. "That lovely redhead in the dark green dress over there, for instance."

"Ah, yes, Marisa Newtown," Jason said. "A treacherous stretch of water, if you ask me. Makes a habit—or perhaps it's become a hobby?—of bedding down with her best friends' husbands. Told me a week or so ago that she was Miranda's very best friend. I've been keeping quite a distance between us, you can imagine."

"So morals among the rich are everything we bourgeois are led to believe?" Cassie asked.

"I don't know what you believe," Jason replied, his voice hard-edged once more. "Mine are in good working order, if that's what you mean."

"Lord, you are touchy, Mr. Darin," Cassie said with a laugh. "I was casting no aspersions whatsoever, I promise. I was just trying to be friendly. It's a fatal flaw among us Southerners, I'm afraid."

"And I'm afraid I'm being a bore," Jason said, shaking his head. "Come, let's find the hostess. She's probably working the crowd in the library." Jason led the way through the high-ceilinged room with its lush oriental carpets, beautiful austere antique Shaker furniture, and glassed mahogany bookcases. It was jam-packed with people, though Miranda was nowhere in sight.

Cassie trailed behind him as he impatiently pushed his way down the hall, briefly toured the ornately decorated dining room, and circled the huge ballroom with its rococo mirrors and marbled floors. Every few feet someone would greet him.

"Jason, how're you doing?"

"Back in town for long this time, Jason?"

"When are you going to get a haircut, darling?"

And he'd respond with a clipped: "Just fine . . . Great . . . Yes, soon."

Finally she found herself alone with him, following him down the same carpeted corridor they'd transversed when he'd first shown her upstairs. He pushed a swinging door open an inch. He listened intently to a muffled conversation taking place in the next room. Suddenly the voices behind the door rose, and Cassie recognized one of them as Miranda's.

"I'm not prying, damn it. I'm only doing my job."

"I find it ridiculous to have to remind you, Miranda, that I dictate the parameters of your job. What I'm telling you is that this time you've gone too far. I want this silly so-called investigation to stop now. Here. Do you understand?"

"Over my dead body."

The other voice, a man's, rose with anger. "Don't you dare contradict me, Miranda, not now. After everything I've done—"

Abruptly Jason pushed the door open. Bright overhead lights from the butler's pantry spilled into the corridor, blinding Cassie for a second.

"Why, here you are," Jason said. Cassie already knew his voice well enough to know his tone was one of barely controlled anger. "All your guests are asking for you."

"We were just talking—" Miranda began. Cassie saw her then: a tall angel of a woman, dazzling blond hair haloing a perfect face. Like Cassie, she wore a powder-blue dress, but where Cassie's was all fitted angles and tailored curves, Miranda's was a sheer swirl of sensuality. Crepe de chine caressed her full breasts and fondled the still-boyish thighs. She was so beautiful! Cassie thought, feeling a rush of fierce pride, followed as it always was by a crushing wave of envy. She was so stunning. No wonder Jason stared at her with such an open look of anguish and need. He loved her. And in a flash of insight, Cassie realized that Jason was not the only man in the room to love Miranda Darin.

The stranger was tall, his mane of silver hair carefully groomed to show off its rich fullness. His face was lined, tanned, and overtly handsome. Unlike Jason's, his were the kind of good looks that called attention to themselves. He was the sort of man people turned to watch as he strode down the street. Was he a movie star? A singer? Cassie tried but couldn't place him. He was impeccably dressed, in a dark suit and faultless shirt and tie that in their extreme understatement spoke loudly of custom tailors, butlers, limousines.

"Cassie," Miranda said, "when did you get here?"

"She's been here over an hour," Jason cut in, "as you'd already know if you'd bothered to check in with your other guests."

Ignoring her husband, Miranda crossed the room to take Cassie's arm. "You look sensational, Cassie. Love that scarf. I've one just like it." She led her toward the tall man who was smiling now, Cassie decided, a very false smile. "I'd like you to meet a good friend of mine. Vance Magnus."

"As in Magnus Media?" Cassie asked, trying to stay cool as she shook hands with one of the most powerful men in the communications industry. His logo—a lion clutching a sword—was emblazoned across the letterheads of more television, radio, and cable networks than anyone else's in the country.

"As in Vance to you, I'm sure," he said graciously. His grip was firm and warm and very dry.

"Oh, I'm sorry," Miranda said with her low seductive laugh. "Why should I expect you just to know? This is my sister, Vance. This is Cassie. The one I told you so much about."

"Of course, Cassie," Magnus repeated, his hand still enfolding hers. "I'm so pleased to meet you at last. Delighted." And though he stood there beaming down at her, Cassie felt a shiver pass through her body. When Cassie was growing up, that sort of feeling—a premonition, really—was known as "someone stepping on your grave." And though she smiled bravely back at Vance Magnus . . . she felt her hands and her heart go cold under his overly warm and penetrating gaze.

Four

"I hate you, I hate you!" Heather's high-pitched whine reverberated down the hall the next morning. Cassie sat up and listened as her niece continued to wage what seemed to be an entrenched campaign against her long-suffering Swedish nanny.

"You will come now, young lady." Cassie heard Miss Boyeson's lilting voice follow Heather's footsteps down the corridor toward Cassie's room. "You will get into your bath this minute, do you hear? Or else you will soak in cold water, this I promise."

The door to Cassie's bedroom opened abruptly and clicked shut. Cassie could hear Heather's quick, excited breathing across the room. The maid had drawn the heavy brocade curtains the night before, cloaking the enormous guest bedroom in darkness, and Cassie guessed that Heather thought she had the room to herself.

"I'll take your bath if you don't want it," Cassie called out. She heard Heather gasp, open the door, slam it, and continue her rampage down the hall. It was just the beginning of a long day of siege.

"Where is my Easter basket?" the seven-year-old demanded shortly after coffee was served in the oval sun parlor that was used as the Darins' informal dining room.

Tall French windows faced out on a back garden whose bushes and flower beds were still shrouded in burlap for the winter. The rounded walls were painted a rich eggshell enamel, drawing in and reflecting the bright morning light. Enormous tropical ferns perched on plaster pedestals, their tendrils moving gently in the warm moist air that circulated from hidden floor vents. This was Cassie's favorite room in the Darins' enormous town house: bright and intimate, it was one of the few places in the house designed for comfort rather than show.

"You have to look for it, Heather," Jason said, folding the paper and reaching for his coffee. He had on jeans and a dark blue wool turtleneck. He hadn't shaved, and Cassie found herself watching him surreptitiously whenever she had the chance. He was so very different from the man she imagined Miranda would have chosen for a husband. When he and Miranda first married—a fact that Cassie had learned about in a brief telegram—Cassie had decided to do a little research on her new brother-in-law. She'd needed to dig no further than a long profile in the *Wall Street Journal* to discover that Jason Darin was something of a business renegade: a fiercely independent developer whose high standards in architecture and construction had gone against the grain of the 1980s building boom. When others threw up retail and office space as quickly and inexpensively as urban growth demanded, Jason Darin created buildings for the long haul. The insistence on quality paid off: there were waiting lists for Darin-made buildings at a time when twenty-five percent of commercial real estate in the city remained empty.

Still, the lengthy analysis of the Darin success story, even the meticulous line drawing that accompanied the article, had done nothing to prepare Cassie for the man. The sarcasm, the brooding temper, followed by sudden bursts of warmth and tenderness—Cassie was beginning to realize that it would take more than a long weekend to understand him.

"I don't want to look," Heather cried. "I want my basket—and I want it now."

"Don't whine, darling," Miranda said as she drifted into the room. She had on a peach-colored satin kimono, her snowy blond hair drawn back from her forehead in a silk scarf. She looked fresh and luminous; the sweet smell of lily of the valley trailed her into the room. Cassie, who'd gotten one of the maids to iron out her gray suit, felt both badly and overdressed.

"But, Momma, I want my basket!" Heather continued.

"You've made that abundantly clear, Heath," Jason replied. "Now I'm going to make myself clear: if you want your basket you're going to have to—along with the rest of the children in the world—go . . . and . . . look . . . for . . . it!"

"Jason, don't," Miranda said, frowning.

"Don't what? Discipline my own daughter? Try to teach her some manners? I swear to God, Miranda, you're going to—"

"We have a guest," Miranda cut in, nodding toward Cassie who tried to look thoroughly involved with buttering her English muffin.

"No, we have family. And I have the feeling that Cassie doesn't mind in the least having some sense knocked into her bratty little niece."

"I've an idea," Cassie said, pushing back her chair. The venom in Jason's tone, the distaste in Miranda's, made Cassie feel slightly ill. "Let's both of us go find that basket, Heather. Come on . . ." Unwillingly, Heather followed Cassie out of the sun parlor.

"I bet it's in here . . ." Cassie called, opening up a glass-covered drawer of the breakfront in the huge darkened formal dining room. Two twin Venetian glass chandeliers glittered dimly overhead.

"Momma wouldn't like you looking there," Heather told her as she came up behind Cassie.

"Why not? There's just linen and silver," Cassie replied, standing up. "Nothing from the Easter Bunny."

"Don't be stupid," Heather said as she followed Cassie into the library. "There's no Easter Bunny. Even I know that."

"You know an awful lot, don't you?" Cassie said, pulling up the cushions on one of the built-in window seats.

"I know that Momma wouldn't want you doing that."

"Well, if you don't start looking for it somewhere, Heather, you're never going to find it."

"Oh . . . I know where it is."

"You do?" Cassie turned and faced her niece. She would have been a lovely little girl if not for the sour expression she generally wore. Her hair was something like Cassie's—a light strawberry-blond—tumbling to her shoulders in neatly curled waves that Cassie guessed were set by hand. She had her mother's green eyes. In fact, her entire genetic makeup seemed drawn from Miranda: the creamy, almost porcelainlike skin, the determined chin, and the wide mouth that offset the slightly too-thin lips. Even her voice—husky and rich—reminded Cassie of Miranda. Not to mention her determination . . . and temper.

"Yes. I got the new cook to tell me this morning," Heather said proudly. "Dumb old cow. Told her I'd tell Momma she'd been stealing unless she did. Daddy hid it downstairs in one of the clothes washers. I should have known. He always hides it in the basement."

"Were you born this awful," Cassie asked, "or have you just been working very hard at it ever since?"

"What did you say?"

"You heard me." After all, Cassie thought, she had nothing to lose by speaking her mind except Heather's affection. And that was something she very much doubted she was ever likely to receive. How in the world did the child—who seemed to have been given every luxury known to man—turn out so grasping and mean?

"Momma!" Heather cried as Cassie had known she would. "Momma! Aunt Cassie called me names. I hate her! I hate her!"

Easter Sunday wasn't a particularly happy occasion for anyone in the Darin household, as far as Cassie could tell. Jason disappeared after breakfast. Cassie was grateful when Miranda invited her up to her bedroom to pick out something to wear to church, but Miranda left Cassie to rummage through the dressing room alone as she pretended to write letters at the antique secretary by the window. Cassie couldn't help but notice that Miranda sat staring down at the same blank monogrammed page—pen loosely held in the carefully manicured hand. In profile, Miranda's features looked overly defined and somewhat drained, the fine blue veins showing through the translucent skin at her temples. Cassie, who accompanied a silent Miranda and a complaining Heather to the Episcopalian church on Madison Avenue, found the inspiring, music-filled service the high point of her morning.

In the afternoon, with Miranda at her office and Heather out visiting friends, Cassie found herself wandering through the downstairs feeling aimless and bored. What was the point of Miranda dragging her up to New York for the weekend if she was too busy to spend any time with her? Cassie wondered as she sat down in one of the window seats looking out over the elegant side street. Lord, but this fabulous house was filled with such unhappiness! Cassie reflected. She could almost feel it drifting through the handsome, high-ceilinged rooms: a heavy fog of misunderstanding and recrimination. It was clear to Cassie that something was wrong with Miranda and Jason's marriage. Was that why Cassie had been asked up for the weekend? Had Miranda hoped to confide in her, to seek advice? If so, it seemed to Cassie that Miranda had changed her mind. Courteous yet distant, Miranda treated her like some business subordinate, someone she had to pretend to like for appearance' sake.

Then there was Heather. Well, Cassie told herself, trying to be fair, when a marriage is on the rocks supposedly the first people to get hurt are the children. Heather was a bright kid. She no doubt had picked up on her parents' hostilities toward one another. Perhaps her awful behavior was just some playing out of fears based on the adults' problems.

"Where is everyone?"

"Jason! I didn't hear you come in." Cassie shook her head, trying to hide the fact that he had the power to make her blush. "Miranda had some work at the office. Heather's at a friend's place."

"And they left you here alone."

"I was just . . ." Cassie stood up to face him. He had a battered leather jacket slung over his shoulder. "Actually . . . yes, they did."

"What you must think of us," he said, shrugging on the jacket. "I'm afraid you decided to visit at a rather bad time. A shame you couldn't make it at Christmas, but that can't be helped now. I was about to go out myself. I need a drive. You're welcome to come if you like."

It shouldn't have surprised Cassie that Jason had a Harley-Davidson motorcycle. Nothing he did or said was anything like what Cassie had expected. Not that he said anything as he buckled her helmet and nodded for her to climb on after he'd revved the motor. They spun out onto the street with a roar, the wind whipping at Cassie's hair.

She didn't pay much attention to where they were going . . . she just knew they were going there fast. Jason snaked his way impatiently through idling traffic, shot past changing lights, accelerated onto a highway ramp, and then really put on speed. He seemed wholly intent on what he was doing, and Cassie, her arms circling his waist, felt the power of that concentration pumping through layers of fabric and leather. He felt tense and strong and yet distant. Cassie sensed this ride was some private ritual—a way of working out aggression and anger—and that she had been invited along simply out of pity. It should have bothered her, but it didn't. It should have bothered her even more that she found holding on to him, tightening her arms and legs around him, so dangerously exciting. But she told herself it was a harmless fantasy. No one but she would ever know how thrilled she was to accidentally touch the cold surface of his belt buckle, or to breathe in the pungent smell of his leather jacket. No one need know. And, besides, the next day she would be gone.

Dinner was a less tense and slightly livelier affair. Heather, exhausted no doubt from a full day of misbehaving, sat quietly—her eyelids occasionally drooping—across the table from Cassie. Miranda and Jason faced each other at either end of the long linen-covered dining-room table. Even though it was just the four of them, the multicourse dinner was formally served by the cook and a pretty, young maid Cassie hadn't seen before. She still couldn't figure out how many servants Miranda employed; the faces seemed to change as rapidly as the moods of the two employers. For that night, at least, their moods were on an upswing.

"Mrs. Fitzgibbon has asked us for lunch next Sunday," Miranda announced, smiling at Jason through a forest of burning candelabras.

"Is that right? Well, congratulations. You've finally won, then. We should have some champagne."

"Oh, you're so vulgar, Jason. You make it sound as if I came in first in a livestock contest."

"How different is it really?" Jason asked. "Most people old Fitzie favors come with strong bloodlines and top-drawer breeding pedigrees. You're one of the dark horses, you know, Miranda. Someone who wins the race on guts and stamina alone."

"Should I take that as a compliment?"

"Take it any way you like," Jason told her. He turned to Cassie. "Fitzie is the doyenne I pointed out to you last night. The keeper of the gate?"

"Yes, the one in blue sequins," Cassie said.

"I hope you haven't been paying any attention to the pure

vitriol Jason directs at my friends," Miranda told Cassie. "I'm afraid my husband is antisocial."

"No," Jason answered, "just antisocialite. There is a difference. I tend to like people for who they are, not whom they know. I suppose we should raise a glass to Magnus for his contribution to your success."

"Yes, I suppose we should," Miranda replied after a moment's hesitation. Cassie felt the chill in her sister's voice. "I'm sure he thinks he deserves all the credit."

Jason stared down the table at his wife. "Don't tell me you've actually discovered a dent in his glamorous armor."

"Several, actually," Miranda replied, meeting Jason's gaze with a small smile. "We'll talk about it later."

Was there something a little sinister in the look Miranda gave her husband, or was Cassie just imagining it? Or, to be honest with herself, was she hoping that what seemed to be a warming trend between them was really just that—an appearance? With a sudden sense of shame, Cassie realized that she had been happier with the situation when Miranda and Jason seemed less happy with each other. She knew why, and she felt the shame dig deeper. "Thou shalt not covet," were among the first words Cassie had put to memory. And yet, from the earliest moment she could remember, she had coveted everything about Miranda. And now this gnawing jealousy—this ugly claw of need—was reaching out and clutching at Jason.

Much later that night, Cassie woke up suddenly. She didn't know what had roused her until she heard the voices. Vicious and accusing, they ricocheted down the hall.

"How dare you . . ."

"What else are you hiding? I wonder."

"Why are you doing this? The girl meant nothing to me. Why do you want to ruin me?"

At that moment Cassie's door opened, light from the corridor slanted in across the room, and a small crouching figure ran toward her bed. Heather, her face slick with tears, shivered beside Cassie's pillow.

"Climb in here, honey," Cassie said, drawing back the sheets.

"I hate this," Heather whimpered, her face burrowing into Cassie's pillow. "I hate this."

"I know," Cassie said, smoothing back her niece's fine soft hair.

"I don't hate you," Heather mumbled.

"I know that, too," Cassie said as she rocked her weeping charge to sleep in her arms.

Five

"*W*here's everyone?" Cassie asked nervously as she faced her sister the next morning.

"Heather left for school, of course. Jason's at his office. It's just as well. I've been wanting to talk to you alone." Miranda was waiting in the sun parlor, breakfast things laid out around her with all the thought and precision of chess pieces arranged across a board. Dressed for the office in a pale green gabardine Armani suit, Miranda looked impeccable. It was impossible for Cassie to square this haughtily beautiful woman with the screeching harridan of the night before.

"So have I." Cassie felt her hand shake as she poured out coffee and cream.

"Why don't you go first, then," Miranda suggested as she squeezed a lemon wedge into her tea. "Have you had a good time? Jason and I are a little—argumentative— sometimes. I hope you don't take that too seriously. It's just our way."

"Your way seems to be hurting your daughter to an extent that I would take seriously if I were you."

"I don't know what you're talking about."

"Last night Heather came into my room, crying."

"Really? She probably had a nightmare. Odd she came to you."

"That's because you and Jason were too busy screaming at each other."

"Don't be ridiculous, Cassie," Miranda replied. "We had a little fight. Every married couple does. It airs things out is all. You'll discover that soon enough when you and— Kenneth, right?—get married. What are your plans? I'd really like to be a part of them if I can. I mean, help you with the wedding. And I think you should have a big ceremony. I regret I didn't now."

"Why didn't you, Miranda?" Cassie asked. It was obvious that Miranda was determined to deflect any further discussion of the previous night's uproar. But Cassie was equally determined to lead them back to it. "Was that just another one of those little things you and Jason disagreed about?"

"Lord, you are ruthless this morning, Cass. Okay, I give in. Jason and I had a whale of a fight last night. We've been going through a rough patch, as I'm sure you've noticed. It's mostly my fault. I'm just too busy for his taste. But I love my job and I love going out. And I don't feel like changing. He's such a homebody. I know he comes across as this sort of dashing, mysterious type— still waters running deep, and that sort of thing. Actually he's very straightforward. Honest, upright."

"You're making him sound almost boring."

"We've been married eight years, Cass. I'm successful. And sought after. I like to stretch my wings. Perhaps I'm just growing a little faster than he is."

"Or perhaps he doesn't like what you're growing into."

Miranda put her teacup down abruptly and folded her hands in her lap. She looked down at her beautifully manicured nails for a moment, then back up at Cassie. "I'm not blind, Cass. I see that Jason's worked his magic on you. He does that to women without even knowing it. He's like one of those magicians who hypnotize people in the audience without realizing it. I can't tell you how many women— friends of mine—he's unintentionally smitten. I'm just hurt you automatically take his side. I didn't mean to get into all this now. But I can assure you that there's a lot going on here you know nothing about."

Cassie knew she was blushing furiously and could do nothing to stop it. There was no point in denying what Miranda said; obviously she, Cassie, had made a fool of herself over Jason. Had he noticed it as well? she wondered. She felt silly and dull. All the fight went out of her. Once again, she was nothing more than Miranda Darin's little sister.

"Oh, stop looking so abashed," Miranda teased. "What's wrong with taking a shine to someone? I'm sure Jason was flattered. You know, you've turned out to be a very attractive woman."

There were all sorts of implications in Miranda's words that Cassie struggled to process quickly: Jason knew—how horrible! And Miranda seemed genuinely surprised that Cassie had "turned out" as well as she had. That meant she must have had a fairly low opinion of Cassie before. It also indicated that Cassie had passed some sort of test in Miranda's mind.

"I'm glad you approve," Cassie replied stiffly. Then she heard herself at last saying what she had felt for so long: "You know, it hasn't exactly been easy following in your huge footsteps. It's like trying to fill the tracks of some enormous dinosaur."

Miranda laughed. "You make me sound so horrible, Cass. Sometimes I think you hate me . . . I wouldn't be surprised. Lord knows I've been the most inconsistent sister in the world. I hope I can start to change that now. I want to play a bigger role in your life. I really loved having you here. I want you to feel welcome—anytime, all the time."

There was something so patently false about Miranda's speech that Cassie sat in shocked silence for a moment, trying to think of some way to react to her sister's insincerity. Miranda had barely seen Cassie over the weekend— so how could she pretend to have loved having her there?

How in the world was she supposed to feel welcome when her two hosts spent most of her time there tearing each other apart?

Before Cassie could frame a plausible response, Miranda added, "Actually, Cass, I want you to stay."

"Stay? Here?"

"Yes. The most terrific job has come up at the network, something that's just so right for you. It's a newswriting slot. I talked it over with Magnus yesterday afternoon, and he agrees you'd be perfect for it."

"But he doesn't even know me. How in the world can he—"

"I told him all about you, of course," Miranda cut in. "He's very impressed with what I said. He's actually rearranged his schedule to meet with you this afternoon to talk it over."

"The head of the network wants to talk to me," Cassie repeated slowly, "about some lowly newswriter position. Miranda, I'm no fool. You talked him into this, didn't you?"

"Well, my word does carry some weight there, Cass. But I also know you'd be terrific at the job. It's such an opportunity for you. It's the kind of position I started out in."

"I'm sorry to disappoint you, Miranda, but I'm not interested. I've already got a job, in case you haven't noticed. I'm a GA now, you know, not some little inexperienced starter. Besides, I've no interest in television. I'm a newspaper reporter."

"You've just never considered it," Miranda said. "You never thought you'd get the chance. It would be so exciting to have you here . . . in the city . . . with all of us."

"It's just not what I want."

"But think about it for a second," Miranda continued persuasively. "Wouldn't it be fun to live up here? Think of what a great time we could have. We've a million spare bedrooms. You wouldn't even have to look for a place of your own."

"And what about my life in Raleigh, Miranda?" Cassie asked. "What about my job? My friends? Kenneth? It's . . . just impossible." And yet, even as Cassie said it, she knew how incredibly easy it would be for her to cut herself loose. Start fresh. All those things that she had assured Miranda were impossible for her to give up actually held her very tenuously. In another moment or two, with a bit more encouragement from Miranda, she might have allowed herself to consider the move. It was seductive. New York. The Magnus network. Even in the few short days of her visit, she'd picked up on the intensified rhythms of city life. Her blood ran quicker here, she knew. Her complexion was more vibrant, a little flushed. She'd felt more attractive, more interesting than she ever had in Raleigh—especially in Jason's presence.

"Damn it, Cass, you know what's wrong with you?" Miranda broke into her thoughts. "You're afraid to succeed. Afraid to take risks. You'd rather stay in some backwater town doing safe local coverage than take a chance on a real challenge. You're afraid to take the leap . . . because you're afraid to fail."

"Lord, but you know all about me, don't you?" Cassie said hotly. "What right have you to dictate what's important and what's not? I hate to tell you, but *Breaking News* is not the be-all and end-all of electronic journalism. If anything, it's oversensationalized and overformatted. When was the last time you had a truly spontaneous segment, Miranda? You know what's wrong with it? You're just too much in control. You have to manipulate everything, Miranda—Heather, Jason, and now even me. Well, count me out."

"I won't, Cass," Miranda said simply. "I want you to reconsider all this. Not right now. It's obviously not the right time. I'll cover things with Magnus. But I beg you to think about it this afternoon on the plane. Tonight when you're alone in your apartment. I'm offering you a whole new life . . . new friends . . . amazing possibilities."

"Why, Miranda?" Cassie asked, realizing at last that this was the question she should have asked at the beginning. "We've just barely been on speaking terms for years. Why would you suddenly want to start helping me now?"

"Maybe you've got it all backward," Miranda said sadly, rising to go. "I'm already a half hour late for a production meeting. Have a safe trip home. Call me when you're ready." Then she was gone. Without a kiss. Without so much as a touch on the shoulder.

It took Cassie nearly a week before she could think back calmly enough on her conversation with Miranda to wonder what her older sister had meant about Cassie getting "it all backward." It seemed an odd response after Cassie's impassioned outburst. It was the sort of oblique and curious statement that Miranda didn't traffic in. Her manner was usually so direct and clear. And the tone of voice had been off as well, Cassie reflected. She'd sounded almost defeated.

Nothing had gone right since Cassie's return to Raleigh. For one thing, it had rained steadily the entire week, causing a drainage pipe above her living room to burst. A big wet stain the shape—and it seemed to Cassie almost the size— of Texas covered the ceiling. The wall-to-wall carpeting had been ruined by the flood, the plush pile fabric a soggy mess that squelched every time Cassie walked on it. The floor below was probably a disaster as well, though Cassie wouldn't know until the carpet removers came, and they were apparently backed up two weeks.

The entire apartment—so recently a source of pride— seemed shabby and small. The furniture, which Cassie had lovingly collected from antique stores and tag sales, now appeared scuffed and mismatched. And what in the world had enticed her to paint the walls light blue? Stains showed up so quickly, and especially on a rainy evening, the blue just seemed so blue, so depressing.

Then there was Kenneth. He'd been upset with her that she hadn't called ahead to tell him what flight she'd be taking back from New York so that he could meet her, and it seemed they'd fought about everything since. Not full-fledged fights, just dull little bickering quarrels that never seemed to reach a climax.

"Why don't you come by the hospital when you're done at the office and we'll have dinner together?" he'd asked her nicely enough in the middle of the afternoon a week after her return.

"It's Thursday."

"So?"

"Kenneth. It's Thursday." She hated the put-upon sound of her voice, but was unable to change it. "Thursday night, remember? It's when Miranda's on."

"Oh, the show, of course. Well, I'll come by your apartment, then. We'll have take-out. What do you want? Chinese or Mexican?"

And that's what it seemed her life had boiled down to: dispiriting choices, dull evenings in front of the television, the accommodating affection of a man she no longer loved. That was the real crux of everything that had gone wrong since her return: she didn't love Kenneth and she realized now that she probably never had. She no longer felt attracted to his tall, lean body or his hands that were a little too big for his long wiry arms. His face, like hers, was lightly freckled. His lips were wide and pale. She no longer wished to touch his face or kiss his lips. He suddenly seemed altogether too rawboned, too tall, too fair-skinned. No, Cassie had to admit as she woke up the following Friday morning, the real problem with Kenneth was not what he was, but who he wasn't. He wasn't Jason.

How awful, she told herself as she leaned over the basin to brush her teeth, how awful and trite. She'd fallen in love with her sister's husband. She found herself dreaming nightly of the one man in the world she could never have. Jason Darin. She adored the very sound of his name! Oh, how awful, how wrong! As she rinsed her mouth out with water she flicked on the little transistor radio on the shelf beside the sink to hear the early morning news. At first it was just another tragic story.

"Found this morning. On Montauk Highway. Car apparently overturned and destroyed by fire. Local police officials put the time of Miranda Darin's death at about . . ."

She stared at herself in the mirror, seeing nothing.

" . . . Miranda Darin, host of the widely acclaimed *Breaking News* television show, one of the most beloved and respected newscasters of her generation, dead today at the age of thirty-eight. Beautiful, poised, Ms. Darin got her start in television news at . . ."

Somewhere Cassie heard a phone ringing. She walked out of the bathroom, leaving the water running, and into her bedroom where she picked up the receiver. She listened for a second or two without comprehension.

" . . . and Jason asked me to help with the arrangements," the deep, somehow familiar voice was saying. "We've booked a flight for you at eleven. Should get you into La Guardia a bit past noon. One of the network limos will be waiting. Does that give you enough time? Cassie? Did you hear me? Are you okay?"

"Magnus . . . Vance," she said. "Yes, I heard you. You know, I just now realized what she meant. Just now . . . when I heard. I didn't understand before. I was so wrong."

"Didn't understand what, Cassie?" the voice said. The tone was both patronizing and concerned. "Are you sure you're okay?"

"When Miranda said I'd gotten it all backward. It wasn't that she was trying to help me. I just this minute figured it out."

"I'm sorry, you're upset." He was trying hard to be sympathetic, but his impatience was beginning to wear through. "I've got a lot to do here, I'm afraid . . ."

"Don't you see? She was hoping that I would help her."

Six

*E*verything looked the same. But Cassie felt the difference as soon as she arrived. It wasn't Jason, but a maid Cassie vaguely remembered from her first trip, who opened the elegant wrought-iron front door.

"They're in the library," the uniformed woman told her. The late March wind swept in behind Cassie and swirled around the circular front hall. The Murano crystal chandelier tinkled overhead as the maid pushed the door shut.

"You go on in. I'll take your things upstairs." There was a reverence in the maid's voice that Cassie had not heard before. Or was it just sympathy? From the moment she stepped aboard the plane that morning and discovered that she had been booked into first class, she had felt that she was being treated with particular kindness and concern. She wasn't used to being pampered and felt silly sitting in the sleek leather-covered backseat of the stretch limo Magnus Media had provided for her trip in from the airport. The car had been equipped with a full bar, telephone, and miniature television set tuned to the Magnus network. The *News at Noon* was on, but they were still carrying only the sketchiest details about Miranda's death.

"A terrible accident," was how the anchor described it as a close-up of a mangled husk of a car was shown. When the newscaster went on to say that "Miranda Darin apparently burned to death," Cassie had quickly turned the television off. She had spent the remainder of the drive sitting silently in the huge backseat of the limo, her hands folded tightly in her lap. She felt nothing: no sorrow, no anger. She realized vaguely that she must be in a state of emotional shock. She kept forcing herself to remember that this was real, not a dream. Miranda was dead. And though everything looked the same, there was one major difference: Miranda was gone.

"What you're describing is a media circus." Cassie could hear Jason's deep rough voice as she made her way down the front hall toward the library.

"Come on, you're being unfair, Jason." Magnus's tone was smooth, reasonable.

"That's my right as her husband. I don't want a million curious spectators waiting outside during my wife's funeral. I want it small. And private. Is that so hard to understand, Magnus?"

"Cassie." Magnus turned to greet her as she walked into room. There was a fire going in the marble-topped fireplace. The crimson-walled library was warm and filled with the nostalgic aroma of burning logs. A vase of freshly cut pussy willows sat on a low, ornate side table. The careful arrangement was so obviously the work of her sister that Cassie felt tears running down her cheeks before she realized she was crying.

"Cassie." Suddenly Jason was beside her, and his arms were around her. "Cassie, I'm so sorry." And then he let her go and made his way back to the couch where he had been sitting.

"I had every intention of being strong and resilient," Cassie said, shakily taking a seat on one of the chintz-covered ottomans. She rooted around in her shoulder bag for a tissue. "Sorry."

"I'm relieved someone around here is showing a little emotion," Magnus said dryly.

"And what the hell is that supposed to mean?" Jason shot back, standing to face the tall, silver-haired man who leaned against the mantelpiece.

"Just that it seems to me you're not thinking about what Miranda would have wanted in all this." Magnus turned to Cassie and said, "We're trying to make plans for your sister's funeral, and I'm afraid that Jason and I are at loggerheads. Perhaps you can help us sort things out." He seemed so much in control, so elegantly powerful, Cassie was beginning to see why Miranda and he had hit it off so well. They were alike in many ways, smooth and self-aware and yet undeniably charismatic. They both had the kind of elusive appeal that used to be called "star quality." It was hard for anyone to resist. Cassie, who was beginning to feel the first real waves of emotional pain flood through her, felt grateful for the strength he was projecting so effortlessly.

"Of course," she said. "Whatever I can do . . ."

"Your sister had millions of admirers, Cassie," Magnus said. "Her death is a shock to everyone—not just her family. I know that doesn't mean a great deal to you, Jason. I've long been aware that you wished Miranda did something else—perhaps anything else—for a living."

"I thought we were going to keep my wishes out of this," Jason replied coldly. "Just make your case, Magnus. I want Cassie to hear it and help me decide. Go on."

"Magnus Media believes that Miranda Darin's many, many loyal fans—like her family—need the ritual of a funeral to start them down the road to mourning and acceptance."

"Don't kid yourself," Jason interrupted. "In two weeks they'll have forgotten her name. But you'll have racked up some impressive Nielsen points by putting what should be a deeply private moment on public display. I say no."

"And I say I thought you agreed to at least hear me out."

"Wait a second," Cassie said. "Are you saying you want to televise Miranda's funeral?"

"Not the actual live service, my dear, of course not. But, yes, some footage before and after. Perhaps an edited taped version of the address spliced into later coverage. We're also working on a tribute to her, putting together spots from *Breaking News* and other places, reminiscences from people she worked with, people who loved her."

"Didn't you manage to exploit her enough while she was alive?" Jason demanded.

"Please," Magnus said, at last showing some anger of his own. "I'm only trying to do what I feel she would want, Jason. She was a public figure and she loved being one. She thrived in front of a camera. She lived for the excitement. The lights. The avid attention of her viewers. Did you ever watch her open her fan mail? Did you ever see her face a moment or two before broadcast? That's when she was most alive, Jason, glowing, happy. Perhaps you don't want to face it, perhaps you can't. But what I'm proposing—an afternoon-long tribute to one of America's most beloved media stars—is precisely what she would have wanted for herself. She loved being adored. I'm giving her fans one last chance to do so."

Jason sighed, leaned back, and ran his hands through his dark hair. "What do you think, Cassie?"

"I hate to say it," Cassie replied slowly, "but I think Mr. Magnus is right. I do think she would have wanted something. But can't we compromise? Have a private ceremony somewhere that's kept very secret, then maybe do a more public thing elsewhere later?"

Magnus seized on her suggestion. "That's a terrific idea, Cassie. I was planning a reception anyway after the service, at my place. We can arrange to have the media and the fans congregate there. Perfect. Thank you. Jason . . . how does that sound to you?"

"Just the way it sounded before. But then, perhaps I'm not the right person to ask. I always did know a different Miranda than anyone else." He rose wearily from the couch and added, "I'll let you two sort out the details. I think I'd better get some sleep."

It was a chilly afternoon with a hint of rain riding beneath a chaotic wind. Bitter, seemingly without direction, the breeze rattled through the branches of the leafless trees along Madison Avenue, whipped at awnings, and wreaked havoc on the expensively saloned hairstyles of the mourners as they moved slowly up the steps of the church. The line of people waiting to get in stretched around the corner. It wasn't until Jason helped her and Heather out of the backseat of the limousine, until they were hurrying to the side entrance of the church, that Cassie noticed several people in the crowd had cameras.

"Mr. Darin!" a man cried out. "Jason Darin . . . there he is . . . quick . . . tell us how you feel, sir . . ."

"Get out of our way." Jason pushed brutally through the crowd, herding Cassie and Heather in front of him. As the heavy oak door closed behind them, Cassie heard Jason swear under his breath. "Goddamn vultures."

"How did they know?" Cassie demanded. "I thought we'd all agreed the service would be private."

Jason stared at her a moment before saying, "As far as the media is concerned, Cassie, nothing is private. I would have thought you knew that by now."

His tone was cold, dismissive. Cassie felt tears sting along her lids. She squeezed her eyes shut quickly, determined not to cry again. He could be so cruel without knowing it. Or was he treating her like this on purpose? For the last few days, since the moment she had agreed to let Magnus televise his tribute to Miranda, Jason's mood had progressively darkened. He had simply withdrawn himself from her . . . and the household. When he wasn't working alone in the large private office next to his bedroom upstairs, he retreated to the even more carefully guarded inner sanctum at his business complex in the World Trade Center. Jason had handed over the funeral arrangements to Magnus and the running of the town house to Cassie. The only person he spoke to, or seemed to care about, was Heather.

"But she didn't want to leave us, sweetheart." The previous night Cassie had overheard Jason's hoarse, distinctive voice in Heather's room. Even if he left her alone most of the day, Jason was there to wake his daughter up in the morning . . . and tuck her into bed at night.

"I did something wrong, didn't I?" Heather asked.

"Oh, no, Heath, you didn't. Don't ever think that."

"But I'm sure it was me, Daddy," Heather told him sadly. "The afternoon before Momma went away she got mad at me because I left my room a mess. She said she was sick and tired of me not being neater. I think . . . I think . . . she just got sick of me. I made her leave."

"Listen to me, Heather, and listen hard," Jason told her. "Your momma loved you very, very much. What happened to her had nothing to do with you. You've got to believe that. She loved you . . . and I love you. And believe me, sweetheart, nothing you could ever do would change that."

But for all the affection and concern he showed Heather, Jason barely seemed to register the fact that Cassie was there: dealing with the house staff, keeping a distraught Heather active and entertained during the day, coping with the endless flow of flowers, telegrams, and letters from Miranda Darin's countless friends and fans around the world. And, not least, helping Magnus coordinate Miranda's funeral and the enormous reception he was hosting after the church service.

"I'm sorry to keep bothering you, Cassie," he told her on the phone the morning after she had flown back. "But Jason is not returning my calls, and I feel that someone in the family should have a say in what happens. Do you know offhand if there were any hymns—or any pieces of music—that Miranda particularly liked?" And then, fifteen minutes later, he'd call back saying: "Me again. What about flowers? Miranda loved roses, but we won't be able to find anything fresh this time of year. And I know Miranda hated those almost fake, refrigerated ones."

"She loved the smell of flowers almost more than how they looked," Cassie said. "Perhaps hyacinths? I remember she had some here the night of the party."

"Marvelous, yes. I'll always associate Miranda with some sweet scent or other . . . that perfume she wore. I don't know if I'll ever be able to smell it again without . . ."

That was the first moment that Cassie registered the fact that Magnus, too, was suffering. How deeply he had loved Miranda and in what ways, Cassie doubted she would ever know. And yet, despite his polished control, behind his take-charge manner, Cassie could feel the powerful man's anguish. In the end, Cassie began to realize that half his calls—and questions—were unnecessary. Magnus needed to talk to someone about Miranda. He managed to work her name into the conversation as often as he could. Cassie sensed it was his way of holding on to Miranda.

Miranda . . . Miranda . . . As Cassie followed Jason and Heather into the first pew of the church, she realized how little time she had had to herself during the past few days to think about her older sister. To mourn her. To accept the fact that she would never again hear her voice or her laugh. She was gone. The last of her family. The final link Cassie had to the past, to her childhood.

As the minister began his eulogy, Cassie found she had a hard time concentrating on his glowing, yet somehow empty, words. His praise was for the Miranda everyone saw behind the camera: the dazzling blond media goddess, the carefully packaged television personality, the gracious, smiling society hostess that Miranda had done everything in her power to become.

And yet Cassie knew that that image of Miranda was as thin and insubstantial as the videotape used to project it. In truth, Miranda had been ruthlessly ambitious. She had been hard, selfish, driven. She had had very few real friends. She had kept her own family at a distance. Her marriage, at least what Cassie had seen of it, had been rocky at best. She had allowed her daughter to become sadly spoiled. As far as Cassie could see, Miranda had sacrificed every human relationship she ever made on the altar of success.

Cassie had always accepted the fact that she idolized Miranda. She had envied her deeply. But she had lived so much of her life in Miranda's shadow, so overwhelmed by her sister's brilliance that she had never really seen clearly just how much Miranda mattered to her. The truth was, Cassie realized as she felt tears slide down her cheeks, she had loved Miranda. She had loved her in spite of all her faults. She had loved her as only one sister can love another, with feelings that went beyond words, with roots that probed deeply into the subconscious and the past. It was a tie heavy with responsibility, weighted with guilt. And as the congregation rose for the closing hymn, Cassie realized that it was a bond too strong ever to be broken. Even by death.

Seven

What Vance Magnus's co-op lacked in warmth and charm it made up for with a conspicuous display of extreme wealth. His duplex was on the upper floors of one of the new sleek marble-and-plate-glass monoliths on West Fifty-seventh Street, a building that had many commercial as well as residential owners. From the elaborately wrought Miro wall hangings and Noguchi-like sculpture in the two-story, pink-marbled lobby, to the Olympic-sized pool and fully equipped gym that comprised the two top floors, the building had an aura of hidden power, of secret deals being conducted behind polished teak doors.

There was very little about the shiny coal-black exterior of the place that spoke of family or domestic comforts. There was an unspoken rule among the building's board members, of which Magnus was chairman, that people with children or pets, as well as a certain class of foreigner, were subtly discouraged from buying in. The Japanese, of course, were welcome, and several Tokyo banks and brokerage firms had purchased co-ops to house their top executives while on business in the city. A sheikh owned the floor below Magnus, though it seemed to be permanently occupied by a series of mysteriously beautiful and extremely young male models.

Magnus had moved into the apartment three years before,

the month the building was completed, from the Park Avenue town house he had owned with his late wife, Millicent Fairborn, who had been dead now for more than ten years. Fairborn money had helped Magnus get his start, though no one denied that Magnus's own iron will and brilliant business sense had forged the multibillion-dollar media empire over which he now ruled. Everyone spoke of the fact that Millie's slow, agonizing wasting away with cancer had been difficult for Vance. They had been an obviously devoted, very socially prominent couple. No one with any class paid credence to the rumors that Vance had been sleeping around for years, throughout their marriage. And not a soul—except Vance Magnus—knew that the reason the Magnus union was childless was because dear, sweet Millie had never been able to drum up enough courage to do "that terrible thing" with her husband. Millie's guilt over this inadequacy led her to be especially generous with Vance when it came to money . . . and essentially blind to his relationships with other women.

Vance Magnus had had his way with so many things for so many years that he had almost forgotten what it was like to find his needs thwarted . . . to be forced to give in to another dominant personality. In fact, Miranda Darin— beautiful, dangerous, demanding Miranda—had been the first woman since his late adolescence with whom Magnus had been seriously smitten. And it had actually felt like a physical blow, Magnus recalled, as he mechanically greeted the crush of socialites and movie stars, politicians and business leaders, who were putting in an appearance at his reception following Miranda's funeral.

Oh, Miranda, Miranda . . . As Magnus clasped yet another pair of hands between his and flashed yet another sad smile, he thought back to the first time he had ever spoken to her.

Elevator Number One in the Magnus Media Building was reserved strictly for the transporting of executives. It was an express, luxuriously padded in wine-colored leather, that went directly up to the top four floors of the plate-glass-covered skyscraper. The building was one of several corporate media headquarters that marched like a conservative, gray-suited army up Sixth Avenue. The Magnus Building, taller and more masculine in tone than the rest, was widely recognized as reflecting the personality of its owner to the extent that Elevator Number One was known as the "Magnus Mobile." Even secretaries who worked on the top executive floors were not allowed on this exclusive elevator; they were forced to take the time-consuming local with the rest of the Magnus Media drones. At first Magnus was surprised when an unknown young woman, a striking platinum blonde, had stepped into the elevator with him one morning nearly fifteen years before.

"This is the executive elevator," Magnus informed her abruptly, cracking his *Wall Street Journal* down the middle to more easily peruse it during the half-minute ride to his penthouse suite.

"I know," the blonde replied, her voice sweetened with the seductive vowel tones of the South. The doors swished shut as she added, "That's where I'm going. To the top."

"Personnel is on Fourteen," Magnus said, pretending to scan the national news but actually letting his glance slide up and down the young woman beside him. She was tall and breathtakingly beautiful. But Magnus was almost bored by most glamorous and available female companionship at this point in his life; what intrigued him about this woman was her composure. She seemed so absolutely sure of herself, so confident of who she was and where she was heading.

"I know," she said simply. "I'm going to see Vance Magnus about getting a job here." He heard himself laughing before he realized that he should be irritated by her attitude. What gall on her part to assume she could just waltz in and demand a position. What balls! He realized that he was strangely taken with her brazenness. Most of the people who worked for Magnus tended to fear him and respect him in about equal measure. Demanding, opinion-ated, he was a self-made billionaire who had gotten that way by bending everyone's wishes to fit his own. His employees were the type who always laughed at his jokes . . . but never felt comfortable kidding him back. And though this was how Magnus had arranged his working relationships, he was growing bored by his own power to manipulate and control.

"It's nothing to laugh about, I assure you," she said with a sniff. He loved the dismissive look she shot him! "I'm superbly qualified. I've just graduated from Columbia Journalism with some of the highest marks ever given. Fred Friendly himself will give me a personal recommendation. I think Mr. Magnus will be impressed."

"I doubt it," he told her. "There are hundreds of people—just as qualified as you, just as eager—who'd be willing to do anything to get a foot in the door around here."

"But I'm better than anyone else," she assured him. "I'm brilliant. I'm hardworking. I'm photogenic. And I'm deter-mined. Magnus is my first choice. But if I don't get a start here, I will get one somewhere else. Believe me, Magnus will see the light in due time."

The amazing thing was that she had been right. He hadn't hired her that day simply because there were no positions open. But Magnus, first and foremost a businessman, had kept an eye on her. Within a year of their first meeting, he read that she had been promoted from newswriter to assis-tant producer at CBS News. A few years after that he had watched as her occasional general assignment reports for the local CBS affiliate became increasingly more polished and professional.

He could tell just by looking at her that she was self-made: the hair, the voice, the whole image was something she was carefully honing into a "look." The year Millie died, Miranda was promoted to local news anchor at CBS, and he found himself looking forward to the eleven o'clock slot with something bordering adolescent puppy love. He told no one of his innocent infatuation, watching the competitive show from behind the locked doors of his oak-lined study. But when one of his executive producers suggested an exposé news hour for the Magnus network based loosely on *60 Minutes,* Miranda's was the first—and only—name Magnus dropped in the hat for head anchor.

He had never told her the truth about why she was hired. He had let the president of the news division handle the negotiations. Though he had worked almost obsessively on helping to craft the *Breaking News* format, he kept his distance from her. He was terrified that she would see straight through him. He knew that she was smart and proud enough to walk away cold if she learned she'd been lured to Magnus for less-than-professional reasons. His care had cost him dearly. Two months after the premiere of *Breaking News,* she met Jason Darin at a Democratic fund-raiser; six months later they were married.

He thought back on that earlier heartbreak and what had followed as he moved now through the crowd that packed his usually commodious duplex. Two different film crews, lights ablaze, roamed through the rooms as well, interviewing friends and associates for the video tribute the Magnus News division was furiously pulling together. Miranda's network of acquaintances had been wide indeed: besides the crème de la crème, there were the usual media luminaries, Broadway producers, some high-visibility literary types, an opera star, a smattering of the more presentable actors and artists, a select group of liberal politicians, several well-known fashion designers, even a rock star. There were only a few faces that gossip columnists Suzy and Liz Smith wouldn't recognize. Stopping to greet guests along the way, Magnus now approached one such unfamiliar face.

"Cassie," he said, coming up behind her. She stood alone at a floor-to-ceiling window that faced west toward a dramatically setting sun. "You're all alone? Didn't Jason come?"

She turned to face him, and he could tell by the state of her eyes and lips that she had been crying. It struck him suddenly that in all the years he had known her, he had never once seen Miranda cry.

"No," she said, "he . . . just couldn't. He felt he should be with Heather. This has all been so hard on him." Cassie was not about to tell Magnus that Jason had said he'd "rather be boiled in oil" than attend the reception.

"It hasn't exactly been easy on you either," Magnus said. "And I can imagine how Jason reacted when he saw the reporters at the church. He no doubt blamed me. I've acted as his scapegoat for so many years."

"You? The entire news industry. The whole world," Cassie replied. "He's like a wounded animal right now. Lashing out at everything near him. Even those who are trying to help." It was terrible to be so close to him— just inches away in the backseat of the limousine—and feel so closed off from him. Cassie knew all too well what it was like to lose people she loved. She had lived for years in a gray fugue of depression after her parents died. She, too, grieved for Miranda. But never had she seen someone act with such unforgiving fury in the face of death as Jason.

"I hope that doesn't mean you as well," Magnus told her. "He has a bad temper. Quick to judge."

"Oh, I'm getting my share," Cassie said caustically. She sounded so like Miranda at that instant, Magnus realized, that he felt momentarily confused . . . and oddly comforted. She was as tall as her sister and, like her, she possessed a kind of coiled suppleness. But while Miranda's body always seemed ready to spring, Cassie's was reined back, held in check. Miranda's beauty had been something that dazzled people instantly—like a mirror flashing in the sun. Cassie's was less obvious. Her face was not conventionally pretty; but the full lips, the arching brows, the angular cut of her cheekbones, the almost invisible dusting of freckles across the brow of her nose, were definitely appealing. By the time Magnus took all this in, he realized Cassie was blushing.

"I'm sorry," he said, unconsciously taking a step back. "You do remind me of her. You can't help it, I know."

"I find it so odd that people think we're alike . . . or were alike." Cassie hesitated a second before she added, "She was always so far ahead of me. She was always the one to lead the way. The place to be. Losing her . . . it's like losing my direction."

"Any idea where you might be heading?" Magnus asked. "Miranda mentioned you were interested in the newswriter job we have. Are you thinking of moving to New York?"

"I wasn't. But I don't know . . ." Her first thought was of Jason. Not the way he was now but of the slightly sardonic man who had haunted her dreams up until the moment of Miranda's death. The fiery explosion that took her sister's life had obliterated the sweet longing she had had for Jason as well. It was not that she wasn't still drawn to him; oh, she was, all too strongly. It was just that there were too many dark forces swirling between them, too much unfathomable emotion, for Cassie to know what she was feeling. The only thing she knew for sure was the extent of her confusion.

"Think about it," Magnus told her. "I'll tell my people to keep it open for another week. Judging from what Miranda told me, you'd be perfect for the job."

"I know," Cassie said. "She told me the same thing. I've got to tell you that I'm not half as sure about that as Miranda was. She sprung the whole thing on me the last morning I was up here at Easter. It was the oddest conversation . . ."

"Yes, you mentioned something to me on the phone," Magnus said, "when I called to tell you the news. Do you remember? You said you realized now that Miranda wanted you to help her. What did you mean by that, Cassie?"

"Her very insistence about me taking this job was strange. She'd never tried to help me before, or even shown particular interest in my career. Then that morning she was so persistent . . . almost demanding. When I asked her why she suddenly wanted to help me out she said, maybe I had it backward."

"But she told you nothing specific?" Magnus asked.

"Specific? No. About what? What do you mean?"

"Nothing . . . I just thought maybe something was bothering her that she didn't tell me about. You can't help but feel guilty when someone dies . . . so suddenly. I keep worrying that I could have stopped it . . . could have done something."

"I know what you mean," Cassie replied. But something in his tone bothered her. Magnus didn't give her much of a chance to linger on that concern. Taking her by the elbow, he steered her into the crowd of celebrities. For nearly an hour he stayed at her side, introducing her to a rising film star one moment, a bestselling author the next.

"So like Miranda," an opera impresario murmured as he kissed her hand.

"We must have lunch," Lucinda Phipps, one of Miranda's society friends, said after they'd been introduced. "And have a long, long talk about poor dear Miranda."

"My dear." Senator Haas leaned over to kiss her cheek but missed. His dry lips brushed her nose; he reeked of after-shave and alcohol. "I can't tell you how terribly, terribly sorry we all are . . ."

It wasn't until much later, while lying awake in the guest room of the huge, darkened house, that Cassie was able to sort through the events of the difficult day behind her. She thought about the funeral. The lost look on Heather's face as they made their way out of the church. Jason's frigid manner as the limousine dropped her off at Magnus's residence. The overly bright and jam-packed reception. The host of luminaries she had met. In the end her thoughts kept returning to Magnus. His tantalizing job offer. His obvious interest in and protective attitude toward her. And yet, behind everything, the feeling that there was a great deal about Magnus and the world that surrounded him that Cassie couldn't begin to understand. Half-lies seemed to linger in the air. So many of the smiles that greeted her that night seemed forced, perhaps even false. She was tired, she told herself, emotionally beat. And yet she couldn't help the childish fear that some unspecified danger hovered . . . just beyond her range of vision.

Eight

$\mathcal{D}$erek Hattery, a senior partner in Hattery, Hattery & Sloan, was clearly uncomfortable. He shuffled through the papers in front of him on the spotlessly clean antique rosewood desk.

"Shall we begin?" Jason asked, crossing his arms and tipping back in the sturdy leather armchair facing the lawyer's desk. Cassie sat next to him, silent and composed, dressed in the same gray suit she had worn the first time Jason had ever seen her. It seemed like years . . . and yet it was less than a month ago that he had opened the front door for her. He had known immediately who she was because she reminded him so vividly of Miranda when they had first met. Before the fame. Before Magnus. During those fleeting first weeks when everything had been so dreamlike and sweet. Amazing, but he remembered that he had actually felt protective of Miranda in those early days. Actually believed that she had needed him.

"Yes . . . well, uh, I thought it best to have the will read with Mrs. Darin's sister in attendance," the lawyer said, nodding toward Cassie while looking at Jason, "just in case there is any, uh, problem."

"Why should there be, Derek?" Jason asked. "I believe I'm familiar with the terms of Miranda's will. We both rewrote ours when we married."

"Yes, well." Hattery swallowed again and reshuffled the papers. "Mrs. Darin rewrote it again. Recently, as a matter of fact."

"How recently?" Jason asked, his tone suddenly wary.

"Uh, two weeks ago," the lawyer said, not meeting Jason's gaze. "Most unusual. I asked her at the time if she was absolutely sure, not acting in haste. I tried everything, but . . . you know, she could be quite determined." The law firm of Hattery, Hattery & Sloan had handled Jason Darin's extensive and increasingly lucrative business affairs for over twenty years. When the outcome of Miranda's meeting with Derek Hattery had been made known to the firm's executive committee, mayhem had ensued. Partner was pitched against partner in the argument over whether or not Jason should be informed of the drastic changes in the dispensation of his wife's extensive personal fortune. Lawyerly wisdom— to do nothing until absolutely necessary—prevailed. Unfortunately necessity had reared its ugly head far sooner than anyone had suspected.

"And you didn't tell me, Derek?"

"I, we . . . didn't think it particularly prudent at the time. Lawyer-client privilege and all that. But we urged her to reconsider. We hoped she might at some future date change her mind."

"I see." Jason sighed. "Well. Let's get it over with, then." She had cut him out. Totally. It was hardly that he needed the money; her comfortable fortune was less than a twentieth of what he was worth. It was far more than that: it was he, after all, who had helped her invest part of her salary . . . taken pride when the stocks he'd chosen for her took off . . . advised her when to sell . . . saw her savings swell into a substantial nest egg . . . urged her to reinvest. It was he who had made her savvy about money in general, forced her to keep her own checking and savings accounts, and invest through her own broker. Like so much else, he'd given her everything he could, and she had taken . . . and then taken some more. Now she had taken him one last time. She left everything she owned—clothes, jewelry, cars, houses, investments, bank accounts—to her only sibling, her half sister Cassandra Hartley. Half of the estate would be turned over to her daughter, Heather Darin, when she reached twenty-one; all of it would revert to Heather upon Cassie's death. There were numerous clauses and subclauses, but the gist of the will remained the same: Jason's name was not mentioned once.

" 'As soon as possible upon this reading, my sister, Cassandra Hartley, will collect the contents of a safe-deposit box at the main office of my bank. Enclosed with this will is the key to aforementioned box. No one but Cassie will be allowed to open the box or be present when she does.' " Derek Hattery cleared his throat, before adding, " 'This is my final will and testament. Signed, in sound mind and body, on this day . . . ' " His voice trailed off as he named a date two weeks before. The room became so quiet that for the first time Jason could hear the sound of traffic on Madison Avenue twenty or so floors below. It could have been worse, Jason told himself. At least she had not hurled any of her accusations at him from beyond the grave. It could have been much worse. At least the sad, ugly secrets they had shared would remain their own.

Derek Hattery leaned across the desk and held out a tiny key to Cassie.

"This is yours. Remember, she wants you to open the safe-deposit box immediately."

Cassie stared down at the key, cold against her palm. With it and the terms of the will, she realized, she was about to unlock a world as outsized—as beyond her grasp— as anything Alice had seen beneath the looking glass. She would be rich. Miranda had left her everything. Her thoughts flew immediately to the dressing room full of clothes: the hundreds of pairs of shoes, the shelves stacked with hat boxes, the rows of silk blouses, the racks of evening dresses, the chestful of jewelry. She would be very rich. The lawyer had mentioned cars and checking accounts. She stared down at the key: it was all hers . . . and it was also all wrong.

"The clothes and jewelry I understand," Cassie said, looking from the lawyer to Jason. "But the rest? The investments, the houses. Don't they belong to Jason?"

She sensed immediately that she had said the wrong thing. Hattery cleared his throat and shifted uneasily in his chair.

"As I said, this is what she wanted as of two weeks ago. It's true that prior to that time . . ."

"I'm sure she thought this through carefully," Jason cut in. "Miranda was deeply attached to you, Cassie. I know she always felt guilty that she didn't get to see you more. I'd guess this was her way of making up for that. Of making sure you were taken care of no matter what happened." Jason was improvising, Cassie knew. Hattery knew it as well. Jason was as shocked by what Miranda had done as any of them: Cassie had seen it on his face when Hattery read the will. Why was he pretending differently? she wondered. Was he just trying to make things easier for her?

"So, there'll be no contestation?" Hattery asked, obviously relieved.

"Of course not, Derek. Listen, if Miranda hadn't made these changes, I probably would have myself. Cassie is Miranda's only living relation . . . besides Heather. She absolutely deserves everything." His tone was a bit more believable now, Cassie felt. She longed to trust him. Why did she continue to sense that he was hiding something?

Jason and Cassie rose to go.

"Uh, one last thing," Hattery said, standing to shake hands. "Remember, Cassie is to open the box . . . by herself. You're not to be in the room, Jason."

"Of course not, Derek. I heard you the first time. I have no intention of being anywhere near the damn place. I've a meeting downtown. Come on, Cassie. I'll drop you at the bank on my way."

*   *   *

The barred door banged shut at the end of the hall as the bank clerk left and Cassie was alone in the small, overbright room. She hesitated a minute, looking down at the oblong metal tray the clerk had taken down from the wall of safe-deposit boxes. She had learned from the clerk that Miranda had last opened the box two weeks before. The day Cassie had left, refusing the job. The day Miranda had changed her will. Whatever Miranda had been going through, whatever secrets she had been unable to share, the answers, Cassie sensed, lay in the contents of this metal tray. Why else had Miranda insisted Cassie open it alone? Her fingers shook slightly as she pulled the tray toward her.

She raised the metal top slowly, expecting to see . . . what? Cassie searched through the carefully folded papers—birth certificate, marriage license, passport, stock certificates—but there was nothing unexpected. She pulled the sheath of papers out of the metal box, spread them across the top of the table, and went through them one by one. With growing disappointment, mingled somewhat with relief, Cassie realized that there was nothing unusual about any of the documents as far as she could tell. Certainly nothing that demanded the kind of privacy Miranda had stipulated. What had Miranda been thinking of? She felt around the inside of the tray one last time. Far at the back, to the left, her fingers brushed up against something cold . . . smooth . . . square. She pulled it out slowly.

There, smiling up at her, were her parents, herself, and Miranda. It was Cassie's graduation-day picture, beautifully encased in an ornate antique frame. What was it doing here? Cassie wondered, turning it over, searching for clues. What was Miranda trying to tell her . . . if anything? That family mattered? That Miranda wished she and Cassie had been closer—as Jason had insisted was the case? As Cassie transferred the various papers and the photo to her shoulder bag, she once again tried to come to terms with Miranda's strange bequests. But no matter how she tried to view her older sister's actions—as a burst of generosity for a sister she had ignored, as a way of landing one last blow in a long-running battle with her husband—Cassie remained confused and more than a little troubled.

She took a taxi back uptown to the town house. She could easily afford taxis now. She could afford a great many things. But the thought, rather than lifting her spirits, made her feel burdened. The choices before her now seemed harder, not easier. Her quandary about taking the job at Magnus Media, for instance, only intensified with the realization that a better salary, greater benefits, were no longer important. She now had the luxury of deciding what she really wanted to do for a living, and where she wished to do it. As she slowly climbed the front steps, she realized how much more difficult and complicated her life had suddenly become.

"Where's Heather?" Cassie asked as the maid took her coat.

"In her bedroom, I believe, ma'am. With Miss Boyeson."

"Heather?" Cassie called as she climbed up the front stairs. "Heather . . . I'm back." Cassie opened the door to her niece's large, chintz-covered bedroom. No one was there, but she could hear water running in the adjoining bathroom. Miss Boyeson was alone in the spacious pink-tiled room, arranging fresh towels on the heated rack.

"Where's Heather?" Cassie asked.

"She's not in her bedroom? I told her to start in on her homework."

"No, she's not there," Cassie replied. "How long since you've seen her?"

"Five minutes," the older woman said. "Ten at the very most."

Cassie hurried back down into the corridor, opening doors as she went and calling, "Heather . . . where are you?"

She found her at last where she least expected to: in the guest bedroom she had taken to thinking of as her own room. Heather was sitting cross-legged on her bed, clutching a throw pillow to her chest, her face blotchy from crying.

"Heather . . . what are you doing here?"

"Waiting . . . for you."

"Miss Boyeson told me you were supposed to be doing your homework."

"I know," Heather said. "I told her I would. I told her I'd do anything she said, so long as she didn't tell on me. But . . . I don't think I can stand it anymore. I have to tell someone. I tried to tell Daddy, but . . ." Tears started to flow down her cheeks.

"Okay," Cassie said, sitting down beside her niece on the bed. "What's all this about? Come on, honey . . ."

"I . . . was the reason Mommy died."

"And what makes you so sure of that?"

"She . . . she . . . told me," Heather explained, trying to keep her sobs in check. "The last time I saw her. She came to my room to say good night and got really mad because it was pretty messy. She said . . ." Heather hesitated, tears welling up again.

"What did she say?"

"She said I was going to drive her to an early grave." Heather said the words in a whisper, her eyes wide with fear. "You see? And that's exactly what happened."

"Oh, Heather," Cassie said, laughing with relief. "That's just a turn of phrase, a sort of joke. It's nothing to take seriously. Believe me, you had nothing to do with the car accident."

"That's not what Miss Boyeson said," Heather replied gravely. "She was in the room when Mommy told me. She remembered. She told me it was my fault, but she wouldn't tell if I was good and did everything she said. But I don't care anymore. I feel too terrible. I'd rather everybody knew. And punish me. Do you think I'll go to jail, Aunt Cassie?"

"No, Heather," Cassie said, pulling her niece into her arms and smoothing back her hair. She tried hard to keep the anger out of her voice. She'd have to get to Jason right away. If she had anything to do with it, Miss Boyeson would be on the street that night, her bag of ugly little threats beside her. The world could be so very treacherous. Nothing was safe. Hatred could be hovering behind the nicest smile. The darkest thoughts could be at work in the brightest places. You never knew where you might find a Miss Boyeson, bending over the bed, carefully pulling back fresh white sheets for a child she'd already filled with nightmares.

Nine

"She's leaving now. I told her to get her things together. Charles will drive her to a hotel downtown. I gave her two weeks' pay. What I really wanted to give her was . . ."

Jason paced in front of the fireplace in the library, his hands thrust deep into the pockets of his jeans. His face was dark with anger.

"I know," Cassie said. "I felt the same way. Where did Miranda find her? From a service? We should call and tell them what happened. This woman should never be allowed anywhere near children again."

"I should have listened more closely to Heather," Jason went on bitterly. "I kept telling her everything was all right, the whole time not even knowing what was wrong."

"We both should have listened. I sensed something was off with her. But I've been so caught up in my own problems—"

"No, that's not true," Jason stopped her. "You've been wonderful, Cassie. Don't think I haven't seen it. The way you've taken care of the house. The servants. Heather. I just left it all in your hands. I've been . . . I've been in hell."

At last, Cassie thought, *he's going to open up to me.* She sat on the couch, hardly breathing, waiting for him to begin. He stopped pacing. He stood in front of the fire, looking down. The antique Austrian grandfather clock in the corner chimed the half hour. It was nine-thirty. Heather was, at last, safely asleep upstairs. Everything seemed ready for Jason to finally explain so many things to her. The silence continued. One minute, two. Cassie realized how tense she was, how concentrated her thoughts were on the man in front of the fireplace. His shadow spread across the far wall. She realized, too, what a looming, outsize role he now played in her life. The images of his face, his infrequent smile, were never far from her thoughts. And at the sound of his voice—her whole body felt lighter, freer. She felt flushed when she was near him, as if his presence alone could warm her. The silence stretched. Cassie could hear the sound of cars passing below in the rain. And still she waited.

When he spoke suddenly, he was unexpectedly direct: "You must wonder about me, Cassie."

"Yes," she said. What was the point of pretending? "I do."

"I can almost hear your thoughts sometimes. It's funny. I can hear you asking—who is this man my sister was unlucky enough to marry?"

"Unlucky? Why is that?"

"Surely you guessed." Jason turned to her, his face half-hidden in shadow. "We weren't exactly happy together."

"Why not?"

His laugh was bitter, self-mocking. "I doubt you have time to hear all the reasons."

"Actually, I have all the time in the world. I've just inherited a small fortune. Solely for the reason, as far as I can tell, that Miranda was too angry to leave it to you. That's really why, isn't it, Jason? It had nothing to do with her caring about me."

"I don't know. She didn't consult me, though I suppose that was more than a little obvious by the way I acted today."

"You didn't answer me," Cassie replied. "But I think I already know the truth. Miranda didn't go to all the trouble of changing her will in order to leave me the money. She did it to keep you from getting it. My question now is why? And why, specifically, two weeks ago?"

"I can't tell you."

"That's not the same as saying you don't know."

"I can't tell you, Cassie. There are many things I just can't talk about. I'm sorry. I don't mean to be evasive or cold. I've been going through such a black time . . ." His voice trailed off as he stared into the fire.

She longed to cross the room, to touch his arm, turn his unhappy face toward hers. If only he could feel how warm she was, how much she cared.

"Why can't you tell me?" she asked finally.

"Because it wouldn't do me any good," he said. He turned to her. "And it might do you harm."

"Oh, for heaven's sake, Jason." Cassie felt exasperated. She also felt a little scared of him suddenly. His look was so intense, and yet impossible to probe. "I'm not asking about national security matters or industrial secrets. I just want to know about my sister, about her life, why she suddenly turned to me just before she died."

"I already told you." His tone had turned cold in a split second. "She realized that you mattered. That family matters. We both realized that. Too late."

"I want to believe you."

"Then do. I don't understand . . . why all these questions? These doubts?"

"Why? Because I'm not a fool. From the moment I stepped into this house, the two of you were at each other's throats. I heard bitter fighting here that weekend. The next thing I know, Miranda's dead. Then she leaves everything to me. The will didn't even mention your name, Jason. And I'm supposed to believe it's because she suddenly discovered she loved me. I don't think so."

"You think it's because she hated me. Is that what you're saying?"

"No . . . well, I don't know." What did she mean? She

stopped a second and tried to pull her disparate thoughts together. "I'm just saying that something must have happened. That weekend I visited. Something was going on. She was so anxious that I move here. That I take the job at Magnus Media."

"What job? She never mentioned this to me."

"It's a newswriter position."

"And? Is it worth your while? Are you considering it?" He left the fireplace and came over to sit beside her on the couch. Why did she feel that he was changing the subject on purpose? Whatever his intentions, Cassie found it impossible to distrust him when he was only inches away.

"I haven't had much time to think about it," she said, feeling the heat rise in her cheeks. She was grateful the room was so dark, that he couldn't see how he affected her.

"I want you to think about it, Cassie."

"Okay," she said, swallowing hard. "Why exactly? What difference does it make to you?"

"I think you know. I think we both know."

Cassie could hear her heart beating. No, it was crashing. Pounding in her ears. Roaring through her veins. He took her right hand. Her fingers were hot against his cold palm. In one unbelievably quick movement, he pulled her to him, strong arms encircled hers, cool lips closed over her mouth. It was like drowning. No, it was like diving—deep down into the clearest, coldest water. She felt a tightness in her chest. She couldn't breathe.

"Please . . ." She pulled away briefly, her hands pushing against his chest. "This is wrong."

"No, it can't be." He pulled her to him again, his right hand caressing her neck, her cheek, smoothing back her hair. "I've been thinking of holding you since that first night."

"No, please . . . Jason . . . don't . . ." But it was too late. She felt herself give way to him, drift with the shimmering current of his touch. It was impossible. It couldn't be true.

But his kisses—demanding and needful—told her otherwise. He had been drawn to her, too. He had been thinking of her, too. Those nights in Raleigh when she had woken breathless from dreaming about him, when her arms and lips had ached to touch him, he had been dreaming of her, too. And now this. It was like one of those dreams. She felt herself sinking deeper and deeper: here were the demanding lips, the probing tongue, the powerful arms pinning her against the back of the couch. She felt his hand move down her arm, caress her waist, drift down her thigh . . . without thinking, she felt her legs spreading.

He broke away. He sat up, leaned back, breathed deeply.

"Oh, Lord." Cassie sighed, struggling to sit up as well. Distractedly she tried to brush her hair back into some semblance of order. She ran her fingers over her tender lips.

"I'm sorry," Jason said, touching her arm. "I wasn't thinking. I didn't mean . . ."

He didn't mean anything by it, Cassie concluded silently for herself. The realization spread through her body as quickly as pain. Of course—he was lonely. He was suddenly terribly, bitterly alone. Yes, he and Miranda had had their problems. Their life together had not been happy, as he himself had admitted. That didn't mean that Jason hadn't loved Miranda. How could any right-thinking man not have adored her beautiful older sister? Cassie asked herself. She thought back on the ugly fighting she had overheard, the outrage in both of their voices. For the first time she thought how closely longing and jealousy could be intertwined. How easily passion could pass for anger, love for hate. What in the world had she been thinking of? It wasn't Cassie whom Jason had wanted to hold, had longed to kiss. It was the memory of Miranda.

"Don't worry," Cassie replied, standing up, tugging her sweater into place. "I guess we both got a little carried away."

"Come back here, Cassie. Sit down."

"That's not a good idea, Jason," she said, and to reinforce her resolve she walked across the room to the large bay window overlooking Fifth Avenue. The rain had stopped, leaving a black sheen of water on the street. Her limbs felt heavy, and her lungs ached. She felt as though she had just managed to pull herself free from a forceful undertow. She realized how close she had come to giving in to Jason. No, it was far worse than that. She had been a breath away, a touch away from urging Jason to take her . . . to make love to her with ridiculous abandon on his own library couch. How foolish she must look to him!

"Okay," Jason said. "But we've got to talk about this."

"About what?"

"Us, Cassie. The . . . situation. Your future. That job."

"I've already decided about that," she lied. "I'm not going to take it."

"Why not?"

"It would mean moving here. Leaving everything I have in Raleigh. Totally changing my life."

"Whether you like it or not, your life already has changed."

"I know that . . . and I have to get used to that. There's a lot to think about."

"Then I want you to think about this, too," Jason went on. "I want you to stay here. Heather needs you."

"That's impossible," Cassie said, turning to face him. "Especially now . . . after tonight." Lord, he looked so tired, so vulnerable, Cassie thought, as she watched him lean forward and rest his elbows on his knees. When he ran his hands through his unruly hair, Cassie saw for the first time that he was starting to go gray. He sat back again, his arms flung wide across the couch cushions. His face looked washed out, his eyes rimmed with fatigue. The lips—just minutes ago so hard, so demanding—looked thin and parched. *He's in pain,* Cassie thought, her heart going out to him. *He's in trouble, but he's not looking for my help. Heather needs you, he had told me. But he doesn't.*

"You don't have to worry about me," he told her wearily. "I won't be here enough to bother you. I'm going abroad at the end of the week. I've business meetings in France and Japan. Most of my real estate dealings are in Europe and Asia now. I'm away more than half the time . . . and this year it will be even more than that. Miranda didn't mind it, in fact I think she welcomed it. And Heather seemed fine about it. But now, well, the choice is to take Heather out of school, make her leave her friends, and travel with me. Or . . . have you stay."

"I see," Cassie said. "As her nursemaid."

"No, damn it," Jason shot back, "as her aunt. As someone she trusts . . . and can grow to love. How can I leave her behind to the Miss Boyesons of this world? It's impossible. So I'm asking you, Cassie."

"As a convenience to you."

"That, of course," Jason replied, his expression darkening, "if that's how you choose to view this. It could also be convenient for you, if you decide to take the job Magnus offered."

"I see," Cassie replied. No wonder he had seemed so pleased about the newswriter position. It bolstered his chances of her taking this other job as Heather's guardian. So what was that impressive display of passion all about? A way of sealing her affections? Of ensuring her loyalty to him? Thank God, she thought, their lovemaking had gone no further than it had. "I'll need to think about it."

"Of course," Jason said, rising from the couch with an effort. "I won't be leaving until Friday. That will give you five days. Enough time to decide?" It was phrased as a question, but he was gone before she could answer. She heard him climbing the stairs.

The fire had gone out. "Yes," she said to the empty room.

Ten

"And this," Magnus said proudly, "is the newsroom. It looks relatively sane right now. Chaos starts to descend around three in the afternoon." Cassie stood beside Magnus in the spacious glassed-in corner office of Frederick Marshall, Magnus Media's anchorman, overlooking a cluttered, near-empty circular arena below. In contrast to the battle-weary newsroom, the anchor's suite was luxuriously decorated with Old West accents—a Remington bronze, a series of sepia photographs of Iroquois, a row of cowboy hats neatly arranged on wooden pegs—that to Cassie seemed about as genuine as a Ralph Lauren commercial.

Frederick Marshall, the network's silver-haired, baritone-voiced anchor, had long ago discovered that his Colorado boyhood could be turned into an effective prop for his public persona. He drawled his words. He called his audience "folks." He signed off each broadcast with an avuncular "Happy Trails, America." Off the set, he wore mostly denim and leather, custom-tailored to a broad six-foot frame that grew more rotund with each successful season. Most people in the media considered him a corny writer and an even sloppier reporter. Luckily he was supported by Magnus Media's vast professional staff. The only thing Marshall had to do was read what ran before his eyes on the teleprompter, and this he did to actorly perfection.

But whatever his shortcomings, America loved him. The *Nightly News with Frederick Marshall* had pulled down impressive Nielsen ratings for the last five years.

And for the last forty minutes the CEO of Magnus Media had been squiring Cassie through the fifteen floors of his domain: the research library, the promotion group, the publicity department, personnel, the company's private canteen. When Magnus had called the morning after Miranda's will had been read, inviting her for "a little tour" of his media empire, she had no idea that the emperor himself would be the tour guide. Or that he would turn out to be such a minutely informed and subtly ironic one.

"I hope you weren't counting on meeting our superstar anchorman," Magnus told her as they stood together in Frederick Marshall's darkened showcase of an office. "The old boy usually doesn't put in an appearance until it's time for makeup. Not our strongest workhorse, Mr. Marshall."

"But I guess you don't meddle with success, right?" Cassie asked, pleased that Magnus had seen fit to confide his real opinions about the anchor.

"Actually I had been planning to do just that. Nobody knew this except Miranda and myself, but I don't suppose it would hurt to tell you, Cassie. We were going to try your sister as a co-anchor next season with the hope that she would take over the *Nightly News* in another season or two."

"But what about *Breaking News*? That's your highest-rated show. Wouldn't you be putting it in jeopardy?"

He turned and looked at her, his usually smooth features wrinkling into a sudden smile. "I like the way you think. You're cautious. Quite unlike Miranda, I'm afraid. She felt she'd done everything she wanted with *Breaking News*. And, as usual, she was looking for her next step up. For her that meant anchor. And, well, you know Miranda. She was a force of nature . . ." His voice softened with emotion.

Looking away, Cassie said, "I hadn't even considered what a blow her death is to you professionally. What's going to happen to *Breaking News*? Have you decided yet?"

"For the time being," Magnus replied, clearing his throat as he regained his composure, "we're going to try a rotation of hosts. Give some of our better people a chance to prove themselves. Maybe mix in some new blood from outside. I'll give it six months or so, then select whoever tests out the best."

"Well, you seem to have it all worked out."

"That's what I do, Cassie," Magnus replied as he escorted her out of Marshall's office. "Work things out. Find the right people for the right jobs. Search out fresh talent. We may be working in an electronic medium, but it's people who make or break a network. Writing talent. Tough reporting. That's what I'm looking for. Computer graphics are never going to replace the right face and a voice that inspires trust."

He led her down the spiraling staircase that joined the newsroom to the executive eagle's nest above. Marshall's suite had exuded luxury and prestige, but the large circular newsroom was all practicality and function. Brightly lit with overhead fluorescent tubes, a mismatched collection of standard-issue desks and computer terminals, this was clearly the chaotic nerve center of the news department. The Magnus Media Building might tower above Sixth Avenue, employ thousands, generate news around the world, but this jumbled pie-shaped room on the eighteenth floor had a familiar, comforting appeal to Cassie.

"This looks just like my newsroom back in Raleigh," Cassie said, stopping at a paper-strewn desk. A photocopied message was taped to the side of a modular wall: "Never forget: without free speech . . . we'd all be out of a job."

"Of course," Magnus said as he guided her through the warren of equipment and furniture. "News gathering, writing, rewriting, reporting—it's pretty much the same whatever the medium. Television just happens to reach millions more people than newspapers."

"This sounds like a sales pitch to me."

"No," Magnus replied, suddenly somber, "it's a fact. Electronic news has a tremendous amount of power. It's colorful. It's live. It can bring a changing world right into the living room."

"True. But it also has no depth. It offers up little sound bites of information as thorough coverage. It never looks beyond the obvious." For a moment she was positive she had gone too far. Though Magnus hadn't mentioned the writing position yet, it was surely the hidden agenda of his guided tour. This was partly a job interview, Cassie reminded herself, not always the best time to speak one's mind.

Double swinging doors opened to a bank of elevators. Magnus walked to the far elevator and pressed the UP button. In silence they rode the elevator to his penthouse offices. Even as the doors swished open, Cassie could feel a difference in the quality of the air. It was thinner, cooler, scented with something ferny and masculine. Light flooded the reception area, pouring down from a skylight cut into the diagonal ceiling. Antique Kashan carpets hung on the walls. The matronly, impeccably dressed woman behind the reception desk took in Cassie as she addressed Magnus.

"I was able to juggle the board meeting to four today, but the *Newsweek* lunch is a noncancel. Sorry. Your speech is all typed, so you can glance at it in the limousine on the way over."

"Damn. Well, thanks for trying, Charlene. No calls for the next half hour, okay?" But even Cassie knew that an answer wasn't expected, compliance was. She followed Magnus down the thickly carpeted corridor and into a corner office with magnificent two-story floor-to-ceiling plate-glass walls. Wordlessly Cassie went to a window that offered a breathtaking panoramic view of the West Side and the Hudson River. Here, midtown seemed distant and serene, the grid formation of avenues and streets a well-organized and successful plan. The taxi horns and sirens didn't carry this high up. The exhaust fumes and grime disappeared like morning mist. Across the river, the flatlands of New Jersey faded into a bank of clouds. A flash of lightning shot vertically through the encroaching wall of storm.

"You can actually see the weather change from up here," Cassie said, turning around to face Magnus as he clicked the door shut behind them.

"It's magnificent, isn't it? The sunsets are the most amazing. You'll have to come back sometime to see one. Have a seat, Cassie." He nodded toward the group of Bedermeier chairs arranged around a huge round table of black polished slate. Red-and-yellow tulips, drooping artfully over the sides of a Ming Chinese bowl, sat in the center of the table. With the sense that everything she touched was priceless, Cassie pulled out a chair and sat down, facing in to the room and Magnus, her back to the beautifully distracting views below.

"Miranda loved this room," Magnus said as he walked over to the south-facing window. "I must sound like a sentimental fool to you," he added harshly, "always going on about her."

"No, you don't. I can hear in your tone how much you cared about her. She wasn't . . . an easy person to be with, to care for. I admire anyone who was strong enough to be a real friend to her."

"She wasn't easy," Magnus said. "But then you aren't either, Cassie. That crack about the shallowness of network news was hardly kind." Cassie sensed that he was offering her the chance to take back what she had said, or to at least soften it. A month ago she would have fallen all over herself to please him. A few weeks ago she would have thought of something accommodating to say that would take the sting out of her criticism. She would have seen both sides of the issue; now she only saw her own. Miranda's death had changed her, hardened her in ways that she did not yet understand.

"It's how I feel," Cassie told him. "I think your half-hour format sells the news short. And I think for the most part *Breaking News* overly sensationalizes the facts."

"Ouch. Did Miranda know you felt that way?"

"Actually, yes. I told her the last time we spoke. The morning she tried to convince me to work here."

"That's interesting," Magnus said, turning from the window. "That very afternoon she told me that you had a lot to offer to the network. That we should hold the job open until you had a chance to reconsider."

"I'm sorry to have wasted your time," Cassie said. "It's been a confusing couple of days for me. I'm still trying to sort out how I feel about a lot of things. Did you know that Miranda left me everything in her will?"

"No. I had no idea. When did all this happen?"

"The will was read yesterday. It was really pretty odd. She made a big point of leaving me the contents of a safe-deposit box, except nothing but the usual sorts of documents were there."

"You've gone through them carefully?"

"Well . . . yes. But what would she have left me that would be so important?"

"I'm not sure," Magnus said thoughtfully, walking to the table. He pulled out a chair facing Cassie and sat down. "But Miranda was working on a pretty sensitive story just before she died. Apparently she was dealing with sources who didn't want their identities known. All very hush-hush. She refused to tell even me what was going on."

"Nobody knew what the piece was about?" Cassie asked. "Isn't that pretty unusual?"

"With anyone but Miranda it would have been unheard of, frankly. But she was special. She convinced me that her sources needed the protection . . . and I gave in to her wishes. As I'm sure you've guessed, she could wind me around her little finger."

"You don't think this had anything to do with her . . ."

"With the accident?" Magnus asked with a sigh. "No. I suppose it would all be somehow easier to deal with, if we could blame somebody for it. Accuse. Convict. But, no, I'm afraid not. The police report states that it was just . . . one of those terrible freak things: she was going too fast on an icy stretch of road."

"But you think she left me notes or something about this story, don't you?"

"Well, maybe," Magnus admitted. "When you mentioned the safe-deposit box and Miranda's desire for secrecy, it seemed a distinct possibility."

"I'll look through everything again if you like," Cassie said.

"I want you to do more than that, Cassie."

"What do you mean?"

"I want you to take the writing job. No, wait . . ." Magnus interrupted when he saw that she was about to object. "I want you to take it on your own terms, Cassie. Develop stories that dig deeper, hit harder. In more ways than you can imagine, I agree with you: the news department is far too mired in hype and ratings. We need an infusion of fresh talent, strong ideals. I'm willing to take a chance on your lack of television experience to get just that."

He had so quickly and cleverly punched all her buttons that for a moment Cassie didn't know what to say. Then she met his amused, calculating look and laughed. "And what if I fall flat on my face?"

"We pick you up, dust you off, and send you back to North Carolina. But I don't think that's going to happen."

"I really get to do the kind of stories I think are important? And go in-depth?"

"Yes, within limits. You'll be reporting to a managing editor, of course, and working with a production crew. It's far more of a team effort than newspaper writing, I'm afraid. But you'll see. The important thing is, I'm here. I believe in you. If you don't think you're getting the kind of support you need down there, just let me know. I'll help you get it."

"And in return?" Cassie asked, sensing there was something left unsaid.

Magnus stared past her shoulder to the oncoming storm that had just breached the Hudson. Rain clouds massed on the horizon; a rumble of thunder echoed up and down the river.

"Just stay in touch, Cassie. Remember that I'm a friend. And, at this particular moment, a sad and lonely man."

It was the end of their discussion. She rose to go. Through the intercom he instructed Charlene to arrange for Cassie to meet with Personnel. He accompanied her to the door of his office and added, as if in an afterthought, as he told her good-bye: "Let me know if you find anything in those documents, Cassie. Or if you hear anything around the newsroom about that story of Miranda's, okay? Good luck, now."

Eleven

*N*othing was going Cassie's way her first day at Magnus Media, and it had started even before she got out of bed.

At six that morning, a few seconds before her alarm rang, she had heard Heather calling: "Good-bye, Daddy . . . bye!" Then the echo of Jason's steps on the stairs, an exchange with the chauffeur, and the sound of the front door slamming. He would be gone for over three weeks. Didn't she at least deserve a quick knock on her door? A whispered "good luck with the new job"? But he had left without a word. And, once again, as she often had over the last four days since she had agreed to stay, she began to doubt the wisdom of her decision.

The night of her interview with Magnus, when she informed Jason quietly after dinner that she had taken the job, he'd merely said, "I'm glad." A silence followed Jason's clipped response. He stared down the table at her. Searching for what? Signs that she was staying because of him? It occurred to her he was worried that she was now going to try to entangle him emotionally.

"It seemed like a great opportunity," Cassie went on quickly. "Even though I was positive I'd blown it at one point. I told Magnus I thought his newsroom could use a little more substance and a bit less style. I was sure that was it."

"Obviously it wasn't if he ended up offering you the job."

"That's what's so great," Cassie went on. "He wanted me to take the job because of how I felt. He wants me to do what I think is right: work deeper, go after more serious stories. I couldn't believe it."

"And, frankly, I don't," Jason told her, pushing back the heavy oak dining-room chair.

"What do you mean?"

"Just that I know him better than you, Cassie. The one thing he's truly accomplished at is getting what he wants."

"You mean he was lying?"

"I mean he's remarkably skilled at manipulating the truth."

"Why do you hate him so much?" Cassie heard herself asking. "Is it because of Miranda?"

"I'm ignoring that last question." He stood behind his chair, his arms folded across the headrest. He looked down the table at her for a few seconds before he added, "But I admit there's no love lost between Magnus and me. We go back a long way . . . I knew him years before Miranda did. It's not necessary to go into all the details, but I will never forget—or forgive—certain things about the man. That's all I want to say about it, except to assure you my feelings toward him—hate is too shallow a word—have little to do with Miranda."

"And yet you let her work for him and become his friend?"

"I was never in a position to let Miranda do anything. She did what she chose."

"And you don't mind me working for him?"

"As you said yourself, it's a great opportunity for you. And it will keep you in New York."

He was turning to leave, when Cassie asked, "Shouldn't I at least be allowed to know what went wrong between you and him? I could be on guard against it myself. I could be more careful with him. I don't like living in the dark."

"It happened a long time ago, Cassie. It has nothing to do with you . . . or Miranda. Besides, we all live in the dark. All the time."

Cassie, sitting alone in an empty, windowless room on her first day at work, was beginning to agree with Jason's assessment of life. More than two hours before, the eighteenth-floor receptionist had shown her to the claustrophobic closet of an office, a full corridor away from the newsroom. She had realized as soon as she stepped off the elevator that she was too early. The place was deserted, except for the sleepy-looking young woman at the switchboard engrossed in a current copy of *People* magazine.

"Oh, yeah." The girl's interest had sparked when Cassie gave her name. "Miranda Darin's sister. I'm really sorry what happened to her. Well, nobody's here yet, but come on . . . I'll take you down to the room Mr. McPherson cleared out for you yesterday."

Ian McPherson, Cassie had learned from her visit to personnel, was *Breaking News*'s executive producer and her immediate superior. She remembered snippets of things Miranda had said about him over the years. "That prima donna, McPherson . . . He looks so harmless, but he has the temperament of a piranha . . . What a perfectionist! For chrissakes, this is a television magazine, not a symphony orchestra."

As Cassie waited in the overheated and stuffy room, she tried to imagine what McPherson had said, in turn, about Miranda. Or what everybody on the *Breaking News* team had thought of her high-powered, demanding sister. Would they expect her to be the same way? Would they resent the fact that she—a relative nobody without television experience—had stepped into this job as easily as Cinderella into the glass slipper? Would they know that the Prince Charming who'd made it all possible was none other than Magnus? Of course they would, Cassie told herself. In any business, but especially in one as tight-knit and pressurized as broadcast journalism, that kind of gossip was as common as the air people breathed. Before she even started this job, she was going to be resented. And, even worse, she was going to be held to a standard she could never hope to meet: Miranda's.

"I simply don't understand," Kenneth told her when she had called him that past weekend in Raleigh to tell him about her decision to stay. "This is just totally unlike you, Cassie. What do you want with New York? Television? Your life is down here . . . with the paper . . . with me."

"Right now I feel it's here, Kenneth," she explained gently. "Heather needs me. And this job is . . . well, it will be a challenge."

"Since when did you want a challenge?" he demanded. "What happened to my sweet-natured, easygoing girl? What's going on up there, kitten?" If Kenneth had hoped that by evoking his pet name for Cassie he was going to be able to reach her emotionally, he was wrong. Cassie felt herself shrinking from the image he had of her: the long blond hair, the dreamy expression, the honey-tinged voice. That's not who she wanted to be anymore, she realized. More to the point, that's not who she was.

"Haul ass!" The sudden explosion of the loud voice, along with a sharp knock on the door, snapped Cassie back to the present. The door opened and what at first appeared to be a mop of dark curly hair perched precariously atop a skinny black body leotard burst into the room. It took a second for Cassie to make out the large olive-black eyes beneath the bangs, because what registered first about Sheila Thomas was her smile; it was as large, toothy, and knowing as the Cheshire cat's.

"C'mon, move it!" the woman yelled, assessing Cassie with one quick, dismissive up-and-down glance. "McPherson's on the warpath."

Cassie followed the woman as she hurried down the hall, knocking on doors and barking out orders.

"Conference room. Now. Mac's pissing mad. Be prepared for massive bloodletting."

Within five minutes, more than twenty people had crowded into a conference room dominated by a scuffed table
and twelve chairs in various stages of disrepair. The room
looked out on an airshaft and a solid gray wall of cement
blocks. Cassie was among those who arrived too late to
get a seat. With one swift glance around the room she
understood why Sheila Thomas had eyed her so critically.
No one had told her about the dress code. It was a motley
combination of jeans and work shirts for the men, baggy
sweaters and stretch pants like Sheila's for the women.
Only one other woman wore a dress, and she, Cassie soon
realized, ran the coffee concession and left after she'd filled
everyone's orders.

No, it wasn't turning out to be a great day. Determined
to be taken seriously, to follow surely in Miranda's footsteps, she had raided her sister's dressing-room closets that
morning to find something new and distinctive to wear.
She'd opted for a gray-and-blue-paisley Lacroix jacket,
a short, tailored charcoal-gray wool skirt that showed off
her long legs, and a pair of dark blue suede Ralph Lauren
heels that added an extra inch to her already impressive
height.

She had so wanted to fit in, to feel like a team player
from the start. As she tried unsuccessfully to hide behind
some people in a far corner of the room, she felt she
looked about as inconspicuous as an ostrich among a flock
of pigeons.

"Guys and gals . . ." He was so soft-spoken that Cassie
didn't hear the rest of Ian McPherson's greeting. What
she did hear was that an immediate, defensive hush spread
through the crowded room. His ginger-colored hair was
receding. His rimless glasses seemed to have slid down
permanently to the tip of his nose, and over them he eyed
the room with a jaundiced smile. His fingers fumbled at
his breast pocket where cigarettes once had been, traveled

through his hair, then drummed nervously at the top of the conference table.

"I have just spent an enormously instructive hour upstairs with our esteemed leader," McPherson began. "We exchanged views on a wide-ranging number of topics."

"Whenever he starts talking like the Secretary of State," Cassie heard a man in front of her whisper to another, "I know we're in trouble."

"Hush, children," McPherson continued, holding up his hand. "First, listen to what your betters have to say. Then, if you're good, we'll take questions. I'll start with the good news. Magnus is firmly behind the continuance of *Breaking News*. He believes, as I know we all do, that it is bigger and better than just one person. That's not to say that Miranda will be easy to replace. I'm not saying that at all. Thus, we come to the so-so news. Her replacements. Yes, that's a plural. Magnus believes that we should give some of you guys a chance to show us what you can."

" 'Guys'?" a female voice demanded.

"I meant that figuratively, of course," McPherson assured her. "Tamara Wilkenson . . . Manuel Cortenzo . . . Phillip DeMott. You'll each report segments from now on."

"That's great!" someone yelled.

"What's so-so about that?" someone else asked.

"Well, dears, just one thing," McPherson replied. "Susan Dearborn from NBC is also being asked to do a piece each week."

"Shit."

"The damned thing's rigged!" Sheila Thomas cried. "Magnus is just toying with us. Dearborn's going to take over. It's just a matter of time."

"Actually, that's not necessarily the case," McPherson replied evenly. "No one person will decide who ultimately takes Miranda's chair again. As usual, when it comes to television, the ratings will decide. Each of the four temporary hosts will be given an hour-long show of his or her own in the next few months. The good people of America will let us know. The one thing Magnus and I agree on is that *Breaking News* should ultimately have just one host. One style. One voice asking the questions, setting the tone."

"So what's the matter with that?" someone asked who was struck, as Cassie was, by McPherson's look of disapproval.

"It's about that tone . . ." he went on slowly. "Our esteemed leader suddenly feels it's not deep enough. He seems to feel that we've been dealing too much on the surface, going after the easy sensationalistic side of the stories."

"And who the hell's fault is that?" a man near Cassie demanded.

"I'm not interested in assigning blame, Darrell," McPherson replied. "But I am damned eager to make one thing absolutely clear to each and every one of you. Guys . . . gals . . ." Once again his tone softened so that everyone had to lean forward to hear him. "You have a problem with *Breaking News* . . . you have a criticism of some sort—an idea—anything at all—where should you go with that sort of thing? I'll tell you where you go. You come . . . to me. Okay? Got that? Understood?" He was looking straight at Cassie, cold blue eyes unblinking in their anger. It was clear that Magnus had let him know from whom he'd gotten his new ideas.

"Yes," Cassie whispered, her cheeks burning. He glared at her another second or two, nodded in dismissal, and then strode out of the room. Slowly the others filed out after him.

"You Miranda's sister?" Sheila Thomas had lingered behind.

"Yes. I'm Cassie."

"And you actually had the balls to tell Magnus what you thought of the show . . . that's why McPherson was foaming at the mouth, right?"

"Yes."

"All right. Okay." Sheila's smile seemed to take up most of the bottom half of her face as she extended her hand to Cassie. "A fellow traveler. Welcome aboard."

So, Cassie told herself, the day had not started out that well . . . but who knew how it might end?

Twelve

$\mathscr{C}$assie made friends easily. She always had. As a little girl growing up in Raleigh she had been so easygoing and openhearted that she'd been everyone's favorite. Perhaps because her competitiveness and jealousies were thoroughly directed at Miranda, she had avoided the petty rivalries common among girls her own age. She was a joiner, always in the most popular crowd, though never the leader. That had been Miranda's birthright, and Cassie had learned her place. She had long ago accepted the fact that she would be second best, play the supporting role. It was a position that made friendship easy; people always felt comfortable confiding in Cassie. She had no axes to grind.

"God, I cannot believe you emerged from the same genetic pool as Miranda," Sheila announced one afternoon about a week after Cassie started at Magnus. They were working together in the editing room on a piece that Sheila had originally produced for Miranda a month before and that had never aired. Miranda's part had now been edited out, and it was Cassie's job to rewrite the segment that would then be narrated by Manuel Cortenzo, one of the new temporary guest hosts.

"Why do you say that?" Cassie asked, then added, "Whoa . . . rewind about fifteen seconds, okay? Take a look at the man's expression. If looks could kill, huh?"

93

The piece they were editing was about the volatile relationship between the brown-uniformed traffic cops—known as "brownies"—in midtown Manhattan and the so-called "violators" whom they were paid to track down to protect the limited parking spaces for law-abiding citizens. In fact, as Sheila had produced it, the piece showed how the average taxpayer was more often than not harassed, bullied, fined, sometimes even jailed—and usually frustrated—by these brownies when trying to find a place to park in the city.

"Why don't we freeze on him right there, okay?" Cassie went on as they both examined in close-up the outraged expression of a man who—having run into a stationery store for change—came out to find his car being hooked up to a tow truck. "The subtitle could be something like 'Why are you torturing me like this?' or . . . 'Maybe we should move to Denver after all.' "

"Yeah, that's good," Sheila said, running the tape forward again. "Then we could speed up here as the car gets towed . . . and you could have Manny come in with some pithy round-up. This is good. I'm impressed, Cassie, and I like to think that I don't impress easy. It's this kind of thing that makes me think maybe you were adopted and nobody told you."

Cassie had thought of the Keystone Kops routine the first time she saw Sheila's piece, and since the segment had to be reedited anyway, it had been a simple enough matter to go back and cut in spots that could be humorously subtitled. It was a breeze to construct tongue-in-cheek narration for Manuel. It was really just a matter of fitting the words to the pictures. Once she'd learned how to use the Steenbeck machine, she'd spent hours running Sheila's film back and forth, rewinding, speed-forwarding, and she now knew the nine-and-a-half-minute spot by heart. Actually the work had been more than easy, it had been fun.

"You're just being nice."

"No, I don't do nice," Sheila retorted. "And I'm sorry to be the one to tell you, but neither did Miranda."

"She was . . . hard to work with?" Cassie asked casually. Though she already felt comfortable with most of the *Breaking News* staff, Cassie couldn't help but notice that nobody mentioned Miranda in her presence. After the initial expressions of regret over Cassie's loss, Miranda's name had been simply edited out of the office. At first Cassie thought it was done out of kindness to her; perhaps people felt it would be easier on Cassie not to keep bringing up a painful subject. But lately she had begun to suspect that the subject of Miranda was a painful one for everybody. That, like any difficult or traumatic experience, Miranda was something these people wanted to get behind them— fast. Sheila was the first person in a week to raise Miranda's name voluntarily.

"That would be putting it mildly," Sheila replied. "Now, what do you think about music? How about some upright piano stuff, you know, a little ragtime maybe, like in the old movies?"

"Great," Cassie said as the film rewound. "But could we go back to Miranda for a second? Why is it that no one ever talks about her around here? I never hear any—well, you know—Miranda stories. And her office. I stopped by just to take a look at where she used to work. It's just totally empty. Almost scrubbed out. It's almost like—"

"We all wanted her to go?" Sheila finished Cassie's thought for her as the film flickered before them in the darkened room. "Well, that's exactly what each of us did want, Cassie, to tell you the truth. And now that we all got our secret wish, I think we're all—collectively and individually—feeling guilty as hell. Things were bad. We were all miserable. But believe me, nobody wanted her to go that much."

"But . . . what was so bad? *Breaking News* has been one of the ten top-rated shows for the last three years. And its Nielsens were only climbing. What was so terrible?"

"Cassie, she was your sister, and I'm sure you loved her a lot. But let me tell you, Miranda Darin was a living hell on wheels to work with. She was just a grab-all-the-glory bitch. On every piece I ever did for her the one thing she ever really cared about was how she was going to come across. She didn't give a fuck about the story, or the truth, or the problems of whatever poor schlub we were interviewing. She didn't even mind ruining a guy's life if it made her look good."

"You're being pretty tough, Sheila."

"I'm calling it like I saw it. You asked, baby, and the truth of it is, this is a pretty tough business, especially if you're a woman. Maybe Miranda started out different, idealistic and kind, but believe me by the time I was put on the show, your sister had developed balls of steel. She had one of those iron-clad contracts that insured her more perks than a G.M. executive: personal hairdresser, makeup artist, wardrobe mistress, recently even a fucking personal security guard, for chrissakes . . ."

"Why a bodyguard?" Cassie interrupted. At first, terrible as it seemed, Cassie had been somewhat relieved by the news that Miranda had not been universally adored. Hate, however, was another matter, and something far deeper than professional envy simmered beneath Sheila's embittered tone. "Had she been getting threats?"

"Oh, sure, we all get threats. I mean the reporters, the anchors, the network in general. I doubt it was anything more than the usual looney tunes. She probably heard Barbara Walters had got a bodyguard clause in her last contract deal."

As they ran the reedited tape again and made notes together about the subtitling and score, Cassie tried to imagine what it would have been like to work for her sister. Like so much else in television, news had become big business, each Nielsen rating point worth millions in potential advertising revenue. Consequentially, news anchors and the hosts of news magazines like *60 Minutes* and *Breaking News* had become far more than just reporters. They had become part of the very news they were hired to report. Like movie stars, they had high-powered agents and multimillion-dollar contracts. They existed in that rarefied celebrity world that made their names household currency, their lives the property of tabloid newspapers.

"There's something you're not telling me about you and Miranda," Cassie said at the end of the afternoon as Sheila and she cleared up their papers and threw away the foam coffee cups in the editing room. Cassie had felt the unfinished conversation hovering in the air all afternoon, the intensity of Sheila's feelings an unwanted yet palpable presence between them.

"Yeah," Sheila muttered, smashing out a filtered cigarette. Trying desperately and largely unsuccessfully to stop smoking, Sheila had taken the tack of smoking only half of each cigarette. The ashtray was a graveyard of broken smoldering stubs. "But it's, like, not something I want to talk about."

"Okay," Cassie replied, surprised by the hurt she felt at Sheila's terse reply. Within a few short days of working with the generally talkative and clearly talented producer, Cassie had felt an easy, mutually admiring friendship take root. Sheila had been the only one on the *Breaking News* team to speak honestly about Miranda. At least up to a point. What could she be holding back?

The answer came, unexpectedly, that Friday, the morning after their reedited piece aired. From McPherson to Manuel Cortenzo right down to a temporary file clerk, Cassie and Sheila had heard only compliments on the segment. Having decided to go out to lunch together and celebrate, they were waiting for the elevator when the eighteenth-floor receptionist came running down the hall, crying: "Cassie! I've a message for you!" She was so excited that she had to stop and gulp in air before she could add in an awed, lowered voice: "Mr. Magnus called. Himself. Personally."

"Yes?" Cassie replied, and then when the girl just stared at her speechlessly, she prodded, "I assume he said something?"

"Oh, yes. Yes! He called to congratulate you on a job well done. Those were his very words."

"What's wrong, Sheila?" Cassie demanded as they slid into a booth at Hoover's, a glorified diner on Seventh Avenue that attracted a combination of media and fashion clientele. Sheila, who'd been chattering nonstop all morning as they discussed the logistics of doing another parking violations piece—this one on city employees who took advantage of their perks—hadn't said a word since they stepped into the elevator.

"Nothing," Sheila replied, hiding behind the enormous menu that Cassie suspected she already knew by heart.

"Let me rephrase that," Cassie replied. "Sheila, what the hell is wrong?"

"I'm just hungry," Sheila mumbled behind the plastic-covered menu.

"You're always hungry," Cassie pointed out, which was true. Sheila's capacity for food was legendary. A normal eating day for her would include two cream cheese-encrusted bagels for breakfast, half a pizza for lunch, buckets of take-out Chinese for dinner, a pint of Häagen-Dazs before bedtime, with any number of little noshes—from a Snickers bar to a half-dozen David's chocolate-chip-and-pecan cookies—in between.

"I think I'll have a chef salad," Sheila announced, folding the menu and staring out blankly at the jam-packed room.

"Now I know something's really upsetting you. Since when do you voluntarily ask for greens? Are you feeling sick?"

"I'm fine, damn it. About the new piece . . ."

"It's something to do with Magnus," Cassie interrupted. "You started acting weird when you heard he'd called me."

"It's nothing to do with anything," Sheila retorted, meeting Cassie's look dead-on. "Damn it to hell, Cassie, you have no right prying into my life like this. Absolutely none. Who the hell do you think you are to come snooping around my personal affairs, implying this, inferring that—"

"I merely asked what was wrong. But now I think I know."

"—no fucking right whatsoever. I do not, I never have, let my hair down, so to speak, to other women about deeply private things. I can't abide this heart-to-heart bullshit routine where everybody talks constantly about how they feel about every little thing. All that 'getting-in-touch' with your emotions garbage. I hate that. I really do. What goes on between a man and a woman, in my humble opinion, is strictly between them. What happens behind closed doors is no one's fucking—"

"You had an affair with Magnus," Cassie interrupted quietly, "that ended when Miranda came along."

"—business."

"That's why you hated Miranda so much. Of course."

"No," Sheila replied, tapping out a cigarette.

"Yes, I think so."

"No, I hated Miranda because she just used Magnus. The way she used all the rest of us." Sheila sucked deeply on her cigarette and squinted at Cassie through the smoke. "Listen, I never kidded myself about Vance. When I started with Magnus ten years ago, his affairs were already the stuff of myth. If you were halfway pretty and more or less willing, you were going to end up one morning in that king-size bed of his on Fifty-seventh Street. He didn't love me any more than any of the others. But I do believe he liked me. A lot. We had . . . fun together. I made him laugh."

"How long did it go on?"

"Seven and a half years." Sheila sighed. "Oh, I wasn't the only one during that time. You see, I didn't kid myself. But I was the only one he kept coming back to. It was a stable, yeah. But, well, I guess you could say I at least had a permanent stall. Pretty pathetic, huh?"

Cassie shrugged and tried to smile; she was thinking of Jason and the little crumbs of affection he had scattered her way. Not only was she content to feed off them, all she wanted was more. That was pretty pathetic.

"At first I didn't know what was wrong," Sheila continued, her mind's eye fixed firmly on the past. "He just became so fucking moody. Unresponsive. I was worried he was sick. Well, I guess in a way he was. I began to realize that he was totally obsessed with her. He talked about her all the time."

"To you?"

"Yeah." Sheila laughed. "Can you believe I actually sunk that low? Listening to a man babble on about another woman. I turned into his comforter . . . it was the only role left. And then I guess she woke up and saw that he could help her get what she couldn't on her own."

"*Breaking News*? But wasn't she hired on as host?"

"Oh, no, Miranda could make her own way in the network. She didn't need him for that; she already had Magnus exactly where she wanted him. No, it was all that la-di-da society stuff she was so involved with: opera fund-raisers, ballet benefits, or whatever. She couldn't break in. In the eyes of those people, Miranda was a total nobody. She needed Magnus—who knew everybody in that world from his first marriage—to get her entree."

"So he opened the right doors for her," Cassie said, thinking of the old woman in blue sequins whom Jason had pointed out to her that first night as "the keeper of the gate."

"Exactly," Sheila said. "The ultra-sophisticated, hugely successful, universally admired Vance Magnus became Miranda Darin's glorified butler. And the truly terrible thing? He loved every minute of it."

Thirteen

*H*e was tired. It was more than just jet lag, though Lord knew flying across seven time zones in four days would wear anybody down. It was more than the nonstop meetings, or business dinners that were really just more meetings, or informal breakfasts that were even further meetings. He was dead-tired. Bone-tired. Weary down to his very marrow. He had extended the trip by one week. Then two. But he finally realized that it was hopeless. For well over a month now he had tried as hard as he knew to run away from what had happened and for not one single second of the time had he escaped it. Miranda was dead, but she was not gone.

"Air France Flight 077 boarding for Kennedy." A Swiss-accented voice interrupted his dreams. He must have dozed off in the bright sunlight that flooded the departures terminal at Zurich International Airport. "First class passengers, please have your boarding passes ready."

"*Bonjour,* monsieur," the flight attendant said, smiling with sudden pleased recognition as he handed her the boarding card. Jason Darin's face was familiar to any Air France in-flight veteran. He was one of those rare, wonderful male passengers who always flew first class, rarely asked for anything besides his privacy and the *International Herald Tribune,* and never made a pass at even the prettiest flight attendants. Although, mused the attendant as she handed Jason back his stub, a show of interest from someone as attractive and—there was no other way of phrasing it—sexy as this clearly exhausted man would not be unwelcome.

Later, as she worked the spacious and comfortably appointed first-class cabin, the attendant tried to figure just what it was about Jason Darin that made him so appealing. Being French and therefore more than a bit experienced in these matters, the attendant liked to think that she held rather high standards when it came to *les hommes*.

Firstly, a man must not be too obviously sensual: no exposed chest hairs or gold chains, no overly long or overly groomed head or facial hair, nothing too flashy when it came to clothes. Monsieur Darin had avoided each of these faux pas. If anything, as was often the case with the American male, he was dressed haphazardly. Not that he looked poorly groomed, he was just clearly a man who had other things on his mind besides what he put on his back. Today he was wearing a handsome tweedy sports jacket that unfortunately should have been retired several seasons back: an inner lapel was frayed, and a cuff button was missing. His olive corduroy pants, too, were impeccable in taste, but worn in appearance. The eggshell-blue Oxford cotton button-down shirt was perfect—especially when offset by the dark, unruly hair—but it really should have been accompanied by a tie. A green-and-gold silk patterned one by Hermes perhaps, the attendant decided, quickly and expertly redressing him.

And then with equal pleasure, as she skillfully served cocktails through a patchy stretch of air turbulence, she mentally undressed him. She could tell by his eyes—the liquid gold of a first-class cognac—that he would be a generous, knowing lover. His well-muscled frame was larger than most European men, and yet he had none of that clumsy bearishness that afflicted so many athletes. He was comfortable with himself, at ease with a musculinity that was as potent as any cologne. But what made this man so ridiculously appealing, the flight attendant finally concluded, was the sadness that had transformed his all-American handsomeness into something altogether darker, perhaps even a bit dangerous. Someone, something, had closed down this man's heart. There was a remoteness about him that made him seem unattainable . . . and therefore just that much more attractive. She stole little glances at him as she served lunch, but he seemed thoroughly unaware of her presence, or of the excellent cut of fillet that he barely touched.

As she cleared away his tray, she asked in her most discreetly seductive tone, "Would you like anything else, monsieur? Believe me, you would be most welcome to whatever your heart desires now . . . or later."

"Excuse me?" He glanced up at the cabin attendant and saw the frank invitation in her smile. "No," he replied, sorry to see her bright expression fade, "but thank you. You've been very kind." After she'd hurried down the aisle with a disappointed shrug, he sat back and closed his eyes but he soon felt the familiar tightening of anxiety in his chest. He hadn't had more than an hour or two of restless sleep each night of the trip; why should he suddenly expect to drift off now?

One of the bankers who had accompanied him to Thailand and with whom he'd become friendly had advised him that he was pushing himself too hard.

"You should delegate more, Jason," Eric Loniman, a vice president at the German investment bank that was backing Jason's new development efforts in Bangkok, had told him. "You Americans drive yourselves so hard. And for what? Another million or two?"

"I like to work, Eric," he'd responded automatically. And as recently as a month ago, that would have been true. For years, Jason had thrived on challenges, on the marathon working days, the equally demanding social nights. He had relished the trigger-quick negotiations that could make or break the crucial bridge loan. He had prided himself on being the calm, cool center of the vortex of bankers, lawyers, architects, engineers, and investors who played key parts in each of his development deals. But this time, though the negotiations had gone well for developing an industrial park outside of Bangkok, he had hardly enjoyed himself. A virus of guilt—as feverish and nauseating as any flu—had weighed down his limbs. Each morning he had to steel himself to face his image in the mirror. Every night he had to climb into bed knowing his conscience was waiting for him: eager, voracious, ever wakeful.

He'd traveled from London to Tokyo to Manila to Bangkok to Prague to Berlin, and now at last he was en route to New York, and yet he knew he had gotten nowhere when it came to facing the truth about Miranda. His mind had circled the subject, ceaselessly, with nightmarish intensity, and yet everything was still unresolved. He was coming home from a thoroughly successful business trip feeling utterly defeated. There were only two things that sustained him—two faces and two voices he carried with him in his heart everywhere he went. One he knew as well as his own. Heather: his pretty, demanding, spoiled daughter. She was his pride and his despair, because though he loved her as much as life itself he knew he was failing her.

"Daddy, when are you coming home?" she had demanded on the phone two nights before, her voice a reproachful whine. "I miss you. I want you here. I hate it when you go away."

"I'll be home soon, pumpkin," he'd tried to soothe her. "I'll be back for your birthday, I promise."

And the other face, the other voice . . . he knew he had no right to treasure. He should not think of her. Because of Miranda, it should never be allowed to happen. He knew this, he kept warning himself. But the only times he had been able to edge himself into unconsciousness was when he tried to conjure up Cassie's face: the exact tilt of her chin, the shape of her lips, the muted color of her eyes. And then, for a brief moment, he would be able to escape from the memory of what he had destroyed . . . by dreaming about what he would never be allowed to touch.

"Now, you're sure you don't want to invite some of your friends back to the house?" Cassie asked Heather the afternoon of her niece's eighth birthday when she picked her up at the Dalton School. Despite her busy schedule, Cassie always dropped Heather off at Dalton in the morning and took a forty-five-minute break around three-thirty each schoolday to collect her niece from that posh bastion of wealth and privilege on East Eighty-ninth Street. She usually raced uptown from Magnus Media in a taxi to wait for the uniformed horde that—despite its impeccable social credentials—was as loud, messy, and boisterous as any group of children anywhere. Except for Heather. Frequently among the last to leave the school, she was always quiet, perfectly turned out, and unfailingly alone. It had long since occurred to Cassie that a girl as self-centered as Heather probably didn't have any friends.

"No, for the last time, no!" Heather snapped as Charles, who came from the town house to meet them, held open the door of the BMW for her. Cassie usually had Charles drop her back at the office after she'd made sure Heather was safely inside the town house. "I hate everyone in that stupid school. And I hate you doing this, Aunt Cassie. Why don't you just stay at work where you belong?"

"I belong here with you," Cassie replied, picking up her end of an argument that had started the first day she'd shown up at Dalton. It just didn't seem right to Cassie, who had been raised in a quiet friendly suburb, to leave a little girl basically on her own in the middle of a dangerous city.

"Mommy never picked me up," Heather would usually respond sullenly. "I'm not a baby. And Charles knows the way home by now."

"No one said you were a baby, Heather." It would be

Cassie's turn to reply. "I just like to see you, okay? Hear how your day went and so forth." A sulky silence would greet all her attempts at warmth and companionship. "So, Heather, how'd your day go?"

"You know, I think I hate you, I really think I do."

"Then we're making progress. Last week you said you were *sure* you hated me." It had not been smooth sailing with Heather, to say the least. Not having any experience with children, it would have been difficult enough for Cassie to cope even if Heather had been a generous, sweet-tempered eight-year-old. It was almost impossible for her to manage this selfish, mean, and thoroughly unhappy little girl. The brief détente that had existed after Miss Boyeson was dismissed ended the minute Jason left on his business trip. Nothing was good enough for Heather. "Hate" was her favorite word, whether used in reference to a pineapple upside-down cake the cook had made or a cable-knit cotton sweater that Cassie bought as a surprise for her niece at GapKids.

"I hate green," she'd told Cassie, unceremoniously dumping the sweater on the solarium floor. "It's pukey."

"You little brat!" Cassie shot back. "Pick that sweater up now or you don't get any dinner."

"I won't."

"Go to your room."

"I won't."

"Then I'll just have to take you up there myself."

So, with Heather kicking and crying, Cassie gathered her luckily feather-light, golden-haired niece in her arms and carried her up the stairs. There had been plenty of sniffling and pleading that night, but Cassie refused to let Heather out until she said she was sorry.

"Aunt Cassie, are you still there?" Heather demanded querulously a little after ten o'clock.

"Yes," Cassie said, folding the newspaper she'd been reading on the landing a few feet from Heather's door.

"Okay. You win. I'm sorry. Now can I have dinner?"

A part of Cassie was tempted to demand a more heartfelt apology, but a wiser part of her prevailed: slowly but surely, she told herself, she would force this badly spoiled little girl into learning some manners. It had been slow all right, but not particularly sure. Clearly Heather needed a lot of help emotionally. She had the demanding, defensive tone of someone who was terribly insecure, and Cassie was smart enough to realize that nothing she could say or do would change that. Heather needed friends her own age. She needed to belong. But she had flatly ignored every attempt Cassie had made to get her niece to do things with girls her own age. At her wit's end, Cassie had called on one of Heather's teachers and several of the mothers of girls in Heather's class. Then, a week ago, Cassie had started to hatch a somewhat desperate plan to celebrate Heather's birthday.

In the weeks since Jason had been away the town house had undergone a series of subtle but, on Cassie's part, purposeful changes. She'd never before lived in such a vast and luxuriously appointed house, let alone been asked to run one, and her first move was to seek rapport with the live-in staff. Charles, the talkative and warmhearted Jamaican chauffeur, had been easy to win over. It was clear he was devoted to Jason and the household; his only complaint was that he didn't have enough to do when Jason was traveling. Henrietta, the cook from the Philippines, was a more difficult challenge. She jealously guarded the kitchen, pantries, basement, and wine cellar as her terrain and waged numerous internicine battles with Nancy, the downstairs maid.

"She's a lazy no-good," Henrietta complained to Cassie in somewhat garbled English one night after a particularly combative day with Nancy. "And Tom is a no-good, too," she said, enlarging her scorn to include Nancy's husband, who acted as the Darins' butler and handyman. "Both no-good-for-nothing bodies."

After another week or two, and a close monitoring of

the household expenses, Cassie realized that Tom was purchasing certain items—expensive sanding equipment, an electric hedge clipper—that never actually found their way into the downstairs workshop. After consulting with a jubilant Charles and a victorious Henrietta, she gave the maid and butler their marching orders. And it was agreed that outside, part-time help would more than adequately cover the cleaning that Henrietta and Charles couldn't get to themselves. Immediately the atmosphere in the town house relaxed and turned more friendly, and Cassie was able to enlist two grateful allies in her crusade to humanize her monster of a niece.

Cassie was the first to admit that she could never have planned Heather's surprise birthday party without the two of them. Henrietta had been furiously baking for days. Charles had cleared the entire ballroom, carefully packing up the furniture and putting it into storage. He'd also arranged to have a friend of his pick up the twelve little girls Cassie and Heather's teacher had targeted as the best possible friendship material for Heather.

The night before, Cassie, Henrietta, and Charles had been up well past midnight decorating the ballroom with hundreds of bright pink helium balloons, bowers of pink paper flowers, and thousands of tiny silver-and-pink lights provided by a specialty party outfit recommended by Marisa Newtown, the mother of one of the girls. A clown, magician, and organ grinder with a live monkey had also been procured for the event. It was the first time Cassie had thought to spend any of the money left to her by Miranda. And though she was smart enough to know that real friendship could not be brought, she was wise enough to realize that the vast fairyland they'd created in the ballroom couldn't help but put a group of excitable little girls in a somewhat friendly mood.

"I want you to go take a look in the ballroom," Cassie told Heather when they got home after running enough unnecessary errands to ensure that the guests had arrived ahead of them. Henrietta and the two or three mothers who had agreed to join the party were clearly doing a fine job keeping the girls quiet.

"Why should I go in the ballroom?" Heather began in her high whiny voice. "Mother never let me go near the ballroom. It isn't allowed. I hate—" But Cassie cut her off.

"Your birthday present's in there."

"Why there? That's a stupid place for it."

"Well, it was too big to put anywhere else."

"Oh."

As they approached the closed ornately carved white double doors, Cassie said, "You have to knock first—very loud—okay? It's important."

"This is so stupid," Heather said, but she did as she was told, and Cassie heard muffled whispers and scuffling as the guests hid behind the thick brocaded curtains.

"Okay, let's see what's in there," Cassie said, pushing the door wide.

"Oh, it's all dark," Heather started to complain. "Nothing's here. I don't want—"

And then lights sparkled on—the ballroom chandeliers as well as the thousands of silver-and-pink pinpoint lights—and the pink-and-silver fantasy of paper and flowers flashed alive. In the middle of the room was a round table, set for thirteen, with a centerpiece designed by a specialty baker Marisa Newtown had also recommended: a large, perfectly sculpted pink swan cake.

"Surprise!" a chorus of excited voices squealed. "Surprise!" the girls cried as they raced out from behind the thick curtains to greet Heather whom, it was true, until now they'd always thought of as prissy and cold. But—between the amazing ballroom, the spectacular cake, and the enticing-looking party favors arranged around the room—Heather Darin was certainly starting to look like someone they could warm up to.

Fourteen

"*I* don't know how you do it," Cassie said with a sigh, slipping off her low heels as she sank gratefully against the chintz-covered pillows arranged on the velvety mauve-colored couch. Cassie didn't spend much time in the living room. She told herself that its ultra-feminine aura—the preponderance of chintz, the fragile-looking coffee tables cluttered with porcelain objects, the gilt-framed original Audubon prints that crowded the walls—reminded her too vividly of Miranda. In fact, she found the atmosphere in the large, fussy room overly affected and uncomfortable. She kept worrying that she'd knock over one of the precious little knickknacks that always seemed to get in the way of her elbows. And she never quite knew what to do with her long legs: the couches were too soft and low to cross them gracefully, and yet the room seemed far too formal for her to tuck them beneath her on the cushions. Until she watched Marisa Newtown, seated across from her on a matching settee, do just that.

"You mean, raise Laurel?" Marisa responded with a laugh. "Oh, I get plenty of help. Which reminds me, Cassie, you seemed a little shorthanded today. What happened to Miss Boyeson? And . . . Nancy, wasn't it?" Cassie studied the effortless way Marisa arranged herself against the cushions: one beautifully manicured hand reaching for the coffee cup

110

Henrietta had laid out on the table in front of her, the other brushing back a stray wisp that had detached itself from her severely elegant French knot. Cassie was beginning to realize that it didn't matter what clothes a woman wore—in Marisa's case that afternoon it was a simple red blazer and charcoal-gray flannel trousers—but how she wore them. Marisa carried herself with the studied poise of royalty; each movement, every gesture, seemed a minimalist ballet of perfection. Even her smile—a rather wide and toothy one—seemed calculated to inspire, perhaps not friendliness, but certainly admiration. Miranda had exuded the same quality: in a glance, you knew that she was somebody.

"I let them go," Cassie told Marisa, tucking her legs up beside her on the couch. "It's much more fun this way. With just Charles and Henrietta."

"But, my dear . . ." Marisa hesitated, studying the woman across from her. She had changed somehow from the evening she had first met her in this very room at Miranda's last party. Then, Cassie had seemed ridiculously naive, without a scrap of class. Now she was definitely more sure of herself, if not altogether at ease. She'd cut and shaped her hair to a far more becoming a style—though one could hardly deem that long, straight look she'd had before a "style." The thick gold mass was now tamed into a shoulder-length cut with delicately feathered bangs. And though she still looked like she was dressing up in her older sister's clothes, she was at least starting to select items from Miranda's wardrobe that suited her, like the simple gray Calvin Klein jersey dress she had on at the moment.

The girl would never be a clotheshorse, Marisa decided judiciously, but at least she was smart enough not to do herself up like a painted pony. Inheriting a few million no doubt did wonders for one's self-esteem. Though merely having money was not the point, Marisa had long ago realized. Knowing how to spend it—now that was the real art. "Who looks after Heather when you're working? What will you do about the house in East Hampton? The Berkshire cottage? Does Jason know . . . what you've done?"

"Well, the houses, you know, are actually mine now," Cassie said, feeling a little foolish. She hadn't yet seen the two other enormously expensive showcase homes that she'd inherited; getting the town house under some semblance of control had been more than enough to keep her busy. "And I take care of Heather myself when I'm not working. She needs a lot of . . . attention at the moment, as I'm sure you've noticed."

The birthday party, winding down noisily under Charles's supervision in the ballroom at the end of the corridor, had seemed a great success. Heather, overwhelmed by all the attention and presents, had behaved in a manner Cassie would almost call shy if she didn't know her niece any better. She'd mumbled thanks as she opened up her gifts. She'd been polite and helpful during the games. She'd clapped and laughed through the clown's performance, sang along with the organ grinder as the monkey danced. She still seemed guarded, though, when it came to playing with the other girls; she spoke in whispers when everyone else felt free to shout. She'd taken a step in the right direction that afternoon, Cassie decided, though time must pass before Heather would let go of her inhibitions and go running full tilt into the hurly-burly of childhood.

"Poor little girl," Marisa murmured, "losing her mother so suddenly. It was a terrible blow to all of us, of course. We miss Miranda dearly on the Parks Committee. In fact, Cassie, that's one reason why I wanted to linger on this afternoon."

"Oh?"

"We—the committee, that is—were wondering if you'd be interested in taking Miranda's place on the board."

"I . . . well . . . Jason!" Cassie had no idea how long he'd been standing in the doorway, his trench coat tossed over his shoulder, an oversize briefcase resting next to him on the carpet.

"Cassie," he said. "What the hell is going on in the ballroom? It sounds like the tag end of a particularly horrible parade down there. Mrs. Newtown," he added formally, nodding as Marisa turned around on the couch to greet him, her wide smile at full wattage.

"Heather's birthday party," Cassie started to explain as she extricated herself from the chintz-covered cushions. "It was a surprise . . . I wasn't sure when you'd be getting in, or we would have waited." Disconcerted by Jason's sudden appearance, Cassie was already halfway across the room before she realized she was still barefoot. Somehow, when Marisa rose from the couch, her shoes were on. Cassie didn't know what to do with herself. Should she kiss Jason on the cheek? Should they shake hands? What she really wanted to do was so impossible that she felt her cheeks flushing at the thought. With perfect aplomb, Marisa stepped around Cassie and pressed her cheek briefly against Jason's.

"Good to have you home again, Jason, darling," Marisa murmured, and then, after collecting Laurel and instructing Cassie to think about her request, she departed in a swirl of mink and Patou.

"Insufferable woman," Jason said as Charles closed the door behind her. "What the hell was she doing here?"

"She helped me with the party," Cassie replied, trying to adjust herself to Jason's difficult presence. There was something about him that always threw her off balance, made it impossible for her to breathe normally, as though the very air surrounding him was denser, heavier.

"That doesn't sound like the Marisa Newtown I know," Jason replied, but his expression brightened when Heather came running down the hall toward him.

"Daddy, Daddy! I had the best birthday party ever!"

It took hours for Cassie to settle Heather down that night, another full hour before Jason convinced his daughter to close her eyes and at least try to sleep. Though exhausted himself, he came back downstairs to find Cassie in the ballroom, cleaning up. Henrietta was trying to repair the damage done to her kitchen, and Charles was busy returning the party things to the rental warehouse in Brooklyn.

"With all the parties we've had in here over the years," Jason said as he leaned over to pick up a crushed pink party hat, "I don't think I've ever seen this room so thoroughly trashed."

"That's a big part of kids having fun," Cassie said, sighing. "Destroying things, I mean." She knew she didn't have to explain herself to Jason; there was no need to apologize for what she'd done. Yet she couldn't help but hear in his comment an implicit criticism of her party. Miranda, clearly, would never have allowed things to get so far out of control. She would never be as good a hostess as Miranda, Cassie knew, thinking back to the perfectly orchestrated evening she had first spent in this house. She would never be as good at anything as Miranda.

"It was really sweet of you to go to all this trouble," Jason said as he sorted through the debris on the table. "What had this been . . . I mean, originally?" he was staring down at the remains of the birthday cake, now a mass of yellow cake crumbs surrounded by clumps of pink icing.

"A swan. I remember that I'd always wanted a swan when I was a kid. You know, for a pet. I was about Heather's age then. I spent all my time drawing these stupid swans on anything I could find. Pink swans, until Miranda pointed out there was no such thing as a pink swan. I guess I'd gotten it all confused with flamingos."

"Well, Heather had a wonderful time. I have you to thank for that, Cassie."

"And Henrietta and Charles. They were both wonderful."

"Charles told me you let Nancy and Thomas go." Though his words were flat and uninflected, Cassie was sure she detected a note of reproach in them.

"I think Thomas was stealing, and Nancy couldn't get on with Henrietta." Cassie turned to face Jason, determined to stand up for her actions.

"You sound so defensive," Jason said. "It's your house now. You can do whatever you like with it."

"You know that's not true," Cassie replied. "It's your home. These are your things. I just did what I thought was right because you were away."

"Cassie," he interrupted her. "It's okay."

"I'm just not used to living like this," she went on, gesturing toward the Steinway baby grand that had been pushed into a far corner, then up at the enormous chandeliers. "All these priceless things."

"It doesn't matter. Things don't matter. People do. And you made one person very happy today." Somehow he had found his way across the room to stand in front of her. They were the same height, just as Miranda and he had been. It took him until that moment to realize that something was different about her. Her hair had been cut for one thing, shorter, more stylish, her bangs lightly framing her face. She looked even more strikingly like Miranda now. Her large hazel eyes met his gaze, openly questioning.

"You look . . ." He took another step toward her. No, he told himself. Remember, he reminded himself. But he found his hand reaching out, touching the slight cleft at her chin. "Just great . . . I missed you."

"And you look," Cassie said, "like you haven't slept for about three weeks."

"More like a month."

"Why? Was the trip that bad?" His hand had fallen away from her face though the place where he had touched her burned from the contact. She felt her body lighten and soften. She felt herself swaying toward him.

"No, business is great. It was . . . other things."

Miranda, Cassie told herself, automatically taking a step back, away from him, as if to leave in reality the space her sister already occupied in Cassie's mind.

"How's the new job?" Jason heard himself ask.

"Oh, great, really," Cassie replied, trying to think of how she could escape. She needed to get away from him, or she would make a fool of herself. How in God's name had she thought they'd be able to live together under the same roof? She needed to touch him. That's all. Just to feel the rough surface of his cheek beneath her fingers. Just for a second. No, this would never work. She felt panic rising in her like a fever.

"Really?" he asked, glancing by mistake at her lips, and knowing in an instant he was lost. "Really?" he repeated, but he knew he was asking about something very different. He took the step toward her. She met him halfway.

Fifteen

*J*ason had become so accustomed to Miranda's demanding, impatient ways that he had almost forgotten what it was like to be with someone who thought of him first. Without realizing it, he had come to view sex—as so much else in his marriage—as just another weapon to be used in their endless, pointless war.

"Are we going to fuck or what?" Miranda would demand after one of their scorching arguments. Threats would thicken the air between them, vicious and palpable. Over the years, the atmosphere of hatred that followed their uglier battles more and more frequently ignited into sexual episodes. After a while Jason began to wonder if either one of them could become aroused without fighting each other first.

"I don't think I have the energy for it, Miranda."

"Fuck energy," Miranda would reply. She loved to talk dirty when she was turned on. "All I need is a stiff cock and I can do all the rest." She moved like a wave, one long gliding, swelling motion toward him. Her hands were like warm, small animals, rubbing at his crotch. He would feel his penis stiffen in his pants. Defeated, he would hear himself moan.

"You're such a bitch."

"That's right," she'd whisper, sliding down to the carpet

and licking the bulging fabric around his zipper. She would weigh his balls in her palm and then knead them, as though they were soft mounds of dough, into his crotch until he was hard, tight, and thrusting against her lips and hot hands. Then she would pull down his trousers and jockey shorts and take him briefly into her mouth. But not for long. Just enough to wet him for her own pleasure.

"Come on down here where you belong," she'd say as she pulled him to the carpet. Her eyes bright, her lips glistening, she'd struggle out of her clothes until she'd be wearing nothing but a flimsy strip of brassiere and a scrap of bikini underpants. "Touch it," she'd tell him, thrusting the lacy mound toward him. "You see? It's all wet . . . it's all ready for you." And she'd slip out of the pants and, straddling him, slowly ease her long body onto his. She would start to rock up and down, back and forth blatantly, blindly seeking her own rhythm and release.

"Suck them," she'd tell him, frantically unhooking her brassiere and letting the small fleshy orbs droop toward him. He'd take the breasts, one after the other, into his mouth, working the nipples until they were hard as pebbles, as she started to buck spasmodically on top of him.

"Fuck me, fuck me," she would whimper, her hair sticky with sweat, her lips stretched against her teeth in a deeply private smile. But in truth, it was really always Miranda fucking him. Toward the end, to heighten her orgasm, she'd pull herself off him an inch or two and lay with her cheek against his lightly matted chest. Could two people get any closer physically, he would ask himself, and yet remain so emotionally apart? Finally she would push herself upright again.

"Yes, oh, yes," she'd mutter as she lost herself in her own rhythms, riding him loosely, jerking him roughly from side to side as she pulled closer to climax. What gave him pleasure in all this besides the raw, wet texture of unbridled sex? Only one thing, that thing a man knows instinctively: looking up through half-closed lids as his wife brought herself to orgasm, he knew, he was absolutely sure, that no other man could give her this. No, it was not love that they offered each other. And these protracted sessions could hardly be called lovemaking. It was more a kind of meting out of justice, almost a bloodletting. They would ride each other mercilessly. They would be cruel and crude as animals. But, in the end, only they could give each other the release they both needed.

The only difference between them was that for Miranda it was never enough. As restrained and elegant as she appeared in public, Jason knew how voracious and needful she was in private.

"I want to be sucked off," Miranda would tell him not five minutes after she'd collapsed with a relieved grunt on top of him. "I want you to suck my cunt."

"Jesus, Miranda, who taught you to talk like that?" he'd demand, then immediately add: "No, don't tell me. I really don't want to know."

Because there were other men, of course. Almost from the beginning, there were others. He knew they existed, although he never bothered to learn their names. He would just feel their existence—sometimes even catch their smell— emanating off Miranda. She wore lovers like perfume; they were a constant, elusive, invisible presence in her life. She changed them frequently, dropping one as callously as an out-of-date handbag, picking up another simply because he was something new and different. But those men were never enough for her, either, Jason knew. In the end, nothing ever was.

"Don't you want to fuck me, baby?" she'd demand after he'd slowly, carefully brought her to orgasm for a second time. She was always grateful when he—as she crassly put it—"sucked her off," because her satisfaction depended so much on him.

"No, I don't want to," Jason would tell her. "But I'm going to have to do something soon . . . or I'll probably die. Turn over, okay?"

"Yes, baby," Miranda would murmur, "please fuck me, fuck me . . ."

Jason couldn't remember the last time he'd been in the guest room where Cassie was staying. Had he ever actually stepped foot in there before? he asked himself as he closed the door as quietly as possible behind Cassie and him. The first thing that hit him was how good the room smelled. He had become so accustomed to Miranda's elaborate fragrances—orchid, mulled spices, Chinese tangerine— that the simple smell of talcum powder and new shoes in Cassie's room filled him with happiness. Holding her against him in the dark didn't hurt either. A pale sheen of light, reflected from the street, revealed the basic layout of the room: an overstuffed armchair, a cherry-wood desk stacked with books and neatly organized papers, a double bed blessedly free of lacy throw pillows, and a bedside table on which stood a reading lamp and a small silver-framed photograph. That was it. None of Miranda's endless bric-a-brac. No artful flower arrangements. Not one single piece of chintz.

It was so quiet he could hear the sound of her heart beating. Or was it his? He kissed her forehead, that wide cool field of white, like a perfectly iced pond that nobody knew about but him. He kissed the bridge of her nose—such a precisely straight, elegantly long, definitely patrician shape. It was a nose that showed breeding, a classic nose, the kind that would look as wonderful at eighty as it did now. He kissed her chin and realized for the first time how sexy a chin could be. You didn't expect it—becoming aroused by a simple chin—but this small, carefully crafted, softly mounded one did him in. He kissed her lips.

"Could we . . ." he said, breathing in the smell of her. She didn't wear perfume that he could tell, but she had her own maddeningly seductive aroma: warm skin, clean hair, mixed with something altogether deeper and elusive. He realized she smelled like freshly washed sheets drying on a clothesline. Her scent made him nostalgic, remembering everything good about his childhood. She smelled like Christmas. He was afraid to let her go for even a second.

"Do you think it's wise?"

"No," he told her, "definitely not. But you're a little too young to be wise."

"Am I . . . are you . . . are you sure?"

"Yes," he said. He'd never been more sure about anything. He'd known as soon as he saw her: she was the one. Not Miranda. Never Miranda. If he'd met both sisters at the same time, he would have chosen Cassie from the beginning. He'd made a terrible mistake but he was being given another chance. No, that wasn't true. He knew how little he deserved this. It had been just weeks since Miranda's death, and Cassie was still grieving. He knew he was stepping way beyond his bounds, that in a very real sense he was out of control. But he had to do this. He had to have her. He'd never been more sure about anything in his life. And then it occurred to him in a wounding flash: what if Cassie didn't want to sleep with him? What if she wasn't ready? He took her hand as lightly as possible in his own, ready to let it go, prepared to step away.

"But it's up to you. Are you sure?"

Cassie had kissed many men in her life. She had always enjoyed the feeling: the tough warmth of a man's lips, the lovely intimacy of shared breath, the sudden thrill of tongue meeting tongue. But what she was doing with Jason was nothing like that. True, all the sensations were the same. They just meant something entirely different. Deeper. Far more serious. From the moment they first kissed that night, Cassie accepted the fact that it was the beginning of something they had no power to stop. Or control. It just had to be. That's why Jason's question—are you sure?—made her laugh. A tidal wave was about to crash down on top of them; it was not as though they had the choice to step away.

Hand in hand, like two children, they walked slowly to the bed.

"Let me . . ." He brushed her hair back off her shoulders and leaned into the delicious task of unbuttoning the front of her dress. He planned on doing everything as slowly and carefully as he knew how; he was horrified to see that his fingers were shaking. Her fingers closed over his as she guided his hands from button to button. It was an ordeal that seemed to take eons and by the time it was done, the soft jersey dress open to the waist and curtaining her breasts, they were both a little breathless. They sat down together on the bed, turning to each other at the same moment.

"Tell me what you like," he said as he started to kiss her again; he then immediately forgot what he had asked. Words seemed so unimportant now. Thoughts, ideas—he knew he would soon be incapable of putting together the simplest sentence. With a swift acceleration of urgency, they had crossed over into the language of touch. He tugged the clinging fabric off her shoulders, exposing the delicious hollows of her neck. He explored the country of her throat—that long taut expanse of warmth that drifted like some desert isle from her chin to the hidden coves of her collarbone. His mouth lingered there as his hands massaged her shoulders with reined-back strength.

It felt so wonderful—rippling shocks of delight—that for a long time she gave in to the utter pleasure of his kisses. She drifted with the incoming tide of desire, feeling the slow, sure building, the waves cresting higher. Then she realized he was hesitating, holding back.

She pulled his hand from her waist and pressed it against her left breast—his rough hands scraping the delicate edging of her brassiere. He eased her down on the bed, watching her face intently in the darkened room. Then he sat beside her on the edge of the bed and ran his right index finger down her cheek and against her lips. She caught his finger between her teeth and sucked on it, her eyes

locked on his as he unhooked the flimsy cotton brassiere
and massaged her breasts.

He had not known that he had been subconsciously com-
paring her with Miranda until that moment, but it was then
that he realized the essential physical difference between
the two sisters. At a glance they had the same long, slim,
athletic builds. But where Miranda had been all smooth
angles and glistening edges, Cassie's body turned out to
be constructed of hundreds of secret curves and unexpected softness. Her breasts were larger and fuller, her skin
softer. Her nipples were lush mounds that tightened under
his touch. He leaned over and kissed her breasts, his lips
moving in grateful pilgrimage from one to the other.

She cradled his head in her hands, running her fingers
through his hair, breathing in his deeply masculine scent:
warm skin, after-shave, something herbal and ferny in his
hair. She felt herself arching beneath him, and from somewhere she heard someone groan.

"Yes . . . Oh, please . . ." She tugged impatiently at his
shirt collar and heard a husky voice barely recognizable as
her own ask, "Does this come off by any chance?"

"Just watch how fast." He sat up, unbuttoned the top
two buttons, and pulled the whole thing over his head.
Then he shrugged out of his white T-shirt. He turned back
to her.

"And is this a removable piece?" he asked, running his
hands down the soft fabric of her dress. "No, let me,"
he added as she started to unbuckle the suede belt at her
waist. His hesitancy was gone now, need replacing caution.
Within seconds the belt was on the floor, the dress was
draped over the far side of the bed, and he was tugging
down her panty hose and cotton bikini underpants. He ran
his hands up the inside of her calves and her thighs and
then let them rest lightly on top of the triangle of hair so
light it was barely distinguishable from her skin. He slid
his hands beneath her buttocks, brought his lips down to
nestle in her hair, and allowed his tongue to explore this

most hidden and precious territory.

Cassie had always enjoyed sex as a kind of healthy one-on-one sport. Lean, well muscled, at ease with her own nakedness, she rarely failed to have an orgasm; when she didn't reach a climax she'd simply conclude that her game was a bit off. During the last year with Kenneth, she'd found her game slipping more and more frequently, but she'd managed to explain the problem away. Consistent sexual satisfaction was not all that important, she'd told herself, when compared with compatibility and shared mutual goals. She recalled her self-delusion with a shudder of pure pleasure as she felt the warm pressure of Jason's tongue moving within her.

Now this, oh, this, was not something Kenneth had ever considered trying. His approach had been direct and clinical, almost as if he were still performing surgery. But this, yes, this, was not sport—it was the timeless, perfectly synchronized, totally absorbing process of mating. She felt her hips rise and fall; she felt the sleek warmth of Jason's head in her hands as she guided him lightly, though he seemed to know far better than she where they were going. They were in a jungle of touch, a primal forest of sensation. She had never been there before—this place where every nerve in her body sang, where her blood hummed, where her heart ran like a wild animal. She heard someone cry out once, twice.

And then Jason was there with her, there within her, and they were riding together. He filled her completely, moved in her so knowingly. She could feel him trying to slow them down, make it last, but she was suddenly ready again, needful, shocked by the depth of her hunger.

"Please . . . oh, please," she murmured, pulling him tighter, moving beneath him. He hesitated a second, trying to gain composure, but she kept arching toward him, hurrying the pace, and soon he had found his rhythm, taken his path, soon he was beyond the thought of turning back. Furiously, gloriously, he crashed toward the hot dark horizon of his being, carrying her with him, pushing her to the edge with him until—with a sudden sound of shattering glass—he felt himself lose all control and pump violently into the sweet warm darkness beneath him.

Sixteen

Shameless. They were shameless. The way they looked at each other. The way Jason's lips stayed curved in a secret smile, even as he shifted gears and pulled swiftly past a dairy truck on Route 17.

"Daddy, you're going too fast again!" Heather cried from the backseat where she sat surrounded by her birthday presents—dolls, games, the beautiful musical jewelry box Jason had brought from Germany—to keep her occupied on the nearly three-hour trip to what everyone called "the Berkshire Cottage."

"Yes, ma'am," Jason said, taking his foot off the gas pedal. Subconsciously he was thinking that the sooner they got to the house, the sooner he and Cassie could make love again. Yes, it was shameless; he had to force himself to keep his eyes on the road—and his hands on the wheel—so urgently did he need to touch Cassie. They had managed to brush fingers once or twice, but Heather's eager voice kept interrupting their voluminous shared silence.

"And Mindy Faberstein wants me to come to her house next week," she chattered on, winding up the jewelry box for the ninth or tenth time and opening the lid as the opening bars of "Für Elise" trilled through the car.

"You're going to break that if you wind it too hard," Jason said as he glanced in the rearview mirror. Was it his own newfound happiness, or was Heather looking some-how . . . more cheerful? Usually not much of a talker, she'd filled the last couple of hours with an almost nonstop monologue about her birthday party. She looked better, too, somehow. Miranda had dressed her in frilly dresses and insisted on rolling her naturally straight hair in curlers, but Cassie had let her wear jeans and a simple green cotton sweater. Her hair was pulled back from her forehead by a pretty cloth-covered band. Ignoring Jason's warning, she rewound the box and opened the lid. A few tinny chords tripped out . . . then the music stopped.

"It's broken!" Heather cried. "It's already broken. I hate it!" Tears stood out in her eyes as she slammed the lid shut.

"Your daddy told you not to wind it too much," Cassie said, turning around to face Heather in the backseat. "It's your own fault for not listening. And you don't hate the box. It's beautiful. Say you're sorry."

"I hate it. And I hate you," Heather muttered under her breath as tears slid down her cheeks.

"Liar, liar, pants on fire," Cassie said, laughing. "Come on, give me that box, and I'll see what I can do with it. But I promise you that you're not going to get it back until you say you're sorry."

Heather's pouty silence and sniffles filled the backseat as Cassie fiddled with the delicately carved box. Jason glanced at Cassie, her golden head bent intently over her task, then into the mirror to see Heather's tear-stained gaze trained hopefully on her aunt. He could not recall one instance when Miranda had disciplined Heather as Cassie had just done. As usual, Miranda had preferred others to do her dirty work for her.

"Let the nanny spank her, if you like," she'd told Jason when he insisted that some sterner measures had to be taken to combat Heather's increasingly obnoxious behavior. "I won't have her despising me years from now, pouring her heart out to some horrible psychiatrist. I much prefer she hate her nanny."

"But you're her best example, Miranda. It's you she looks up to . . . and wants to emulate. You're single-handedly turning her into a little horror show, do you realize that?"

"Oh, Jason, please, can't we agree about anything, darling?" The truth of the matter was no, they couldn't. From disapproving of each other's friends to disliking each other's clothes, they were constantly at loggerheads. Tension and anger built up as each refused to give an inch. Their sense of humor and playfulness died. In the end they held on only because neither one wanted to give the other the satisfaction of escape. And Heather, of course, was the real victim. Jason had been so deeply infected by the disease of the marriage that it took him years—really, it took Cassie—before he realized just how sick the relationship had been.

With Miranda, all touching halted after the sexual act was complete. Last night with Cassie, exploring each other had been just the beginning. She'd run her fingers across his chest, caressing his nipples, massaging the lightly matted muscular surface.

"Was it my imagination," Jason asked in a near whisper, "or did the earth actually move beneath us? I thought I heard something crash."

"Oh . . . my God . . . that's right." Cassie sat up in the dark and fumbled for the light. The photograph of Cassie's graduation that Miranda had left in her safe-deposit box had fallen off the bedside table and lay shattered on the floor.

"I'm sorry," Jason said, pushing up on an elbow. "I'll buy a new frame for you, Cassie."

"No, that's okay," Cassie replied, slipping out of bed to gather the pieces of glass, silver, and the oddly bulky picture and backing together; she slid them carefully into the shallow drawer of the bedside table. "I'll just have this one fixed. I was so touched that Miranda kept this picture—and actually had it framed. It makes me realize that, in her own way, she did care about me and Mom and Dad."

Of course Jason would never tell her that he'd never seen the picture before, that Miranda had never displayed it . . . or anything else that had to do with her family or her past.

"Listen, I couldn't get out of there fast enough, okay?" Miranda told him when he tried to find out more about her childhood in Raleigh. "It was just your typical boring middle-class upbringing. I never really was a part of the family—I was always the half sister with a stepfather. It was pretty dreary, darling, believe me."

Would he ever be able to tell Cassie the truth about her sister and his marriage? Jason wondered as he turned off the highway and started down the long circling drive around the lake that led to the house. He glanced across at her again, and she caught his look with a smile. No, he told himself, as he turned his attention back to the road, sometimes the truth was too ugly. Sometimes silence was the kindest response.

The bright sounds of the restored jewelry box broke into his thoughts. Cassie turned to the backseat with the prettily carved gift poised triumphantly in the air.

"What do you say, Heather?" she asked lightly. Jason glanced in the rearview mirror to see his daughter look hungrily from the music box . . . to Cassie.

"Okay, I'm sorry," Heather answered grudgingly as she reached out to reclaim her birthday present. She didn't really hate her aunt all that much. At times—like when Cassie read her stories at night or helped her with her homework—she didn't hate her at all. Ever since her birthday party the day before, she was beginning to think she might even—almost—like her.

When Cassie heard the word "cottage," she immediately thought of something small and shingled, a porch or two, and a chimney plumed with smoke. What she saw instead as they crossed a small stone bridge that connected the island property to the mainland was a majestic white-brick colonial farmhouse, meticulously restored, a large barn converted into guest apartments, an Olympic-size pool, a pagoda, half a dozen gardens, and at least one tennis court. Beyond the house and outbuildings, fields of wildflowers nodded in the light breeze. At the bottom of the sloping hill they were climbing, the lake shimmered as one of the first sailboats of the season tacked into the wind.

"What were you expecting?" Jason asked Cassie as he saw her slightly dismayed reaction to the property. Far more than the town house and the East Hampton beach house, the Berkshire cottage was Jason's creation. Miranda had been against buying it from the beginning.

"It's hardly more than a farm, for chrissakes," Miranda complained when she first saw it. Jason had fallen in love with the rural solitude of the Berkshires five years before, when business dealings in Boston gave him an excuse to commute back and forth on his motorcycle. Though it took him several hours longer than the Massachusetts Turnpike—and half a day more than the shuttle—racing down these lush back roads and rolling hills restored his sense of humor and self in a way that nothing else could. He had learned about the farm from associates in Boston— it was in an estate sale of one of the senior partners of his law firm there—and made an offer the afternoon he first saw it. He'd intended it as a surprise birthday present for Miranda.

"Nobody goes to the Berkshires anymore," Miranda would complain whenever Jason suggested they weekend there. "They're all in the Hamptons."

"That's precisely why I like the cottage," Jason would reply, "because nobody will be there but us. Don't you ever want to get away from it all, Miranda? Lie out in the backyard and look up at the stars? Swim naked in the lake at midnight?"

"You know I prefer the pool, even at the beach," Miranda replied. Although Jason had wanted to keep his Berkshire retreat as natural as possible, he'd put in the Olympic-size pool, tennis courts, sauna, and Jacuzzi to make the farm more palatable to Miranda. Not that it had helped much; she still had found every possible excuse not to visit.

"It's . . . wonderful," Cassie murmured as the car slowed in the cobbled courtyard in front of the house. Despite the showiness of the pool and tennis courts, it was obviously a home that had been carefully tended for many years. Arbors of roses arched around a side door; rhododendron bushes flanked the entranceway. The pungent aroma of freshly clipped box hedges and newly mowed grass drifted in the cool mid-May breeze.

With Heather trailing behind, Jason spent the afternoon showing Cassie the property: the boat house, the pebbled swimming beach with its brightly colored umbrellas and chairs, the small fish hatchery where Jason and his groundskeeper were trying to breed freshwater trout, the old original barn—which Miranda had declared an eyesore and demanded relocated out of sight of the house—now housing a noisy contingent of pigs, geese, wild turkeys, hens, and a cock. They ended at the stable and paddocks. Four thoroughbred horses grazed quietly in an adjoining field.

"Do you ride?" Jason asked as one of the horses trotted up to the fence.

"I usually manage to stay on," Cassie replied, watching as Jason caressed the horse's mane and scratched knowingly behind its ears. She remembered the gentleness of his touch the night before and—though she had tried all day to fight it off—felt a powerful surge of longing break through her resolve. As if reading her thoughts, Jason glanced at her, his gaze lingering on her lips.

"Okay, let's go, then," he said, swallowing hard. "Heather, you ride with me on Juno. I'll get some help, and we'll saddle up the horses."

The trails led around the lake, winding through the hills, sloping across the fields, meandering down dirt roads still muddy from a recent rain. The golden slanting sun of late afternoon filtered through trees that were just starting to sprout their green leaves. Here and there a wild patch of daffodils—or a hedge of forsythia—dabbed a hillside with color. The cooling air was filled with the promise of spring:

the rich scent of pine needles and fertilizer, the sound of blue jays and a distant chain saw. They rode until it was almost dark, arriving back at the stable just as the sun was turning the lake a dark, volcanic orange.

They all made dinner together from provisions stocked by the caretaker couple who lived in the gameskeeper house across the lake: vegetable soup, grilled ham-and-cheese sandwiches, a salad of wild greens, and bowls of strawberry sherbert topped with freshly picked strawberries.

The temperature had fallen swiftly after sunset, and they ate in front of a roaring fire Jason built in the living-room fireplace. The room was furnished—as was most of the house—with starkly simple Shaker furniture, origi-nally built, Jason explained, less than five miles from the house.

"There used to be several Shaker settlements in the Berk-shires, some very large and powerful. But it was a religion bound to die out. They believed in chastity, you know, the men and women living in separate quarters."

"How odd," Cassie said, feeling the smooth work of the ladder-backed rocker she was sitting on. "What they created was so beautiful. It seems to be made with such love."

"Mommy hated these chairs," Heather said sleepily. "She hated this house, too. She said it was way out in the boon-docks. Is that a bad thing, Daddy?"

"That depends, pumpkin, on where you want to be," Jason said, getting up and pulling his daughter into his arms. "And I think I know where you ought to be about now."

After Jason carried Heather upstairs, Cassie cleared away the dishes, rinsing them in the double tin sink in the oak-paneled kitchen. There was no dishwasher. No food proces-sor. But the room was large and cheerful with a big Franklin stove in one corner and an impressive collection of antique pewter mugs and earthenware bowls running across a top shelf. Cassie had a hard time imagining Miranda here; she could hear her ridiculing the austere rooms with their rough wooden floors and tiled fireplaces. Her sister clearly hadn't spent all that much time in the house—there was no sign of her signature chintz or porcelain pieces—and yet Jason obviously loved the place.

She wiped down the countertops, then went back into the living room, put another log on the fire, wrapped herself up in an afghan blanket that had been draped over her rocker, and curled up in front of the fire. She hadn't gotten much sleep the night before, and between the trip up and the long ride that afternoon, she was bone-tired. She meant to just close her eyes for a moment. She was grateful for a few minutes alone to think about Miranda and Jason . . . to try to imagine them together in this house.

Everything was moving very quickly—her need for Jason, her growing, almost painful physical desire for him—and soon she was going to have to come to terms with what Jason meant to her. No, that she already knew: he meant everything. But what did she mean to him? All that they had done so far together—each word, each kiss, every touch— was shadowed by Miranda's memory.

Poor Jason, she thought sadly as her thoughts began to drift, having to settle for a half sister . . . only half as good . . . only half a life.

Seventeen

She was asleep when he finally came back downstairs. She was curled up in front of the fire, her head resting on the crook of her elbow, the firelight casting the room in a warm glow, shadows dancing along the ceiling and walls. Shadows . . .

He knelt quietly near her, careful not to touch her, and studied her face: the fine infrastructure of cheekbone and chin, the velvety expanse of skin, the spun-gold hair. He tried to memorize the exact curve of her eyebrows, the slight indentation at her temple, the lovely complexity of her chin and throat. His gaze and thoughts strayed to her hips . . . her waist . . . her thighs . . . and he felt the heat that he had been trying to tamp down all day within him start to rise. He tried to remind himself why it should end here, why it should never have been. He forced himself to remember who he was and what he had done in the past. He pushed himself to think of the darkness, of the shadows. He heard himself say: "Miranda . . ."

Cassie stirred. She was suddenly cold, unaccountably sad. Something had jarred her awake from her deep, dreamless sleep. Then she remembered: he had said Miranda. She saw Jason watching her, his expression so dark that she quickly sat up. She pulled him into her arms.

"It's okay," she said, although it wasn't. *Miranda*. That

134

one word was like a blow, a sharp cruel punch that knocked the breath out of her. She wanted to cry. For herself. For him.

"It's not . . ." Jason started to say as he pulled her tightly to him, breathing in the smell of her hair.

"Jason . . ." She turned away, hugging the blanket to her. "We have to . . . we should talk . . . about Miranda."

"What do you want me to say?"

"I don't know. We're moving so fast. I feel a little stunned. I just think we should talk about what's happening."

"What's happening is I want you," Jason said, touching her shoulder. "Now. Rather desperately, as a matter of fact."

"So that you can forget?" Cassie turned to look at him, the terrible question clear in her eyes.

"No, Cassie, no . . ." he told her, but he knew she didn't believe him, wouldn't believe him until he told her the truth about Miranda. And that he could never do. He would have to convince her some other way. He would have to make her forget. He took her right hand in both of his and held it to his lips. He opened her palm, smoothed back her fingers, and brushed his lips across the soft mound of skin. He felt her shudder as he ran his tongue over her palm. He heard her moan as his right hand moved up her leg.

"Please," she murmured, unsure herself if it was a protest or a plea.

"Please, what?" he asked roughly, his hand drifting up the inside of her thigh.

"Please . . . Let's just talk for a while."

"Talk . . ." Jason ran his hand through his hair and sat up beside her.

"Yes, you know. I say something. Then you say a few words. It's not that hard once you get going."

"Sure. Fine," he said, but he felt as though he were drunk, everything off balance, out of focus. He wanted her so badly it was ridiculous, a physical craving that was just barely within his power to control. He got up and busied himself with the fire, putting on another log, all the while trying to pull himself together. It occurred to him that he was frightening Cassie with his outsize needs, his terrible longing. He wasn't acting normal, he knew, but then he had long ago left behind the signposts of acceptable human behavior. For so many years his world had been ruled by hate and anger, the need to control and the desire for revenge. Now, faced with someone good, his passion was all-consuming. He was starved for love and suddenly panicked that his hunger would only drive Cassie away. *Slow down,* he told himself, *follow her lead, find her pace. Don't let her see how desperate you are.*

"So . . ." Cassie said, feeling a little ridiculous. "What . . . should we talk about?" She felt as though she knew him so thoroughly in some ways. She knew him by touch and taste. She was uncannily attuned to his presence. Even with her back turned, she would know when Jason walked into a room. Yet in so many ways he was a stranger. She knew nothing about his past—his upbringing and background—except for the fact that he had married her sister.

"Whatever you say," Jason replied, taking a chair a few feet away from her. He loved the way the firelight painted her face a warm rose, the way the shadows played against her skin.

"Okay . . . where did you grow up? Did you come from a large family?"

"Bronx. Five kids. Dirt poor. My father was a second-generation Italian stone worker. Unfortunately there were not a lot of stones to work in the fifties, so he took odd jobs. We all helped out."

"You were the oldest?"

"It shows that much?" Jason laughed. He felt himself relaxing a little as his thoughts turned back to his childhood. "Yeah, I was the oldest with a vengeance: aggressive, ambitious, determined to get ahead."

"College?"

Jason nodded.

"But how did you manage? Without any money, I mean?"

"I had a—what should I call him?—a patron. Senator Haas, though he was just a junior assemblyman then. I worked for his office a couple of summers when I was in high school. He took a liking to me."

"Haas! My parents idolized him," Cassie said. "He represented everything they believed in—civil rights, freedom of speech. It must have been wonderful to work with a man like that."

"Yes, I learned a great deal from Anthony Haas." If Cassie had not been so caught up in her own memories at that moment, she would have heard the irony in Jason's tone.

"And after college? How does one get a start as a real estate mogul, anyway?"

Jason laughed and said, "A stint in Vietnam is pretty decent training. I learned the basic business tactics there: guerrilla warfare, camouflage, midnight raids."

"It's really that cutthroat?" Cassie asked.

"No, I was just kidding, honey," Jason told her. It had been a long time since he had talked about his work to anyone who wasn't directly involved in it. Miranda, once she had been satisfied that what he did was immensely lucrative, had only pretended to listen to his talk about deals and closings. Early on in the marriage, he had stopped trying to explain the complex, fragile layers of loans and contracts, tax breaks and union deals that comprised the real raw materials of his empire. Now, sensing Cassie's genuine interest, he tried to think of a way to explain the essence of his work.

"I'm really just a broker in a way. A middleman. I'm the one who brings everyone—bankers, investors, architects, contractors—together. I'm like the glue—the one that everyone sticks to."

"So what was your first big building? That must have

been quite a feeling. Seeing that go up."

"But what about you?" Jason replied. "Do you remember the lead in your first story?"

"You just rather abruptly changed the subject," Cassie said, studying his profile.

He turned to meet her gaze. He smiled. "It's my turn now," he told her. "Tell me about yourself. Your parents. Growing up . . ."

"But you already know all that from Miranda. I'm really not interesting . . . What about your first building? Where was it?"

"I guess . . . I'm a little ashamed to admit that I don't really remember all the details. It was a long time ago . . . twenty years or so. An office complex in Manhasset out on Long Island. Nothing very glamorous or exciting."

"But you must have been so proud. And your parents— your father, a stone worker watching his son put up entire buildings—they must have been thrilled."

"They were. They are. They're in Florida now . . . living in a retirement resort I helped put together."

"You're so lucky to still have them . . . I miss my parents so much."

"I should see them more. I will see them more. Miranda . . ." Miranda had wanted nothing to do with Rosa and Tomasso, or any of Jason's brothers and sisters. Like Miranda's own family, Jason's relatives were people Miranda felt were best "left behind."

"You have to pick and choose, darling," Miranda would tell him. "Hone your list of friends. Keep the best relationships polished and bright . . . let the others tarnish. What in God's name do I have in common with your mother? Or with mine, for that matter? Why waste time pretending? If you feel you must visit, then go. I'm not stopping you. But I'm not going, and neither is Heather. They'll feed her all sorts of unhealthy things." The subject had been the source of numerous arguments, ones Jason always lost.

"Miranda . . . what?" Cassie asked, studying Jason's face

in the firelight. His expression was cold, inward-looking. The lines etched around his eyes and mouth made him look older and tired, a man who had already seen the best—and the worst—of what the world had to offer. And yet the night before when they were making love, she had seen his face transformed—alive and joyful, his rare smile lighting his eyes.

"I'm sorry," Jason replied, shaking his head. "What were we talking about? Oh, yes, my parents . . . You'd like them, Cassie. Maybe I'll fly them up this summer. We could all spend a week or so together here. Would you like that?"

"Jason, please, no more excuses. Can't we talk about Miranda?"

"No." The word came out with far more force than he intended, and he immediately tried to soften his tone. "I mean, Cassie, I'm not ready. It's . . . too close. Painful."

"But you know that we . . . I can't . . . we have to talk about her if we hope to stay . . . I mean, have any future together." She was stumbling over her words, afraid of sounding pushy or possessive, yet anxious that he face the truth. Every time Miranda's name came up, he changed the subject. And the closer they were drawn to each other, Cassie was beginning to realize, the more solidly Miranda stood between them.

"Cassie . . ." He was sitting next to her again suddenly, brushing her bangs back off her forehead, running his hand down the curve of her cheek. "I am . . . I have a lot of things to sort out. I'm sorry. I wish this were easier—"

"Just tell me, Jason, now," Cassie broke in. "Am I just . . . am I simply a substitute for Miranda? Because if that's the case, it's better I know. It's better things end here."

He could lie, of course, he told himself. It would be such a simple thing to do . . . and it would be so much better for her if he wasn't in her life. He could lie . . . and who would ever know the truth? He could just continue the lie that Miranda had been so good at perpetuating: the devoted Darins, that perfectly matched couple. Oh, there had been cracks in the facade—but people were always willing to believe in hype. And Miranda had been such a good little self-promoter, even to her own sister. Cassie actually believed that he had loved Miranda . . . and he could let the lie stand. He should let the lie stand, except . . .

"No, Cassie," he said, pulling her to him. It was selfish. He had no right. Yet he heard himself saying as his lips found hers, "Things don't end here . . . they're just beginning."

Eighteen

Jason was home for ten days straight, the happiest days of Cassie's life. Careful and discreet by day in front of Heather and the staff, they were voracious lovers by night, often not falling asleep until dawn filtered through Cassie's guest room curtains. No one in the house seemed to notice. But Sheila Thomas nailed Cassie first thing Monday morning after the weekend in the Berkshires.

"Who is he?"

"Excuse me?"

"Who's the lucky man? It's written all over your face—love, or at least some very excellent sex."

"I don't know what you're talking about," Cassie replied with a laugh. "Let's get to work."

"Okay, be like that," Sheila said with a sniff. "But don't expect mine to be the shoulder you cry on when the time comes."

"What makes you think I'll be crying, Sheila?"

"Experience. The harder they fall, the longer they weep. Now, about this school-board thing . . ."

They were in the middle of an in-depth piece on a scandal-plagued Bronx school district that had thrown out its entire board a few weeks before. It was a choice assignment: timely and important. Magnus himself had suggested that Sheila and Cassie cover it as a team.

141

"He said some real nice things about your work on the traffic violations things," McPherson muttered when he gave them the new assignment. "Thinks the two of you are hot stuff."

"Do I detect a note of disagreement?" Sheila demanded.

"Not really," McPherson admitted. "I just don't like to be told by anybody who should be doing what in my department. I don't like favoritism. Or interference. It can backfire, you know. You two damn well better keep your noses clean."

They had been given a camera crew and a project allowance. They had also been given a larger office to share: the empty corner suite that had been Miranda's.

"Man, we're really moving up in the world," Sheila said as she ran her fingers across the pristine keyboard of Miranda's high-powered computer terminal. "These babies can just about write the stories for you."

"And it's a great view," Cassie said, standing at the plate-glass window that looked down on the sea of traffic rolling up Sixth Avenue. Across the street the windows of Rockefeller Center glinted in the sun. The benches and sidewalks below were clogged with sightseers and early lunchers out to get some air. In another week it would be June. Cassie's thoughts drifted: to Jason . . . summer . . . the Berkshire cottage.

"After this trip, I'll try to take some time off," he'd told her early that morning as they lay together in her bed. "Maybe you can get a week away yourself . . . and we can all just escape to the country. Really relax." His grip had tightened as she turned to him and ran her index finger lightly across his heavy brow.

"I'm not sure you're relaxable," she told him as she kissed his chin, then his lips. "I don't think I've ever actually seen you asleep."

"Wonder why," he murmured as his hands drifted down her shoulders and cupped her breasts. "Oh, Cassie . . ." She shivered, feeling his touch still . . . the memory of his mouth on her nipples making her weak with longing.

"Snap out of it, kid," Sheila said, watching her from across the room. "Christ, I wish you'd get some sleep one of these days."

"I don't know what you're talking about," Cassie replied evenly. "I'm perfectly fine." And she was. She put in long tough hours, commuting back and forth to the Bronx with Sheila and the crew, and yet she still had more than enough energy left for Jason at night. She was too happy to sleep, too excited. There was also a part of her that was afraid to stop. Things might catch up with her if she did. Like Miranda. They had not mentioned her name since that night in the Berkshires when they had been alone together. It was an unspoken pact between them to let the subject drift. In fitful dreams, Cassie would push Miranda's memory away. Later, they would face her together. Later. But for now, all she wanted was to feel his arms around her again: safe and strong.

The morning he was scheduled to take the Concorde to London, Jason didn't sleep at all. When Cassie woke up after drifting off around four in the morning, he was watching her, his head resting on his elbow, a half smile lingering on his lips.

"Don't tell me," she whispered, "I was snoring, right?"

"No." He smiled at her, and he suddenly looked years younger than when she'd first met him. Could she really be responsible for this change in him? Her whole heart longed for it to be true. "I was just lying here worrying that I don't have a decent picture of you. I'll need something I can take to London with me. God, it's going to be hell being away from you for two weeks. Maybe I should cancel."

"No," she said, putting her finger to his lips. "I won't be held responsible for bringing down the Darin empire. Anyway, there's some jam I'm particularly fond of that you can only get at Harrod's. You see, now you have to go."

"Okay," he said, "but I'm going to buy cases of it . . . so I don't have to go back too soon. I'm going to miss you, Cassie."

In the end, because she had nothing else, she'd given him her graduation photo, the one that had been in the frame that Miranda had left her, the one that had smashed on the floor the first night they'd made love.

"Here," she said, tugging it out of the bent frame, "I have to take this in to be fixed anyway. I'm the washed-out one in the middle," she added uncertainly. For there, once again, was beautiful Miranda, standing a little apart from the rest of her family and yet somehow, in Cassie's mind at least, dominating the photograph.

"Thank you, Cassie," Jason said, carefully and quite conspicuously folding the photo so that only Cassie was visible. He slipped the edited photograph into the first plastic sleeve of his wallet.

The evening after Jason left, Cassie spent several hours in her room, sorting through the documents that Miranda had left her. Though she'd tried to push Miranda from her thoughts when she was with Jason, now that he was gone she found herself thinking about her sister almost obsessively. After all, she was now working in Miranda's office. Taking care of Miranda's daughter. Having an affair with her husband. Though the word "affair" seemed all wrong—or not half enough—to describe what Cassie and Jason did together. They simply were together. They belonged together. They were . . .

In love. Cassie knew it was far too soon after Miranda's death for Jason to fall in love again. Anyone would tell her this obvious truth, and that was one reason why she so jealously guarded the secret of their relationship. She didn't want to hear that she was nothing more than a substitute for Miranda, or that Jason was clinging to Cassie in order to stave off the task of facing his wife's death. Of course that's what everyone would think. But they were wrong. Weren't they?

With Jason beside her, she didn't have to ask herself these questions. When Jason was with her, she was sure of herself . . . and them. But now, with Jason away less than a day, she felt a relentless uncertainty take hold. She wandered around the room, trying to imagine Jason there, sitting on the corner of the bed, laughing, talking, brushing back her hair.

She stopped at the night table where the broken, photoless frame lay in several pieces. She picked up the oddly bulky backing and turned it over a few times. It consisted of two pieces of cardboard taped together on all four sides. On closer inspection, it seemed clear that the two pieces of cardboard weren't just backing for the photograph; they were protecting something wedged between them. Cassie found a nail file and slid it under one of the taped edges. A 3½" computer disk slipped into her hand. It was unlabeled and looked perfectly harmless. But it had certainly been put there for one reason: to keep it hidden.

Though Cassie slept soundly that night, she jerked awake at dawn from a recurring nightmare that had plagued her since childhood. She was drowning, going down for the third and final time. Fully awake now, she decided to dress and go into work early, leaving a note for Heather, telling her she'd pick her up after school as usual.

Not even the receptionist had arrived before Cassie. She turned lights on as she made her way down the corridor to Miranda's office, trying to shake off the spooky feeling that had colored her morning since the nightmare. Before she even took the plastic cover off her coffee, she turned on Miranda's computer and watched it beep into life. Various icons flashed on the screen, naming the software programs and protective devices installed on the hard drive. She clicked on the hard-drive icon, rummaged through her shoulder bag for the broken picture frame and the 3½" disk she had brought with her, and inserted the disk into the drive. A document icon appeared on the upper-right-hand corner of the screen: it was titled FOR CASSIE ONLY.

A part of her knew even before she opened the word processor and retrieved the document that she had at last found what Miranda had wanted no one but her to discover. Her fingers shook as she clicked the OPEN command and a flood of numbers filled the screen. She had to scroll up and down on the document for a full minute before she realized it was divided into three sections. The first was headed "Darin." The second, "Magnus." The third, "Haas."

How long did she study the document before she finally realized what she was looking at? An hour at least, because when she finally heard people talking in the corridor she'd already accepted the fact that the dream world she'd been living in for the past two weeks was gone. In its place was this field of amber facts glowing against a flat black screen.

Under the Darin heading, Miranda had made notes on Jason's real estate transaction's during the mid-seventies. She had bank account numbers, dated entries, and amounts that added up to slightly more than $100,000, all made out to "A. Haas."

Under the Magnus heading, Miranda had kept track of Magnus Media's phenomenal growth through the seventies as well as numerous payments to "A. Haas" amounting to more than a million dollars.

The "Haas" section was more descriptive, a capsule résumé of a young unknown state representative who would eventually become one of the most influential senators in the country. But not without help, Cassie thought sadly. Not without money. Kickbacks. Payoffs. It was obvious from Miranda's notes that the very first building that Jason put up—the office complex in Manhasset he had been so reluctant to discuss—was given zoning clearance because of payoffs Jason made to Haas. The extent of Magnus's kickbacks was broader and more complicated, though it was clear that Haas had secured favorable F.C.C. rulings for Magnus in exchange for cash.

Cassie stared at the bottom of the last "Haas" entry for several seconds before she saw from the cursor at the bottom of the screen that there was more to the document. She scrolled down the page, until she came to the following message:

Cassie:

I'm sorry if you ever have to read this because it will mean two bad things: 1) all my suspicions are confirmed and 2) I'm in trouble. All I know is what I've been able to outline above. Senator Haas has been on the take for years, and Jason and Magnus are both involved. You'll find photocopies of papers supporting all this, in case you don't believe me, out at the East Hampton place under the flagstone in the far right corner of the wine cellar. I figure if you find this and I'm not around to help, you'll know what to do. But be careful. Trust no one.

M.

Nineteen

Her first impulse was to run. Out of the office. Away from New York. Back home to North Carolina. To Kenneth. Safety. She clicked on SAVE to store the information and ejected the disk from the computer. She slid the disk into the zippered pocket of her shoulder bag. She could leave right away. Leave everything behind. Heather. The job. Sheila. Magnus . . .

"I find it ridiculous to have to remind you, Miranda." The very first words Cassie had heard Magnus utter had been in anger. The night of the party. "I dictate the parameters of your job. What I'm telling you is that this time you've gone too far. I want this silly so-called investigation stopped right now. Here. Do you understand?"

And Miranda's response? It had seemed so harmlessly flippant at the time.

"Over my dead body."

He had known she was looking into his financial relationship with Haas. He had wanted her to stop. But just how badly?

Her second thought was to forget the whole thing. What did any of it matter now? Miranda was dead. Cassie might never have found the disk. Or opened it. She could pretend she'd lost it. Misplaced it. Who would know? Miranda was dead.

Cassie could just leave. Say she'd changed her mind. Missed her old life . . . old friends. She could catch a flight to Raleigh that very afternoon. She could run. Away from Heather. Magnus. Haas. Jason . . .

"Why are you doing this?" She remembered Jason's bitter tone late Easter night. The argument between him and Miranda had echoed loudly down the hallway. "Why do you want to ruin me?" Jason . . . she thought of his smile, the taste of his kiss, the almost unbearable tenderness of his touch. Jason, who didn't even want to mention Miranda's name now.

"No," he had said. "I'm not ready. It's too soon. Painful." But hadn't Cassie known even then there was something else? Jason was holding back. He had been hiding something from the moment they met. Jason and Miranda. The tension between them had been electric. You could just about see the sparks. Of passion . . . or hatred? A dark unexplored part of Cassie had always wanted to believe the latter. That there'd been only negative currents between them. That Jason was Cassie's alone to love. But now that thought terrified her. Jason's moods could darken in a second. His eyes would go cold. She didn't want to think about his strength, the tight coil of muscles on his arms and back. She didn't want to think about the feel of his hands on her skin.

She could just leave. Miranda was dead. Three months ago Cassie hadn't met any of the people who dominated her life now: Magnus, Heather, Jason. She didn't have to stay. This wasn't her responsibility. She could go anytime. No one back home would be surprised. Kenneth would forgive her and take her back. She could forget about this. She'd pick up her old life. And then the truth of what she had seen on the screen finally hit her: Miranda was dead . . . but it wasn't an accident.

"Actually, Cassie, I want you to stay," Miranda had told her their last morning together. In the end, she almost begged her to take the job. "Maybe you've got it all backward," Miranda had told her when Cassie assumed her older half sister was belatedly trying to help her, forward her career. It was Miranda who had needed Cassie's help. And now, at last, Cassie knew why.

"You're in early." Sheila Thomas didn't enter a room—she exploded into it: juggling morning newspapers and her take-out bag of coffee and bagels, shoulder bag flapping at her back, curly hair bouncing, headset buzzing. "Uh-oh." Sheila dropped all her things on the desk next to where Cassie was sitting. "You don't even have to tell me. It's written all over your face."

"What is?" Cassie said, relieved to have Sheila there. She felt as though she'd spent the last two hours in another dimension, existing in an altogether different and terrifying reality. Sheila's loud voice brought her back to the eighteenth floor.

"Your guy. You had a fight. Or he dumped you. Something. I recognize that look all too well." She sat down, swiveled the chair around, and propped her black boots on the desktop as she lifted an oversized cup of coffee out of the brown paper bag.

"Sheila, did you know anything about a piece Miranda was working on right before the accident? Something sort of hush-hush? Off the books?"

"So, you don't want to talk about it even? I was just kidding about my shoulder. Use it as a hankie if you like."

"No, I mean it. About Miranda. Anything odd you can remember? A fight with McPherson? A blowup with a staffer?"

"Cassie, kiddo, honey pie. Miranda was always fighting with McPherson, nothing unusual there. And she blew up at staffers with the regularity of Old Faithful. I even heard her take on Magnus one night. Must have been about a week before . . . she died."

"What was it about? How did you happen to overhear it?"

"I wasn't snooping if that's what you mean. We'd finished taping for the week. Magnus occasionally came down for the final session in the studios on the fifteenth floor. She had a full fucking dressing room down there: shower, sauna, walk-in closets. I think they'd often go out for dinner together afterward. I remember he had on a tux. Christ, he looks good in black tie."

"I'm more interested in what he said than in what he was wearing."

"It was Miranda who did the talking. She said he could damn well go on alone if he didn't give her what she wanted. I assumed they were going out to one of their society dos."

"And Magnus? What did he say?"

"Basically to keep her voice down. It was hard to hear him, but you could tell by his tone that he was trying to humor her. I think he even said something about being reasonable."

"No idea what they were talking about?"

"Nope. But I could tell she had him going. He's pretty circumspect about his language, but I remember him saying that someone had really fucked up. Not your usual silver-tongued Magnus by any means."

"But nothing specific?"

"No. It got real quiet then. Awful quiet. About ten minutes later they emerged all glittery and dewy-eyed. She had on one of the full length evening dresses she kept down there. You can bet your ass that thing cost more than my annual salary."

"Where's all that stuff now? Where are her project notes and scripts? What happened to all her files?"

"How should I know?" Sheila replied as she peeled back the paper encasing her bagel. "Someone from personnel swept up in here. I assume McPherson has her old files. Pieces she was working on and so forth. What's all this about anyway?"

"I need to see those files," Cassie said.

"That's too bad. McPherson has this weird thing about security on upcoming projects, you know? Like he doesn't want *60 Minutes* or *48 Hours* to know what we're up to. Stuff is in a safe, Cassie. Forget it."

"You're close to McPherson. You're probably the only one around here he trusts."

"Like I said. Forget it."

"I can't tell you how important this is," Cassie began, sitting down on the edge of Sheila's desk.

"Sure you can," Sheila said, licking cream cheese off her fingers. "You can start by telling me what it's all about. But for starters, let me clue you in on something. You say Miranda was working on some big deal story right before she died? I hate to tell you, but I doubt it. Miranda hadn't generated an original idea for *Breaking News* the whole time I've been here. Sure, she had her name down as producer on three or four pieces a year, but it's mostly stuff she usurped or inherited. She was too fucking worried about how she looked to give much of a thought to what we covered. That's our job. The great unwashed, unloved slugs offscreen."

"And you're still so sick with envy you can't see straight."

"Bull. Like, I'm just trying to give you the score, Cassie. Sorry if it offends your delicate sensibilities. But your sister was a first-class, full-blown bitch."

"I know." Cassie stood up and walked over to the window. The morning rush was easing. Only one person got off the bus across the street. An elderly woman, well dressed in a linen suit. She walked slowly up Sixth, stopping to look in a store window. Retired, Cassie decided, with plenty of leisure time. She'd shop all morning, perhaps meet a friend for lunch or a matinee. Something Miranda would never do now. "That's not a good enough reason to have her killed."

Sheila stopped eating. She sat up. She took her boots off the desk. "You know what you're saying?"

"Yes. I'm afraid I do. I don't know who did it for sure. But I do know why. She had information that could destroy the lives of at least three powerful men. I wish it were coincidence. But it's not. You see, she tried to get me to help her. She knew she was in danger. That contract bodyguard you told me about wasn't going to do any good. These were men she knew. Well. Intimately."

"What are you saying?" Sheila's voice was a whisper. She glanced at the open door, got up, crossed the room, and quietly closed it. "Are you sure? How do you know?"

Cassie stared across the desk at Sheila. "I just do. Believe me, okay? It's better for you not to hear the details." Sheila was a friend. A fast friend. A pal. But would she really want to learn that Magnus was corrupt? Could she put her own feelings and loyalties behind her for the sake of a woman she'd despised? How much did the truth really matter, Cassie asked herself, when it came to the pull of the heart? She thought about Jason and realized that she didn't know the answer herself yet. How could she possibly trust Sheila?

"What . . . do you need from McPherson?" Sheila asked.

"You're going to help me?"

"Yes. But not because of Miranda. I'm sorry. But if what you say is true, we're sitting on one hell of a hot story. And it sounds like it's ours. Exclusively."

"You could say that." Cassie thought about the disk in her shoulder bag. She was going to have to find a very good place to hide it now.

The opportunity arose to get into the safe, as Sheila knew it would, two days later. The programming meeting was scheduled for three that afternoon, and McPherson would need to glance over his notes, memorize his proposed line-up, and have the file returned to the safe sometime before the meeting began. She waited until he was comfortably seated at his desk, eating his usual lunch of take-out sushi.

"When are you going to schedule our Bronx piece, Mac?" Sheila asked, poking her head around his office door. "Oh, sorry, didn't know you were busy."

"As if anyone around here ever cared," McPherson replied glumly. "I don't believe I've eaten lunch in peace since the Mets were in the World Series back in 1986. Loved that team. People spent their lunch hours reordering the lineup, so I was able to eat uninterruptedly for at least a week."

"I said I was sorry," Sheila pointed out as she leaned against the doorjamb. "I'll come back when you're done."

"Well, you're here now. Get me the programming file, will you?" McPherson held out the key to the safe. Everyone knew the safe was hidden behind the Matisse poster above his cracked leather sofa at the far end of the room.

The painting obscured McPherson's vision just long enough for Sheila to find the file she needed and slip it inside the elastic band of her stretch pants. Her oversize cotton work shirt hid it from view. She dropped the program scheduling file on McPherson's desk and walked casually to the door.

"Is it as good as the traffic violations thing?" McPherson asked, flipping open the file in front of him.

"It's better. It's tough. We'll have a rough cut by Friday."

"Okay, I'll pencil in a tentative for the week after next, okay? And would you mind closing the door as you go out, honey?"

Later than night, long after the cleaning crew had gone, Cassie opened the slim manila file marked "M.D.—In progress." It consisted of two yellow legal-sized pages filled with Miranda's large, childish scrawl.

"Seems to be about a primary," Sheila said, reading over Cassie's shoulder. "The senatorial race, I think. See, there's a note about Haas. Anthony Haas. He's up for reelection next year."

"What are his chances?" Cassie asked.

"A shoo-in, I'd say," Sheila replied, yawning and stretching. "You find anything there? Looks to me like Miranda was planning on doing a piece on Haas. Big deal. He's a buddy of Vance's."

"Yes, I know." Cassie closed the file. "It seems he's been a lot of things to a lot of people over the years."

Twenty

"Senator Haas's office."

"Is he there?"

"Who's calling, please?"

"It's . . . personal."

"This is his office, ma'am. The Senator has a very full schedule. Personal matters should be directed to his home."

"I'm sure he'll want to talk to me. I'm Miranda Darin's sister."

There was a moment of hesitation, then: "I'll put you through to one of his aides. Hold please."

"Geoffrey Mellon, how may I help you?"

"Yes, hello. I'm Cassie Hartley, Miranda Darin's sister?"

"Right. How can I help?"

"I need to see the Senator."

"This is his office, Ms., uh, Hartley, is it? Surely it would be better to try him at home."

"No. I need to see him today. It's . . . quite important. Tell him it's urgent. Please? I'll hold."

She thought her voice would shake. Or that her nerve would melt. Instead she felt extraordinarily calm. Confident. She'd been awake most of the night going over the little she knew about Anthony Haas, and deciding it wasn't enough. All the frayed threads of information she had led back to him. And if she was going to find out what happened to Miranda, she'd have to learn a lot more about Anthony Haas. What better way to start, she finally decided, than where Miranda had left off?

"We'll squeeze you in at four-thirty, Ms. Hartley." Geoffrey Mellon's voice was terse with disapproval. "For fifteen minutes. This better be good."

Senator Anthony Haas's New York offices were in the Lincoln Building across from Grand Central Station on Forty-Second Street. The stately, ornate lobby with its elaborately gilded arched ceiling appealed to the Senator's sense of ceremony. The excellent five-year lease for his ten-room suite that he'd recently negotiated with the managing agent appealed to a more grasping side of his character. Anthony Haas, born to impoverished German-Italian parents in the Bronx, had learned at a very early age the importance of pinching pennies. And even though he was now worth more than six million discreetly invested dollars, he still hungered after money. It was an insatiable, all-consuming desire, one that he knew he could only satisfy—the way some men ease the need for women or drugs—in the more shadowy corridors of human commerce.

Elected government officials, alas, earned very little when compared to businessmen, corporate lawyers, and even most doctors. How far could a $150,000 income stretch, after all, when there were so many trips to finance . . . parties to give? So, through the years Tony had learned the power of his political currency. While brokers traded stocks and bonds, and businessmen pushed products and technology, Anthony Haas dealt in influence. A government contract here, a successful plea bargain there . . . and it began to add up. There was also one highly sensitive connection, relating to the Italian part of his heritage, that gave Tony ready access to any cash he might require.

Initially, when Tony was still a struggling representative, his influence peddling gave him occasional pangs of guilt.

He had set himself up as a defender of the downtrodden, an inspiring civil rights advocate whose rugged good looks propelled him into the front ranks of those who marched behind John Fitzgerald Kennedy's liberal banner.

Sure, years ago he asked himself once or twice if what he was doing wasn't somehow . . . corrupt. He even admitted that, seen from a certain perspective by uninformed people, it might look as though he was taking graft. But the truth was that's just how things in government—in every level and type of government—were handled. He was a realist, that was all. A pragmatist. A man who got things done. If, in the doing, people felt obliged to compensate him somehow . . . what could he do? Refuse the two-week vacation in the Bahamas? Wouldn't that be small-minded, even churlish of him? Of course it would.

The self-doubts, however, lingered. The wealthier he got . . . the more grasping he became. Vodka helped, blunting his appetite. He'd progressed with amazing speed from the martini cocktail before dinner to the bracing gulp from the toothbrush glass before breakfast. Nowadays he required almost hourly pit stops in the men's room for a refresher from his sterling-silver hip flask. Not that it showed, really. He did his work. He got through the day. If his nights tended to blur, if he often forgot how he got home—or with whom he slept—well, he was a year or two beyond sixty. Not that he was past his prime by any means, but still he had come to see himself as an aging hero.

His personal staff had nearly doubled in the last ten years. He was now surrounded by bright young aides who crafted bill proposals in his name, arranged his schedule, dealt with his constituency, and interfaced with his fund-raising committees. These clear-eyed, athletic young men and women with their Paul Stuart suits and eighty-dollar haircuts briefed him each morning on how he should vote, when he should speak, what he should think. A part of him knew that he was only a mouthpiece now. An actor who spoke other people's lines. He was still essential to the play, of course.

Where would a senatorial staff be without their senator? But in some way he did not yet fully understand, the fire had gone out of his words, the light out of his eyes.

Election years were always difficult, but this year's campaign felt particularly wearing. For one thing, his strongest opponent, a female special prosecutor with a tough crime-busting reputation and a hard-hitting personal style, was raising several ugly questions about the Senator's fund-raising techniques. Though his aides told him not to worry, the Senator's financial dealings were actually the one area of his life that his staff knew very little about. Haas still held very tightly to the purse strings, and for very good reason.

Senator Anthony Haas, waiting in his oak-paneled corner office for his next appointment and already worn out though it was just four-thirty, took the opportunity of being alone to swivel around in his custom-made black leather chair, squirm forward to fish out his hip flask, and then tilt his head back for a long deep gulp of vodka. He chugged it, nearly choked, and wiped his chin just as the door opened and one of his sleek-voiced aides announced: "Cassie Hartley."

"Ah, yes." The Senator swiveled back around as he stowed the flask in his pants pocket. "Ms. . . . Miranda! No, of course." Haas rose to cover his confusion and held out his hand, saying: "Cassie, of course, we met at Miranda's. We were all so sorry to hear of her death. Please . . . sit down. What can I do for you?"

"Well . . . it's rather personal," Cassie said, glancing sideways at Geoffrey Mellon whose smug, clean-shaven face she'd disliked on sight.

"You can go, Geoff."

"Perhaps I should stay and take notes, Senator?" Geoffrey suggested with a smile. "To relieve you of any worry about details. Remember the tax reform bill." How long would the staff hold that blunder—a vote he'd cast incorrectly because he'd forgotten their instructions—over his head?

They'd been able to salvage the bill, but not the fact that he'd appeared on cable television acting both bewildered and uninformed. Not the greatest look for an incumbent senator running for reelection, his staff relentlessly reminded him.

"Ah . . . yes. Good idea. Now, Cassie, what's all this about? Geoff told me you said this was . . . urgent?"

"Yes, Senator, it is. But first, I just have to tell you that you've been a kind of folk hero of mine since I was a little girl. My parents were both deeply involved in the Civil Rights Movement in North Carolina where we lived. And you were always a guiding light . . . their inspiration."

"That's very nice, Ms. Hartley," Geoffrey Mellon cut in, "but can we get to the urgent part? The Senator is very pressed for time this afternoon."

"I see," Cassie said, glancing from Haas to Geoff and noting that the Senator hadn't objected to Geoff's bullying tone. It became clear to her suddenly who was really in charge there. "Okay, I'll get to the urgent part . . . but it does relate back to the high regard with which I hold the Senator—and all he stands for. I'm working for Magnus Media now. I'm a writer for *Breaking News*."

"Oh, Christ, the media." Geoff Mellon sighed. "You've got some nerve barging in here under personal pretenses, Ms. Hartley. Let's cut this short, okay? You want to get a line into the Senator, go through channels, okay? Call Rita Kirbie, our press secretary. I'll be happy to give you her number on your way out." Geoff rose to go.

"I'm sorry if that's your attitude, Senator," Cassie replied, ignoring Geoff. "I believe that an in-depth, moment-by-moment piece on how you spend your time—and the taxpayers' money—could only help in an election year. Considering the allegations that Ruthie Nester's making about your fund-raising committee. And especially when you know that it's being put together by a true admirer of yours."

"Does Vance know you're here?" Haas demanded, his face flushing. "Because he should have damn well given me a call himself if—"

"No, sir," Cassie answered softly. "Mr. Magnus doesn't know anything about my visit. I came, as I said before, for personal reasons."

"This is preposterous, Senator!" Geoff broke in. "I regret letting this woman barge in here to try to railroad you into—"

"Geoff, sit down and shut up. Since she is here, let's hear Ms. Hartley out, shall we?" A dull gleam of self-determination appeared in Haas's eyes as his surprised aide took his seat.

"Continue," the Senator said, nodding at Cassie.

"Senator, sir," Cassie began, "many of the people in my generation don't remember J.F.K., the sixties, or much of anything that took place when you first became a household name. They have no understanding of the hope, the charisma, the pure idealism of that time. They have no understanding of what you're really made of . . . what you believe in. These people—a huge voting block that's poised to take over the country in the next decade or two—have grown cynical and disillusioned with politics and politicians."

"We are fully aware of all this," Geoff said.

"Then I'm surprised that you object to my proposal of a *Breaking News* piece that will—for the first time in many years—reveal the Senator's true giving nature to his voters. He's under attack, no doubt unfairly. Unless something is done, this state is going to lose one of the finest leaders it's ever had. I want to help. I *can* help."

"*Breaking News* is known as a sensationalist, mud-slinging program," Geoff replied. "It's absolutely the last place I'd suggest the Senator consider."

"Exactly!" Cassie replied, almost laughing. "Don't you see? Millions of people are going to tune in, ready for a scathing exposé of their senior senator. Expecting blood. Assuming he's going to be thrown to the lions. And what will they watch? A balanced, admiring report on one of the last true liberals in the country. Homage to a great man. A man who not only demands our respect, but who deserves our support for as long as he wishes to serve the public."

"And what," Senator Haas asked quietly, "do you get out of this, Ms. Hartley?"

"Did you know, Senator," Cassie replied, "that Miranda wanted to do a segment on you herself? I found her notes at the office the other night."

"I don't think so," Haas replied, shaking his head and looking puzzled, "though we might have discussed the idea at some point. But not recently that I can recall." But then there were many things, too many things, that tended to blur in Tony Haas's memory, especially if the events took place at night, after drinks and dinner. Had Miranda said something to him about an interview at that last party she'd put on? He remembered speaking to her at the end of the evening—at some length—about his past. He vaguely remembered a look of triumph on her classically beautiful face, but why? Perhaps he'd agreed to such an interview then?

"You don't seem very sure," Cassie observed. "But, believe me, she had hoped to do a piece on you, obviously to coincide with your reelection bid. You ask what's in this for me? A chance to finish something that Miranda had started. This wouldn't be just an homage to you, Senator. For me . . . it would be one to Miranda as well."

"Senator, please," Geoff interrupted, "we're running way behind schedule. Let's turn the proposal over to Rita's office. She's in the middle of planning your publicity schedule for next month, though I doubt there's any time to fit this in."

"I'll decide about that," Haas replied, standing up. Cassie stood as well, and they shook hands. He felt his hand tremble slightly as it closed around hers. He felt exhausted suddenly. It took a lot out of him, going up against people like that cocksure Geoff. He wished he didn't need to surround himself with such barracuda. If only he could pull together a staff of true believers, like this young lady here. Good, honest people who remembered, as Cassie put it, what he stood for. Though sometimes, especially these days, the Senator himself forgot what those things were. He needed to clear his head. Get a grip on himself. He needed to go to the men's room before his next meeting. Lock the stall. Unscrew the top of the silver flask and take a big gulp from his private store of burning integrity and courage.

Twenty-one

At first Magnus was absolutely furious after the call from Haas. But when he phoned down to McPherson and learned that Mac had not okayed Cassie's meeting with the Senator, in fact hadn't even known she'd had one, Magnus's anger faded, replaced with . . . What was he feeling exactly? Melancholy? Nostalgia? The truth of the matter was, Cassie was turning out to be a lot more like Miranda than he would ever have imagined.

"What do you want me to do?" Mac had asked him. "Take her off the Bronx piece as punishment, maybe? I don't know why the hell she's running around after Haas when she's in the middle of the school-board thing."

"That is the question, isn't it?" Magnus replied. "Why Haas . . . and why now? No . . . let me handle this. Our little girl is getting some big ideas. Perhaps I'm responsible for putting them there. Tell her I want to see her. Around seven tonight."

Charlene and the rest of the executive staff had gone. Magnus was standing at the westward-facing window, watching the sun stain the wetlands of New Jersey a bloody red, when the elevator doors swished open, then shut. He didn't turn as he heard her footsteps in the corridor. She had Miranda's sure, swift walk. He could almost imagine it was Miranda coming to him again, as she had so many other

163

evenings at sunset. He would never forget the first night she had visited him here. It was two and a half years ago. She'd come to give something . . . and to get something else.

"This is quite a power view," Miranda told him, standing where he was standing now, facing a brilliant sunset. "It's like being on Mount Olympus."

"Except we're not gods," Magnus said, handing her a flute of champagne mixed with kir. He would learn that it was her favorite drink. He would always keep a bottle or two of champagne chilled for her. He would become addicted to the taste of champagne on her lips and tongue.

"Oh, no?" she replied, laughing and turning toward him. "I see a lot of similarities between us and them. For instance, we don't play by the same rules as most mortals."

"Meaning?" Magnus asked, studying the smile on her lips. He had wanted her for so many years. He had waited for so long.

"We're both ruthless, Vance," she told him, tipping back her head as she drank from the long slim glass. Her neck was so white and soft, he longed to run his fingers along it. "You don't mind if I call you Vance?"

"Not at all, Miranda," he told her. "I'm just sorry that it's taken you such a long time to do so. But go on about our ruthlessness . . . what do you mean? I like to think of myself as being reasonably moral." And he had been, hadn't he? Up until the moment she elected to enter his life.

"We get what we want," she replied. "And we don't really care how we do it. I'm surprised you've waited so long to go after what you really want, Vance." She put her glass down on a side table. She stood facing him, right hip cocked, hands behind her back. Submissive, inviting.

"I'm not sure . . ."

"Cut the bullshit, Vance," she told him. In one swift movement, she unzipped the back of her dress, pulled it down over her shoulders, and tossed it on the floor. She stood before him in a frothy concoction of expensive black lace underwear. She had guessed correctly about his tastes; she even wore a garter belt.

He stepped toward her . . . no, in truth, he stumbled. He was blind with desire. She guided his hand between her legs. In her heels, they were nearly the same height. She was not wearing any panties beneath the tight black sheath of garter. His fingers trembled against her, massaged slowly, until her hand closed over his . . . guiding him inside her. He had always taken what he wanted from women, rarely considered their pleasure except as a lazy afterthought. How could she have known how much this would excite him? Forcing him to hold himself back. He stood against her, fully clothed, as she guided his fingers in and out of her—faster, then slower, then in the mad, irrhythmic motion of orgasm.

"Yes, fuck, yes." He watched her face contort with pleasure as he could feel her flesh ripple against his fingers below. She made him feel so powerful, so virile. Hardly skipping a beat, she jerked down his zipper, tugged off his pants.

He made love to her on this very carpet, a violent, explosive session that left them both panting and sweat-soaked.

"I was right, wasn't I?" she said as they sat together later on his leather couch. She was sipping another glass of champagne; and she had never looked more beautiful. Her usually perfectly tamed hair now hung wild around her shoulders, her blue eyes bright with satisfaction. "You have wanted to do that for a while now."

"Ever since you rode up with me on that elevator. When was that . . . twelve years ago? Yes, Miranda, I've wanted that."

"Why did you wait?"

"I'm not quite as ruthless as you think. You're married, after all. I assumed that meant something . . ."

"Yes. It means I have a husband. And a daughter. I like having things. I've never understood why Americans are so puritanical about all this. But I'm not like most mortals, as

I told you. When I see a man I want . . . I take him."

"You've seen me for a long time now, Miranda," Magnus replied. "Why now?"

"It's more than just wanting you . . . it's wanting something only you can give me."

"I'm afraid I don't understand," he said, sitting up. He felt suddenly drained, satiated, beyond his depth.

"No matter what I do, Vance, what committees I serve on, what donations I make . . . I just don't seem acceptable to your society friends."

"My friends? You mean old Fitzie—that crowd? I wasn't even aware that you wanted to be accepted. It's all so stodgy, Miranda."

"You won't do it." Her voice turned cold, her face a mask of disappointment.

"Do what?"

"Escort me to the ballet benefit next week? Show them I really am somebody? That I'm worth letting in?"

"Darling, that's truly all you want?"

"Of course, Vance. That's all."

It seemed so wonderfully easy to make her happy. For months after that they glided smoothly together from fundraiser to opening night . . . benefit to ball. Then slowly Miranda's interest faded. She became easily distracted, irritated. He was terrified that she'd taken a new lover, that he'd lose her. Then one night six months ago when she arrived at his office a full hour later than they had agreed upon, he demanded an explanation.

"I'm just so bored. Can't you tell? I feel like I've done almost everything I've ever wanted."

"Some things," he told her, reaching out to touch her hair, "are worth doing more than once."

"Oh, not now, please," she muttered, pulling away and walking across to the window, sipping her drink.

"Darling, I hate to see you like this," he said, despising the pleading note in his voice. "Isn't there anything I can do?"

"Actually, there is one thing . . . I've been thinking lately that I might like to anchor the evening news. Oh, I realize I'll have to co-anchor for a season or two until we can ease Marshall out. But I want to be solo anchor. The first woman in the business to do it. That's something you could do for me."

He was shocked at first. Hurt. Once again it was clear to him that she didn't actually want him, just what he could give her. But even before he could sort out these feelings, she crossed the room and started opening his shirt, kissing his chest, making him hard. She hadn't allowed him to touch her for several weeks before that, and he had been almost desperate in his desire to make love, crying out her name, losing more ground with each kiss, every touch. He lived only to feel himself inside of her. She had him where she wanted him. She outwitted him at every turn. Except one. She made the mistake of telling him exactly what she wanted. And he was smart enough this time to realize that once she had that—once he'd made her anchor—he would have nothing else left to give or interest her. And so the long, inevitable contest had begun.

"Hello?"

Magnus turned at the sound of Cassie's voice. "Come in," he said, walking over to his desk. "Sit down, Cassie."

She was wearing one of Ralph Lauren's deceptively-simple-looking linen sheaths. The navy-blue material, cinched by a bright red patent leather belt, accentuated her graceful slimness. A red leather bag was slung over her right shoulder. She was carrying a legal manila folder. She'd cut her hair shorter, feathering her bangs, softening her features and at the same time making her face more interesting-looking. Where before she could be easily pegged as another tall, pretty blonde, now her look was harder to define. She was more mysterious and less accessible. Before, she was all out front: open, friendly, a modern Southern belle. Now she was holding something back—some key part of herself—and that restraint made her infinitely more attractive.

"I got a call from Anthony Haas this afternoon," he said, watching her closely for a reaction. She nodded, as if she had been expecting him to say exactly those words.

"Yes, I supposed he would call you."

"Of course he'd call, you little idiot!" he exploded, deciding it was time to crack her new facade. "He's a long-time friend of mine. What the hell do you think you're playing at? You had absolutely no right to contact him on your own. You made me look like a fool to Haas. McPherson's furious. And so am I. This ridiculous move has done you a great deal of harm . . . just when I was beginning to believe you had real possibilities. I think I deserve an explanation. Now."

"I'm sorry I've upset you," she replied, meeting his angry stare. "I—I just wanted to show you what I could do. I don't know what I thought would happen. I guess I just imagined that I'd walk in, tell the Senator how much I admired him and wanted to do an interview, and that he'd say great, let's do it."

"Cassie, I can't believe you're that naive. You know damn well that McPherson decides who does what stories. These things are very carefully plotted out. What got into you?"

"This," Cassie said, holding out the manila file.

"What the . . ." He stopped talking when he saw Miranda's childish scrawl on the yellow legal sheets. "Where the hell did you get this?"

"Well, you told me to poke around, remember? See if I could find anything about that 'highly sensitive' story you said Miranda had been working on. This was all I could come up with. Not much, but I wanted to take it another step—try to pin Haas down on an interview— before bringing it to you. Sorry it got so screwed up."

Magnus scanned the handwritten notes quickly. "Nothing particularly new here. Just background on Haas's reelection efforts. Certainly not anything to get upset about." Magnus sighed and handed the file back to Cassie. "If this was the story Miranda told me about, she hadn't gotten very far with it."

"You're sure there really was a story?" Cassie asked, tucking the folder under her arm.

"What do you mean?"

"Just that . . . some people on the show have implied that Miranda had gotten . . ." Cassie hesitated, glanced at Magnus, then at the floor.

"What? Out with it."

"Lazy. She let others go after the stories. According to what I've heard, she hadn't done any of her own legwork for some time. She'd do this kind of thing." Cassie held up the folder. "Easy celebrity interviews. But the hard-hitting stuff? The pieces that need a ton of research and digging? No."

"So you're saying . . . what? Miranda made up the idea of a big, explosive story to impress me? String me along? Isn't that a little absurd?"

"Not if she thought you weren't taking her seriously as anchor material. You yourself told me she was pushing you to make a decision. I could see her using whatever leverage possible to get that slot. It's just office politics, really. I imagine she knew how to play those games very well."

"Something's telling me it runs in the family," Magnus said, smiling for the first time since Cassie walked in. That stupid fool Haas, Magnus concluded silently; he saw a conspiracy behind every tree. It was time they all stopped worrying about Miranda. "Why don't you sit down, Cassie, and tell me exactly what you have in mind."

"Just what I told the Senator," Cassie said, taking the leather Eames chair across from Magnus. "A sort of 'day in the life' portrait of him at work . . . at home. Of course, we'll cut in footage of the Kennedy years—the peace marches and civil rights rallies. I grew up with his politics. My parents were among his biggest supporters. It's something I want to do for them . . . as well as for me. And, of course, it's something I want to do for Miranda."

"You're aware, of course," Magnus said, looking down at his steepled fingers, "that Haas is under a certain amount of fire? There are some questions about his fund-raising techniques."

"Sure," she said dismissively, "doesn't that sort of thing come with the reelection territory? It's so mean-spirited, like Willie Horton. I'm hoping our segment will give the Senator a chance to set the record straight."

"Okay, but we don't want a puff piece here. It shouldn't be too obviously pro."

"Absolutely. I intend to ask some hard questions."

"You intend to ask them?"

"Yes." Cassie smiled. "I want to do the whole thing: research, write, and do the on-camera interview."

"Oh, my." Magnus laughed and leaned back in his chair, shaking his head. "I do believe I'm creating another monster."

Twenty-two

"Okay, you two." McPherson glared at Cassie and Sheila over his half glasses. "What's going on?"

"Good afternoon to you, too," Sheila replied as she walked calmly into McPherson's office and sat down in one of the chairs facing him. Cassie took the other, though with less confidence. The grungy corner office was flooded with sunlight, accentuating the dirty windows and the dried-up spider plant on the windowsill.

Though McPherson was a perfectionist when it came to all things video, he barely saw the actual world around him. He would scream bloody murder if a *Breaking News* segment was ten seconds too long, throw a temper tantrum if some obscure fact was misstated on the show, and yet his own office was utter chaos. He could never remember the names of his secretaries, and he ran through them as he once went through cartons of unfiltered Camels. Many blamed his irascible humor on the fact that—after many decades of smoking—he had finally given up cigarettes the year before. Sheila, who'd worked with him in one capacity or another for nearly ten years, knew differently. Mac had been born dour and demanding. He was always prepared for the worst. And though many people, including Magnus, considered him one of the best executive producers in the business, he was convinced that any day, at any moment, he was going to be fired.

"Jesus, Mac," Sheila said, pushing aside a stack of books so that she could cross her leg, "why don't you tell Judy to get in here and clean this mess up?"

"Judy?"

"Your new secretary," Sheila replied.

"What's the point?" McPherson said, sighing, "she'll be gone in a day or two. I doubt I'll be around much longer myself. Not the way things are going. What the fuck are you two up to?"

"Can you be more specific?" Sheila demanded, meeting his sardonic gaze with perfect equanimity. "Are we just supposed to deduce from your rather vulgar accusations what you're referring to?"

"Don't you dare sass me," McPherson said, glowering at her. "You know perfectly well I mean this Haas business. Political bio crap. I was almost beginning to think the two of you had a modicum of talent, a smidgen of investigative flair. And what do you come up with? Senator Haas. Not even a dirt-digging expedition. Just your typical puff pastry pastiche. Christ, Sheila, this is the kind of thing Miranda would have done. In fact, come to think of it, I remember her telling me she had something like this in mind. There were even some notes around here . . ." He began to pick up stacks of papers and files, then put them down again. "Somewhere."

"Exactly," Cassie cut in with a glance at Sheila. Cassie still hadn't told her friend who exactly was implicated by Miranda's disk. "She mentioned something about it to me, as well. That's why I talked Sheila into helping me out with it. As a sort of homage—"

"To Miranda?" McPherson's bushy, ginger-colored eyebrows shot up. He turned his faded blue gaze on Sheila. "You in on this homage routine or you have a reason of your own? Magnus wants it done to help his friend the Senator out of a tight squeeze. You realize, Cassie, don't you, that Haas is under some fire at the moment?"

"Yes. And we'll touch on that."

"But lightly, right?" McPherson shook his head sadly. "Once you lie down with the lions, friends, it's very hard to get up unscathed. Our competitors are going to take some real mean swipes at you if you go soft on Haas. Now, your Bronx school board piece. That's good investigative reporting. Did you know the Mayor's office has already asked for a screening tape? They're going to have to work overtime on spin control after it airs on Thursday night."

"We're proud of it, too, Mac," Sheila assured him. "And we're going to do a terrific job on this Haas piece. We're going to really surprise you."

"Magnus expects a certain kind of program here, Sheila," McPherson warned her. "I really don't want any surprises if it means upsetting the man. So please, don't do me any favors. I just want a straight-ahead competent job. I'm giving you a mobile unit and your own team back in the studio." McPherson turned to Cassie. "I understand you'll be making your on-camera debut with this one. Ever been in front before?"

"No, not really . . . not at all," she concluded, meeting McPherson's withering stare. "But I can do it. I know I can."

"Yeah, sure." He sighed, his gaze moving from Cassie to Sheila to Cassie again. "I just wish someone would tell me what the fuck is really going on."

Jason decided on impulse to leave a day early and surprise Cassie. It was not the kind of thing he usually did, and his London office was thrown into a tizzy.

"But, Mr. Darin, we had a breakfast meeting scheduled with you and the new Undersecretary of Commerce. Surely you'll not wish to break that?"

"Sorry," Jason replied, staring out the window at the rain-swept sidewalk clotted with brightly colored umbrellas. It had poured every day he'd been here. He usually didn't notice the weather, rarely let such external circumstances affect his mood. But he'd grown irritated with this damp, foggy city and its overly correct denizens. Jason had learned over the years that despite their beautiful manners, the English could be as shrewd and grasping as any of their colonial counterparts. He never seemed able to relax totally in London, he reminded himself, as he turned from the window to face his impeccably groomed male secretary. Especially this trip, when he found his thoughts wandering in the middle of the most intense negotiations. When his body ached to be elsewhere. Cassie.

"I'm sorry, Evan," he said, trying to sound more convincing. "I'll call his office directly if you like and personally extend my apologies. Something's come up at home . . . I've got to get back." Though he really didn't. He was letting a whim dictate his schedule. Or was it more than the impulse to surprise? In fact, something had bothered him about the way Cassie sounded the last few times they had talked on the phone. It was as if someone were standing beside her, listening in. Her tone had lost all sense of intimacy.

But surely he'd just been imagining it, he told himself as he sorted through the morning's mail. He'd become far too sensitive lately. Cassie's doing. Within a few short weeks of falling in love with her, she'd managed to strip away his emotional armor. He now felt exposed and vulnerable. Two nights before, he'd gone with business associates to the opera for a rather pedestrian performance of *Carmen*. He was horrified to find himself crying through the final tragic—and in this case, not even particularly well-sung— scene. He knew that everyone thought he'd been mourning Miranda.

In fact, he tried not to think of her. These days, that was easy. With that almost extrasensory perception that love often brings, Jason felt Cassie's presence everywhere. He made it through his days by trying to imagine her beside him. In the taxi in from Heathrow. Sitting across from him in a little Italian restaurant in Soho. Alone at night, in his spacious corner suite at the Royalton, he found himself seeing his world through her eyes. She would think Harold such a pompous ass, Jason would tell himself as he listened to his Scottish architect go on about his plans for the underground garage in the office complex they were building in Bayshead. Or: she'd tell him to say something conciliatory to Evan because he looked so crestfallen.

"Good work on the Bristol contracts, by the way," he told his secretary as he started to sign the letters Evan had positioned before him on the desk. "I don't think we would have gotten that zoning approval without your efforts."

"Thank you, sir." It was impossible to tell from Evan's tone if the compliment had mollified him at all. Damn the British with their stiff upper lips, Jason thought, you never knew what they were really feeling. He longed for Cassie's honesty. The openness of her smile. What was it in her voice that had worried him? Or was it all in his imagination?

He was so impatient to be on his way that he barely glanced at the letters he signed. He was at the airport an hour earlier than necessary and managed to catch a delayed flight that landed at Kennedy a few minutes past ten o'clock.

He took a taxi in from the airport, fighting back a rising tide of anxiety during the whole ride. There was no reason to think anything was wrong, and yet, the closer he got to home, the more sure he was that his life was once again spinning out of control. The night air was thick with heat and exhaust, the low cloud cover lit with an unnatural-looking pink—like cotton candy. As he paid the taxi driver, he realized that he was sweating heavily, and the bills he handled were damp and warm.

The side windows of the town house were dark, but as he let himself in the front door he saw light coming from the library. He dropped his two bags in the foyer and quietly followed the noise of the television down the hall. The late news from the Magnus network flickered on the screen, casting an eerie pall across the two figures asleep on the couch. He gathered his daughter in his arms and carried her up to bed without waking her.

"Cassie," he said, coming back downstairs and sitting beside her. He studied her face. She was dreaming, her eyelids fluttering, her lips forming silent words. He leaned toward her, gently brushing her hair off her temple. Her skin felt sticky, almost feverish.

"Hey, I'm home," he said, gently shaking her shoulder. "Surprise."

Her eyes flashed open. For a second she stared up at him, terrified, still trapped in unconsciousness, struggling to escape. Then she saw him. And she screamed.

Twenty-three

$\mathcal{J}$ason read the *New York Times* review aloud at the breakfast table the next morning after Heather had left for school: " '*Breaking News* Toughens Up. Known of late for its sensationalist supermarket-tabloidlike stories and celebrity interviews, tonight's *Breaking News* segment called "Spare the Child" comes as a welcome surprise. With investigative honesty and a hard-hitting style, the piece offers a look at a scandal-ridden high school in the Bronx. Although P.S. 196 has been extensively covered in the print press and on evening news broadcasts, *Breaking News* takes us into the battered playgrounds and stripped-down schoolrooms to talk to the true victims of this continuing urban crime: the kids. The result is a powerfully moving portrait of the lives of these deprived young people, most of whom come from broken homes, many of whom see little hope in their future. Sensitively directed and beautifully produced, "Spare the Child" is first-rate journalism, a piece that not only forces us to face a certain truth, but also provokes us into wanting to change it. If this is the direction *Breaking News* intends to take in the future, I say lead on.'

"Well, congratulations."

"I don't believe it. Here, I need to read it myself," Cassie said, reaching for the newspaper. As she buried herself in its pages she realized that she had found just one more place to hide from Jason. She'd been avoiding him in one way or another since his unexpected return. It was ironic: before, it was she who was constantly urging him to talk, open up. Now their roles were reversed.

"Cassie, quiet, shh—what in the world were you dreaming?" he'd said, pulling her to him the night before. He had no idea yet that her nightmare was still continuing, though she sat rigid and unyielding in his arms.

"I don't remember," she lied, fighting the desire to relax and be held. He smelled so familiar. He felt so warm and strong. She longed to close her eyes and forget everything she suspected, but she couldn't. Almost every night now, Cassie woke from the same terrible dream: she wasn't just drowning, somebody was pushing her underwater, holding her down. That person, she now realized, was Jason.

"Sometimes it's better to talk about nightmares," Jason told her gently. "What was it? You can tell me . . ." He started to kiss her temple, run his hands through her hair.

"No." She pulled away and swung her legs to the floor. "I'm sorry. I guess I'm really pretty shook."

"Come on, let's go up," he said, standing and holding out his hand.

Pleading exhaustion, she'd been able to keep him from her bed, but she knew he sensed something was wrong. With Haas and Magnus it had been easy—almost exhilarating—to pretend to be something she wasn't. She was able to hide her anger and suspicions behind a professional manner, leaving them no reason to suspect her motives. But with Jason, every move she made seemed patently false. Haas and Magnus had made her nervous, but Jason made her afraid. Each time he touched her, every look he gave her deepened the dread.

"This is great," she said as she folded the paper. "Mac's going to be forced to be pleased for once. And Sheila really deserves some praise. I hope you don't mind, by the way, but I invited the whole crew here tonight to watch the broadcast."

"Sure, but—didn't you think I was coming back tonight?"

"I don't plan the programming, Jason. *Breaking News* happens to air on Thursday nights."

He stared at her for a moment, then said, "You sounded just like Miranda then."

"What's that supposed to mean?" she demanded, realizing suddenly how she could keep him at bay. It was almost as if Miranda were whispering in her ear: *Pretend you're me, darling. Act ambitious, selfish. Flaunt your success. He'll be furious, of course. But isn't that better than being suspicious?*

"Just that you don't sound like yourself, Cassie. And you seem, well, edgy. Is something wrong? Have I done something—or not done something? Tell me. I really hate this feeling."

"I'm sorry, but I don't know what you're talking about," Cassie replied evenly. "Perhaps it's jet lag, Jason. Everything seems a little unreal after a long flight across the ocean. I've got to run. See you tonight. We'll all come up from work around seven-thirty. Oh, and thanks so much for the jam," she added, tapping the decorative little jar—one of two dozen—that Jason had brought back with him from London. Then she dropped her napkin on the table and hurried out of the room.

"Mac." Jason shook the editor's hand. "Good to see you again. Sounds like a terrific show."

"Yeah, at least we've done one thing we can be proud of," Mac replied, then added morosely, "it's going to be hard to beat."

The rest of the *Breaking News* crew was gathered around the boxes of take-out pizza, bowls of tossed green salad, and bucket of iced beer that Henrietta had set up on a folding table at the far end of the library. Jason, who vaguely recognized most of the guests, knew only Mac by name. After their initial exchange, Jason could think of nothing further to say, and they stared across the room at the noisy, happy crowd around the buffet for several minutes.

"Beautiful woman, that Cassie," Mac finally got out. "Of course, no one could touch Miranda when it came to looks. But I'm excited to have Cassie on board."

"I thought nothing excited you anymore, Mac." Jason laughed, trying to hide the rush of pride he felt at the editor's praise. Yes, Cassie was beautiful. He watched her talking animatedly to a short wiry brunette, her blond head bent to listen to the other woman's words, her mouth set in a tight line of concentration. He regretted the awkward scene between them that morning, and his thoughtless words. He had to remember not to criticize Miranda in front of Cassie, not to show his bitterness or anger.

"Yeah, well, you know we were hit pretty hard by Miranda's death," Mac was explaining. Jason turned his attention back to what the editor was saying. "And I know we're all jumping to conclusions. But, publicity-wise, even I've gotta admit it would be great. A coup."

"I'm sorry, but I lost you somewhere. What would be a coup?"

"Cassie," Mac replied. "She'll be hosting her own piece on Senator Haas. And if she can pull it off, between you and me I know Magnus has something more permanent in mind."

Jason felt his heart go cold. "What's the Haas thing about? You have an angle on this fund-raising business of Ruthie Nester's?"

"I only wish." Mac sighed. "Nah, it's nothing like that. Unfortunately it's going to be very flattering. You know, Vance is a big pal of the Senator's. Personally I'd love to nail the son of a bitch. But, hey, I also want to keep my job."

"This Vance's idea, then?"

"No, actually, I heard Cassie came up with it. Apparently Miranda left her some notes or something. I'm a little disappointed after this Bronx piece, but it will give her a chance to get her feet wet in front of the camera. I'd say she's got a future, that gal . . ."

By the time *Breaking News* came on, the party was in full swing. Charles had set up all the house television sets—five altogether—around the room, and the crew gathered in front of them to watch weeks of work flicker across the screens for less than an hour.

"Hello, everyone!" A familiar baritone sounded down the hall as the credits for the Bronx segment scrolled up the screen. Dressed in black tie, brandishing a magnum of champagne, Magnus made a grand entrance into the library.

"Who invited him?" Cassie asked under her breath.

"I'm sorry, I saw him in the lobby as I was leaving," Sheila whispered. "I told you I couldn't resist him in black tie."

"Watch yourself," Cassie warned, seeing the flush of anticipation on Sheila's face.

"Don't worry. Like, I'm a big girl now, okay?" But it wasn't Sheila to whom Magnus presented the champagne or whom he held in an extended embrace.

"My dear, I am so proud," Magnus said as he finally let Cassie go. "The piece was terrific. And so are you."

"I hardly did it alone, Vance," Cassie replied, blushing and taking a step back. "Everybody here deserves a lot of praise."

"Of course," Magnus replied, unwiring the bottle. The cork flew across the room, landing near Jason. "To *Breaking News,*" Magnus cried, holding up a glass and smiling at Cassie.

"Got a sec?" Jason asked, taking Magnus's elbow almost an hour later. With increasing anxiety, he'd been watching Magnus monopolize Cassie's attention. Each time Jason tried to catch Cassie's eye, she'd turn with seemingly renewed interest back to Magnus. If Jason didn't know Cassie better, he would think she was actually flirting with the man.

"Of course, Jason," Magnus replied, following his host into the front hall. The party roared on in the other room as

Jason led Magnus down the corridor. "What is all this secrecy?" Magnus asked a little nervously when Jason looked over his shoulder to see if they were being followed.

"The Haas business, Vance."

"What about it?"

"Do you really think it's a good idea?"

"I didn't initially, but it's starting to grow on me."

"I can see Cassie's growing on you, too."

"Jealous again, are we?" Magnus laughed pleasantly. "Are you more worried about Haas or her? I wonder."

"You know how I feel about Tony. I don't like the idea of Cassie tangling with him. Is he sober enough these days to know what's going on?"

"Just barely. That's why Cassie's going to come in so handy, you see. Whatever ugly little facts Ruthie Nester manages to dig up, Cassie's flattering interview is going to help whitewash them."

"You better have a lot of whitewash. Why protect him? You can't have any use for him anymore."

"Don't bet on that. You never know when you're going to need a favor, Jason."

"I know all about Senator Haas and his little favors. I'm getting the feeling that Ruthie Nester and others do, too. I think this whole thing might blow. I don't want Cassie in the middle of it when it does."

"You don't want her in the middle of what, Jason? Excitement? Success? All seem a little too familiar to you now? I think the problem here is that your little country mouse is turning into a city slicker, and you don't like it."

"I'm not worried that she's changing, Vance, I'm worried about what she's changing into."

"Something a bit more like Miranda, right? Well, I'm sorry you're disappointed. Personally I'm delighted. She's far more to my taste now, Jason."

"Don't you dare touch her, Vance. Don't corrupt her."

"Oh, my, we are vicious tonight, aren't we?" Magnus took a step back, pretending fear. "And just who are you to dictate who does what to whom?"

Later, when everyone had gone home, Jason tried again to break through to the Cassie he thought he knew.

"What's going on with you?" he asked gently as he came up behind where she stood, looking out the French doors to the street. "I feel like we're a million miles apart."

"Perhaps we are," she admitted.

"But why, Cassie?" he demanded. The fear he'd been trying to control rushed through him. "What's happened to us? What have I done?"

"Why do you assume that you've done something?" she asked, turning to face him. "Isn't it possible that I've done something instead? For the first time in my life, I've found a bit of success in what I do. I like the sensation, Jason. I feel whole for once, and very strong. I feel that I can really make a difference here. In New York. At Magnus. Like I'm finally headed somewhere."

"You sound so much like Miranda," Jason replied wretchedly, staring beyond her to the street. "I know what you're going to say next: I'll hold you back. I'll clip your wings. You're not ready to settle down. Something like that, right?"

She met his gaze; his dark eyes were almost black, cold and flat. He raised his hand uncertainly, and for a moment she was afraid he was going to hit her, but instead he brushed his fingers lightly down her cheek.

Cassie shivered. Was it fear or desire? She didn't know, and at that moment it didn't matter. Jason stepped toward her, and she found herself incapable of moving away. She had been so determined not to give into him, not to give in to her own unquenchable longing. But as he took her into his arms, she knew it was impossible.

"I've missed you so much," he told her as he leaned down to kiss her. As his lips met hers, she knew that—despite Miranda, despite all her darkest suspicions—her need for this man went beyond reason or caution. Her mind kept telling her to be careful. Miranda's words rang through her thoughts: *Trust no one. Trust no one.* Briefly her nightmare about drowning resurfaced, flooding her with dread. But Jason, sensing some renewed resistance, drew her closer, held her tighter. And she felt herself relax in his arms as all her fears were overruled by the fierce, quickening demands of her heart.

Twenty-four

"Did you get him shaking hands with the girl in the wheelchair?" Sheila asked as the camera crew climbed back into the van.

"We got him shaking hands with the entire fucking school," Harvey, one of the two cameramen assigned to the project, replied. "The man does a very nice handshake. His hands also shake all by themselves, I've noticed."

"What's that supposed to mean, Harve?" Cassie demanded from the passenger seat in front. Freddie, the other cameraman, climbed in on the driver's side. Sheila, Harvey, and Cal, the sound technician, were squeezed together in the back of the van with all the mobile equipment.

"Just that our esteemed senator has a major thirst problem," Harvey replied as he capped his camera. "I ran into him in the rest room before. The man carries a flask the size of a canteen."

"I hope you didn't say anything to him," Cassie said as the Senator's limousine pulled away from the curb in front of the junior high school in Brooklyn where they'd been working.

"Nah, I just asked him for a swig."

"You what?"

"He's kidding, Cassie," Sheila intervened, pretending to punch the cameraman in the stomach. "Harvey has a very warped sense of humor that not everybody appreciates."

"Yeah, well, we need a little humor to get us through this one," Harvey grumbled. "I don't get it, you guys. The man's major fuck-up, and we're supposed to make him out like he's the Pope or something. Next time I'm following him into the men's room with my camera. Shoot the bastard chugging it down."

"No, you won't, Harve." Sheila sighed. "No, he won't, Cassie," Sheila repeated when Cassie turned to the backseat. "Harvey's a pro. He'll do what he's told."

"But I'll think what I like," Harvey grumbled. "And personally I'm thinking that I'd reelect my mother-in-law before I'd vote for that pompous son of a bitch."

No one could blame the cameraman, Cassie thought as she watched the limousine pick up speed in front of them. Haas was just about impossible to capture in a flattering light. They'd been filming all week at various goodwill and fund-raising events, and Cassie doubted that they'd canned more than five minutes of usable video.

For one thing, Anthony Haas didn't look well. His face, already puffy and flushed, would appear almost balloonlike once television added its standard ten pounds to his figure. And though his staff gave Cassie's crew drafts of the Senator's speeches before each event, the words delivered frequently had little relation to the printed ones. The worst moments were when Haas was forced to ad lib.

"Stay in school, that's the most important thing you can do for yourself, your parents, and the nation," the Senator said to end his prepared speech that morning before asking for questions.

"Why stay in school, Mr. Senator?" a third-grader asked. "My brother got shot in this school last month. Sometimes I'm afraid to come here."

"Because it's important," Haas responded evasively, glancing down at his watch.

A teacher stood up and said, "The child has asked you a question, sir. I think she has a right to a decent answer.

Our public schools are becoming more dangerous every day. What are your plans for changing that if you get reelected?"

"We're working on some legislation now that would do a lot to protect these children from the outrages of the gun-toting, drug-dealing predators who are feeding off and, uh, feeding off these . . . kids. We're doing everything possible to stem the tide of corruption and abuse that has decimated the very core of our educational system. We're . . ."

"But what exactly are you proposing?" the teacher demanded. "More police protection? Metal detectors? After-school counseling?"

"Uh . . ." Haas turned uncertainly to where his staff was standing near the side entrance. Geoffrey Mellon, trim and handsome in tailored pinstripes, had a bounce in his step as he hurried onto the stage.

He smiled at the Senator with seeming affection as he took the microphone.

"I'm working closely with the Senator on the legal aspects of all those important possibilities you've raised, ma'am. The Constitution, though an amazing document, also has a way of throwing up certain roadblocks on what might seem the straightest path to a solution. Drug counseling, sex education, job discrimination—all these issues, as you know, are central to the Senator's beliefs. They're also key to helping these children grow into mature, responsible adults. With a conservative Supreme Court now sitting, it is essential that we elect leaders, like our Senator, who will fight for our liberal causes, who are unafraid to speak up for the poor and underprivileged . . ."

With almost boyish charm, Geoffrey had talked on extemporaneously for another five minutes, saying things that sounded important without proposing anything the least bit concrete. Not for the first time, Cassie saw how effectively the Senator's staff directed their man. They were like a powerful, smoothly oiled machine attached to a faulty and deteriorating figurehead, keeping him alive and viable. But, especially with Geoffrey, Cassie sensed a ruthlessness and cynicism that made her uneasy. How far would they go, she wondered, to protect Haas's reputation and power base?

By the time the assembly was finally dismissed, Cassie sensed that—due primarily to Geoffrey's damage control—most of the teachers and administrators in that room were convinced that Haas should be reelected in November.

"What's next on the agenda?" Freddie asked as their van followed the Senator's limousine up the ramp to the Queensboro Bridge.

"A Democratic Women's Caucus lunch," Cassie told him, scanning the computer printout that Haas's press secretary Rita Kirbie faxed Cassie's office every morning. "He's giving the keynote."

"That prick Mellon stopped me back at the school," Sheila added, "and informed me we're allowed to record audio, but no video. The hostess is apparently some society type who doesn't want her precious belongings advertised on television."

"Great, so you won't need Freddie and me," Harvey said. "I wouldn't mind getting the stench of politicos out of my nostrils for a while."

"Take the van, then," Cassie told him as Freddie pulled up to the curb behind the Senator's limousine on Park Avenue. "Let's meet back at the studio around five and see what we got on tape today."

"Cassie, hon, I can already tell you what we have," Harvey said as Sheila, Cassie, and Cal climbed out of the car and started to organize the equipment, "but I don't like to use that kind of language in public."

The Senator seemed decidedly more at ease and credible with the elegantly dressed women attending the catered luncheon fund-raiser than he had been at the school. Though Sheila, Cassie noticed, seemed suddenly uncomfortable and out of sorts. With access to Miranda's wardrobe, Cassie blended seamlessly with the crowd in her silk crepe beige Armani suit; Sheila, in black cotton stirrup pants and a B52

Bombers T-shirt, definitely did not.

"Christ, finger bowls!" Sheila snorted as she plunked herself down next to Cassie at a table in a far corner of the hostess's large oval music room, the only table with a place card, labeled in an imperative hand: "Press."

The French doors connecting that room to the dining room and living room beyond were all open, providing almost everyone with a view of the Senator at the head table near an ornately carved eighteenth-century fireplace. A collection of French furniture was pushed to the sides of the room; oriental carpets were rolled; only the sedately lit oil paintings, several of which Cassie was able to identify as minor works of major masters, remained on public view. In decor and spaciousness, the apartment wasn't that much more elaborate than Jason's town house. And the guests, several of whom seemed vaguely familiar as friends of Miranda's, no longer intimidated Cassie as they once would have done.

"What's the matter with finger bowls?" Cassie asked, dipping her hands into the warm, lemon-scented water as she surveyed the chattering, expectant crowd. Waiters in white jackets moved from table to table, serving small plates of smoked salmon cornets filled with crème fraîche and caviar.

"Like, they're utterly passé."

"And since when did you become the expert?"

"I've been reading up on this crowd, Cassie," Sheila replied, pushing her unused bowl to one side as she dug into her salmon. "Library microfiche of the society pages comes in handy. As does *Town & Country* and *W*. I wish *Vanity Fair* hadn't stopped with their party section. It was an excellent resource for finding out what to serve to an intimate crowd of your five hundred closest friends. Also, it's the one connection I got between your sister and Haas." Sheila lowered her voice, turned to Cassie, and added, "I don't mean to push, babe, but someday soon you're going to have to let me in on what we're doing here. Harvey's right. The thing we're doing on Haas is pure bs. I know enough to guess that we're digging for the three men you say Miranda's notes threatened. It doesn't take a genius to guess one of them is—"

"Not now," Cassie cut in as she saw Geoffrey Mellon snaking his way around the tables toward them. "Here comes the Senator's wet nurse."

"How's it going?" he asked, his smile taking in all three *Breaking News* staffers. "Getting everything you need from Rita's people? I see you're following our itinerary pretty closely."

"Day in the life," Cassie said, smiling back, "just like I promised."

"Great, terrific. Well, the Senator himself asked me to invite you to an event that's not on the official schedule. We're having a party at his Brooklyn brownstone for his reelection volunteers. Next Saturday night. Strictly social though," he added as he waved across the room to somebody. "Leave your techies at home."

"That man even manages to make an invitation sound like a threat," Cal observed as Geoffrey moved on through the crowd. "You should hear his voice—without video—sometime. Gives me the creeps."

The Senator's luncheon speech, though the same stump script Cassie had been hearing all week, was received on Park Avenue with polite applause and such flattering questions as "Do you ever aspire to an office higher than the Senate, Anthony? Several of us hear your name is in the hat for vice president next time out."

"Buffy, darling," he replied, his beefy face flushed and smiling, holding up a restraining palm, "one thing at a time, please. Just help carry me back to old Washington this year, that's all I'm asking for here."

"Plus a couple of million for the kitty," Cassie murmured under her breath. The luncheon finally broke up around three, and Cassie, Sheila, and Cal shared a cab back to the office.

The screening of the day's footage was as unusable as Harvey had predicted, and the subsequent meeting was short and depressing.

"Mac's going to skin us," Freddie said. "Maybe I should put in for early retirement."

"I don't think you're eligible at thirty-two," Cassie replied. "Now, come on, guys, it's not that bad, really. I mean, after we cut in stock footage from his civil rights days. Once it's all edited, it could very well be . . ."

"Awful," Harvey concluded for her.

"He's right," Sheila said after the others had left. When Cassie, labeling the tape canisters, didn't respond, Sheila went on, "It's my ass as much as yours, okay? I ripped off those notes for you from Mac. And I helped talk the man into letting us do this ridiculous piece. In other words, since I'm already in this over my neck, how about telling me just what it is I'm drowning in?"

"You don't really want to know."

"Bullshit."

"I don't want you getting hurt."

"And I don't like you coming on like my mother here, Cassie. Enough of this mavericking around. If you want me to stay with you on this, I need to know everything. Now."

"Okay," Cassie said, realizing what a weight had just lifted from her shoulders. "Let's go back to our office. But, I promise, you're in for some disillusionment."

"Hey, like I was born knowing I was in for that," Sheila said as she turned out the lights in the editing booth and followed Cassie down the hall.

Twenty-five

"*I* just don't get it. Why would Vance need to pay Haas that kind of dough under the table? If he liked the man, just contribute to his political war chest."

"These notes clearly state the money went into Haas's private savings account," Cassie pointed out. "Whatever's going on between them, I don't think it has to do with politics."

"Blackmail?"

"Perhaps," Cassie agreed. "But look at this," she added, leaning across Sheila to move the cursor farther right on the computer screen. "Miranda cross-referenced Magnus's deposits to several favorable F.C.C. rulings Haas helped manipulate on his behalf. See, back in 1979 that $10,000 deposit follows shortly after Magnus was granted permission to buy that cable network in Georgia."

"Bribes."

"I think so," Cassie said. "Jason is part of the picture, too. It's just too much of a coincidence that he gets zoning approval for a major development a month after these deposits were recorded."

"But there's not much on Jason after the mid-seventies," Sheila pointed out. "Looks like Magnus's payoffs have only increased over the years."

"Jason might have been paying in cash," Cassie replied.

"Would have been a lot safer. Harder to track."

"I guess you're right. And, man, Miranda sure does sound spooked," Sheila added, rereading the warning at the bottom of the document. " 'Trust no one.' "

"I can't believe she'd suspect Jason," Cassie said, "unless she had a really good reason. They were married. Had a child. You don't go around digging up dirt on your husband unless you're pretty convinced there's something buried underneath."

"Sounds to me like you're trying to convince yourself of that," Sheila said, turning to look at Cassie.

"Maybe. I . . . we . . . Jason and I . . ."

"I kind of guessed," Sheila said, cutting off her embarrassed explanation. "How serious was it?"

"For me, very," Cassie said, walking over to the window. Though nearly eight-thirty, it was still dusk: a liquid sunset flooded the windows opposite with a burnt orange wash. "From the moment I first saw him . . . I knew."

"And with him?"

"He claims to feel the same way," Cassie replied unhappily. "And initially I believed him. I wanted to, rather desperately, despite the fact that he'd been married to my incredibly beautiful and glamorous sister for eight years. I still wanted to believe him, and did, ignoring the odds. And then, damn it, I came on this"—Cassie gestured at the screen—"and realized how important it would be for him to make me think he loved me."

"You mean, it would keep you from telling anyone if you suspected he'd somehow arranged Miranda's death?"

"Yes."

"And this was all it took for you to suspect him?" Sheila demanded. "Miranda's notes? Nothing more? Suddenly— boom—a great love dies?"

"No, you're right. I sensed from the beginning that he was hiding something. His moods can change so quickly. And when I stayed with them for a weekend a few weeks before Miranda died, they fought terribly. There was this passion—this electricity. There was so much between them—I don't know if it was love or hate—but it terrified and attracted me at the same time. I wanted it. I wanted him."

"It's ironic," Sheila said. "That's exactly how I felt about Magnus and her. He was so obsessed by her, so totally enthralled. I thought, if only he'd wake up and see that she didn't love him, wouldn't take care of him the way I could. She was just using him, dazzling him."

"I accused you once of being so jealous of her you couldn't see straight," Cassie said, crossing the room and leaning against the desk beside Sheila. "The truth of it is, so was I. From the time I was a little girl, I envied her. Tried to emulate her. Wanted everything she had. I've spent my life trying to be her. And now she's gone, leaving me everything I wanted. Even her husband."

"Except you can't enjoy any of it, right?"

"Enjoy?" Cassie said bitterly. "Ever since I found this disk, I feel I've been living a lie. Miranda begged me to move to New York the weekend I visited here. She hinted that something was wrong, but I chose not to hear. I really believe that if I'd stayed, if I'd helped her, she wouldn't have died. I feel utterly guilty."

"And you're going to absolve that by finding out what happened to her . . . and why?"

"Exactly. It's my fight. It's a personal one. You're free to step out of it now that you know what's at stake. In fact, I really wish you would."

"Forget it with your noble sentiments. I've got a few of my own, you know, though none are particularly elevated. Vance, for instance. I knew he was far from perfect, but this?" Sheila tapped the keyboard a few times. "This is downright illegal. Scummy. It would do me a hell of a lot of good to discover he was a slime. An instant cure for heartache. And, like I said before, this could be one sensational story, though I somehow doubt Vance would want it on *Breaking News*."

"You're taking this very lightly, Sheila. It could be dangerous."

"Correction. It is fucking dynamite. Wrong person finds out we know what we know? Boom, we're dead."

"You take my point," Cassie said with a faint smile. But the feeling of isolation and despair that had surrounded her like a fog the last few weeks had lifted slightly. She put her hand on Sheila's shoulder. "Thanks for helping me. It means a lot."

"Hey, I'm not doing this for you, okay?" Sheila replied with an embarrassed shrug. "This thing could land me a job on *60 Minutes* if I play it right."

"Aunt Cassie! Daddy!" Heather shrieked from the other side of the sea lions' pool in the Central Park Zoo, "Mindy and I are going into the penguin house!"

"Okay," Jason called back. "We'll see you back out here." Then, lowering his voice, he said to Cassie, "Unless, of course, you want to go in . . ."

The enervating mid-August sun dazzled the surface of the large pool in front of Cassie, worsening the headache she'd had all morning. It was a Saturday. Jason had been back a week.

"No, thanks," she replied. "I've spent enough time with Heather and her buddies and those damn penguins over the past few months to last several lifetimes."

The zoo, just a few streets down and across the avenue from the town house, had become one of Heather's favorite places to take her new friends. Along with Mindy, Heather's constant companions included Laurel, Marisa Newtown's daughter, and two other giggling, enormously energetic eight-year-olds from Heather's Dalton class. Though Cassie could trace the advent of Heather's social life from the afternoon of the birthday party, she also realized that it was the change in Heather herself that kept her popular. The poutiness, the selfishness, had evaporated with the first few friendly phone calls from classmates.

"You've been great with her, Cassie," Jason said. She knew he was watching her, though his eyes were hidden by dark glasses. Every time they were together, she felt his gaze on her: weighing and analyzing her moods. Jason surely had to wonder about how quickly her feelings could swing—from cool and distant, to needful and yearning. Because, try as she might to erect a wall of reserve between them, the thin emotional structure gave way the moment he touched her. She sensed that he didn't entirely believe her story of wanting to concentrate on her career, that he knew something deeper and far more complex had come between them, but that he didn't want to pry into the problem. He seemed willing to let things drift, content just to have her near, even though he had to sense that she was withholding a large part of herself from him. Surely he realized she no longer trusted him, Cassie told herself, but did he know why?

"She's growing up, that's all," Cassie replied, starting to walk toward the trellised colonnade on the far side of the pool. As always, being too close to Jason made her anxious and confused. His physical presence intoxicated her. When he was within touching distance . . . she longed to reach out. Instead, as often as possible these days, she forced herself to move away. He followed her across the park, his hands in the back pockets of his worn blue jeans, the sleeves of his faded denim work shirt rolled up to his elbows. Cassie often felt other women turning to look at him, and her heart contracted with jealousy.

"Yes, she is," Jason said, leaning on the rail next to where Cassie had stopped to watch an extended family of monkeys roam over their rocky island home. Swans drifted in pairs around the little pond that separated the island from the walkway where Jason and Cassie stood. "Much too fast, as a matter of fact. I feel as though I've missed most of her childhood."

"Because you were traveling?" Cassie asked, shielding her eyes with her right hand as she looked at him. She shouldn't have. His lips turned down in the smile she knew so well. He must have sensed her reaction; he took off his sunglasses.

"That and because I wasn't paying enough attention," he said, his eyes searching hers. "The way I obviously wasn't paying attention to what matters to you. I can see now that I forced my own values on you, my own experience. Work doesn't matter much to me anymore. It's odd, but especially this past trip, I found my thoughts constantly wandering . . . back to you. I've canceled my next business trip. I'm sending one of my associates to complete the Bangkok negotiations. I want . . . I want us to work things out."

She looked away from him, across the man-made pond, into the dense green backdrop of distant trees. It was the worst possible news; each day—torn by her desire for him and her growing suspicions about Miranda's death—she'd been waiting for him to tell her he was leaving again.

"It will be good for Heather to have you back."

"That's not what I wanted to hear you say."

"It's all I can tell you."

"That's simply not true, Cassie. I know you better than that. I know *us* better, damn it. Listen. Look at me . . ."

"Please don't . . . force me to say—"

"Okay, I'm sorry," he said to cut her off. "But I just don't think I can go on like this. I'm ready to do whatever you want to bring us together. Cassie, I'm in this private little hell—you must know what you're doing to me."

"Jason, I thought I made it clear before that I'm not ready to get . . . too close."

"What were we before, Cassie? Don't tell me our time together didn't mean anything to you. Our weekend in the country? What was that? Casual friendship?"

"We moved too fast," Cassie retorted. "I told you at the time I was getting in over my head."

"That's what it's all about—losing perspective, getting lost in someone else's life, letting go."

"I'm just finding myself," she said, turning to him, but unable to meet his gaze. She directed her words to the man-made mountain where a family of monkeys laughed and played in the sun. "I'm just getting my sea legs in a very rough business. I'm in the middle of my first big assignment. That's what I'm thinking about. That's my priority."

"Why is it that I don't believe you?" he asked, his gaze taking her in. "I believe you when you kiss me, Cassie. I believe you when I hold you in my arms." His tone had softened; his voice felt like a caress.

She longed to feel his mouth on hers. She inhaled deeply; it took a monumental effort for her to say: "Perhaps it would be better if I moved out."

"No, don't." Jason turned away, leaning his back against the railing. He ran his hands over his face, massaged his temple, and put the sunglasses back on. "Did you know I was going to ask you to marry me this afternoon? I have a ring in the back pocket of my jeans. I knew it was probably too soon. I kept telling myself you weren't ready. Christ, you don't have to say it, Cassie. In your own way, I know you've been trying to warn me off. I'm not a total fool."

"I'm sorry, Jason." She was grateful that he didn't see her expression.

He was silent for a long time, staring out across the hot sea of children, balloons, gardens, and fountains. Cassie studied his profile—the high forehead and overgrown brow, the slightly too long but somehow elegant nose, the wide, mobile mouth—and let herself briefly feel how much she was losing. *No, don't think about it,* she told herself quickly. *Remember Miranda. Consider what Miranda lost.*

"I was thinking before," he said at last, "of asking you to take some time off and spend the last two weeks of summer up in the country with Heather and me. I realize that's impossible now. But I think Heather and I should go."

"It will do her good to get out of the city."

"It'll do us all good, I suspect," he replied, glancing at

her with his down-turning smile. "Don't worry," he added. "I won't put you through this again. I've spent my life being aggressive, going out and grabbing what I want. I can't pretend I don't want you, Cassie. But I am prepared to wait. I've never been a very patient man, but I'm willing to learn. I'm not returning the ring. I want you to know that. It will be here with me. Because in my heart I know, even if you don't, that we belong together."

"Daddy!" Heather cried, running through the crowd toward them. "We've been looking all over for you!"

"It's just a matter of time," he added quietly.

No, Cassie told herself, *it's a matter of life . . . and death.*

Twenty-six

Senator Anthony Haas's "little party" turned out to be a posh by-invitation-only fund-raiser, and as soon as Cassie and Sheila saw the limousines double-parked along the Senator's tree-lined Brooklyn street, they realized that they should have insisted the production unit be allowed to accompany them.

"Damn, that son of a bitch Mellon," Sheila muttered as Cassie paid off their cabdriver. "He knew we'd be pissed when we saw how big this thing is. Look over there—that's the Channel 5 news van. I'm going to strangle the man."

"Forget it," Cassie replied. "It will give us a chance to concentrate on Haas. How he lives. What his tastes are."

"Where his personal financial files are stored," Sheila added, climbing out of the cab.

"Now, don't concentrate too hard," Cassie said.

"You mean, don't get caught at it," Sheila replied. "Listen, if I happen to run smack into a list of his 1974 campaign contributors, is that my fault? Oh, don't worry," Sheila added when she saw Cassie's expression. "I'm not about to do anything foolish."

"I wish I didn't know you so well. I might be able to believe you."

Even from the sidewalk, it was clear that this was an expensive, fully catered affair. A bright green-and-white-striped awning led across the lawn and up to the front lacquered green door of the Senator's brownstone. Valets in white tuxes waited at the sidewalk to open car doors, help people out, and escort the older guests up the steps. Urns, filled with freshly potted geraniums, and ivy flanked the front path, and pinpoint white lights, wrapped around the sycamore trees, gave the carefully groomed front yard the otherworldly look of a fairy garden.

Inside, the high-ceilinged rooms had been likewise transformed for the party with elaborate flower arrangements and more strands of tiny white lights. The front hall led straight through the brownstone to the backyard where a Dixieland jazz band was playing. Though the front rooms of the house were crowded, the noise level emanating from the back indicated that the real party was taking place out there.

"The Mayor's here," Sheila whispered to Cassie as they made their way toward the music. "And his wife. She never puts in an appearance at night if she can help it. Haas must have a lot of pull down at City Hall."

"Isn't that the publisher of the *News*?" Cassie asked, nudging Sheila and nodding toward a group of well-dressed men in the far corner of the dining room.

"Yeah, and, oh, God," Sheila said with a sigh, "there's Magnus."

"Come on." Cassie pulled Sheila's arm. "We're supposed to be mingling, remember? Him you can see anytime."

"You don't fool me, Cassie," Sheila replied as they continued down the hall and out into the noisy backyard, "I know him well enough to sense when he's hot for someone."

"And?" Cassie already knew, but didn't want to hear, what Sheila was going to say.

"'Baby, it's you.'" Sheila sang the old doo-wop song under her breath.

"I've done nothing to encourage . . ."

"Hey, don't get me wrong, I'm not laying this on you," Sheila said, lifting a glass of white wine from a waiter passing with a silver-plated tray. Together the two women moved into the milling crowd. Cassie had borrowed an off-the-shoulder, above-the-knee Mizrahi sheath from Miranda's wardrobe for the black-tie occasion. The fabric—woven with tiny beads and strands of gold—shimmered as she moved. "It's not your fault you look so much like Miranda. You even sound a bit like her. And now, in his eyes anyway, you're stepping into her shoes at the network."

"That's absurd. I'm doing a single temporary host slot, hardly anchoring the show."

"The word is you're it," Sheila told her, sipping the wine and watching the couples dancing on the grass in front of the band. Sheila, for whom formal attire meant black, was wearing a jet-colored cocktail dress with a pouffed skirt that dated the purchase at least three years, high spiked heels, and long dangly ebony earrings. Though the two women couldn't look less alike, they had one thing in common: every male head turned to watch them pass.

"Did you see Susan Dearborn's segment last week?" Sheila went on. "She was so stiff, boring. But you—you're a fresh new face. Even Mac thinks so. He told me yesterday," she insisted when she caught Cassie's disbelieving look. "Why be so shocked? You're gorgeous enough. You've got the presence . . . the right 'look.' And the emotional currency for the viewers—I mean your being Miranda's sister—is pay dirt for the network. Plus, as far as I'm concerned, you've twice the investigative stuff Miranda ever had. Barring some terrible mistake or other, I'd guess the seat is yours."

"Why are you telling me all this . . . suddenly?"

"Because some people would view our little hidden agenda . . . as just such a terrible mistake."

"Do you?"

"In terms of your career?" Sheila asked, glancing at Cassie. "If Magnus found out? Or Haas? I mean, forget

Miranda's file for the time being and whether or not either one of them is guilty. They find out what we're up to . . . you can kiss Magnus Media good-bye."

"You're getting cold feet," Cassie concluded.

"Hell I am," Sheila shot back. Then, looking around, she lowered her voice. "What have I got to lose? I'm just trying to point out to you what you're risking by going ahead. No one's telling me I get to host *Breaking News* if I keep my nose clean. I've never kidded myself. I'm nobody's golden girl."

"I'm not either," Cassie told her, "if it means whitewashing Miranda's death. I thought I made that clear to you."

Sheila looked at her a long moment over her wineglass, her dark eyes dancing with the tiny, reflecting lights. Then she held up the glass in a toast and said, "You've got a hell of a lot more guts than she had, too. Okay. So, let's get mingling."

A year before, even six months earlier, Cassie would have had a hard time attending a party on her own, let alone attempting to meet new people and make friends at one. It was proof of how much more self-confident she'd become that she drifted that night from group to group with apparent ease. Shaking hands, introducing herself, she slowly made herself a part of whatever circle she chose to enter. In each, she'd manage to innocently ask: "Have you all known the Senator long? My network's doing a segment on him. We'd love to hear any stories or memories you might have . . ."

And though Cassie pretended to seem most interested in those who eagerly responded with their various anecdotes, it was really those who closed up suddenly, who moved quickly away whom she mentally marked down. Around eleven, the relentlessly upbeat Dixieland combo was replaced by a louder, electrified band. People's high heels and ties came off. Cassie, unable to hear herself speak, was working her way back toward the house when she felt someone touch her elbow.

"Care to dance?" It was Geoffrey Mellon. His red bow tie hung loose at his neck, and his white dress shirt accentuated the deep tan of his face and neck.

"Not my kind of music," Cassie replied.

"Good. I really wanted a chance to talk to you, anyway," he said genially. "Let's go in." He propelled her in front of him; his grip firm on her elbow.

"Great party," Cassie said when they'd reached the back hall. "Too bad our crew wasn't around to film it. Would have made terrific footage."

"Doubtful," Geoffrey replied, opening up a door, flicking on a light, and talking over his shoulder as he led her down a flight of carpeted steps. "No taxpayer likes to see his money hard at work drinking and dancing."

"You've got a point," Cassie said. "But that begs the question why Channel 5 is out in the front yard."

"I was afraid you might notice," Geoffrey replied, opening a door at the bottom of the steps and turning on another light. He pushed the door wider and stood aside for Cassie to enter. It was a large, pleasantly masculine room with wood-beamed ceiling and an enormous flagstone fireplace that took up one entire wall. Floor-to-ceiling bookshelves covered another wall, hundreds of photographs of the Senator with the influential and famous covered the third, the fourth was taken up by eight metallic-gray four-drawer filing cabinets. At the far corner of the room a door opened to a short flight of stone steps that led up to the backyard.

"That's why I wanted the chance to see you alone. Relax, Cassie," he said, gesturing to one of the comfortably worn Strickey chairs in front of the fireplace. "Can I get you a drink?"

"Only if you're having something."

"Don't touch the stuff," he said, leaning on the arm of the chair next to hers. She sensed he'd taken a standing pose in order to—literally—get the upper hand. He folded his arms across the pleated white fabric at his chest, and added, "I've seen what alcohol can do to people."

"Anyone in particular?" Cassie asked as she stood up—deciding two could play at power dynamics—and walked over to the wall of photographs. The framed shots covered the wall, depicting Haas over more than three decades in Washington: standing beside Kennedy in the Oval Office, as a freshman congressman with an almost military crew cut and a wide, optimistic smile. Next to that, taken fifteen years later, there was a gold-framed photo of Haas—with sideburns and slightly thinning though stylishly long hair—shaking hands with a dazed-looking Jimmy Carter in the Rose Garden. Alongside the shots of other political Washington celebrities were those of politicized Hollywood: Haas with Jane Fonda and Tom Hayden in the seventies, flanked by Meryl Streep and Debra Winger in the late eighties.

"I think we can talk frankly, Cassie," Geoffrey replied, watching her across the room. "It's clear Tony overindulges from time to time. He's under a great deal of pressure, especially now with all the endless demands of his reelection campaign."

"Don't worry. We don't have an incriminating tape of Haas dancing with a lampshade on or anything."

"I'm sure you don't," Geoffrey replied pleasantly. "Believe me, I'm well aware what you do—and don't have—on the Senator."

"And by that you mean?"

"We run a tight ship, as I think you're beginning to notice. I imagine you're getting a bit frustrated by it as well. Believe me, it's necessary. You're aware that rumors are circulating—ugly, partisan mud-slinging ones—about illegal contributions for Tony's campaign."

"Ruthie Nester's a liberal Democrat," Cassie replied, turning to look at Geoffrey. "I somehow don't think of her as particularly partisan."

"Then you're far more naive than I thought. Nester's getting ready to run herself in another four years. I don't intend to let her get carried into the Senate on the broken back of Anthony Haas."

"You don't?" Cassie turned back to the wall of photos. There was a shot of Senator Haas surrounded by the Mets at the end of their 1986 World Series championship. He wore a baseball cap and was smiling, but the photo showed how time and drink had finally blurred and broadened his once handsome features. "Sometimes, Geoffrey, you sound just a little bit like a one-man political band. It must be tough, having to stake all your hard work on the fate of another man. What will you do if the Senator doesn't win? Or if he decides to retire?"

"Neither possibility gives me the least concern, actually. Tony's only in his mid-sixties. I know him well. I'll wager he'll be in there fighting twenty years from now." His tone was so patently false that Cassie found herself staring at him with open surprise, but Geoffrey's expression was as bland and unreadable as always.

"And where will you be? I wonder. You strike me as someone who wouldn't make a bad candidate yourself."

"You flatter me," Geoffrey said, rising and walking over to stand beside her. "I'm second string, Cassie. The prompter in the wings. I like to work behind the scenes. Helping draft legislation, cut deals, work out compromises."

"Some people would call that being the power behind the throne," Cassie said, turning to a photograph of Senator Haas, with his mid-seventies sideburns, flanked by two men Cassie recognized, but couldn't immediately place. Geoffrey glanced from her to the framed picture.

"That's Vance Magnus," Geoffrey told her, pointing to the tall, bronzed, smiling man on Haas's left dressed in an expensive three-piece suit. Like Haas, his hair was longer; but unlike the Senator, Magnus had the kind of patrician good looks that could carry off any style—however faddish—with graceful elegance.

"Who's that?" Cassie asked, pointing to the bearded man with intense dark eyes on Haas's right. There was something so penetrating and knowing in the man's look; Cassie felt he was looking right at her, now, in this room.

"You don't know?" Geoffrey asked with an amused laugh. "That's your brother-in-law. Jason Darin. Apparently those three were really tight back in the early seventies. Thick as thieves, you might say."

Twenty-seven

"When was the picture taken?" Cassie asked, stepping closer to examine the shot. Haas had his right arm around Magnus's shoulders, his left hand wrapped around a neck of a champagne bottle; there was something about the way he was standing that made Cassie think Magnus was helping to hold Haas upright. Jason, hands thrust deep in his pockets, looked angry and uncomfortable, as though someone had forced him to pose for the picture against his will. There was a banner behind the three men, though the words running across it were cut off by the top of the frame.

" 'Magnus for Mayor,' " Geoffrey told her. "Don't you remember? Back in the mid-seventies sometime?"

"I had no idea Magnus was ever in politics."

"It was a very brief stint from what I understand. It was way before my time, but my impression is that he got his feet wet, then decided he didn't want to take the final plunge. He never made the ballot. Just another businessman getting in a bit over his head."

"In what way was Jason involved? I wonder."

"At the time I know he owned the hotel where they held a few of Magnus's fund-raisers. The Savoy in midtown. Those were the days when you could pick up Manhattan real estate for a song, the way Jason did. He was even smarter to sell most of it off in the late eighties. Too bad he lost interest in politics. We could use someone with his connections on our reelection committee."

"I get the feeling that it was more than just his losing interest," Cassie said. "Somewhere along the line I think he lost respect for Haas. Do you know what happened?"

Geoffrey gave her a look, then a smile. "You're fishing in the wrong river, Cassie. Tony's as tight-mouthed about Jason Darin as I've ever known him to be about any subject. They had a sort of father-son thing going there for a long time, I know. Something happened, and their relationship ended. That's about the best I can do, I'm afraid."

"But Magnus and Haas have stayed good friends," Cassie said, turning back to the wall of photographs.

"Yes," Geoffrey answered, his voice suddenly taking on the slick, slightly insincere tenor of the efficient aide. "Vance Magnus is one of the Senator's most influential supporters."

"I suppose that works both ways," Cassie replied. "Influence, I mean. Vance needs something done in Washington, I guess he just calls you guys for the favor."

"In its broadest sense, it's called lobbying, Cassie," Geoffrey replied smoothly. "It's probably the one growth industry in the capital right now. Totally legal. In fact, absolutely necessary."

"I stand reproved."

"Not really. Just better informed, I hope. I can't help but feel that you're looking for something in the Senator that simply isn't there. And I don't necessarily mean anything negative," Geoffrey continued quickly as he turned back to the fireplace. He massaged the base of his neck, sighed, and relaxed into the chair Cassie had vacated. "There's no room left in Washington for the kind of idealized politics Tony once preached. It's far more complicated now—subcommittees, special interest groups. Bureaucracy—rather than rhetoric—rules the roost."

"And that's all it was before," Cassie asked, "rhetoric?"

"Don't get semantic on me," Geoffrey told her. "I'm just trying to help. I know you probably feel that the Senator's schedule is a bit overorganized, his speeches perhaps too calculated. It's true, we currently have more people on staff doing p.r. than constituency liaison. But that's how the game's played these days. It used to be that a Senator like Haas would take his message to the people. Now we take it to the media. In the long run—it's more or less the same thing. Except voters can now watch a speech in the comfort of their own living rooms, rather than at a rally."

"Which makes a relationship like Magnus and the Senator's all that much more important. And the *Breaking News* segment pretty crucial."

"You've got it." Geoffrey smiled across at her. "That's why I wanted to make sure we—your team and mine—are all still on the same wavelength. I sometimes get—how should I say this?—funny vibes from you. As I said, like you're looking for something that isn't there."

"Well, one thing we had been trying to locate," Cassie replied lightly, tapping the wall, "were some good photos—old ones, in good condition—to use as background. Could we get our crew down here sometime during the next week or two, maybe? To shoot this wall?"

Geoffrey glanced briefly around the room, his gaze hesitating at the filing cabinets, then back at Cassie. "I think that can be arranged. But just the photos, of course. The rest of the house is off-limits. Understood?"

"Oh, absolutely."

By the time Cassie and Geoffrey had made their way back upstairs again, the party had started to wind down. Haas, flanked by Rita Kirbie and another aide, was saying good night to guests at the front door. Swathed in a black tuxedo that could not quite conceal his girth, the Senator looked unhappily sober, and it seemed likely to Cassie that Rita and her colleague had been designated watchdogs.

"Where've you been?" Sheila materialized at Cassie's side and took her arm. "I've been looking all the hell over the place for you. Magnus has offered to drive us back. He's waiting outside in his limousine." From the emphasis Sheila put on the last word, Cassie knew that her friend was not as immune as she pretended to be to the trappings of wealth and power. There was also a look in her eye, an intensified energy about her smile, that made Cassie realize she was still far from cured of the charms of Vance Magnus.

"I've some interesting news about our new chauffeur," Cassie told Sheila once they'd shaken hands with Haas and started down the front steps. "And I think I know where Haas keeps his personal papers."

"In the basement," Sheila told her as they stood at the curb looking for Magnus's black stretch Mercedes. "I've been busy, too, making nice with a disgruntled house-keeper."

During the drive along the Brooklyn-Queens Express-way, Magnus, seated in the middle of the plush backseat, chatted mostly to Sheila on his right while Cassie stared out the window at the massive glittering shell of lower Manhattan across the river. But if Sheila had hopes that Magnus's interest was more than transitory, it was surely dashed when he leaned forward to instruct the driver to drop Sheila off first.

"You've been very quiet," Magnus said as he climbed back into the car after seeing Sheila to her door.

"Tired," Cassie told him. "It's been a long couple of weeks."

"Haas told me tonight that you've been tracking him like a bloodhound."

"That may be so, but we haven't yet picked up much of his real scent. Haas's staff has him so sanitized, he's barely human. He can't open his mouth without a prepared speech in hand."

"These days politicians have to be so careful," Magnus told her. "Appearances are everything unfortunately. It used to be that certain things—a candidate's home life, his financial history—were off bounds to the press. Would Kennedy have ever been elected, for instance, if people knew how much he played around? But since Gary Hart, the thing's a free-for-all."

"You sound as if you don't approve," Cassie said. "But I distinctly remember Magnus Media joining in on the Hart feeding frenzy."

"Still playing Little Miss Morality, are we?" Magnus laughed and turned to her, his arm moving along the back of the seat, grazing her hair lightly. "Well, you're quite right. I'm constantly having to employ a double standard: what's best for the corporation as opposed to what I really believe. In the case of your piece on Tony, I feel we have the opportunity to right a few of the wrongs I see at work out there. The man deserves a better break from the media— some respect and acknowledgment. I'm delighted we can give him that."

"And if the piece comes out looking totally orchestrated and rehearsed, you don't care?"

"In this case, my dear, no," Magnus said, his arm dropping to settle against her back, his left hand curling around her shoulder. "I know you'll do your best. A positive segment is never as interesting as a negative one. Oldest rule in my book."

"I've some rules, too," Cassie said, sitting forward suddenly, breaking his embrace.

"I understand."

"I'm not sure you do," Cassie said, turning toward him. "Would you like to come in to talk about them?"

"I'd love to, but I somehow doubt Jason would second the invitation."

"Jason has nothing to do with this, and besides, he's not here," she replied as the limousine pulled up to the curb. A light was on in the front hall for her, though Cassie knew that both Charles and Henrietta had left hours before. Since Jason and Heather had decamped for the Berkshires, the town house felt ridiculously large and suddenly empty to Cassie. She had had no idea that she would miss Heather's high, demanding voice so much, the sound of her footsteps pounding down the front stairs to breakfast. But far more fiercely and painfully she missed Jason. His smile. His touch. His rare laughter. The far-off sound of his voice on the phone in his study, all the indistinguishable background noises of people living together.

Now, essentially, Cassie lived alone again. And though her nonstop working hours kept her from facing it, she was deeply lonely. More than the house, her heart was empty.

"Armagnac? Brandy?" Cassie asked Magnus as she switched on the lights in the library.

"No, I won't keep you. I just want to know what you meant . . . about me not understanding." He was leaning against the fireplace, looking down at the immaculately clean marble hearth: a tall, impeccably dressed man with silver hair and a thin smile. His attraction, Cassie had long ago decided, was the aura of compressed power that he wore as easily as his custom-made suits.

"I'm not unaware how much you've done for me," Cassie said, pouring herself a splash of brandy from the small bar unit built into the wall of bookcases. She was nervous, and the balloon glass acted as a handy prop. She rolled the base back and forth between her palms as she walked across the room to join him at the fireplace. She knew that in the low light her dress shimmered seductively. She shook her bangs back and looked up at him. "I'm also not unappreciative."

"You make me sound like some rusty old professor who's given you a good mark."

"And what would you rather be . . . for me?"

"Honestly?"

"Yes."

"I want to take you into my care. I want to make you into a media star—first as a host of *Breaking News,* then eventually in the role Miranda had wanted, as the first woman to anchor the news alone. I've been watching you, Cassie. You have all the raw abilities to do it: you're smart, creative, you've good reporter instincts. You've also got something Miranda never had: a way with people. I've seen how you and Sheila work together, how hard the crew was pulling for you on the Bronx segment. I could help you become the first woman megastar in network news. Like Rather and Cronkite, only a hell of a lot prettier."

"And in turn," Cassie asked, "what do you want from me?"

"Nothing you're not ready to give," he said simply, his gaze moving from her face, down her body, and back to meet her eyes. "I won't lie and say that I'm not interested in you physically. I am I have been since we first met. But in the beginning, I'll admit, it was because you reminded me so much of Miranda. Now, my dear, it's because you're so definitely you: beautiful but kind, intelligent but not haughty. And your sense of morality . . . it's . . ." He shrugged and smiled almost boyishly. "Just so charming."

"I don't know what I'm ready to give," Cassie replied, holding her glass against her chest, "but I am ready to take: I accept your offer. I'll work like hell not to let you down. The other . . . let's just start slowly and see what happens."

"Is this slow enough for you?" Magnus asked, stepping toward her. His arms slid around her waist, and he held her lightly, the brandy glass nestled between them. His thin, hard lips covered hers. His tongue invaded her mouth, lingered briefly, then withdrew.

"Yes," Cassie replied with a forced smile, hiding her distaste with a sip of brandy, "and enough, too, I think, for tonight."

Twenty-eight

"*T*hat's the connection all right," Sheila said the next morning. "The one time all three of them worked together, knew each other. It's also when the paybacks to Haas started."

"Something must have happened during Magnus's run for mayor," Cassie went on. "It blew Magnus's chances, and it bound Jason and Magnus to Haas."

"Whatever it was, they managed to smother it publicly," Sheila said. "I've had Research pull all the important files on Haas for the show. He looks to be lily-white."

"It's got to be there," Cassie insisted. "It has to be. And we're going to find it, whatever it takes."

"Why don't you just ask your new boyfriend?" Sheila demanded, trying—and not quite succeeding—to sound ironic and cool. Cassie had decided it was important to tell her friend everything that had happened the night before, down to the last detail.

"When the moment is right, I promise you I will."

The following Wednesday evening presented the first such opportunity. When Magnus had learned from Marisa Newtown that Cassie was on the invitation list for the Parks Committee benefit that Marisa was hosting, Magnus asked Cassie if he might escort her.

"It's always easier at these formal affairs to have some-one at your elbow with whom you can make fun of every-one else," Magnus told her rather stiffly as if to offset any appearance of eagerness on his part.

"I couldn't agree more," Cassie replied. "I'd be delighted." She wore a deep pink strapless organdy Laroche evening gown, long sheer silver gloves, and ballet-style silver slip-pers that allowed Magnus to tower a full two inches above her. She pulled her hair back in a French twist, then offset the simplicity of the look by wearing oversized platinum-and-ebony earrings that dangled all the way to her shoul-ders. She felt a bit like Cinderella the entire evening: the ball crasher, the new face, the woman with a secret.

"Who is that heavenly creature with Vance?" she over-heard one middle-aged woman ask Marisa as the guests filed into the ballroom for dancing after dinner.

"That's my dear friend, Cassie, Miranda Darin's sister, you know."

"Oh, of course. Poor darling. Though I heard she inher-ited everything. Do you suppose that includes Vance?"

He kissed her at the end of the evening—once, quite gent-ly while they were still in the backseat of the limousine—before walking her to the door. She didn't invite him in; he didn't ask. But despite the mildness of his approach, she'd felt his eyes on her the entire evening: keen and possessive as an eagle spotting prey.

Her second date with Magnus was to a private party honoring one of the men who sat on the Magnus Media board of directors. The guest of honor, a publishing warlord well into his eighties, presided over a sit-down dinner for five hundred in the grand hall of the New York Public Library. The poet laureate read a poem in the man's honor. Magnus held Cassie's hand when the lights were lowered and the hundreds of guests rose to sing "Auld Lang Syne." Besides that, his behavior remained entirely circumspect, though once again she'd felt his predatory gaze and sensed something clamped-down about him.

And then, quite suddenly, Jason and Heather were back. Cassie, of course, had been aware of their expected arrival. But even though she knew to the hour when they were due to return, even though she had assured herself that she was thoroughly prepared now to face Jason with poise and only friendly interest, the moment she saw him her heart betrayed her. She felt her face flush. She could not control the obvious pleasure in her smile. As Heather clamored all over her, demanding kisses and hugs, Jason and Cassie exchanged glances. He broke the gaze first. The kiss he gave her when Heather finally let her go was on the cheek: brief, almost formal. She knew it was irrational to want more: the pressure of his mouth on hers, the warmth of his arms.

Rather like a couple sharing joint custody of a child, Jason and Cassie managed to spend as much time as they could with Heather during the next few weeks, while avoiding spending any time alone with each other. If Jason noticed that Cassie was out more than before, he showed no sign of it. The renewed demands of his work kept him down at his office to all hours, and though Cassie heard talk of problems with some new deal Jason was putting together in the Philippines, there was no hint that he planned to travel again soon. She sensed a renewed commitment from him as a parent, as well as a new restraint—and almost total withdrawal—where she was concerned.

When Magnus called Cassie for a date, it was usually first thing in the morning, via the office intercom, in a tone that was businesslike and brisk. The third time he invited her out—to a dinner party hosted by the Mayor at Gracie Mansion for leading Republican businessmen— Cassie expressed surprise that he himself had been invited to the event.

"Aren't you a Democrat, or am I crazy?"

"You're crazy," Magnus replied with a smile in his voice. "Oh, I once had some liberal misconceptions. Then I married Millie and saw the error of my ways."

"But you support Haas," Cassie pointed out, then added on impulse: "And you ran for mayor as a Democrat."

There was silence on the other end of the line. "That's very ancient history," Magnus said finally. "From whom, may I ask, did you learn that terribly minor piece of esoterica?"

"From a photograph, actually, taken with Haas and Jason. The Senator has it hanging on the wall of his study."

"The fool."

"I've upset you. I'm sorry. In answer to your question— yes, I'd be happy to go with you. When is it?"

There was something about the day he gave—the second Thursday in September—that tickled Cassie's memory, but her mind was so preoccupied these days with the concerns of the present that she merely jotted the appointment down in her day book and turned back to the manila files of press clippings stacked on her desk. The folders, just a small part of what the Magnus archives had yielded up on "Haas, Anthony," included all major print coverage during the mid-seventies.

While ostensibly working on the *Breaking News* piece, Sheila and she had been poring over every agate line and sound bite of information they could find—including, along with the Magnus material, similar files from the New York Public Library, the Museum of Broadcasting, UPI, and two on-line networks.

"Bingo," Cassie said, looking up when Sheila came in fifteen minutes after she'd hung up the phone.

"You actually found something?"

"No, I heard something. In Magnus's voice. I asked him about the mayoral run when he called a little while ago. And I heard it. But good."

"What?"

Cassie leaned back in her swivel chair and smiled. "Fear."

"Hold on." Cal stopped before the lights flashed on. "I need a level on sound."

"One . . . two . . . buckle my shoe," Cassie spoke into the mike clipped to her jacket label as she glanced around the room, wondering if they could possibly fit another person or piece of equipment into the Senator's basement study. Besides Haas himself, standing solemnly upright while Felice the makeup artist patted his face with matte powder, there was Rita Kirbie, Geoffrey Mellon, and two other assistants from the Senator's staff. The entire Magnus unit was in attendance, as well as such on-location personnel as the makeup artist, wardrobe assistant, and hairstylist. Setup of the lighting alone—especially tricky because the glassed-in photos tended to pick up glare—had taken a full hour. Now, two hours after they had been scheduled to begin, the *Breaking News* crew was ready to start shooting.

"That's fine," Sheila said, standing to the left of Cassie, a headset covering her ears, clipboard folded under her arm. "How're we doing on lights? Ready? Makeup, finish it up, please. Senator . . . Okay, Harve, Freddie, let's do it." Sheila pointed a trigger finger at Cassie and said, "Shoot."

"We're here in the Senator's private study," Cassie began, smiling into the explosion of lights that had—just a few weeks ago—tended to blind her. Now, she'd grown accustomed to their glare in the same way that she'd learned to project her voice and orchestrate her gestures for the camera. Sweeping an arm across a row of photographs, she continued, "and we're standing in front of a wall of memorabilia that represents—as best I can tell—a remarkably extensive photographic history of his years in office. Senator Haas," Cassie said, turning to her right as Harve zoomed back to widen his angle, "perhaps you'd be so kind as to take us on a guided tour of this wall, of your past, of these remarkable memories . . ."

Although carefully rehearsed, with Cassie's relaxed presence, the fifteen-minute interview had a friendly informality about it that was lacking in the Senator's public appearances. With Cassie's arm on his sleeve and her encouraging smile ever ready, Haas found himself speaking with fluency—and even some humor.

"Yes, that's me shaking hands with Gerald Ford. Good thing he wasn't trying to chew gum at the same time, eh?" And once again, Haas felt himself wishing that he could have more people like Cassie on his staff: someone who looked up to him, who appreciated his place in history, who even laughed at his jokes.

"Finished already?" Haas asked when the lights suddenly flashed off. A wave of anxiety—not unlike the reeling sensation of inebriation—darkened his vision for a second.

"We're running a bit behind schedule, sir," Sheila said, stepping over to help him remove the mike.

"Actually we've planned a surprise," Cassie added. "Since this interview gives us just about everything we need to start cutting the segment, we arranged a thank-you dinner for you and your staff. Just down the street at Hudson's Cafe."

"We checked with Rita," Sheila assured him, "and you've nothing on your agenda for dinner. We promise to have you back here in plenty of time to dress for your Meals on Wheels benefit at the Armory."

"Really, Senator," Geoffrey said as he wedged himself between Sheila and Cassie, "nobody informed me of this event. It's absolutely out of the question to—"

"It was a surprise," Cassie interrupted him. "Meant for you, as well. We just wanted to have a chance to show you our appreciation . . ."

"Don't be such a tightass, Geoff," Haas told him, taking Cassie's arm. "Lead the way, my dear. I think we all deserve a good stiff drink."

In the general hubbub of breaking down the equipment, loading the vans, and piling everyone into various vehicles, nobody seemed to notice that Sheila was left behind. Cassie, chatty and slightly flirtatious, managed to keep both the Senator and Geoffrey engaged straight through dinner.

"Where's your production girl?" Geoffrey asked finally as coffee was served. "Come to think of it, I don't remember seeing her leave the house." He sat up, suddenly suspicious.

"She took a cab back to the city," Cassie told him, tearing open a pack of Sweet'n' Low and shaking it into her coffee with a show of unconcern. She smiled knowingly at Haas. "Some hot date."

"I think I'd better check," Geoffrey announced, standing up. For a moment, until he started to jangle loose change around in his pants pocket, Cassie felt her adrenaline surge. "I'm going to call Constance, make sure everything's secure."

"Lord, Geoff, live a little." The Senator sighed and reached for his double Sambuca as Geoffrey hurried toward the wall of pay phones along the corridor leading to the rest rooms. "That boy doesn't know the meaning of a good time," Haas went on, gulping down half his postprandial drink and turning a sloppy smile on Cassie. "All this new crowd cares about is getting ahead. Making it. Winning. No one takes time out anymore just to sit back and smell the roses."

"I bet you used to have some parties," Cassie suggested, "back in the old days. Like when Magnus ran for mayor— that must have been one long good time. Am I right?"

The Senator's lidded gaze dropped, and for just a second Cassie thought he'd fallen asleep. Then she found herself staring into eyes that were suddenly sober, fully alert, and terribly sad.

"Honey, I hope you haven't been trying to play with us big boys," he told her softly. "I really hope not. Because I was starting to get to really like you."

"I'm like totally lucky to be alive," Sheila told Cassie breathlessly. As prearranged, they'd met at Finklestein's, a typical watering hole on First Avenue, frequented by aging, mostly chronic singles. "Thank God I had the good sense to make Constance unlock that back door in advance."

"She okay, Constance?" Cassie asked, nibbling at her cuticles and totally ignoring the platter of club sandwiches in front of her.

"Sure. Believe me, one hundred smackeroos goes a long way these days. And personal disgust doesn't hurt either. The woman is sick and tired of picking up after a drunk. Who can blame her?"

"So she lied when Geoffrey called?"

"Cool as a cucumber. Said a taxi had picked me up not five minutes after they'd left for the restaurant. I should have had the good sense then to get out. Except I didn't find the damn stuff until the very last second."

"I've had enough suspense for one night, Sheila. Please tell me what it is you found before I have to throttle you."

"Interesting you should use that word," Sheila replied, taking a big bite out of her oversized cheeseburger, a multilayered extravaganza of beef, tomato, pepper, cheese, and lettuce. Catsup dribbled down her chin.

"What word? And I'm warning you, I'm prepared to inflict bodily harm."

"Throttle. That's what really happened to the girl. She was strangled to death. Asphyxiated, according to the death certificate."

"What girl? What murder?"

"Not murder necessarily" was Sheila's maddening reply. "Could have been kinky sex. Some guys get off on that, you know. Trussing a woman up. She was just a political volunteer—an aide to Haas. No one knows for sure how she ended up in his room. At least that's what the newspaper article said."

"What hotel? When? Sheila, I'm warning you . . ."

"The Savoy. In midtown. The night of Magnus's big fund-raising party for his mayoral thing. Someone clearly tried to squash the story, but leave it to the *New York Post* to get the gory details." Sheila reached into her shoulder bag and pulled out two yellowing pieces of paper. And there, reproduced in grainy sixty-five-line screen was the picture of Haas, Magnus, and Jason at the party, under a caption that read: "FOUL PLAY AT FUND-RAISER?" Cassie scanned the brief write-up which said, in slightly more lurid language, what Sheila had already told her, except that the story reported the girl had died of an overdose of cocaine. Sheila unfolded the other piece of paper and pushed it across the table.

"In some ways, this is the more interesting piece of evidence," she said. "It's the poor kid's death certificate. But see that—official seal of the Manhattan coroner's office? Copies wouldn't have that. And why is this cause of death different from the one the papers carried? Also, tell me what the original's been doing in Senator Haas's private files all these years?"

Twenty-nine

𝒞assie waited until they were dancing, until Magnus's arms were around her, until he could not walk away or show anger without publicly calling attention to himself. Then she asked sweetly, smiling at him, "So you really wanted to move in here?" She glanced beyond him at Gracie Mansion's rather drearily formal decor. "Seems a bit stuffy to me." She could feel him stiffen, but his expression did not change from the look of studied indifference he'd worn all night. He'd seemed distracted from the moment he'd first met her; as he helped her into the backseat of the limousine, his touch was clammy and cold. It wasn't until he failed to mention, as he had in the past, how lovely she looked—and even she had to admit that the metallic lace Mary McFadden sheath clung to her slim body with alluring grace—that she knew something was wrong. They'd driven to the party in near silence.

"A folly of my youth," he replied. "Not a subject I relish, Cassie. I thought I made that clear."

"I'm sorry. It's just, I guess, because we're here. I couldn't help but wonder about it."

"And what excuse do you have for bringing it up with Haas the other night?" he demanded. Magnus was a superbly accomplished dancer. People stepped back and smiled at the stunning couple—she, tall, blond, shimmering with youth; he, as elegantly handsome as an older Cary Grant—as they moved together with such unstudied perfection.

"Excuse?" Cassie laughed. "Why should I need one? I was just curious about the whole thing, especially when I noticed the other day—when we were shooting at Haas's place in Brooklyn—that he'd taken the picture down—the one of you, Haas, and Jason together at the hotel."

"I'd asked him to."

"But why? What's the big deal?"

"Why all this damned interest in a subject I've made clear to you is painful for me?"

"I'm sorry, Vance," Cassie said gently. "I guess that's why I can't help but be curious. You're so much in control all the time. So seemingly impervious to sudden emotions. I—"

"Please, enough." It was a command. The orchestra segued from "Something Foolish" to "Moon River."

They did not speak for several minutes.

"It was probably the one thing in my adult life," Magnus began suddenly, "that I failed at. I thought it would be so easy. It seemed to make so much sense. At that time, in the early seventies, the city was in such a shambles economically, and I was, after all, a businessman. I thought I'd just step in—a white knight—and save the masses from self-destruction. It's difficult to admit that I just didn't seem to have the necessary common touch. I was—I remember distinctly what the p.r. firm I hired finally told me—'too patrician.' "

"But from what I understand, you threw in the towel before the primary really started."

"From whom do you understand these things?"

"Just background we've been doing on Haas." The orchestra broke for fifteen minutes, and Magnus introduced Cassie to the Mayor and his wife, a State Supreme Court judge, the Manhattan Borough President, as well as numerous business leaders and their wives, all of whom appeared to be close friends of Magnus.

"Vance, darling, you're looking wonderful."

"Tennis Thursday, Magnus?"

"Are you going to the Metropolitan gala next week, Vance? We're having a little dinner after. Bring your lovely new friend."

"Do you know every important person in this city?" Cassie teased him when the music began again.

"No," he said, pulling her lightly into his arms. "They know me."

Somewhere in the back of Cassie's mind, she knew the question would arise eventually, but she was still not quite prepared for Magnus's invitation when he said as the party was breaking up, "It's early. Let's go back to my place for a nightcap, shall we?"

He took her silence for assent, and they rode back through the leafy darkness of Central Park hardly speaking. His hand brushed hers once—a seeming accident—but he could detect no clear physical response from her. Had he ever? he wondered as he unlocked the door to his apartment. His housekeeper had left a few lights on in the foyer. Beyond, the reflected lights of the city cast the huge living room in a slightly eerie dark red glow.

Odd, he thought, that he should at that moment find himself missing Miranda. He hadn't thought of her much recently; in truth, he imagined that he'd almost gotten over her. Cassie and she were so similar in many ways that it had been fairly easy to replace one obsession—one sister—with another. But then in other respects it was becoming clear to Magnus that Cassie was different. She was more subtle, more elusive, her sensual nature far more refined. Miranda had grabbed for what she wanted, whether it was success or sex. Cassie seemed content to let it come to her. He'd practically had to thrust the idea of hosting *Breaking News* upon her. And she didn't seem at all aware that she owed him for it. Of course, he had said they would take their time, let it ride, but no experienced woman could possibly expect to be given so much—without giving back.

Miranda would have known that.

"Drink?" She was standing at the window looking out over the dark rectangle of Central Park. He put his arms around her waist.

"No," she said, attempting to move away, but he didn't loosen his grip this time. He was suddenly irritated by her evasions, her delicately phrased refusals.

"I'm tired, Vance," she said softly when he didn't release her. "I think I should go."

"I'm tired, too," he said, "of you keeping me at arm's length. Give me a chance." He pulled her to him and pressed his lips against her temple. "Please, Cassie."

"I'm not ready. I really don't—"

His lips closed over hers, cutting off her words, her breath. His arms locked around her waist, rocking her against him. He could feel his erection swelling, his need growing with it. He had been dreaming about this moment for weeks now, running the scene over and over again in his imagination. Then tonight, when he picked her up and saw how beautiful she looked in the silver sheath he'd bought for Miranda— he knew that it was ridiculous for him to wait any longer. It was his right.

"Don't." She was trying to pull herself free, turning her head away. A spoiled child. An ungrateful woman. He pushed her up against the wall of glass, trying to hold her steady, his desire mounting. Miranda had sometimes liked to struggle like this, pretending to be his victim. It was all a game, of course, but it had helped arouse his sometimes flagging energies, as Cassie's clenched teeth and tensed body were doing now. He would pry her mouth open, if necessary. Pull her arms away from her chest. Force his knee in between her tightened legs.

"No!" She was thrashing around now, panicked. A manicured hand flailed out, found his cheek, ripped into flesh.

"Christ." He let her go, stepping back. There was blood on his fingers after he touched the ugly scratch on the side of his face. It would show in the morning. Anger flushed his skin. "That wasn't necessary."

"I think it was. I'm going now." She was turning as she spoke, stumbling in her high heels and skintight dress as she attempted to run across the living room. Stupid woman, Magnus told himself as the front door slammed, not to realize that she wasn't really going anywhere without him.

Idiot, she told herself, once out on the street. She'd left her evening bag in Magnus's apartment. She'd have to walk the nearly thirty blocks home. The September evening that had begun almost balmy had grown damp and chill. A wind worked the first leaves loose from the trees lining Central Park South. She hugged her bare arms and walked faster. Almost halfway there, one of her heels broke and she had to take off both shoes and continue without them, the damp cobblestone sidewalk along the park soaking her feet and shredding her panty hose.

A light was still on in the library, the television on low, its images flickering down the corridor. She started to climb the stairs quietly. Suddenly the television clicked off. "Cassie. Is that you?"

She waited on the stairs, keeping within the wall's shadow. "Yes. I just got in. I'm going up."

"Do you have a minute? There's something I wanted to say."

"Okay." She turned to face him, hiding the broken heels behind her back.

"Won't you come down?" She was worried he would ask questions, demand an explanation for her ruined shoes and stockings—but he seemed preoccupied with his own concerns. She followed him into the room. He leaned over and picked up a slim, handsomely wrapped package from one of the coffee tables.

"I didn't realize you'd be back so late," he said, holding the package out toward her. "Heather waited up as long as she could, but I finally had to send her to bed."

Then she remembered. Today had been her birthday. "Thank you," she said, reaching for the gift.

"Go ahead. Open it up. It's something I've been meaning to do for a long time now."

It was Cassie's graduation picture mounted in a beautiful antique silver frame.

"It's lovely," she said, looking down at the familiar faces encased behind the glass. Miranda, looking slightly bored, stared back up at her. She thought of her sister taping the disk to the back of this photograph—and of all the lies and fears that had resulted in Cassie finding it. The incident with Magnus had disturbed her more than she realized. She was tired. She wanted the ordeal to end. And then, meeting Jason's look, she knew what she really wanted: she wanted him to hold her again.

"What is it?" he asked. "What happened to you?" He'd noticed her torn stockings. He moved toward her.

"Stupid me," she replied hurriedly, stepping back. "I broke a heel on my way home." She held the shoe up in front of her. He took it from her, grasping her free hand in his.

"Look at your feet. They're bleeding." He led her to the couch and forced her to sit beside him. "Why the hell didn't you phone?"

"I left my bag—" She stopped, uncertain just how much she should reveal about the evening. That she'd gone back to Magnus's apartment with him alone? That he'd forced himself on her? She realized suddenly how naive she'd been not to realize Magnus's intentions in the first place. She'd been blind to the danger because she was so little drawn to the man physically. In the past when Magnus had kissed her, she felt only mild distaste. Tonight she had felt revulsion.

"You were with Vance?"

"Yes."

"Are you in love with him?"

"It's not—"

"I know it's not my business," he interrupted her before she could finish, taking both her hands in his. He looked down at their entwined fingers as he said, "I don't expect you to accept the fact that I'm telling you this for your own good. It doesn't matter. What matters is that you listen to me and believe me when I tell you to be careful with Vance Magnus. When it comes to women—"

"I know," Cassie said, her eyes on Jason's bowed head. She longed to touch the dark hair, run her fingers down the taut, strong neck, lift his chin toward hers. As if sensing her thoughts, he looked up. He must have seen something of her feelings in her eyes; she heard his quick intake of breath. She felt her gaze on his lips, her whole body tensed with desire.

"Cassie?" It was a question that she knew she wasn't ready to answer, though the need to give herself over to this man raged within her, warring against her doubts.

"I'm sorry, Jason," she said at last, pulling her hands free and standing up. She felt dizzy with regret. But for his sake as well as hers, she knew she could never again give him her heart until she could give him her absolute trust as well.

Thirty

"I thought we could do a voice-over here," Sheila said as the image of Haas smiling and shaking hands at the Democratic Women's Caucus luncheon filled the VCR screen.

"Will it pass as a rough cut, do you think?" Cassie asked, sitting back.

"It has to. Magnus told Mac he wanted to see something tomorrow morning, latest."

"Why the sudden rush?"

"It is almost October, Cassie. The election is hardly more than a month away. If this thing is going to have any positive impact, it's got to air pretty damn soon."

"I know that. I just wondered if somehow Haas found out that you—"

"Have the papers? If he did, wouldn't he—or one of his little henchmen—attempt to contact me? I think he'd try some more radical methods than asking for a green light on our segment."

"You're right." Cassie stood up, straightened, and started to move around the small editing room. "I'm just feeling . . . watched somehow. Under suspicion. Haas, Jason, Magnus—I've been asking too many uncomfortable questions."

"I know what you mean. And we still only have part of the answer."

231

"We need more. Damn, I wish I'd had the presence of mind the other night to poke around Magnus's apartment."

"Actually, I've still got my keys. And I know where to look for his files. In his bedroom, of course, where only us harmless bimbos are allowed."

"What are you talking about? Breaking in? What if he finds you?"

"I declare my undying love. Prostrate myself on his leopard-print bedspread. Don't worry, I have my ways. The doorman still knows me. It'll look like Magnus is just fooling around with me again. Piece of cake."

"You still care about him."

"That sounds like an accusation somehow. One I could make about you as well. You're still stuck on Jason. A part of you wants anyone but him to be guilty, even though he holds all the bad cards: motive, access, zip for an alibi."

"He was home asleep."

"All night? Unless someone was standing over him watching him snore, I say he could be anywhere. At least Magnus and Haas were both busy early in the evening. Magnus at the theater, Haas drinking with some friends."

"Either one could have made it out to East Hampton in two hours if he had to. Or had someone tinker with Miranda's car. Arranged the accident."

"More likely the latter. Which makes me think it's time we picked up those papers Miranda mentioned at her summer place."

"It's long past time I went out there," Cassie admitted. "It's the one place I've been avoiding. But you're right. Without the hard evidence, we only have Miranda's allegations on the disk."

The next morning the executive screening room was standing room only. Senator Haas and Vance Magnus sat in the front row, flanked by their senior staffers. The *Breaking News* team and lesser members from the Senator's office filled the remaining rows of the small, plushly decorated

semicircular auditorium. It was the first time Cassie had
seen Magnus since she'd fled his apartment the previous
Saturday night, and though he nodded to her as he walked
past, there was no warmth in his smile. After everyone was
seated, Mac rose and stood uncomfortably on the stage.

"What you're going to see is what we call a rough cut.
All the basic pieces are here, but we've still a lot of editing
ahead of us. That's not to apologize for what Cassie and
Sheila and their people have done. I'm very pleased, every-
thing considered, with how 'Haas on the Run' has come out.
So, thanks for coming. Relax. Here we go. Lights . . ."

It wasn't half bad, Magnus told himself, as he sat in the
dark, fingering the faint scratch marks on his cheeks. Though
the skin had nearly healed, the anger he felt was still red and
raw. But as he watched Cassie at work on the screen—can-
didly questioning Haas in his office, interviewing friends and
enemies alike—he grudgingly had to admit that she'd done a
good job. Exactly what he had and Haas had wanted. Though
Cassie's questions sounded tough—"We've all read these
allegations about illegal campaign contributions, Senator"
or "There are rumors, sir, that you have a problem with
alcohol"—Haas had been brilliantly prepped on how to
handle his responses.

"It's true, Cassie. And I'm going to admit it here on
Breaking News for the first time. I've come to realize that
over the years my enjoyment of drinking has become, well,
something of a bad habit. Unfortunately it's an easy trap for
those of us in public life to fall into. You've been traveling
with me these last few weeks, and I hope you now realize
how much of what I do involves banquets, dinners, formal
luncheons . . ."

Adeptly, the interview allowed Haas to turn the taint of
scandal into heartfelt confession.

"I'm not embarrassed to say that I'm seeking help. I hope
that my example can inspire the hundreds of thousands of
people like myself—who wake up one morning and realize that something that once was a pleasure has become

a dependency—to find the courage they need to reclaim their lives."

By the end of the segment, when Cassie turned from the gallery of photographs in Haas's study to face the camera, Magnus felt his last reserve of bitterness give way. As all-American as Jane Pauley, as sophisticated and articulate as Diane Sawyer, and yet thoroughly her own person, Cassie's closing remarks were delivered with the finesse of a consummate pro.

"No, Anthony Haas is not a young man. He's not a perfect man. He's been in the front ranks of our political battlegrounds longer than I—and most of you—have been alive. Many say that he's fighting now for his political survival. That's nothing new. Anthony Haas has always been a fighter, whether it be for civil rights or his own sobriety. A seasoned politician. An experienced legislator. And one of our last truly committed political warriors. Anthony Haas. Thank you . . . and good night from *Breaking News*."

"Great, just great." Haas pumped Cassie's hand after the lights came up and the group began to disperse. His flushed face glowed with relief.

"Excellent work," Geoffrey Mellon said next. "I want to thank you . . . and apologize."

"For what?" Cassie asked, looking over his shoulder for Magnus and spotting him at last near the door, deep in conversation with Mac.

"My doubts about you. Your perspective. I had this bizarre idea that you were really in the muckraking business. Using the piece as an excuse to dig up dirt on Haas."

"That wasn't my assignment, Geoffrey. But just out of curiosity—if it was, would I have found anything?"

"Political ground rule number one: know which questions to answer," he replied, squeezing her elbow as he turned away, "and which to pretend you just didn't hear. Senator, sir, we'll have to hurry to make that meeting at *Business Week*."

"Cassie." Magnus held out both hands as she approached. Mac, standing to his left, beamed at her like a proud father. "It was better than I ever hoped. Congratulations." His smile was so affectionate and his expression—an eyebrow cocked at a questioning slant—so apologetic that Cassie couldn't help but wonder if she'd overreacted to his advances after the Mayor's party. As if reading her thoughts, he touched his cheek which still carried faint traces of her fingernail tracks; his smile deepened.

"Thanks," she said, blushing. "But again, I hardly did this single-handedly. Sheila, Harvey, Cal—they were all terrific."

"And they'll all be be properly thanked," Mac assured her, "by being named a permanent part of the new team."

"New team?" Cassie asked, looking from Mac to Magnus.

"The press release will go out with the announcement of the air date for 'Haas on the Run,' " Mac replied. "The screening this morning made it clear beyond a shadow of a doubt. Cassie, you're going to be the new host of *Breaking News*."

"But . . ." She searched Magnus's gaze but could not get beyond his neutral, pleased expression.

"No buts, my dear," he said, holding out his hand again. "It's yours. No strings—or anything else—attached."

A week later Cassie rented a car at a midtown garage. "Just for one day," she said, filling out the rental form. "I'll have it back this time tomorrow."

"Aren't you what's her name? Miranda Darin's sister?"

"Yes," Cassie said, smiling. It was not unusual for people to stop her on the street these days, asking the same question. The press release of her new appointment as host of *Breaking News* had made a local splash; she'd been on two talk shows and done numerous press interviews. All the attention had been exciting—and diverting. It had taken her several days to face the fact that it was probably all in vain. One or more of the three most important men in her life had been instrumental in ending Miranda's. And once the truth was known about how Miranda died, it was not at all unlikely, as far as Cassie was concerned, that Cassie's career would end with it.

"But that's absurd," Sheila had responded when Cassie told her how she felt. "Whomever we nail, it's going to be big news. Front page stuff. A truly to-die-for trial. It's going to put you over the top. Not that you need any more pushing."

"I don't think I'll have the stomach for it," she replied, turning away.

"That's ridiculous. We've gotten this far. We're almost there. Friday night, when Magnus is at the ballet, I'll check out his apartment. You'll do the Hamptons and pick up the rest of the evidence. Like we discussed, Monday morning we visit the D.A.'s office and show them what we've got. We're so close."

Now, as the traffic began to thin out along the Long Island Expressway, Cassie faced what was really bothering her. It wasn't that they would soon have enough evidence to take to the authorities; it was whom the material seemed to indict. The more she puzzled through what she knew of the circumstances surrounding Miranda's death, the more positive she became. Haas, just a social friend, had no motive. Magnus, Miranda's lover and boss, only lost by her death. That left Jason. Bitter and angry Jason who had admitted openly to her that the marriage had been in trouble. And it was easy enough now to guess what had pushed him over the edge.

Miranda had discovered, just as Cassie and Sheila had done after her, the link that bound Magnus, Jason, and Haas: the death of a girl more than twenty years before in a midtown hotel owned by Darin Associates. The death had quickly melted out of the news, followed by all talk of "Magnus for Mayor." A month later the hotel had been sold. Though the murder was never solved, it had lost none of its meaning for the three men most closely involved. Haas had kept the original death certificate in order to blackmail both Jason and Magnus. A thoroughly ugly business, one the guilty parties tried hard to keep buried in the past. But one that Miranda had forced back into the harsh light of the present.

"Why are you doing this?" Jason had demanded the last night Cassie saw Miranda alive. "The girl meant nothing. Why do you want to ruin me?"

Jason. As always when Cassie had a moment to herself, she thought of him. He'd been so obviously pleased for her when he heard about her promotion at Magnus that her heart had leapt with secret joy.

"I'm proud of you, Cassie," he'd said the morning after the screening when she told him her news. He was heading out to the office when she'd stopped him in the foyer, and he put his overstuffed briefcase on the floor as though he meant to free up his arms for something. Her, perhaps? she wondered as they stood a few feet apart. But so much more divided them than the short stretch of carpet and marble that Cassie suddenly felt the essential shallowness of her new position. She felt the need—one she'd promised herself to resist—to break down the barriers that kept her from Jason. To demand the truth.

"For someone who's doing so well," Jason said with his down-turning smile, "I must say you don't look very happy."

"Jason . . ." She tried to stop herself, but he took a step toward her and said with real concern, "What is it, Cassie? What's wrong?"

"Just a funny thing Sheila—you know, my producer on the Haas piece—came upon recently," she replied, taking the plunge. "Involving you."

"Yes?"

"And Magnus. The year he ran for mayor. And you supported him?"

"Yes? What of it?" His voice had lost all its earlier warmth.

"What happened?"

"I don't know what you mean. Magnus made a run for mayor. He got cold feet. Pulled out."

"But why?"

"Ask him."

"I did. It's not a subject he likes any more than you do," Cassie replied. "Why is that? I wonder."

He looked tired, worn down by fatigue though the day had just began. "I'm late," he told her. "I've got to go."

"Was it that girl who was killed at your hotel?" Cassie demanded, her voice sounding overly loud, shrill. For the first time in months, she felt Miranda's presence nearby, listening, smiling. She sensed Jason felt it, too. He turned abruptly, starting for the door, but she grabbed his arm.

"Tell me the truth, Jason!"

"You don't want the truth any more than Miranda did." Jason jerked his elbow free.

"Yes," she tried to tell him, "yes, I do." But he was gone, the door slamming shut behind him.

In the week since, they'd hardly spoken, greeting each other with curt nods, allowing the anger and pain to simmer. When she told him that morning that she'd be spending the night with a friend, he hadn't even looked up from the paper.

"Fine," he said. "Have fun." But there was little to enjoy in the long gray drive across Long Island. By the time she reached East Hampton the sun was a fiery red glow along the horizon that melted—all at once, within seconds—behind a long stand of scruffy pines. The Indian summer warmth went with it as an ocean breeze picked up. The summer resort towns seemed deserted on that mid-October evening. Local restaurants had already closed for the off-season. Cassie stopped at a gas station to ask directions to the house.

"Darin place?" The attendant leaned into the car, studying Cassie's face. "It's been closed up for months now."

"I know. Can you just tell me how to get there?"

"Sure thing, ma'am," the boy agreed, pointing down the highway and explaining the fastest route. "But be careful now. The house is way the hell off by itself, you know."

As Cassie took the ocean drive, the salty nostalgic smell of the sea filled the car. It was pitch-black by the time she pulled up alongside the closed double gates of the house. As she opened the door, she heard the roar of surf and a soulful, clanging sound: just the noise of a distant buoy, Cassie assured herself, though it seemed to be ringing out an urgent, unreadable warning.

Thirty-one

The gate was locked, the property walled off from the road by a tall picket fence, edged by boxwoods. Though she had keys to the main house and guest cabanas, Cassie knew the security system at the main entrance gate was wired to the police station in town, and she didn't want to alert anyone to her visit. As she started to walk down the deserted lane looking for another way in, her heels kept sinking into the sandy shoulder. She finally took her shoes off and pulled her light linen jacket closer. When she'd dressed for work that morning, the temperature had been in the seventies, the city stifling under the unexpected humidity of a late Indian summer. But, just three hours out of Manhattan, East Hampton was already deep into the fall season. Half the tree limbs were bare; the fallen leaves crunched beneath Cassie's feet as she walked. The fence seemed to go on forever, an anonymous wall of naturally bleached wood designed to keep out day-trippers from the city. Cassie had seen photographs of the house; if viewed from the street, it was the kind of modern palatial concoction that would have sightseers stopping, pointing, and taking photographs.

Two summers before, the estate had been featured in a four-page glossy spread in the *New York Times* Sunday magazine. Someone on the Raleigh paper had pointed the article out to Cassie, saying: "Not bad for a seaside shack. Do the guest bedrooms come with their own saunas and whirlpools? If so, feel free to invite me along next time you go."

As usual, Cassie pretended to be a lot closer to Miranda than she really was and acted as if she already knew all about the article, though she eagerly devoured each word of the piece. The four-color photographs had shown a luncheon party in progress: a perfectly tanned Miranda, dressed all in white, mingling with elegant-looking guests on an enormous front deck. White-jacketed waiters carried trays of frosty champagne cocktails. A table, set up beneath a striped awning on the beach, was piled high with a smorgasbord of chilled shrimp, dilled potato salad, wedges of avocado and mango, thin slices of dark grainy bread, an enormous crystal bowl of fresh strawberries, melon, and local blueberries. In the interview accompanying the photographs, Miranda had spoken of her desire to live simply and entertain casually in the summer.

"It's so important to get back to nature. Feel the sun on your face. Breathe in this wonderful, restorative salt air." Her words had been set in italics next to a photograph of her in a filmy peach-colored swimsuit coverup holding a pair of shiny gold sandals.

The wind was picking up off the ocean by the time Cassie finally reached the end of the wooden fence; a lower barbed-wire fence joined it, threading inland along the property line. The land adjoining was undeveloped, running for several miles along the coastline, a silent stretch of rolling dunes and sea grass, crisscrossed by sandy paths. From there Cassie finally had a full view of the sea—the white flank of beach, the slow army of breakers, a new moon cocked precariously above a growing embankment of clouds.

She followed the barbed wire for several yards until she found a spot where it was low and loose enough to dig beneath the sandy bank and crawl under it. The grass on the other side was close-cropped and durable, an imported, carefully rolled natural carpet that, like the grounds themselves, Cassie knew cost thousands of dollars every year to maintain.

"You could sell it, Cassie," Jason had told her when they were still lovers and she had first gone over the long list of properties, paintings, furniture, antiques, and clothing that she had inherited from Miranda's estate. "Even in today's market, I'm sure you could get a very good price." He made no bones about despising the whole Hampton social scene and Miranda's formidable role in it. Partly because of that—but also because it was where Miranda died—Cassie had avoided visiting.

"But she loved it out there," Cassie had replied. "It wouldn't feel right to get rid of it yet. I'll just hold on to it for now . . . and see." But what she'd seen in upkeep bills—the cost of the gardening services alone was more than what she had earned every month on the *Raleigh News and Observer*—made her aware that the "natural life" Miranda enjoyed in the summer came with a very steep price tag.

As Cassie started up the beautifully manicured lawn to the enormous darkened structure looming on the hill, she was reminded of the other reason she could not possibly sell any of Miranda's possessions. Nothing that Miranda had left her—from the tiniest earrings to this multimillion-dollar compound—felt as if it truly belonged to Cassie.

Yes, she gladly wore Miranda's clothes, rode in her Mercedes, and slept in her Porthault-covered bed. But despite the fact that all these things were now legally Cassie's entitlements, in her heart she knew they were still her sister's. In many ways she felt as though she had simply been dressing up in Miranda's belongings the last few months. Pretending to be someone else. Someone far more glamorous and talented and desirable than Cassie Hartley would ever be. And though she had been able to fool so many people—Jason, Magnus, and Haas among them—she knew the truth. She was still Miranda Darin's somewhat shy, not particularly ambitious, easily intimidated younger half sister. As she approached Miranda's towering, oddly angled glass-and-bleached-wood home, Cassie told herself that she would always be what she literally was now: on the outside looking in.

The thin moonlight turned the ground-floor windows into dark mirrors, reflecting the carefully groomed shrub borders and gardens, tennis courts, and pool area. Then, seeing something moving across one of the lower windows, Cassie stopped, her heart racing. The image stopped, too, and she realized that it was herself, a hazy white figure frozen against a nearly black background of lawn and trees.

The pool itself was covered with a tarpaulin, though the surrounding garden of geraniums and ivy was still flourishing. Antique white cast-iron benches and tables ringed the perimeter. Cassie remembered the setting from the *Times* piece: the tables topped with pretty green-striped umbrellas, the long rectangular pool ashimmer with clear, deep aqua water, the enormous sloping lawn with its panoramic view of the sea.

"I stock a lot of the Long Island wines," Miranda had said in the magazine article. "They're very light and fresh-tasting, and I think it's important to try to support the local merchants, don't you? Though we have our share of the serious French vintages, we do try to keep it fairly simple. We've a little cellar in the basement of the pool house over there."

It was a simple white one-story wooden structure with opaque glass windows topped by an antique weather vane in the shape of a sea gull. As Cassie found the keys to the double padlocked door, she thought she heard the noise of an approaching automobile. She stopped, the key still in the lock, and listened. Where would a car be going at this hour? The road dead-ended less than a quarter mile after the entrance gate to the house. But whatever Cassie might have heard, the sound now blended subtly into the other night noises—the rustle of trees, the roar of the distant surf, the overhead creak of the weather vane—and after a second or two she turned back to the door and was shortly rewarded by the lock snapping open. She grasped the cool aluminum of the door handle, turned, and pushed the door in.

It had been a long time since he had felt this way: the white heat of rage pounding at his temples. He looked down at his clenched fists on the wheel and at first hardly recognized them as his own. His knuckles were so bloodless and knobby they looked like some animal carcass, something dead and discarded. Slowly he forced his right hand, then his left, open. He shook each one, working to get the circulation going. He wished that he could do the same with the tight ball in his stomach. He felt sick, feverish. He had been so sure that it was all behind him now.

Of course, as soon as he learned what had happened, where Cassie was going, he knew he would have to follow her. Stop her. What a pity she'd gotten involved. A damn senseless shame. He'd tried to keep her out of this. Tried to make her see that it wasn't in her best interests to pursue the matter. He should have known immediately, when the Haas business started. But he'd so wanted to believe that it was all over, finished and forgotten, that he'd allowed himself to believe what she'd told him.

Fool. His head ached. He tried not to think about the extent of her subterfuge; he tried to concentrate on the immediate situation and how he was going to resolve it. But her face kept swimming toward him: so open, so sweet, so willing to please. How could he have misread her? He should have known when she turned on him—he should have realized then—but he'd been blind. He'd allowed himself to be blinded. Once again.

When it had all happened, he told himself he'd never come out here again. He'd never liked the ocean anyway—the grit of sand between the toes, the potent marshy smell of the sea. He'd only come out for Miranda. Now, as he turned off onto the beach road to the house, the salt air filled his nostrils and he felt another wave of nausea sweep through his system. He slowed and braked. He pulled off to the side of the road. His hands shook as he ran them through his hair; his temples were damp with sweat. He decided to leave the car there and walk the half mile or so up the beach. It would do him good to get some air. He needed to get a grip on himself before he had to face her. He couldn't let her see how thoroughly she'd outstripped him. How completely he'd allowed himself to fall under her seemingly benevolent spell.

Something was wrong with the light. She flicked the switch back and forth several times, but nothing happened. She should have thought to bring a flashlight, of course, but she hadn't. She had some matches in her purse, but they wouldn't do much good, especially with the wind kicking up the way it was. Whatever light the moon had offered was lost now under a thickening cloud cover. The air carried the charge of an encroaching storm. She propped the door open with a cushionless cast-iron lawn chair and slowly edged her way into the cluttered storeroom. Besides the pool equipment—skimming nets, tubs of chlorine, hoses, and filters—there were stacks of deflated rafts and inner tubes, a floating pool chair, a wire basket filled with masks and flippers, a line of fishing rods, scattered beach balls. Cassie's eyes adjusted to the lack of light, and she saw steps leading down to the cellar, barred by an elaborate wrought-iron door. It was locked, and it took her nearly ten minutes of trial and error with her key chain to find the right match of lock and key. The gate groaned as she pulled it open.

There was no railing. She felt her way downward, step by step, crouching and balancing against the wall. The air was musty and damp, far cooler than the floor above. Cassie fumbled in her shoulder bag, found the pack of matches, and lit one. It flared just long enough for Cassie to make out the hundreds of bottles—running in three neatly racked rows down the length of the small room—before it sputtered out. Miranda had said that the papers were hidden under the flagstones at the far end of the wine cellar. From where Cassie stood, that could mean one of two places. Moving by touch alone, she made her way over to one corner and pried open the loose floor stones. There was nothing beneath but firmly packed dirt. She crawled across the floor and began to lift up the stones in the other corner. They came up more easily and—even in the near pitch-blackness—Cassie could see the pale front of the manila envelope hidden beneath.

She didn't hear the steps at first. She knew the wind was strengthening, and mentally wrote off the overhead noises to the effects of the oncoming storm. But then she saw the crisscrossing beam of a flashlight at the top of the stairs. It seemed to take forever: one slow, steady step after the next. The large shape of a man finally came into view, the flashlight flicking around the room—ceiling, walls, wine racks—as if checking for damage. She held her breath, pulling herself into the corner, cradling the manila envelope in her arms. She thought for sure that the intruder would be able to hear her heart beating—its panicky drumbeat was deafening to her ears. But he didn't. He hesitated at the bottom of the steps; she could hear the light whistle of his breath. The flashlight made one last slow journey around the room, passing over her head. Missing her!

And then it flicked back, dropped to her level, and stayed there.

"Cassie, darling," Magnus said as he walked toward her, "I've been looking all over for you." He was pointing something at her. At first she thought it was the flashlight. Then she realized it was a gun.

Thirty-two

"Get up, please. You look absurd—all curled up in the corner, cowering like that."

"There's a gun pointed at my head," Cassie replied, anger giving her courage. "One tends to cower."

"I need those papers, darling, that's all. Just hand them over, then we can both go home. Have a nice long chat."

"I don't think so. Miranda left these for me."

"Ah, I see. Well then, this will take a bit longer than I'd hoped. In any case, get up, please." He held the gun in his right hand; he gestured with it toward the stairs. "You go first."

She stood shakily, clutching the envelope to her chest with both arms. He moved aside as she passed, guiding her way with the flashlight in his left hand. She hesitated at the first step, fear subsiding long enough for her to ask: "How did you know I was out here?"

"I believe, my dear, that given the situation I don't have to answer any of your questions. I also believe that when I ask for something—those papers for instance—you'd really best hand them over."

She looked from his face to the gun. She gave him the envelope.

"Now up the wooden hill."

She climbed slowly, upset to find her legs were wobbly, her heart skittering. She'd been warning herself for months now that investigating Miranda's death could be dangerous, but she'd never seriously believed it. Though ugly and illegal, it had all seemed so abstract, something that existed only on paper: a bank statement, a newspaper article, a death certificate. A gun, however, was a very real thing. And when pointed at one's back, it tended to bring a situation into crystal-clear focus.

Magnus. She'd been wrong to challenge him, foolishly asking him questions as though she still had options. He had all the say now, all the power. Quite literally, her life was in his hands. Would he kill her? Had he murdered Miranda? Suddenly the one thing she cared most about—almost as much as staying alive—was knowing the truth. At the top of the stairs, Cassie saw that the storm was upon them: the door to the pool house was slamming against its hinges, tree limbs were tossing in the wind, and leaves flew.

"It's started to rain," Cassie said, hesitating at the door. "I've the keys to the main house if you'd like to go in." She held the key chain up for him to take.

"You probably think the house has an alarm system that will alert the police," Magnus replied. "Sorry, my dear. Wrong."

She was about to tell him that she knew only the front gate was wired, but changed her mind. Let him think he'd outwitted her. "I could use a little brandy," Cassie told him. "I'm freezing."

"Why not?" Magnus said. "Keep moving, across the lawn. We'll go in through the kitchen. And we'll build a fire to warm you up." He laughed, obviously pleased with himself. "I know just what we'll burn."

He made her find the key to the kitchen door, training the flashlight on her hands, the gun on her back. She was nervous, her fingers slick with sweat, and it took several minutes.

"That a girl," he said when the door finally clicked open. "The light switch should be up on your left."

"It doesn't work," Cassie replied after several tries. "The lights in the pool house were out, too. Do you think the power lines are down because of the storm?"

"Perhaps," Magnus said. "Just as well. I don't particularly want the neighbors seeing the house all ablaze with light. Move in, down this hall, kitchen's on the left."

Did fear sharpen the senses? Despite the lack of light, Cassie found that she could see: the huge, modern kitchen gleamed with glassed-in cabinets and brushed aluminum counters. The air was heavy with the sweet smell of wealth and cleanliness: expensive wood, furniture polish, a ferny herbal bouquet fragrance overlaid with the untamable musk of the sea.

"You'll have to do the looking for us," Magnus said, flicking the flashlight around the room. "The butler's pantry is over there. I assume you'll find some candlesticks with the rest of the silver."

With Magnus following her closely, it took Cassie around five minutes to assemble fresh candles, candlesticks, and two brandy glasses.

"Liquor cabinet's in the dining room," Magnus told her when she had everything on a tray, "down that hall. You go first. And remember, I'm right behind you. Don't even think of trying anything."

"I won't," Cassie replied meekly. Magnus added a bottle of Armagnac to Cassie's tray, and then directed the way to the living room.

"How are you at building fires?" he asked as Cassie moved into the living room in front of him. The soaring cathedral ceiling was oak-beamed, the sand-blasted walls hung with Navaho blankets. The fireplace was built into the far stone wall, and Cassie started toward it.

"I was a pretty good Girl Scout," Cassie said, determined not to show her fear. She set the tray down on a cedar chest next to the fireplace, put both candlesticks on the mantelpiece, lit them, then knelt on the flagstone hearth and busied herself with arranging the kindling and newspaper on the grate. It felt good to be able to do something with her hands, despite the fact that Magnus stood over her with the gun.

"Such a charming picture," he said caustically. "So domestic, so modest. Oh, I had such high hopes for you, Cassie. Whatever possessed you to destroy such a promising career? Surely you knew that's what you'd be doing when you meddled in all this."

"She was my sister. I owed it to her to find out what had happened."

"Why? What did she ever do for you? You were nothing to her—nothing—until perhaps the very end when she thought you might be able to help her."

"You don't know that," Cassie said, surprised at how much his words could still hurt. The hope that Miranda had truly cared about her, but didn't think to show it, had always secretly sustained her.

"Yes, I do. I knew everything about Miranda. Everything. I'm a very intelligent and highly motivated man, Cassie dear, and for many years I made your sister my most serious object of study. I took a post-graduate course in Miranda Darin. I knew her inside out. And a great deal of the reason I found her so fascinating was that she was so much like me: consummately selfish."

Cassie struck a match against the flagstone, and held it to her carefully arranged bundle of papers and kindling. Fire licked along a rolled piece of newspaper, then flared. Dry branches crackled.

"You were unselfish enough to love her," Cassie said, sitting back on her heels and staring into the rapidly spreading blaze.

"Yes." Magnus sighed, uncorking the Armagnac. He poured out two glasses and put one down beside her. "You're quite right, I was. And she wasn't. What a terrible shame. Do you know—the only things Miranda ever wanted were what she didn't already have. And once she got something, it no longer mattered to her. Jason, myself, even poor little

Heather. The more we clung, the harder we held on—the less she cared. Jason was the smart one."

"How do you mean?"

"He let her go. He dropped her. Oh, he kept up appearances, for Heather's sake, I assume, but he gave her as much rope as she wanted. If only I'd thought of that, if only I'd known not . . . to hold on."

"But when you're in love with someone—it's very hard to be that rational. It's a kind of madness, don't you think?"

"Oh, yes! Yes. I was crazy. I even knew I was crazy, but I couldn't do a thing about it. And she knew it. She found it all . . . very amusing. Titillating. In the end I think I was probably nothing much more than a joke for her. A very fancy plaything. An accessory. About as important to her life as a well-made umbrella." Magnus laughed and gulped his brandy.

"Did she have a new lover?"

"No," Magnus said thoughtfully. "That's where I was so foolish. She'd clearly lost interest in me. Even the social life I'd helped create for her—she'd begun to see what I've known for years: it's fundamentally vacuous. No, darling, it wasn't anybody new. It took me such a long time to figure it out, because she pretended to loathe him so. Would say such terrible things about him, about their life together. But she spent so much time bitterly complaining about him. Hours on end, pacing my apartment. It was obsessive, almost deranged. I finally realized that the way she acted about him was very much the way I acted about her."

"She fell in love with Jason—all over again?"

Magnus looked down at Cassie with a sad smile. "You're really so naive, my dear. That's one of the things I find refreshing about you. And so different from Miranda." He sipped his Armagnac and gazed into the fire. "No, it was far more complicated than that. You see, the thing that came closest to love in Miranda's lexicon was—control. When she came up against people who resisted her, who wouldn't let her dominate or manipulate them, she couldn't stand it. She'd have people fired from the show—an editor, one of the writers—if they disagreed too vigorously with her. But she couldn't fire Jason."

"She could have divorced him."

"We talked about it. Idiotically, I urged her to. I wanted to marry her. I offered her everything. But as I said before, that wasn't what she wanted: she longed for what she couldn't have. And that was to dominate Jason—to get him back under her spell."

"But Jason himself told me that he was faithful to her, in spite of everything."

"Oh, I know, but that only made it that much worse. She had nothing substantial to hold over his head. In actuality she was the unfaithful one. But emotionally—he'd stopped loving her years before—and so she'd lost all her power over him. That's what ate into her so: she couldn't force someone to love her. So in the end, I suppose as something of a last resort, she decided she would have to destroy him."

"With the help of Senator Anthony Haas," Cassie murmured, putting a log on the fire. "How did she find out about that?"

"I told her." Cassie turned and stared up at him. He was twirling his empty snifter, seemingly entranced by the way the crystal refracted the firelight. He walked over to the cedar chest and refilled his glass, saying: "Yes, it is ironic, isn't it? I told her because I wanted her to stop obsessing about him—to see he was human, frail, like all of us. Like me. We were having dinner at the Four Seasons—it was in early January to celebrate the new year—and all she could talk about was Jason: how he'd acted the part of the model father over Christmas, how much she despised his holier-than-thou approach to their marriage. And I simply said that he might pretend to be righteous, but he'd not been above getting his hands dirty when he'd needed to. I knew from the esteemed Senator himself about the money Jason had given Haas when he was first starting out. You should have seen the gleam in her eyes—the look of near rapture on her face—when she heard this. She could talk of nothing else all evening. I realized, even then, of course, I'd made a fatal mistake."

"Because she would eventually find out about your own dealings with Haas?"

"Yes, of course," Magnus said, picking up the envelope that he'd left on the couch behind him. "She was out to hurt Jason, but she was going to hang me in the process."

"But that's what I really don't understand, Vance. Why you? Why did you need to give Haas any money? Surely you've always had enough power—and wealth of your own—to buy your own way in Washington."

"Darling girl, you really haven't been thinking this thing through at all, have you? I'm somewhat surprised, actually, that with your investigative skills you haven't come to the obvious conclusion. Miranda didn't either, but then, quite honestly, I rather think you have the sharper mind. Let's just see if these papers"—he flicked open the envelope— "might be of some help."

Thirty-three

"Ah, yes, this does bring back memories." Magnus held up a yellowing newspaper article titled "MEDIA MOGUL MAKES BID FOR MAYOR."

"Happy ones?" Cassie asked, noticing his smile. She sat cross-legged beside the fire while he leaned against the back of the couch a few feet away.

"In the beginning, quite," Magnus said. "By the early seventies, I'd been running the network for over a decade, Cassie. Those days were such a high-water mark for television, it seemed that everything I touched turned to gold: sitcoms, talk shows, sports. I, the whole network, could do no wrong. Naturally I became a bit bored. There's no fun, my dear, in always succeeding."

"So you decided to move into a more public arena?"

"Arena is the word exactly. As in Ancient Roman. And tossing good Christians to the lions. Politics is a dirty business, as I've told you before, though at first it seemed simple enough. Throw parties, pull together a platform, build a coalition. The business community liked me because I was one of their own. Thanks to Millie, I had the backing of the old money crowd. And, of course, with all my network connections, I had plenty of Broadway and Hollywood support."

"I know," Cassie said, "I read up on your bid for the nomination. It looked to me like you had everything going for you, Vance. Why did you back out . . . really?"

"I didn't back out, Cassie," he retorted, gulping his brandy. "I was pushed."

"You sound very bitter," Cassie said softly, "whatever it was. I can tell it still hurts, as though it took place yesterday."

"It hasn't stopped haunting me—in one way or another—since it happened."

"What was it, Vance? What happened?"

"Ah, but surely you've guessed?" he said, looking down at her. "I know you too well, my dear, not to realize you probably figured it out the moment you first saw me tonight. Yes, I think so."

He walked to the fire, leaned over, and threw the newspaper article in. It caught fire and disappeared in seconds.

"For one thing, you have to understand that those were such different times—socially, sexually, whatever you want to call it. These days, you order a martini at lunch and people start saying behind your back that you're an alcoholic. In those years, right after the sixties, it was 'anything goes'—and it did. Booze, drugs, sex, sex, sex—it became so routine in a way, just something you expected."

He poured himself more brandy and leaned back against the couch again, his gaze lost in the fire.

"It was the biggest fund-raiser yet. I mean everyone was there: Liza Minnelli, Frank Sinatra, Sammy Davis, Jr., put on a concert after dinner. The place was absolutely packed. Hopping. Cops up and down Broadway, just to keep people out."

"This was at the Savoy? Jason's hotel?"

"Yes. He'd opened up the ballrooms for us. He believed in what he thought I believed in. Well, he was young and foolish enough to still think he could hold on to his ideals— and survive. That night helped to cure him of that, all right. I don't remember a great deal of what happened after my speech. I'm not a terrific public speaker, I get a bit nervous, and I was so relieved when it was over that I probably drank more than I should have. Vodka, I was drinking then. I hazily remember the concert. Minnelli was stunning—those long, gorgeous legs. I remember feeling quite turned on— and then suddenly there was this girl."

"The newspapers never gave her name," Cassie said, not adding that the death certificate had.

"Felice Ruhl," Magnus said. "She was underage—that's one of the reasons the papers hushed it up—but how was I to know that then? She was an aide to Haas, after all, and looked to be in her mid-twenties, at least. I made some assumptions that I shouldn't have. She was only a volunteer, poor stupid girl, one of those wide-eyed suburban kids who was just out looking for a good time. Some action. Well, she got that, all right . . ."

Magnus looked down at the gun he was holding in his right hand as though seeing it for the first time. He turned it over slowly, the metal nozzle glinting in the firelight.

"As I said, I don't remember a whole lot. I wasn't in the greatest shape. Someone had cocaine, and after the concert we all went up to the suite that Tony had taken and did some lines. I remember ordering room service, as well. Felice wanted a Coke—'to go with her coke'—she'd said. And then . . . we were alone. I remember she'd fallen asleep on this huge king-size bed; she looked so sexy, her tight little miniskirt all bunched up around her waist, exposing those long, young legs. These big tits—just about bursting out of this skimpy halter top. I didn't rape her. She woke up, urged me on. She wasn't a virgin, by any manner or means. When I suggested a little something more innovative than the usual, she seemed interested, eager . . ."

"Innovative?"

"I sometimes indulge in a bit of bondage, Cassie dear, something I rather doubt you've ever considered. All fairly innocent, I assure you. Silk ties, bedposts, that sort of thing."

"But not so innocent here, I take it. Something went wrong."

"I don't remember exactly. I was clumsy, I suppose, or overeager. I had the tie around her neck for some reason—oh, yes, of course, it was a modern bed, no head posts. I suppose I'd become overexcited, though I don't remember the actual act. All I remember is trying to wake her."

"And she wouldn't wake."

"No, she'd . . . slipped away. If I'd been more coherent, I probably could have saved her. Mouth-to-mouth . . . something . . . but I couldn't. I guess I simply panicked. what did I do? I called someone I thought would help me. And he did. He sure did."

"Haas?"

"He was next door, in an adjoining suite, not in such great shape himself. But he pulled himself together fast when he saw what was up. He called Jason up to the suite; kept everyone else out. Just the three of us."

"And Felice?"

"Haas had already rolled her body up in a bed sheet. It was as though he did this sort·of thing every day. He told Jason that the girl had OD'd, and that we were going to have to move fast to control the damage. He said he'd arrange to have the body picked up by an unmarked van and get her to the morgue where he said he had a high-level 'friend,' if Jason could get her carried downstairs in a laundry trolley. At first Jason wanted no part of this. But then Haas made some comment about Jason's business—something about some zoning clearance he needed, and . . ."

"He caved in," Cassie said quietly.

"Actually, no," Magnus replied. "He said that Haas could go to hell, and that he was going to call the police. Haas calmly told him to do just that: call the Commissioner, why not? He and Haas were best friends. Jason just left then—looking sick at heart—and who could blame him? He was a different man after that: tougher, more careful. Never got involved in politics again. Sold that hotel the next month—

at a loss, too, I understand. Probably the only real estate Jason Darin ever lost money on."

"And the body?"

"I wheeled her down myself. Haas was as good as his word. The van was waiting at the service entrance. Next morning the papers all carried the story that the girl had overdosed on coke. But Haas showed me the real death certificate—the one he had his friend at the city morgue fix up. The true cause of death: asphyxiation. He told me that I was dropping out of the race, out of politics altogether, except when he needed my backing for his own campaigns. He also informed me that from then on he would look to me as a major financial contributor to the Anthony Haas political war chest. He made his announcement about running for the Senate less than six weeks later."

"Not exactly the enlightened liberal leader my parents so admired," Cassie murmured.

"I gave him his big break," Magnus replied. "Though he'd made something of a splash in the sixties with the Kennedys, after Camelot faded away he has never been able to find the financial backing he needed to take his show to the big stage. He'd been just another anonymous representative for nearly a decade by the time all this happened—and in the Nixon administration the liberal tag was like a millstone around his neck. With my support and advice he got what he wanted: the Senate, prestige, power. I helped shape his new platform—the liberal causes offset with a more practical pro-business attitude. I put him on the map."

"You sound almost proud—but he was blackmailing you the whole time."

"Oh, the money part was certainly distasteful," Magnus said, refilling his glass once again. Cassie noticed that the bottle was nearly empty. "But it was the first time I realized how much power I had to make somebody— transform the look, reshape the public persona. I created Senator Anthony Haas. And though he may be into me for several hundred thousand dollars—in a more important respect I control him."

"He's your monster," Cassie suggested.

"Exactly." Magnus turned to her, smiling. "As Miranda was. As you were going to be . . ."

"And what you create," Cassie said, rising uncomfortably from her cramped position on the floor, "I suppose you think you have the right to destroy."

"Now, you stay right there," Magnus warned her, raising the gun. For the first time that night he looked uncertain. He swayed slightly. "I wouldn't want to have to hurt you, darling."

"I don't see that you have a choice," Cassie said matter-of-factly. "You killed Miranda because she knew too much . . . why should I be spared?"

"I didn't kill her! I did not. It was an accident. A terrible misunderstanding."

"Like the girl in the hotel room?"

"That was an accident. I was drunk. We were all a little out of control. With Miranda . . . it was totally different."

"How was it different, Vance?" Cassie demanded, finally finding the courage to ask, "How did Miranda really die?"

"Step to the side." Magnus gestured angrily with the gun. Cassie edged away from the fireplace. "That's right. Now don't move." With his right hand he trained the gun on Cassie, with his left he crumpled the remaining papers from Miranda's folder and tossed them into the fire. They caught, flared quickly, curled into ash.

"You know, she really wasn't all that bright," he said, staring into the fire as the last piece of paper flamed. "Or else, over the years she let her ambitions and ego get the better of her intelligence. Lord, the vanity! She lived in this warped world—where everything revolved around Miranda Darin. In the end, it was more than simply being selfish. She was dangerous. Obsessive."

"About Jason, you mean?"

"She refused to let it go. I warned her. I begged her, but she didn't listen. She thought she'd pieced it all together—the Jason and Haas thing. She couldn't wait to tell me all about it—told me to meet her out here, at a little motel we used to go to in Montauk when we were lovers. We called it the shack."

Thirty-four

"*I*'ll meet you at the shack. Around eight tonight."

"But, Miranda darling, we have that black tie for the Brooklyn Botanical Gardens. We can't possibly—"

"It's important. I'm leaving Jason. I've finally figured it out. I've a story, Vance, that's going to blow this city sky-high."

"Miranda—I . . . I'll be there. At eight . . ."

It was a brutally cold night, cloudy, with a knife-sharp wind that sang beneath his tires on the highway. Just outside of Medford, it began to snow. He had to brake to a crawl to avoid skidding, the windshield wipers sloughing off the heavy, unexpected downfall. He knew he should be mentally preparing for what was ahead, what he had to tell her, but his thoughts kept getting caught up in what she had told him: "I'm leaving Jason." It kept going around and around in his brain, like a jingle. It picked up the rhythms of the windshield wipers. By the time he got to the motel, he was in an absurd state of hope and anticipation. It had been months since they'd been there together, weeks since she'd allowed him to touch her, and the thought of seeing her again in one of the many anonymous shabby rooms where they'd spent so many hours making love filled him with desire. He spotted her red Mercedes parked in front of a door at the far end of the complex, turned off on a

261

side road, avoiding the bright lights at the front cottage, and parked beside her car. A light was on in the room.

"The door's open," she called.

"Sorry I'm late," he said, "but this damned snow." He found it hard to breathe. She was curled up on the double bed, legs tucked beneath her, her thick glossy hair loose around her shoulders. She was wearing the deceptively simple-looking sports clothes of the very rich: a beige cashmere sweater, amber-colored tights tailored to her long fine legs, a belt of woven leather with a gold buckle. She'd kicked her shoes off, and they lay like obedient pets at the foot of the bed. Even from the door he could smell her perfume—not that it was strong, just that it was so fine and penetrating that it instantly took control of the room. Just as she did. She smiled and put the dog-eared copy of Reader's Digest that she'd been flipping through back on the chipped bedside table.

"Thanks for coming all the way out. I just needed to get away. From him, that house!"

"What's happened?" He pulled his coat off, draped it over a chair, sat next to her on the bed. He was careful not to make the first move though he longed—with an ache that dug into his very marrow—to take her in his arms.

Then she said it again, "I'm leaving Jason."

"Oh, darling, that's wonderful!" He couldn't help it. He fumbled for her hands.

"We had a dreadful fight." She pulled away, swung her legs over the far side of the bed, and got up. She moved around the room, picking things up—an ashtray, a conch shell—and putting them down as she talked. "I found out about the girl, Vance. The one at the Savoy—when you were running for mayor—who supposedly OD'd? Well, she didn't. She was murdered." She turned to look at him, her eyes bright with excitement. When he didn't say anything, she went on in a rush.

"Don't you see? That's the real reason Jason's paying

off Haas! Jason did it, and Haas was there. He fixed the death certificate. He kept the newspapers at bay. Managed a whole cover-up number."

"I was there, too, Miranda, you know. Perhaps I was the one who killed the girl."

"You?" She started to laugh. "I don't think so, darling. You're far too civilized and well behaved. No, it was Jason. You don't know him the way I do. He has these dark, intense periods—when he'll hardly talk to me. His looks alone can kill."

"Perhaps you drive him to it," he said, rising slowly from the bed. It was absurd for him to be angry that she had it wrong. Ridiculous to be hurt that she doubted his nerve, the animal side of his nature. Jason! Of course she would think of him first—assume it was he. The main protagonist in the ongoing drama that was Miranda Darin's life. While Magnus played a two-bit role. Best supporting actor. Too civilized and well behaved. His head ached at the temples, throbbing with rage.

"No it was him." Miranda turned to the window, pushed the curtain aside. The blizzard continued—the huge wet flakes twirling every which way, like fake snow inside a paperweight. "He's been hiding something about Haas from the moment we met. He'll never talk about the man, refuses to even have his name mentioned in front of him. Practically foams at the mouth when I put Haas on invitation lists. Actually that's one of the reasons I continue to socialize with the old sot—because Jason despises him so."

"I sometimes wonder, Miranda, if that's why you continue to socialize with me."

"Lord, you should have been there tonight when I confronted him with the Savoy business. I've never seen him like that. Totally out of control. I really thought he was going to hit me."

"Did he deny it? When you accused him of killing the girl?"

"Of course! What was he going to do—stand there and

thank me for finally uncovering what he's been hiding from for twenty years?"

"He didn't accuse anyone else?"

"No, he was too interested in trying to convince me to drop the whole story. Drop it! This piece is going to make history, Vance. Just think about it, darling—me exposing my husband and Senator Anthony Haas on national prime-time television."

"You may accuse," Magnus said, coming up to stand behind her at the window, "but you won't be able to convict."

"Don't be absurd, I know that," Miranda said, turning to face him. "The jury will do that—after I'm through with them."

"No, Miranda," Magnus said. His hands curled around her shoulders. "I'm afraid you're not going to be able to do the story as planned."

"Of course I will," she snapped, irritably trying to shrug off his grip. But he held her tightly. "Do let go, Vance. I'm afraid I'm not in the mood tonight."

"I killed that girl," he said. "Felice Ruhl. It was me, Miranda. I killed her."

"Honestly, darling, you're being ridiculous," she replied, though she had stopped laughing. "And you're hurting me."

"You thought I was too civilized to hurt anyone, Miranda. But I'm not, am I? I'm just as much a man as Jason, you know. But you've never really given me a chance to prove it. It's always Jason, Jason, Jason. You fool. You stupid, silly woman. I loved you. I've made you. I would have done anything for you. Anything. And what have you done in return? You've humiliated me, walked all over me. But I can't . . . I'm sorry . . . I can't." He didn't realize he was crying until he felt the tears running down his cheeks. "I can't let you ruin me."

"Don't . . . please . . . please . . ." How long had his hands been at her neck? He didn't know. It had seemed like seconds, and yet she'd gone limp in his grasp, her eyes *rolling up beneath her lids. One second she was alive, and the next—*

"Miranda!" He knelt beside her body, fumbling for her now lifeless hand. Where was the pulse? He leaned over and laid his head against her chest. Her breasts were still warm, but she was dead. He knew as soon as he looked again at her face—she was gone. Her neck was bruised and swollen. Her eyelids were half open. He sat back on his knees. He stared at her for a long time, trying to face what had happened. What he had done. He had loved her more than any other woman he had ever known, almost as much as life itself. He would never have willingly killed her—she had forced him to do so. Because one way or another, what she had discovered about the Savoy would have destroyed him. And that was the only sacrifice he was not willing to make for her.

Magnus had always been a meticulous and highly organized man. Once he'd come to terms with the situation, it did not take him long to figure out what had to be done. He scoured the room, wiping off anything he might have touched. When he was sure that he'd left no trace of himself behind, he turned out the lights. He waited in the dark until his eyes had thoroughly adjusted to the gloom, then he carried her out and put her in the backseat of her Mercedes and climbed in the front seat behind the wheel. He drove to East Hampton, stopped at a twenty-four-hour self-service station, and filled up the gas canister that she carried in the back trunk.

It was still snowing, though more faintly, as he drove back east. In all, he passed only two other cars on the highway, both proceeding slowly on the slippery stretch of road. He stopped and turned around about five miles outside of town at a deserted curve in the highway where the shoulder fell off into a sandy gulch. He got out, dragged her into the front seat, and wiped his fingerprints as best he could from the wheel and dashboard. He let go of the hand brake and pushed the car over the incline. The sandy bank helped *break the fall, and the car with her body slumped over the wheel came to a harmless stop at the bottom of the small ravine. The gasoline filled the chill air with a rank, clinical smell; he poured it over the hood and splashed it across the driver's side of the front seat. He knew that to be sure he should probably wet her down with it as well, but he couldn't bring himself to do it.*

It was hard enough lighting the match from the book he had taken from the shack. As the little flame flared in the darkness, he saw that the front of the matchbook advertised a restaurant/bar in Montauk where Miranda and he had frequently gone after their afternoon sessions at the motel. The front seat caught with the first match. He was only fifty feet away when the car exploded. The sky burned a bright orange behind him as he hurried back to the motel by way of a road that ran parallel to the highway.

His car was where he'd left it in the motel parking lot. The snow had stopped, and the night was dark and silent. A fire truck and police car, sirens wailing, passed him as he pulled up to a stop sign on his way back out of town. He could hear other sirens ahead and saw the flashing red-and-blue lights strobing the night sky before he passed the actual site of the accident.

"How dare you call it an accident?"

"That's how I think of it, darling," Magnus replied. "In so many ways, it really wasn't my fault. I loved her. I didn't want to lose her. She . . . it just happened."

"How did you feel when you drove past that car?"

"Don't be maudlin, Cassie. She was already long gone by then. I didn't feel anything except relief, I suppose. I'd managed to salvage the situation, save myself."

"And now—how do you plan to salvage the situation?"

"I've been thinking about that as we've talked," Magnus replied, kicking the dying fire with the toe of his shoe. "And I'm afraid you're right. I don't trust you to keep quiet. I admire you a great deal, my dear. I could have grown quite fond of you but I've my own welfare to consider. This sounds rather melodramatic, but frankly you know too much."

"I'm not the only one who knows."

"And by that you mean . . . what exactly?"

"Sheila Thomas. She knows everything. We've been working together."

"Oh, yes," Magnus said, laughing and nodding. "I know. Dear Sheila. She was apprehended this evening breaking and entering my apartment. Such a pity."

"What do you mean?" For the first time Cassie felt true panic surge through her.

"I was at the opera. I have a beeper alarm. I left immediately and walked back to the apartment—as you know, it's only a few blocks from Lincoln Center. I keep a gun in the closet near the entryway. Senator Haas helped me get the license as a matter of fact and—"

"Please," Cassie interrupted, "just tell me what happened."

"She was such a live wire, that one. So bright. So funloving. Well, I found her in my bedroom, going through my personal filing cabinets. I made her tell me what was going on. Where you were. She tried to explain that she was doing all this for my own good. That she loved me. She turned at one point, and I was rather afraid she was reaching for a gun. I beat her to it. I shot her in the back."

Thirty-five

"*Y*ou bastard. You're not going to get away with this."

"Yes, as a matter of fact, I am. Now, let's get moving. Keep your hands behind your back where I can see them. That's a good girl. We'll go out the way we came."

"You're crazy. You can't kill two women in one night— four altogether—without someone finding out."

"It depends on who you are. Whom you know. I've already spoken to Haas. He's so very grateful about what the network is doing for him. He'll handle the little problem with Sheila. After all, she had broken in, you know. It was dark. I might have thought it was some dangerous lunatic looking for drug money . . . I'm not really concerned."

"How are you going to explain shooting me?"

"I won't have to," Magnus said as they reached the kitchen door. "Open it up, slowly, now. That's right. Keep on going, out onto the lawn. My goodness, the storm is picking up all right."

The wind raged through the trees and shrubs, though the rain was holding off. The weather vane on top of the pool house was skittering around in circles.

"I'm right behind you, darling," Magnus said as she stumbled across the lawn. "No, not the wine cellar. We're going to take a nice long walk on the beach."

The walk wasn't nice, though it was very long and cold. The wind blew the sand into Cassie's eyes and nose and mouth; the cold took her in its grasp and shook her viciously—her teeth literally chattering against one another.

But she felt all of this from far away—as though she were watching herself perform in a badly lit home movie—while she concentrated all her thinking on the man behind her. She replayed in her imagination what Magnus had told her about Felice Ruhl's death, Miranda's final hours alive, Sheila's ill-fated venture. *Don't worry,* Sheila had assured her, *it'll look like Magnus is just fooling around with me again. Piece of cake.* Sheila, who could never bring herself to blame Magnus for anything, including breaking her heart, was now gone, too. But her death was unlike the others. Up until the moment Magnus admitted that he had shot Sheila in the back, a part of Cassie still wanted to believe that Felice's and Miranda's deaths had indeed been accidents. Fits of passion with fatal results—not truly evil. But earlier that night, Magnus had crossed over the line. He'd drawn the gun and fired, fully intent on killing. Throughout their long night together, Cassie had been afraid of Magnus because he held a gun in his hand. Now she was terrified of him because of what he was in his heart: a murderer.

Cassie lost track of how far they'd walked up the beach, how long she'd been stumbling into the wind. They were deep into the stretch of state park beach that ran for many miles between the Hamptons and Montauk when it finally started to rain.

"This will do," Magnus called out over the wind. "Stop here." Cassie turned. It was too dark to make out his features; he appeared as a looming black silhouette against a churning background of sea, beach, and sky.

"What are you going to do?" she asked, surprised that her voice sounded so steady and strong. "Shoot me and bury me in the sand? You realize that's mad, don't you?"

"I'm perfectly sane," Magnus replied. "And I've no intention of shooting you. You're going for a swim."

"I'm not. I can't swim. I'm . . . afraid of the water."

"Yes, well, that's a pity, but I've worked this all out. I'll say you've been despondent for many months since your sister's death. You have no other family, you're all alone in the world. I'll imply that you tried to step into Miranda's shoes at the network but didn't quite make the grade. I'll admit, to my deepest regret, that I'd told you just this afternoon that Miranda's job was going to someone else. Oh, you became so despondent! Finally, after months of not wanting to face the house and all its memories, you came out here alone. You had some brandy, made a fire. But finally, distraught, perhaps slightly drunk, you wandered outside. You walked down the beach. You went for a swim, right here, where unfortunately there happens to be a particularly strong undertow. My dear . . . I'm afraid you drowned."

"No." From childhood, it had been her worst fear and the source of recurring nightmares: something forcing her head beneath the water, sucking her under; the panicky struggle for breath. "I won't do it."

"I'm sorry but I don't have time for dramatics. Start walking into the surf."

"I won't."

"Cassie, I'm warning you," he cried, "I don't want to have to force you, but I will. I think you know that now."

The rain that had taken so long to arrive now pelted against the sand and churned the surf with an insistent hissing noise. Cassie turned toward the dark, turbulent surf where, as far out as she could see, whitecaps formed and crashed and formed again. Salt air and sea foam stung her eyes. She started to wade in, the first waves swirling coldly against her ankles.

She had never learned to swim, despite endless attempts at YWCA lessons. It had not helped that Miranda, fearless as always, had taken to the water as though the ocean were a second home, riding in the waves on the North Carolina shore like some sea goddess grandly surveying her domain.

Miranda had been on the swim team in high school, even helping the school win a state championship in her junior year. Cassie had never even learned to tread water.

"Come on, honey," her father had encouraged her one summer when she was six or seven and they were vacationing at Cape Hatteras. He couldn't stand seeing the rapt look of envy on his younger daughter's face as she watched her older sister play in the surf with the other children. "I'll hold your hand. We won't go out far."

Perhaps if things had gone differently that summer day, Cassie thought as she felt her knees shaking with cold, she might have had some chance against this storm-tossed night. But just as her father had led her into the surf, she'd tripped and been swept under by a sudden wave. She'd come to no harm, of course, except for a bruised elbow and a noseful of seawater, but that night she'd had her first nightmare.

Her parents, believing nature should take its course in such matters, never pressured her to try again. She thought of her parents now as the waves drenched her, as numbness began to creep up her legs. How hard they had tried to be fair, to love her and Miranda equally, to encourage each to be her own person. They had believed in the power of love, the ability of any individual to grow, change, excel. They had devoted their lives to the idea that all people are created equal—have the same rights. And they had believed that people like Senator Anthony Haas shared and struggled for the same ideals.

I can't die, Cassie told herself, *and let Haas and Magnus continue on. I have to stop them . . . have to . . .* A wave knocked her over, and she stumbled blindly in its foamy wake, her soaked skirt dragging her down until she ripped it off.

"Keep going," Magnus cried from the shore, his voice much clearer and closer than she would have thought. "Keep moving . . . now."

She regained her footing and lurched forward but also sideways hoping any movement would give Magnus the illusion that he was being obeyed. Twice more she was knocked down by incoming waves, the second time floating for several seconds before regaining her balance. She tried floating again on her own in between the breakers. She kicked. She moved her arms. Within seconds, she was swimming for the first time in her life.

"That's right, Cassie darling . . ." She thought she heard Magnus's voice above the roar of the surf, but it might have been the wind. It didn't matter anymore. She was moving outward with the current, floating above her fear. Soon, even the cold didn't bother her that much, though she knew by the strangely weighted feeling in her legs that she was probably going numb. The terror was gone.

I can't die now, she reminded herself as she felt her legs grow heavy and her arms start to burn with fatigue. *I can't because . . .* She struggled mentally to remember why she couldn't die. There was something besides the need to stop Magnus and Haas, someone . . .

Jason, I was wrong about Jason. For the first time that night she let herself think about him, and she immediately felt new energy flood into her limbs. She thought about his mouth, his smile. She thought about his voice, the strange sound of his laughter. She thought about his arms, the feel of them around her. She was wrong, as Miranda had been wrong before her. Even now Jason didn't know what had happened in that hotel room. He'd been told the girl had overdosed on drugs and—despite Haas's extortion attempt—he had refused to have anything to do with a cover-up knowing only that. And he hadn't been responsible for Miranda's death, didn't even know that it had been a murder. He was, after all, the man with whom Cassie had first fallen in love. She had been wrong, as Miranda had been wrong, not to trust him. Though she had never stopped loving him, Cassie knew now that in her own way, Miranda had never stopped loving him either.

"There's a lot going on here," Miranda had told her their last morning together, "that you know nothing about." Now, at last, she knew everything. And it was too late. She tried once again to capture the memory of Jason's smile, but it was gone. A whitecap swept over her, and she swallowed water. She coughed and struggled against the current that had been carrying her out to sea. She could no longer see the beach; she no longer knew in which direction she was swimming. She was tired, so she closed her eyes.

She'd been treading water in a semidoze when a sharp clear report—like a gunshot—startled her fully awake. She thought she heard voices, and there seemed to be a light coming from her left.

"I'm here," she cried, paddling weakly toward the light. "I'm right over here." She called out again and again as she saw the lights crisscrossing in front of her. Once, she was sure she heard the distant roar of an engine. The light came and went, and the voices—or was it just the surf?—were buffeted back and forth in the wind. She kept swimming, despite her desperate feeling that the tide was pulling her farther out. She decided to close her eyes for just a second— she was so tired—but she knew as soon as she did so that she was giving up.

And then—how lovely—she was able to recall Jason's face again. The way he looked when they were making love—his eager, almost boyish smile, the slight indentations at either cheek that would, on a less formidable face, be called dimples. She wanted so to reach out and touch his lips. To tell him she was sorry, that it was all okay now, that everything was going to be fine after all . . .

"What's that—over there!"

"Just whitecaps, sir. I'm sorry, but—"

"No, look, it's something white. Where's that other searchlight?"

"He's right . . . there is something." The small inflatable dinghy bobbed dangerously in the surf, half-flooded by the roiling water and the weight of the three men. The two policemen tried to hold Jason back when they finally reached the floating body. The woman's blond hair was fanned out across the water, her pale arms lifeless.

"Don't, sir, I'm afraid it's . . ." But the man was out of the dinghy before they had the chance to restrain him, his arms around the girl, hugging her to him. With one arm grasping the plastic raft and the other bracing her against him, his mouth closed over the girl's as he worked frantically to resuscitate her.

When the dinghy finally reached the shore, the ambulance was waiting, its red light circling. Two uniformed paramedics ran down to meet them, carrying a stretcher.

Jason dragged her out of the water, his mouth still working against hers until the men pulled her roughly from his grasp.

"I'm afraid there's nothing more you can do now," one of them told him gently.

Thirty-six

$\mathcal{I}$t was a dazzling clear day. Chilly, windless, the sun so bright that it hurt Jason's eyes as he made his way from the house to the police cruiser, his boots crunching on the white gravel Miranda had insisted on importing from Italy. For the first time in nearly a year, he'd spent the night at the beach house, though by the time the police were through he hadn't gotten to bed until after three o'clock. But he'd slept soundly, as he had never been able to in the old days.

Early that morning, when he woke up and went out on the deck adjoining the master bedroom, he realized what was different. He had not dreamed about Miranda. He had been able to sleep the night in the king-size bed they had once shared without once imagining her face. Or hearing her voice. He had come back to the place where she'd felt the most at home and not found her there. The calm white sunlight filled the empty room, flashing against her many mirrors, but Miranda's ghost was gone.

He'd called the hospital, the police, and finally Heather, assuring his daughter that everything was fine. Though he wasn't at all sure of that himself. Cassie was alive. Physically she was going to be fine.

"Her mental condition is another matter," the doctor in charge of her admittance the night before had told him. "She's not coherent. We've sedated her, and we'll keep a close eye on her all night, but I have to tell you that I'm concerned. We don't know for sure how much damage she might have sustained."

The hospital had been just as noncommittal that morning when he'd called, but the head nurse had agreed to let him see her during regular visiting hours at eleven o'clock. In the meantime, the police had arrived to escort him to the station house. The local cops had been as polite as possible, but it was clear to Jason that they all felt this was the kind of ugly, complicated matter best settled in Manhattan.

Representatives from the D.A.'s office, state police brass, corporate lawyers from Magnus Media, and God knew who all else, along with Jason, were being called into an emergency session that morning. As far as Jason was concerned though, the urgency for such a meeting was gone. A rookie East Hampton police patrolman had ended it the night before. He'd shot Magnus square in the heart seconds after Magnus had let fire with his own handgun. It had been a classic police academy hit, one, Jason felt, that should make the young policeman proud. One that Jason would have given almost anything to have administered himself.

Though he had already delivered his statement the night before, Jason was asked to recap what had happened to the haggard-looking group of men and women assembled in the airless station-house conference room. It was not the way any of them had intended to spend that Saturday morning.

"I got a call last night—around ten—from Sheila Thomas, a producer at Magnus Media. She was shot, badly hurt, and left for dead at Vance Magnus's apartment."

"Objection," a balding but very fit-looking lawyer angrily interjected. " 'Left for dead' implies motive."

"And this is not a court of law," the police chief replied. "Nothing's going on any record. We're just trying to get some of the basic details straight in what appears to be a pretty messed-up situation. Now, you don't have to be here if you don't want. But if you are going to stay, shut up until you're asked to butt in. Proceed, Mr. Darin."

He explained how he'd phoned 911, met the ambulance and police at Magnus's, and helped get Sheila to the emergency room at Roosevelt. Although she'd been only semiconscious when Jason had first arrived at the apartment, Sheila had become fully awake—even agitated—during the ride to the hospital. Jason, holding her hand in the back of the ambulance, had tried to calm her down, but she kept gesturing for him to bend down so that she could whisper.

"I didn't mean to tell him. He pretended so well, you know? He blamed you, said he was worried about Cassie. I believed him. I didn't know . . . he made me tell him where she was . . ."

"Sheila, just take it easy. You've lost a lot of blood. We'll talk about all this in the morning."

"No! Now!" She'd tried to sit up, but Jason and one of the paramedics held her down. "You've got to get out there. He's on his way out there now. You've got to stop him. He's going to try to get Cassie next."

"What are you talking about?"

"Magnus is following Cassie out to your summer house."

"Cassie's not out there. She said she was spending the night with a friend . . . she said she was going to be with you . . ."

"Jason, believe me, she's there—and she's in trouble. Magnus—look what he did to me—he's dangerous."

There was a moment of uneasy quiet in the crowded conference room. Then the police chief said, "That's about when you called us, right? From the hospital. Honestly, sir, you were a little bit incoherent yourself at that point—or we would have moved faster."

"It doesn't matter," Jason said, though it might have. They'd resisted going out to the house without him being there, delaying the search for Magnus by the two hours it took Jason to drive to East Hampton. The department's slowness to respond to a situation they'd initially called "domestic" might have cost Cassie her life. He was sick at heart by the thought that his own slowness to understand what was going on around him—his refusal to face so many of his own unanswered questions about Magnus— might have contributed to the disaster. "If you don't need me any further," he said, rising to leave, "I'd like to get over to the hospital."

He was just out of the room when the Magnus Media corporate lawyer was on his feet, saying: "I demand a legal hearing on this matter immediately. This so-called briefing is a travesty. Gross injustice is being done to the memory of Vance Magnus. I demand that this matter be immediately moved to Manhattan where due process can best assure a fair reading—and outcome. I demand—"

A patrolman drove Jason to the hospital where he'd left his motorcycle the night before. The streets of East Hampton seemed so quiet and peaceful, the white steepled roofs and gingerbread porches reminiscent of a Norman Rockwell painting. But both Jason and the taciturn police- man beside him in the front seat of the cruiser knew better than that. The grotesque events of the night before lingered heavily in the air like the smoke of burning leaves. And soon the news would spread from this quiet hamlet to the larger world. The first word, like a pebble cast on the calm surface of the pond, would be that Vance Magnus had been shot to death by a local policeman. But that was just the initial ripple in a story that would widen and widen to encompass and swamp countless lives and careers.

But only one life concerned him now. From the moment he had heard Sheila's breathless explanation the night before, Jason had allowed himself to remember just how much that life meant to him. After he'd checked in at the reception desk, Jason was briefed by a young doctor before he was allowed to see Cassie.

"I understand you initiated mouth-to-mouth resuscitation in the middle of our minor hurricane last night."

"Yes, I did."

"Well, as far as we can tell, it saved your friend's life. She has pneumonia and a number of nasty contusions," the doctor continued, glancing down at his clipboard. "We're not out of the water yet, so to speak, but it looks as though she's going to make it eventually. I wouldn't stir her up with a lot of talk. She needs her rest."

At first he thought she was asleep. Her eyes were closed, her arm connected to an IV, extended in a gesture of helpless appeal. He sat down quietly on the chair beside the bed. Her paleness terrified him, as did the ragged edge of her breathing. He didn't want to wake her, but he found he had to take her hand in his.

"Hi," she said, looking directly into his worried gaze. "What's the matter? You look terrible."

"You should talk," he said, squeezing her hand, and for a moment unable to go on. Her right eye was swollen almost shut, her cheek bruised an ugly purple—both probably caused by his frantic attempts to keep her afloat the night before.

"So tell me," she said, closing her eyes briefly. "How does the other guy look? Nobody around here will tell me anything."

"You're lucky you made it," Jason replied. The doctor had warned him not to stir her up, and news of Magnus's death would certainly fall under that category. "I think we should both sit here quietly and count your blessings."

"You count," she said, "I'm too tired." He held her hand as she slept until the end of the visiting hour. When he came back in the evening, she seemed stronger. She smiled when he walked into the room with his arms full of flowers he'd picked from the house gardens, late-blooming marigolds and mums.

"I should be giving you flowers," she told him. "I understand you're responsible for saving my life."

"A rather alert team of paramedics helped a little."

"That's not how the doctor tells it. I'm afraid I don't remember much, except that I finally learned how to swim."

"I hate to have to be the one to tell you, but your form needs a great deal of work."

She laughed briefly, then fell silent. "He's dead, isn't he?"

"Yes."

"I knew it, as soon as I woke up the first time. It was in the middle of the night and the moonlight was streaming through the window. I felt such peace, I knew either I was dying . . . or Magnus already had."

"He pulled his gun on one of the rookie cops in the search party. He was shot point-blank; died instantly. I'm sorry, Cassie."

"Don't be. I never thought I'd say this, but he deserved it. He was a murderer."

"I know, Cassie. Sheila told me everything."

"But how?" Cassie tried to sit up in bed, but the sudden movement made her wince with pain. "He told me he'd killed her."

"He tried," Jason told her, taking her hand again. "But he missed by quite a bit. She's in Roosevelt, recovering quickly. Last time I checked in, she was raising hell because they wouldn't let her send out for Chinese."

"So that's how you knew where to find me."

"Yes. And why you were out here."

"She told you about Felice? How she died?"

"Yes, but I should have figured it out for myself a long time ago. I was too angry—and then too guilt-ridden—to think it through. You see, the last night Miranda was alive she accused me of killing the girl. I just exploded. Oh, God, it was a truly awful fight. I've always felt, I guess I've always known, that I caused Miranda's accident. We were both so angry—blind with fury—I can see how she would have lost control."

"All these months—you've felt you were responsible for her death?"

"It's why I haven't been able to talk about her. To anyone. Even you. I know . . . how you must feel about me."

"I don't think you do," she said. She reached out. She touched her fingers to his lips. "I don't think you have any idea." It took her a little over ten minutes to recount what Magnus had told her about Miranda's final hours alive. At one point Jason got up and moved over to the window. He stood there silently for several seconds after she was finished, looking out across the moonlit landscape of parking lot and carefully clipped lawn.

"Magnus was right about one thing," Jason said at last. "I stopped loving Miranda very shortly after we were married. She didn't want to have Heather, you see. She said she wasn't ready to be a mother, she had her career to think of, et cetera. I stopped loving her and started loathing her at just about the same moment. But I wouldn't let her have an abortion. I promised her that I'd do anything she wanted—do all the real child-rearing if necessary—of only she'd go through with the pregnancy. I think she realized even then that she needed leverage with me, that she'd lost my respect—and passion. But it was awful. She hated being pregnant, despised giving birth, and blamed me for everything."

"I'm sorry," Cassie said.

"I was at fault, too," he went on. "I demanded things of her she simply couldn't give. She saw the world only in terms of how it benefited her—forwarded her glorious career. Even poor Heather turned into one of her pawns. She knew how much I hated the way she coddled her—so she did everything she could to turn Heather into a spoiled brat. We were a disastrous family, but she refused to let go. Said she'd demand custody—and she'd probably have gotten it—if I sued for divorce. By the time you visited last Easter, I was living off pure venom. And then I saw how sordid the whole thing was, how hopeless."

"Why?"

"Because I fell in love with you. And the more I wanted you, the more I hated her. Magnus might have killed her, Cassie, but in my heart I did, too."

Thirty-seven

$\mathcal{C}$assie had a great deal of time to think during her two-week stay in the hospital. Though her condition was slowly improving, the doctors refused to let her travel until her lungs had thoroughly cleared. It was not an unpleasant place to be: the room blossomed with dozens of flower arrangements from friends and colleagues, and the rich golden autumn sunlight flooded through the double windows. She spent her mornings reading every newspaper she could get her hands on, watching the morning news shows, and talking on the phone, primarily with Sheila who was likewise incarcerated in Roosevelt Hospital. At least twice a day Cassie spoke with Jason and Heather on the phone, and Jason drove out to see her as often as he could.

"You must be exhausted," she said one evening, noticing the smudges of fatigue under his eyes and the tightness around his mouth.

"Not at all," he replied easily, taking her hand. "You know how I feel about the Harley. And the highway's almost empty this time of the year." But a few minutes later, he swallowed a yawn, and half an hour after he started reading to her—a routine he had begun when she complained once briefly of the difficulty of doing so with an IV in one's arm—his voice faltered and his eyes closed.

She was happy for this opportunity to study him without his being aware of the scrutiny. She lived for the moments when they were together, for the rough intimate tenor of his voice. And yet, despite his rather awkward declaration of love, he remained to Cassie—as he did to the world at large—a deeply private man. It was not something she wanted to change about him, rather it was one of the many things she wanted to try to understand.

Another was that, with almost maddening conviction, he refused to discuss anything he felt might upset her. Claiming he was operating under doctor's orders, Jason made sure that their conversations remained light, neutral, loving. They spent a lot of time talking about Heather and the puppy he had brought her—a boisterous little beagle named Satchmo—to cheer her up while Cassie was away. And though Cassie sensed that Heather had taken the news of Cassie's "accident" pretty hard, Jason fed her only hilarious stories of Heather's and Satchmo's latest high jinks. Even the books he chose to read to her were funny and fun. He'd fallen asleep over James Thurber's *My Life and Hard Times*.

But despite his constant attempts to infuse her life with sunlight, the dark side—the murders Magnus had committed, Haas's corruption—refused to go away. Cassie knew that darkness wouldn't lift until it was faced head-on and resolved. Jason would not discuss it with her, but it was clear to Cassie from the news reports that—although information about Magnus's death had spread quickly through the major media—the real story behind it had never caught fire. The funeral service had been small, almost secretive. It had taken place before the papers caught wind of it. Senator Haas's name never came up, except in the various obituaries where he was mentioned as a friend and recipient of the deceased's largesse. Magnus's death was being termed "an accident, pending further investigation by the East Hampton police force and the Manhattan D.A.'s office."

A great many people, Cassie concluded, were working

hard to keep the story quiet. As her health improved, so
did her sense of unease over what she perceived to be
a cover-up. There was only one other person she could
talk to about these concerns; in fact, Sheila and she rarely
discussed anything else.

"Mac dropped in on me last night," Sheila had told Cassie
on the phone that morning. "He looks like hell. Magnus
Media's board of directors has taken over the company
for the time being, and they've involved poor Mac in the
restructuring plans. Mac of all people! One of the all-time
worst administrators in the world. He actually asked me if
I knew anything about project efficiency reports. Like, the
man is running totally scared."

"He knows what really happened? You told him about
Magnus and Haas?"

"I tried, Cassie, but it was really weird and kind of sad—
he didn't want to hear about it. He said he has enough
on his plate without hurling unfounded accusations about
our dear departed leader and the Democratic senatorial
front-runner."

"Unfounded? But surely we have the ammunition to make
somebody listen—whether it's Mac or the D.A. We've just
got to get to the right people. I can't believe this hasn't
come out already. I bet Haas is putting on political pressure
at City Hall."

"He is, after all, best friends or something with the
Mayor."

"Okay, so we'll have to be very careful whom we
approach."

"And, like, what are we going to tell this person when
we meet? If I remember correctly, our hard evidence went
up a certain chimney in East Hampton."

"I still have Miranda's disk. We have the death certificate. We'll just have to start putting the pieces together
again. Sheila, listen, after everything you went through I'll
really not hold it against you if you want to forget about
this. But I can't."

Cassie misunderstood the silence on the other end of the line; she felt her heart drop.

"We're forgetting something," Sheila said at last. "What about Jason? If he would agree to back us up—support our story—it wouldn't matter what we have on paper. All we'd need is his corroboration."

"You're right," Cassie replied uneasily.

"There's an unmistakable 'but' in your voice."

"He won't talk about it. And he won't let me."

"Why? You don't think . . ."

"He's still somehow connected with Haas?"

"Well, it's a possibility. I mean, think about it: Magnus murdered his wife, almost got the two of us. If I were him, man, I'd be dying to blow this thing sky-high! Why else would he want to keep quiet?"

"No, I don't think so. Not him. Now now. How can you say that?"

"You said it, sweetheart, not me."

No, Cassie told herself now, studying Jason's face in repose. Sleeping, he looked ten years younger, the dark circles under his eyes softened by his lashes. His mouth curved in an unconscious smile. She looked at his hands—the long, fine fingers curling around the pages of the book—and remembered the feel of them against her skin. She believed that he loved her, that he wanted to protect her, and yet . . .

"What?" Jason had woken suddenly and caught her expression.

"I think you know."

"We'll talk about it later. When you're better."

"No. It has to be now, before it's too late."

"Darling, I would think you'd know by now that it's never too late." He leaned over to kiss her, but she turned her face away. He sat back. He folded his arms across his chest.

At last, he said, "I'm going to tell you a different kind of bedtime story tonight, okay? It's about a young, ambitious kid determined to make his mark in the world. His father, an unemployed stone carver, is not a good enough model for this kid. He wants to emulate someone powerful. Connected. He works one summer for a junior congressman and thinks he's found his idol. The politician is good with words, knows his way around the city, has a knack for making things go easy for people he likes. Well, the kid adores him. Works for him straight through high school. And after the kid puts in a stint in Vietnam, the congressman does him some favors, and before you know it a building project the kid's been trying to put together—is suddenly a reality. Union problems solved. The guy even cosigns a bank loan for the kid."

"And then, once the construction started," Cassie continued for him, "the congressman hits the kid up for a kickback."

"Oh, you already know this story," Jason said with a weary-looking smile. "What was so horrible about it all was that Haas just assumed I'd buy in. 'It's the way of the world, son,' he told me. 'I'm stunned you're so naive.' He told me if I didn't kick in he'd call back the loan or start union trouble. One way or another, he said he'd manage to shut me down. I couldn't let him. I was too full of myself, too proud of where I'd gotten to see it all taken away. But, believe me, although that was the one and only time I ever buckled under to Anthony Haas, he's been taking it out of me ever since."

"So why don't you help me do something to stop him?"

"No, you're not to get involved." He sat forward again and took her hands in his. "Listen to me, Cassie. For as long as I live I will regret the fact that I didn't do something to stop him sooner, that I pretended not to see what was going on around me—how sick Magnus really was, the scams Haas was still pulling. That I cut myself off from everyone except Heather. But mostly that I let you step in—where I should have months before." He brought her fingers to his lips. "That's what bitterness does to you—it turns you to stone, makes you blind. Well, I'm awake now, even if I haven't got much sleep recently."

Finally she realized what he was trying to tell her. "You are doing something—on your own," she said.

"No, with help. Very professional help. I know Haas too well. He may be greedy, but he's no fool. The only way to make any of this stick is to catch him red-handed. We've got to keep the thing quiet so he won't suspect. That's one of the reasons the story on Magnus got quashed so quickly in the media. The other being that Magnus Media wants to keep its embarrassment to a minimum. They're reorganizing, rethinking their goals, but they very much want to stay in the game. I think they're hoping to pin a lot of what happened on Haas."

"Magnus Media is actually cooperating in all this?"

"The board, yes, with the help of a small army of lawyers. The Feds are involved, too. Even a well-placed person on Haas's staff."

"Not—"

"Yes, Geoffrey Mellon. With a promise of immunity, of course. He's one clever little operator. I wouldn't be the least surprised if he made it to the House himself one day."

"It's terrible what I was thinking."

"That I was somehow still involved with Haas? I'll tell you the truth, Cassie, until we nail him—I feel like I am. I want to be the one responsible for bringing him down. The one he's looking at when he's taken into custody. I want to be the one he blames for the rest of his life."

Two days later, Haas was the top story on every morning television news show in the country as well as the front page national lead of every major paper. Though many of the national editors across the country were surprised by the scope and detail of the information about the episode that came to them over the wire, Ian McPherson was not. He had headed up the team of Magnus writers and editors who had been allowed to help craft the press release supposedly prepared by the F.B.I. In it, the extent of Vance Magnus's role in Senator Anthony Haas's dirty politics was played down considerably. But no one hearing or reading the story would have any trouble sensing that there was more to it than met the ear or eye. Typical of the scandalous nature of the story, the front page headline in the *Daily News* read:

SENATOR STUNG!

New York Senator Anthony Haas, seeking re-election for his fourth term in November, was the target of a successful F.B.I. sting operation yesterday evening that purportedly captured him on video accepting a large cash payment for promised political favors. The operation, which involved the cooperation of several local law enforcement agencies as well as the F.B.I., took place in the corporate offices of Darin Associates in the World Trade Center. The Senator, believing that he had just been handed $300,000 in cash in an expensive attaché case, apparently promised Mr. Darin that certain overseas trading restrictions would be loosened in the near future for Mr. Darin's business convenience.

According to Mr. Darin and, as yet, several unidentified but highly placed sources, the Senator can be implicated in numerous such instances of graft and corruption, including an extortion scheme victimizing the recently deceased CEO of Magnus Media Corporation, Vance Magnus. There is no clear evidence at this point whether Mr. Magnus's accidental death three weeks ago in East Hampton is any way connected with Senator Haas's alleged criminal activities.

Pending his hearing at the Manhattan Federal District Court, Senator Haas is being held without bail in an undisclosed location in Manhattan. A spokesperson for the Senator, Ms. Rita Kirbie, said, "He's devastated by these accusations, an absolutely broken man. Hardest for him to bear is the news that people he thought his friends, even his closest aides, have turned against him in this very dark hour."

Cassie and Jason watched the news together that night, holding hands over the guardrail of Cassie's hospital bed.

"You're not watching," Cassie objected, glancing at her companion during an analysis of the Haas scandal and seeing that he was studying her intently. He looked years younger than he had the night before, relaxed, and—if the word could ever be applied to Jason Darin—content.

"Yes, I am," he said, smiling.

"Should we turn this off?"

"No. I have a feeling I'm going to have to get used to having a television blaring in the background for the rest of my life."

"Why is that?"

"Because I want to spend it with you. And I think television is going to come with the territory."

"You're sure? About me, about us?"

He kissed her before she could go on, and then murmured in her ear as he reached into his back pants pocket: "Would a man who wasn't certain carry a ring around with him for half a year? Tell me, Cassie Hartley, have I waited long enough?"

Thirty-eight

It was, as Miranda had predicted it would be, one of the biggest stories of the year. Its many tantalizing ingredients—greed, sex, the abuses of power, murder, a cover-up—kept Americans across the country rapt in front of their television sets night after night as the Haas trial unfolded on the evening news broadcasts. Like Watergate before it, the investigation led its audience through the shadowy corridors of power and behind the closed doors where the most important deals—in this case primarily illegal—were really cut. Jason testified, and, as expected, Geoffrey Mellon and two other Haas aides turned state's evidence. The outrage both among Senator Haas's long-time constituents and voters in general was phenomenal. Many felt that the high turnover in congressional and senatorial seats that November election was due to a throw-the-bums-out attitude prompted by the Haas trial.

The Senator himself, looking indeed like the broken man Rita Kirbie had described, went through a violent withdrawal from alcohol addiction shortly after being arrested and had to be transferred to a special hospital for several weeks of treatment. Haas emerged from the rehabilitation program a "new man," according to his highly paid team of lawyers. He had found God and A.A. He repented his many sins. Every day of the trial he carried a worn Bible with him into the courtroom. Frequently, when the flow of testimony grew turgid, the television cameras would zoom in for a close-up of the Senator, brow furled, deeply engrossed in the Book of Job.

Of all the many hours of regular news coverage and special investigative reports on the Haas trial, the one that drew the most interest—chalking up the highest ratings of any single television news program in history—was the hour-long *Breaking News* special hosted by Cassie Hartley and produced by Sheila Thomas two months after the Haas story first broke.

Cutting back and forth between the footage taped during Cassie's and her initial interviews with Haas and coverage of his arrest after the sting operation and the subsequent hearing, Sheila Thomas pieced together a brilliant study in contrasts: what the Senator said as opposed to what he was actually doing. One of the high points came when, after five minutes of excerpts from Haas's lugubriously delivered speeches about "justice, honesty, and returning the power to the people," the blurred videotape from the sting operation was played in its entirety.

But the show's main draw, indisputably, was Cassie Hartley herself. When the news hit of her role in the downfall of Senator Haas, every media organization in the country wanted a piece of her. She herself became part of the story. Pale and composed, a little thin from her weeks in the hospital, she handled all the questions and interviews with an intelligence and compassion that impressed even her most cynical fellow journalists. It became clear immediately that she was not interested in the notoriety, except to the degree that it helped her get the truth out. In fact, she disliked the notoriety, though she had little choice. *People* and *New York* magazines fought over her for their covers. Oprah and Donahue each wanted her first—and, of course, exclusively. Magnus Media's public relations department went into overdrive to handle all the requests and scheduling details.

"You're the hottest thing since Schwarzkopf," Mac kidded her during a meeting with the newly formed board of directors. She and Sheila had been called into the weekly board meeting the Friday after their Haas piece aired.

"We want to tell you how grateful we all are," Leon Myers, the recently named new president of the corporation, told her. Leon, like Mac, was a veteran of Magnus Media, someone who had come up through the accounting ranks, whose loyalties were first and foremost to the corporation. And though that loyalty had been severely shaken by the news of Vance Magnus's deeply flawed reign, Magnus Media had become too big and powerful a company to be destroyed by one man. Leon, Mac, and a cadre of middle and top management had for many years constituted the true heart of the company—one determined to beat on.

"You and Sheila have given us a terrific morale boost at a time when we desperately needed one," Leon added.

"Okay," Sheila responded quickly. "So what can we expect by way of gratitude?"

"Whatever you want, actually," Leon said. "We know you're both being courted by other networks. Obviously we don't want you to leave."

"I'll rephrase that," Mac said. "You're not going to leave. So let's get you both good agents and start hammering out a deal we can all live with."

"We've got to get some new stories into production, and I mean immediately," Sheila went on excitedly. "But our kind of stories: tough investigative stuff. No more puff pieces."

"I don't think I'll be able to go ahead with any of this," Cassie announced quietly, though her words had the same effect as a bomb going off in the middle of the executive conference room.

"Cassie—don't worry—we'll work out terrific terms for you," Mac said.

"Whatever you want. Just name it," Leon added quickly.

"What the hell do you mean?" Sheila demanded, turning on her friend. "You can't go ahead? I thought you and I agreed to leave the party with the guys we came in with?"

It was true that when the offers from other networks and news organizations started overloading Cassie's and Sheila's message machines, they'd sat down and decided that they wanted to stay together—and at Magnus.

"I don't know, I feel like the damn place needs us," Sheila had said. "This is where I got my big break. I know this is weird, but I feel like I owe people here."

"I feel the same way," Cassie agreed at the time. But job offers and career considerations were not the only decisions on Cassie's mind. If anything, they were the last. As the board of directors and Sheila glared at her, Cassie decided that the only way she could diffuse the anger in the room was to tell the truth.

"We were keeping it a secret because of all the press coverage, but I have a feeling you won't forgive me if you hear it first from the *Daily News*." Cassie was talking to Sheila only, her smile pleading for understanding. "Jason and I are going to get married next week."

Sheila, who prided herself on her urban cool, shrieked with teenaged abandonment.

"Next week? Where? How? Like . . . when did all this happen?"

"That's great, Cassie," Mac said, extending his hand. "Congratulations." It was Leon who first considered Cassie's announcement in light of Magnus Media.

"Is that why you were worried about accepting the *Breaking News* job?" When she nodded, he went on happily, "Well, don't think twice about it, we'll work around your schedule. Just as long as you intend to come back to Magnus. Take whatever time you need."

It was a statement he would begin to regret three weeks later when the only communication they had received from their new media megastar was by way of a postcard sent to Sheila, postmarked from some obscure Greek island that Sheila was unable to locate on any map.

" 'The sun shines every day. The water is wonderfully clear. Nobody here's ever heard of Anthony Haas. And because of Heather, we're taken for a normal—though perhaps unusually happy—little family. Which is all I've ever wanted in the world. Love, Cassie.' "

"Come to bed, Mrs. Darin," Jason said, watching his wife at the open window, the moonlight outlining the tall, slender figure against the light cotton nightgown.

"I will in a second. I was just thinking about Miranda. She would have loved it here. Surrounded by the sea."

They could talk about her now, and they often did, with warmth and sadness and something akin to nostalgia. Miranda, with all her faults, had brought them together, and a part of Cassie believed that Miranda would be pleased for them now if she knew how happy they were together.

"Yes, she would have," Jason said, climbing out of bed to stand beside Cassie. The moonlight cut a glittering swath across the water. He put his arm around her waist and pulled her close.

"She was such a good swimmer—fearless, strong," Cassie said.

"She told me once," Jason added, kissing Cassie's hair, "that if she could live her life over again she would have chosen to become a swimmer, maybe tried out for the Olympics. She didn't, though, because she was afraid she wasn't quite good enough."

"Oh, she would have been good enough. She was always the best at anything she chose to do."

"Not everything," Jason said, leaning over to kiss his wife, with nothing between them now except love.

Mollie Gregory

__PRIVILEGED LIES   0-515-11266-6/$4.99

When power is the ruling passion, telling the truth can be deadly.

Los Angeles filmmaker Faye Ferray knows her friend Della's death is no accident and that it must be related to Della's work as a lawyer. Faye and her friends from law school—a top Washington attorney and a television reporter—put old rivalries aside as they dig through influential Washington and Los Angeles circles for the key to Della's murder.

__TRIPLETS   0-515-10761-1/$5.50

"Sexy, slick, searing and shocking!"
—Los Angeles Times

The Wyman triplets had everything money could buy, and more—beauty, intelligence and talent. Sara, Sky, and Vail shared a special closeness...until the day their crystal dreams were shattered, turning their trust and loyalty to deception and dishonor.

If you enjoyed this book,
take advantage
of this special offer.
Subscribe now and get a

FREE
Historical
Romance

No Obligation (a $4.50 value)

Each month the editors of True Value select the four *very best* novels from America's leading publishers of romantic fiction. Preview them in your home *Free* for 10 days. With the first four books you receive, we'll send you a FREE book as our introductory gift. No Obligation!

    If for any reason you decide not to keep them, just return them and owe nothing. If you like them as much as we think you will, you'll pay just $4.00 each and save at *least* $.50 each off the cover price. (Your savings are *guaranteed* to be at least $2.00 each month.) There is NO postage and handling – or other hidden charges. There are no minimum number of books to buy and you may cancel at any time.

Send in the Coupon Below

To get your FREE historical romance fill out the coupon below and mail it today. As soon as we receive it we'll send you your FREE Book along with your first month's selections.
